Molly O'Brien
AND THE
Mark of the Dragon Slayer

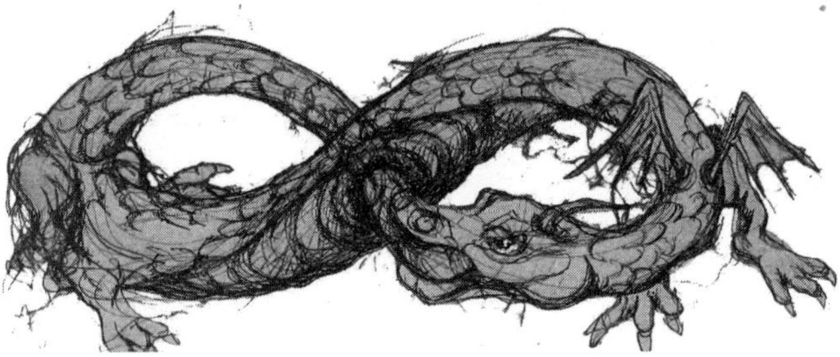

Kathleen Damiani

Larson Publications
Burdett, New York

Library of Congress Control Number: 2011935753

Publisher's Cataloging-In-Publication Data
(Prepared by The Donohue Group, Inc.)

Damiani, Kathleen.
Molly O'Brien and the mark of the dragon slayer / Kathleen Damiani.

p. ; cm.

Interest age group: 013-016.
Summary: Molly O'Brien learns the power of Woman to disrupt the sinister momentum of dark energies and nurture ones that serve what's precious in life. Sophia, the Queen of Wisdom, is eager for Molly to join her on a dangerous mission: saving Earth from imminent destruction by Ialdobaoth, the Great Dragon of crystallized thoughts from humanity's past. Molly ultimately learns to navigate and balance her magical and mundane realities, and find the core strength her destiny requires.
Includes bibliographical references.
ISBN-13: 978-1-936012-55-8
ISBN-10: 1-936012-55-3

1. Young women--Juvenile fiction. 2. Young women--Conduct of life--Juvenile fiction. 3. Goddess religion--Juvenile fiction. 4. Dragon slayer (Tale)--Juvenile fiction. 5. Young women--Fiction. 6. Young women--Conduct of life--Fiction. 7. Goddess religion--Fiction. 8. Imaginary wars and battles--Fiction. 9. Dragons--Fiction. 10. Fantasy fiction. 11. Bildungsromans. I. Title.

PZ7.D265 Mol 2011
[FIC] 2011935753

Cover art: Hrana Janto
Interior art: Rosemarie Quebral

Published by Larson Publications
4936 NYS Route 414
Burdett, New York 14818 USA

larsonpublications.com

20 19 18 17 16 15 14 13 12 11
10 9 8 7 6 5 4 3 2 1

FSC www.fsc.org MIX Paper from responsible sources FSC® C011935 to my husband Paul (1953–1985)

and

to my mother, Katherine Granville (1916–2008)

Contents

PART 1

1

Sophia in the Tree

"Molly!" A woman's piercing strong deep voice split the roar in two, dissolving it. Everything collapsed into darkness.

I slipped away into blackness, like a vast winter night sky, starless, frigid. Suspended in this dark void, these words announced themselves everywhere:

> *I breathe a breath of force—*
> *of wind and roar and howling storm,*
> *I am infinite power.*

The voice now was neither male nor female, just deep and strong, rumbling like thunder through my body.

There was more that I couldn't catch but those words are burned into my memory like a brand. Then I passed out. Or did I? My memory was wiped out for a while. I have no idea how much time passed.

"Moll-lee . . . Molleeee . . ." The sound of my name rolled through the vast emptiness.

"Molly!" The woman's voice dove again into the midnight silence and yanked me back to my senses.

"For heaven's sake, wake up and help me get free of these branches!" she demanded.

Startled, I regained consciousness quickly. Every word she spoke dissolved all traces of mist and noise. This was no nun from my school, teaching our third-grade lessons. I looked closer at the oak tree and saw a large unusual-looking woman pushing branches out of her way.

"Come and release me from these branches."

"Who are you?" I asked. "And what in the world are you doing in that tree?"

"My name is Sophia and I'm doing exactly what *you* probably do every day when *you* climb trees. When you're way up, you try to figure out how to get down!" she said in a huffy tone. She seemed to be sort of in the branches, sort of wound around the trunk—and very high up. I was looking straight across at her from the library in the second story of my high-ceilinged Catholic grade school.

I would've laughed at this strange woman, or wondered how she knew I climb trees, but I was too busy looking at her body. It gave off a green haze that glowed in sharp contrast to the dead brown autumn leaves she was pushing her way through. She was wearing a loose-fitting emerald green dress, so velvety looking that I wanted to touch it. Squinting hard so as not to miss anything, I kept staring at this odd-looking woman. Long black hair fell loose and wavy behind her neck, disappearing below her shoulders. *Where did she come from?* I wondered. Her skin was brown, with a ruddy overlay.

What is that? What is that about her ears? They were large, with big gold earrings dangling from them. I couldn't stop looking at the gold hoops, as big as saucers, and started to imagine tiny blue parakeets swinging in each one. I almost burst out laughing and quickly tried to hold back—threw my hand over my mouth so she wouldn't notice. I didn't want to be rude; but really, this was funny.

I could see her face clearly. It was strong and defined. She seemed pretty big, but not fat. I could see only the top of her body. She had very large breasts pushed together by a tight black bodice laced up with gold ribbon. Around her waist was a gold braided cord.

"It is clear that I haven't frightened you too badly," she said in a gentler tone.

I tried to see where the large woman was standing, but it was impossible to tell how she could stay upright without sitting on a branch or at least holding on to one of the limbs. As I tried to figure out how she was in the tree, I noticed something peculiar, almost like scales, wound around the large branch below her, curling like a gleaming snake.

"Oh, my gosh!" I gasped, pointing to the branches just beneath her. "What is that below you, *a snake*?"

"Never mind the snake! It's not a snake. It's part of my baggage," the woman snorted, annoyed at my question.

"Baggage? What baggage?" I saw no suitcase. Her left hand was on a branch; the right one was pulling at her clothing.

She didn't answer me, probably because she was still trying to untangle her dress. I thought this whole scene was odd, weird. The scales looked way too creepy. *Oh my gosh, I think I see a tail!* I thought with amazement. *She has a tail!*

"Why don't you do something useful instead of just standing there, and help me untangle myself!" she insisted.

"I can't!" I yelled back. "Don't you see I'm stuck here in this school? I can't possibly help you!" Looking through the window to the pavement of the parking lot far below, I shuddered, then shouted, "I'm just a kid!"

"Oh, of course you can help me! Don't be so, so . . ." she paused, looking for the right word, "so *helpless!*" she yelled right back at me.

I blushed and felt stupid, but only for a second. I was too excited to feel self-conscious around this Tree Woman. She didn't scare me at all. Sophia wasn't like any adult I had ever met, just odd and a bit huffy.

"How am I going to fit through this window?" I asked her. "And even if I could, what do I do then? I'm up too high. And, oh yeah, ummm . . . *there's electric wires!*" I suddenly remembered my hand reaching through the window to grab the black wire before being overtaken by the blackness. But any urge like that, whether I was meaning to kill myself or not, had now gone away in the excitement of meeting Tree Woman.

"Just get yourself through the window," she assured me, "and then I'll help you get to the tree. Or would you rather stay in school?"

It took about three seconds to decide I'd rather risk leaping over to the tree than stay one more minute in school. Getting through the window wasn't easy, though. There was only about a twelve-inch space underneath the window when it was open all the way. I squeezed through on my back, feet first. My back scraped on the concrete window ledge, but I was skinny enough to make it. I kept my hands close to my sides to avoid the wires and help wiggle my butt through. The thick electric wires connecting to the second-story brick wall of the school were only inches away from me. With one final push, I made it out. As I perched on the concrete sill and looked down, my heart jumped like a grasshopper.

"Yikes!" I yelped.

"Oh, stop whining and just leap!" Then her voice lowered: "You can do this." She said it firmly, as though it was already done.

How does she know? I'm two stories up and that's concrete down there. My heart beat fast as I forced my eyes to focus on the large branches in front of me, instead of the hard pavement below.

"Just trust your body. It will tell you to jump at the exact moment that *it* is ready to do so safely. What do you think, that your body *wants* to splatter itself onto the parking lot? Hah!" Tree Woman was talking to me as though she could hear my fears.

I knew I could do it, too. I was used to climbing trees, some so tall I could see over rooftops from them. *She's right,* I thought, *there's always a flash, a second when my body sort of sends a signal when to leap—from a branch, or over rocks in a stream.*

I focused on the large branch closest to the ledge and figured out where to put my feet. I saw which branch waving in the wind to grab onto when I jumped. I waited for that signal that said, *now!* And right then I pushed myself off the window ledge. As easily as a monkey on a vine, I grabbed one of the thin waving limbs with my right hand, swung in the air for one scary moment, and then jumped onto one of the oak's big solid arms. Its bark was weathered and stained black in places.

"Well done, Molly. You are a leaper of abysses—in the spirit world, that is. You crossed over to the other side and remained conscious. Congratulations!" Tree Woman, still partially hidden by limbs and rusty brown leaves waving in the wind, reached the long fingers of her strong brown hand toward my hair and stroked it.

"What do you mean? Did you expect me to fall off the ledge and die?" I asked.

"No, of course not! I'm not referring to your rather ordinary jump from the ledge to the tree. You do things like that on your own every day. What I'm surprised and pleased about is that you slid into the spirit world so easily. My, my! It's rare to find one so young who can stay awake, stay conscious when they leave their physical body to travel into the world of spirits."

I looked down at my legs. There was my body, plain to see. "What do you mean, leave my body? Am I dead?" I touched my left leg above my knee with my free hand. "It feels like I'm still here. Tell me, what's going on? Who are you and, uh, what do I do about *that*?" I looked behind me, pointing my thumb back toward the library window.

"Don't worry, dear one. You are between worlds. An image of the densest part of your physical body is back in the room you just left—just in case your teacher comes looking for you. She will think you fainted. The outer shell of your body will be slumped over on the floor. If the ambulance comes to take you to the hospital, your body will not die but will appear to be in a coma."

"What?" I was shaking my head *no*.

"Don't worry, dear, you are still in your own body. But the experience you are now having in *this* body *right here*," she pointed a long brown finger at me, "that you are talking to me from, is more real than your routine reality, trust me. You can still feel pain and fear. Why, you can even die!" She laughed as though dying was a private joke. I didn't find my situation funny at all.

Her face regained its composure quickly. "We have only a short time to be together until your teacher comes to fetch you for lunch. Why don't we get comfortable here for a few minutes and properly introduce ourselves? Then we can help each other get down from this glorious tree." She took a big breath and let it out with a big puff, then swirled her left arm above her head as if she was honoring the majesty of the oak that was protecting us from the gusty wind. "After that, we'll take a walk and get you some lunch."

Lunch sounded like the best idea yet. Relaxing a bit, I looked down at my stomach, still covered by my navy blue uniform, and patted it. It looked and even felt like the same body. I was so hungry and didn't want to go back. Anything but school, the arithmetic class after lunch, and Sister Mary Rose.

Still standing on the limb I'd leaped onto, I slowly, carefully inched my way over to a cozier spot near the main trunk of the oak, where several of its large arms came together. I was getting ever more curious about this woman with the tail.

2

Queen of the Middle Realm

"Well, who *are* you, anyway?" I asked. She was still tangled in the branches, but it also seemed she was somehow on the same limb I was on and had moved closer to me. "And . . . ummm, are you real or make-believe?"

"If you can tell me the difference between real and imaginary, then I'll tell you!" she answered very quickly.

"Who *are* you—*really*?" I asked again, a little embarrassed that she might not like me thinking she wasn't real. I lowered my eyes to the ground far below. Leaves on the parking lot below flew in circles like small buzzards. I hugged my school-uniform sweater tighter around me against the increasing wind.

"I just told you. My name is Sophia. I am Queen of the Middle

Realm . . . and have other titles, too." I looked up just as she threw back her fine strong shoulders and tilted her chin to the stormy sky.

"What's the middle realm and where is it?" I asked, more excited about other realms than that she was a queen.

"The middle, my dear, is where all the fun happens! It's the place 'in-between' two other things. If you have a woman over here and a man over there, but they never look at each other, why then, nothing will ever happen."

So what? I wondered.

"Let me try again. We're sitting in this magnificent oak tree. At one time, it was just a little acorn, the oak's vital kernel all wrapped up in a hard case. The acorn falls from the mother tree, then rolls around and rests on the ground until its shell breaks open. Maybe someone steps on it. Or maybe a squirrel plants it somewhere and forgets about it over the winter. Over time, when conditions are right—sun, soil, water—the acorn splits its shell. Roots grow down and branches up. See what Nature has done?" She squeezed her shoulders in and grinned like a girl who had just won a spelling bee.

Since I loved trees and climbed way up high in the elm tree in our front yard on nice days, I thought about it half a minute and said, "Yes, it's amazing that this giant tree grew out of a little acorn."

"So, Molly, try to see this. People in your world are enclosed in a hard shell, just like the acorn. They haven't had the right conditions to break the shell and start growing into becoming human. The acorn isn't really a tree until it breaks out of its shell and starts the dangerous journey of growing up."

"You're telling me that all the humans on Earth aren't humans, just seeds?" It didn't make sense to me.

"Yes, that's what I'm saying. They *look* human, but the consciousness that makes them human hasn't left the safety of its tiny prison and claimed its destiny, its freedom to grow in the larger world."

"What do acorns have to do with the middle realm?" I asked.

"Humans are in danger of snuffing out their seed of consciousness. They've created a habitat of fear and violence, so the seeds are dying or staying closed. Think of what the little acorn faces when it cracks open and grows: floods, fire, windstorms, lightning, animals, poisons in the soil, insects, lawnmowers—all kinds of dangers could snuff out its young life. So I oversee and protect life when it expands to become itself fully. I also control the boundary between the worlds. As a matter of fact, according to Proverbs in your Bible, I was present at the creation of your world. I am its architect, its designer."

"I thought God did that kind of stuff," I quipped.

"In your mind, God has to do everything, poor chap! Doesn't he sound more like a mother than a father?" She grinned, flashing her teeth wide and white against her ruddy brown face.

I looked away, a bit disappointed at her description of the middle realm. She sensed my interest fading.

"Let's keep this very simple for right now, Molly."

I was still wondering, *Where are we, anyway? What makes the middle realm different?*

"The middle realm is right where you are *now*," she continued. "It's a dimension between two worlds—the world of the living and the world of the dead—a realm where you can see *both* the material and spirit realms. At the moment you reached for the electric wires, you were caught right smack in the middle, between life and death. Your desire to leave the world was just as strong as your desire to live. So, everything in your ordinary school world . . . why, it just came to a stop!" she exclaimed with excitement. "*And*—you remained conscious!" She clapped her hands with glee.

"But I don't want to be in the middle of anything. I want to go back to the world of the living." I was getting worried. As much as I hated school, I didn't want to leave with a woman who had a green haze and a snake tail, even if she was a queen.

"I'm sorry, Sophia, it was a mistake for me to reach for the wire. Honest, I didn't really want to electrocute myself. Can't I please go back now?" I started to get up from my perch, looking back to the library window ledge. Fear bubbled up in me, as I began to feel that I could never jump from the tree back to the ledge.

"There's nothing to be afraid of. I'll explain as best I can what happened. Listen with your wild self, not from your fear, not from your school self."

Her voice drew me back in. I forgot about the chills that went through me with every gust of wind.

"Do you remember reaching for the wire while your attention remained riveted onto my tree?" Her words slowed down and her tone became more serious.

Why is this tree hers? I wondered to myself.

She paused, as though taking note of my unspoken question, then chose to ignore it.

"Well, my dear, at that moment, you were caught between the worlds. Your strong emotion, your desperation, sent out a signal that reached me like an urgent call. Your wail was loud enough to be heard in the Ogdoad—which is one of the places I reside until I'm called forth by one such as you."

I stifled a giggle at the funny-sounding *Ogdoad* word.

"Well, I don't get it." I was hearing but not understanding. "It doesn't make sense to me. Where am I right now? Are you sure I'm not dead? Am I in hell?" I looked around and I was still in the tree outside the second-story window of the school, looking back into the library instead of out from it.

"You are exactly where you see yourself to be—in the tree, not hell! From what I can see, you just left hell. School imprisons children, removes them from Nature!" All of a sudden, she *spit* through all the branches—and it went *splat!* right on the ground! I was amazed by her good aim.

She continued without pause, as though spitting was to be expected in polite conversation. "You are not dead, Molly. There's no such thing—at least not in the way you think about it. The intensity of your distress opened a crack between the worlds. Your acorn shell has split apart. Claim your right to grow into the form of the fully human woman!" She lifted her right arm into what seemed to be a fist of victory.

A gust of wind drew my attention from her words to her glossy black hair. It billowed out around her face and shoulders. I pulled my eyes away from her beautiful face and hair and focused on her words.

"Your fate, my dear," she reached out to touch my hand, "is to begin the journey into another, more dangerous world." She looked at me intently, and a big grin widened slowly across her face. I was pretty relaxed now, considering I was stuck in a tree with a large snakey-tailed woman talking to me like we both had fallen into the rabbit hole in *Alice in Wonderland.*

"Why me? Just me?"

"No, of course not only you. Any truth seeker will eventually cross over to a different state of consciousness and meet me when the explanations their society offers them become too confining, contradictory, or false. You could say," she paused for dramatic effect, tossing her hair among the swirling leaves, "that sanity requires a return to the intelligence of the Life Force . . . and that would be me, Wisdom."

At that moment, the wind gusted strongly, whistling through the branches, shaking them, chilling me again.

"I'm hungry, Sophia, and cold." I started feeling sad. I felt lost and alone.

"We'll go soon. This is too much for you, isn't it?" She seemed worried about me.

"No, it's not too much. It's just that, well, I don't want to leave my school world if it means leaving my family behind."

Gently, she reached over and put her hand on my shoulder. "You already *have* left your commonplace world. You can never go back, Molly. The shell has cracked—no force on Earth or in Heaven can put it back together!"

3

The Mark of the Dragon Slayer

The wind started to sway even the big limb we were on, so I moved all the way to the main trunk. Hugging my knees up close to it to stay balanced, I began to cry softly.

"Listen, Molly," Sophia continued, "this beloved Earth of ours is the jewel of the cosmos! I orchestrate the web of connections between living creatures, their habitats—even men and women—to make it so! But now a great crisis is erupting in all the worlds. I don't know how to fix this problem. I could really use your help."

Hearing that was such a surprise that I forgot my sadness. "Me? What could I possibly do to help you, Queen of Heaven and all that?"

"I will lead you to the place of seeing—but not now. Today we're just meeting each other." She lifted her strong dimpled chin toward the sky and closed her eyes for a few seconds before saying, "I don't want to overwhelm you with my . . . rather vast . . . history."

It was getting harder to pay attention to her odd words. I began to feel wobbly from hunger, not to mention the strangeness of talking with a woman who had a tail. Slowly, I collapsed onto the wide arm of the tree, and let go of the branch I was holding.

"Not so fast, child!" Quick as an arrow, Sophia reached out and caught me before I fell through the branches to the concrete below. She got there just as everything started to go black again. I struggled to wake up, and we both lost our balance as I started to slip off the damp gnarled bark.

I screamed. Sophia didn't. Her dress, still tangled around the branches of the limb we both had been on, was keeping us from falling. She was able to hang on to me, even though now we both were dangling in the air.

"I'm going to drop you onto that branch right below us. Just stay calm. Let go of me and grab it, then shimmy down the trunk. You can do it," she promised.

I had no choice. Waiting for a calm, alert moment, I finally said, "Okay," and she let go. As I dropped, I lurched forward and grabbed the trunk with my knees and arms.

"Ouch!" I yelled. The sticky rough bark, or maybe a stub of a tree branch, scraped the skin on my upper thigh, an inch or two below where my underwear was showing. My skirt had pulled up around my waist.

"You made it! I'm proud of you, dear," Sophia called. "Stay right there. It will only take me a moment to break free of these branches."

Soon she was at my side. She'd somehow untangled herself. My legs had found a limb to support me; my arms were still around the stout trunk. Embarrassed by my exposed underwear, I pulled down my uniform skirt. Blood quickly oozed through the thick navy blue material, turning it wet black.

"Here, grab onto my shoulders and I'll carry you down."

Without any hesitation, I leaped onto her back and clung tightly, then closed my eyes, trusting she'd get me down safely. She went down very fast. I opened my eyes and watched her grab one limb after another down through the branches. Finally, we stopped at the one closest to the ground. She got ready to jump the last seven feet. I shut my eyes again, hugging her neck. Then I felt the jolt as we landed on the ground.

I tilted my neck way back, and my eyes retraced our path back up to the tree top where we'd been. It was so high, so far away. Still I held on. I didn't want to let go of her. And Sophia didn't hurry me. Heaving a long sigh, she bent over to straighten out her clothing and shake the leaves out of her hair.

Slowly unwrapping my arms from her neck, she put me carefully on a small patch of leaf-covered roots and set my head ever so gently upon one of the large roots at the bottom of the trunk. Cold, hungry, shaky, and hurt, my body—or whatever it was—sank into the leaves.

"You got hurt, Molly. Let me fix you."

She knelt down, folded back my uniform, and brought her face down close to my leg. Then she wrapped the bottom of her dress around her right index finger, spat on the cloth, and rubbed around the oozing cut. With very light dabs, she cleaned the torn skin. My eyes got droopy as I relaxed under her care. I felt a warm liquid roll into the cut. Opening my eyes, I was startled to see her face almost touching my thigh—she had *spit* into the wound! Wiping her mouth with the sleeve of her dress, she ignored my shock at what she had done. So, I pretended not to notice. Lying still on the ground, I waited and wondered what she would do next.

A minute or two passed. The wind—invisible, harsh—slapped me with shivers. Leaves swirled around both sides of Sophia as she silently bent over my leg with all her attention on it. Suddenly she squealed with surprise and delight. Raising her face and upper body away from me, still kneeling, she looked me in the eyes and pointed her left index finger right toward my face.

"You!" she said with a surprised, delighted smile. "You! You are a little Spartan. You are a dragon slayer!"

Tired, hungry, and scraped up, I said nothing.

"Let me show you the *mark* of the dragon slayer." She lifted my shoulders with one arm and sat me up. With her other hand, she raised my left knee so I could see the ugly oozing wound on my thigh. The open cut was about an inch and a half across, wet with puffy white spots appearing on either side; but it wasn't bleeding anymore.

"Do you see those two white marks?" she asked, pointing to two fresh welts on the outside edges of the cut. They looked like two crescent moons facing each other.

"Your little scrape with the branch of the tree will produce a scar in a few weeks that will look like two teeth marks. The *mark of a dragon slayer* appears on the body either at birth, or through injury. Mothers in ancient Sparta tattooed the thigh of their boys with a lance or a snake to show that they belonged to the tribe of Cadmus and Pentheus, the Spartans of Thebes.

"You belong to their tribe, little Molly, descended from those individuals 'sown' or 'Earth-born' from the dragon's teeth. You are from the bloodline of dragon fighters."

"But there aren't any dragons to fight," I reminded her. *Where does she think I live?* "Don't dragons only live in fairy tales? And, how come my mark has teeth and not a snake or a lance?" I asked, leaning way over to look closely at the ragged cut. I saw the two raised whitish bumps but the wound was still oozing. It just looked like mangled flesh trying to heal itself.

"The tooth is the symbol of reincarnation. Maybe because a tooth looks like a seed-corn, which is planted and rises again and bears fruit. Ahhh, dear little Spartan, your destiny is to encounter the Great Dragon. I'm so sorry, Molly, but a normal life is not for you."

Smiling sweetly, she pressed my right hand between her own hands. Then she leaned close to me and placed all three hands over her heart. Her eyes looked into mine. Their centers were like deep pools speckled with points of light, just like a night sky.

She put my hand back on my lap, lowered her eyelids, and began to rub the wound so gently I barely noticed.

"Your future is to *bear witness,* to see *all* of life, not just the niceties, the lies, the illusions people create to cover the Great Beast that controls so many of the humans on the planet now like puppets. You will bear witness to hell—and to heaven. Your scar is to be a special sign. You are destined from before your birth to meet the Dragon, but not without training. You will learn to master him." She hesitated only a moment before continuing with a slow and measured tone, "Or he will devour you. Your soul is at stake."

Astonished at her words, I felt a new kind of excitement and hope in my body, driving away the sadness and helplessness.

"You belong to me, Molly. And I'm all yours. This mark only appears when you are ready and willing to find out what is true. For a number of reasons, I have chosen *you* to tell my story, our story, the tale of how a girl can get wisdom and learn to confront the Dragon. Someday you will find a way to get our story told, and its words will have a transformative effect on girls and women everywhere—and on boys and men, too.

"It is a time of great danger in the realms. The survival of Earth and her creatures is at stake. In a universe of millions of cosmoses, Earth is a priceless gem. I oversee the perfection of its physical and spiritual habitat just for this: the miraculous appearance and development of clear perception, that is, wisdom. To be a fully awakened human requires a *conscience*: the ability to discern truth, beauty, and justice. To choose the good is to become conscious."

She stopped to catch her breath. "Ahhh . . . You see! I have told you about the Crisis already! And we hardly know each other. Now, we really must get you something to eat before you faint again."

"I know exactly where we should go!" I said. "Let's go to Rexall's soda fountain. It's down the street here on Electric Avenue. There's a counter there, with high stools to sit on!" With renewed energy at the thought of food, I jumped up and began walking toward the street.

"That's a fine idea!" Sophia said.

I was in a hurry to get there. I could hardly wait and started imagining what I wanted to eat . . . a grilled cheese on rye with pickles and mustard, french fries, and a cherry Coke.

Sweeping up her scaly tail, Sophia placed it discreetly under her emerald-green gown. She hustled to catch up with me and we were on our way. I noticed gold embroidered designs along the hem of her dress, and also down the sleeves that ran all the way to her wrists. Squinting at the gold emblems swirling around the hem near the ground, I stopped in my tracks and gasped, "Oh, my gosh!"

4

Sophia and King Solomon, Women and Men

I was horrified to see her feet: She wore no shoes. Her feet were toeless, hard, and large . . . they were *hooves!* I hadn't noticed them before, all covered up by her green gown.

"What's wrong with your feet?" I have to tell you, even as shocked as I was, that her hooves did not ruin her lovely looks and seemed . . . well . . . to kind of fit with all her other strange protuberances. Her feet took away none of her grace and humanity, although "humanity" may not be the word I'm looking for. *How could she be human and look like this?* I started walking again, and she trotted by my side, keeping up just fine.

"Well, it's a long story about my feet. I don't know why humans are so bothered by them. I was given a horrible name centuries ago in Europe: Bertha of the Big Foot! Centuries before that, when I was still self-conscious and embarrassed about them, I once tried to get them fixed during a visit to friends in your realm. I even traveled a great distance from Ethiopia to Jerusalem to visit a king who, I was told, could fix such conditions. His name was Solomon and he was really, really wise. He had a rather desperate need to understand the meaning of life and, like you, his call reached the Ogdoad and called me to him.

"When I arrived in your world, however, I was far away from his kingdom. There was a signal error of some sort. These things happen. I ended up in my favorite country, Ethiopia. I went there many times."

A big smile lit up Sophia's dark face as a far-off memory returned:

"People back then honored my arrival on Earth. And, of course, I landed exactly where I was ordained to be: Ethiopia, or the Kingdom of Sheba as it was called then. The Ethiopians were so impressed with my size, beauty, and inspiring speeches that they made me their queen.

"Many years passed before I could find out where Solomon lived even though his call—like your stress—kept sending me a signal. I can usually find my way to the person if the signal keeps reaching me. As long as it remains strong, I can find my way through the layers of realms by following it. In Solomon's case, his signal got weak and I kept losing it. It disappeared every time he made love, which was quite often." She laughed softly.

Sophia must have noticed my surprise at this turn in the conversation to sex. She stopped laughing, and turned to me, slowing her pace. She reached out and softly squeezed my chin.

"You're too young, Molly. Too bad! There are important things I have to tell you even though you're too young to understand."

She began to walk and speak more quickly. I could barely digest her words—words so utterly opposite to what I was taught in church and school.

"For a man to become fully human, he needs to open his heart to a kind woman with heart and depth, to allow himself to be transformed by the transmission of the divine feminine through her. That way, he will break out of his acorn shell and grow in compassion, nurturing, beauty, and love. Relationship with such a woman awakens a man's soul.

"But instead of listening to their body, which is alive with the wisdom of the Life Force," she went on breathlessly, "men have been deceived by religious leaders who instill fear and suspicion and disgust of woman, the body, and Nature, and then . . . create millions of books made from the flesh of my trees to justify it!" She stopped walking and angrily pawed the ground with her hooves.

Her tail whipped out of the folds of her heavy gown and beat the ground. I couldn't believe my eyes! I rubbed them, but still the vision was there: hundreds of tiny animals scattering through the air, springing with sparkling dust from her tail, like particles flying off a rug being beaten on a clothesline. My mouth opened in astonishment. I squinted at the sight of falling and flying tigers and lions and dolphins and horses and giraffes and hippos and lizards and birds and dogs . . . trying to identify them; but it all happened so fast, and *zip!* as fast as they whisked through the air, they disappeared in a cloud of scintillating dust.

"Was that . . . did I just see . . .?" I had stopped in shock at what I just witnessed.

She was silent a moment. "My tail? You saw my animals?" She tossed her long black locks and laughed merrily, fluttering her eyelashes at me. "Yes, that is me, as well. My animals, beloved creatures of Earth, are part of who I am!"

Sophia placed her graceful long-fingered hand against her heart in a gesture of fondness and remembrance, then turned to me and said, "Now, where was I? . . . Ah, yes, men and women—my favorite subject!" She lowered her voice more, as though confiding a secret, as though there were nosy people around trying to hear what she was saying. "That was one of my jobs, you know, to get men to fall in love with women. 'I cause men to love women.' Egypt, among my most beloved countries, remembered that about me under my name of Isis." She patted her heart again. "Men have forgotten my magic. The power of love is still there, but perverted. Men no longer have the eyes and heart to perceive the message of their own body—that there is only one Life Force, which is both biological *and* sacred!"

She flung both of her graceful long arms heavenward and her sleeves fell back so I could see the full length of her dark, muscular arms. "And thus does a woman," she smiled broadly, "as well as the man who loves her, connect to *me*, Wisdom!" Slowly bringing her arms back down to her sides, she turned to me. I said nothing and started to walk again. With a voice light and smiling as she trotted slowly beside me, she said, "You see, Molly, there are more enjoyable ways to connect with me than how you did today."

"But what does that have to do with men and women?" I asked.

"Originally, Molly, men *wanted* to serve the Life Force through its highest and most beautiful expression, Woman. I used to work directly with *men,* to remind them whom they serve—the Life Force as the evolution of Life into its greatest possibilities of freedom and creative potential.

"My next job is to work directly with women to reconnect them to me. When women lose their connection to me, they sink into the realm of the Dragon and become its servants. Then men get confused, or they blindly follow the women's errors, and things get all mixed up and troubles abound in your world.

"Here's how it's supposed to be: First, women connect to me, as Queen of Wisdom. Then men connect to me through the agency of women."

The sound of nearby jackhammers made me put my hands over my ears. When Sophia waved at the two men hunched over them, they looked up and smiled. I wondered if they saw Sophia's tail, but it was tucked under her dress. After we were past the noise, Sophia continued, "Truth is found through Woman. Some men see a woman only as an object to possess, control, and discard. But not all men! Those who love Truth eventually find their way to Woman—and through a woman, they find *me!*

"The next stage of my own development, Molly, depends not on man, but upon Woman assuming responsibility for her knowledge and power and vision of life as the treasure it is . . ."

"Wait!" I interrupted, "what do you mean 'next stage of development'? I thought you were Wisdom, you know, like a goddess or something? How come you're not through growing?"

"When I help the human realm, I further my own understanding and growth. Deities and beings from other realms are forever growing into fuller expressions of their powers and glories, just as humans are, only on a bigger, cosmic scale. It's one of those lies perpetrated by malicious or self-serving priests that there is a static God. Anything static is not alive. Insofar as any being great or small has life, it will change, grow, flower, and die, gods included. This cosmic creation . . ." she said as she waved her slender long-fingered right hand through the air above her head, "is a work in progress. Always has been, always will be.

"Now, let's go back to my favorite subject: men and women!" She brought her hand back down and laid it across her left breast, smiling.

"In the old days, right after I caused men to love women, my inspiration and teaching were still fresh in men's hearts, They honored women as the embodiment of the Life Force. But in your modern world, most grown men distance themselves from women, even in marriage—because they are terrified of the power that truth has to dismember them. Well, not *literally* dismember their bodies—just tear apart their belief in their own superiority and separation from Nature."

She turned to see if I understood, which of course I did not. But I nodded as though I did, and she went on. She seemed delighted to talk about this topic whether I cared about it or not.

"And who can blame men for their fear? The glorious energy of truth dissolves not only their little-boyhood but also their attachment to their mother and all the lies and beliefs she inflicts on them to bind them to tradition and rules."

Slowing her pace even more, she sighed. "If a man compulsively acts out the beliefs of his group, he is a tool for the Dragon."

I perked up at the mention of a dragon. Now I was interested. "Where's the Dragon?"

"He's in what is called the imaginal realm or the middle realm. He encircles the Earth like a belt."

I watched her intently. Her left hand went to her waist and fingered a scarlet velvety cloth belt, on top of which was the gold braided cord that ended in a fringe. She wore the belt low between her waist and hips. *Why didn't I notice the red velvet of the belt before?* I lowered my head to get a closer look. A brilliant blue stone with an odd eye-like black mark secured the band in the middle, just below the roundness of her belly. Her hand stayed there only a moment, then she resumed.

"Don't worry, someday I'll show you the Great Dragon. You're not ready yet. If you saw him, you'd melt from the heat. You have to first develop your second sight—everyone has it, but in most it's dormant. Now that you've met me, your third eye is open; but you have to pay attention to it so that the door of clear perception will remain open." Before I could ask her what she meant by three eyes and two sights, she lifted her rich emerald gown with a grand gesture of her arm to expose much of her scaly shiny tail, and muttered under her breath, "Dragon and I have a close relationship!" She let the hem drop.

"What will I see?" I got so excited when she mentioned dragons. I could feel myself on a black horse all dressed in armor with a long spear hunting the dragon that incinerated the village.

"I will take you to the middle realm, that part of the Earth sphere that contains all the residue of life that has ever lived on this planet for all time. "If you're human—which of course you are—you see this swirling massive glob of residue as a Great Dragon. The Dragon is, to your present state of understanding, the totality of lived life. It is spent Life Force, like a dead battery. The problem is that it can get recharged, reactivated by human attention and desire." She frowned and put her hand on her cheek, her voice slowing down, "The Dragon is the image that you see, of all thought-forms that have ever been thought by humans."

"So *where* is this place the Dragon lives?" I was trembling with excitement.

"You can see him as an actual dragon only in the astral world. 'Astral' is the name sages give to one of the dimensions of the middle realm. From there the Dragon controls the actions of men, kings, leaders, and soldiers—and of course, women who are terrified to stand up to men because they rely on them for protection and security.

"In itself, the Dragon is neither good nor bad. It is simply leftover life—in the form of thoughts." She sighed, and then fondled the end of her tail, "It is the past, Molly. It never goes away. But it can be restored to something lovely."

This didn't sound like any kind of dragon I'd read about.

"But let's leave the dragon talk until later, okay?"

5

About My Family

The wind was dying down and the sun peered through restless clouds scuttling across the sky above. We had walked for about fifteen minutes, passing by familiar alleys, streets, and neighborhoods.

"Are we almost at Rexall's, Molly?" asked Sophia.

"Yes, it's on the other side of the street, on the corner of Taft and Electric," I replied, "about another ten minutes. Sophia, I'm freezing cold, though. Can we stop over there to rest a minute and get warm?" I pointed to a laundromat up ahead on our side of the street.

"Of course, dear. You seem to know these streets very well." We hurried through the doors into the laundry. Several dryers were tumbling clothes. The washers in use were large and noisy. It was toasty warm and no one was around. Probably the moms were at the butcher shop down the street or doing errands.

"Well, yes, I do," I giggled. "This is where my cousin April comes to make out with her boyfriend. My brother Billy used to come here, too, but he doesn't hang out on this street or at Rexall's anymore."

"Why not?" asked Sophia, after several moments of silence.

I grinned. "He got in really big trouble last year. He shot out the street lights in front of Rexall's with a friend's BB gun!" I thought it was neat that he caused so much excitement in our quiet neighborhood. It was wild and dangerous, like something a train robber or cowboy might do.

"Was he mad about something?" Sophia asked. We found a wooden bench far from the door, close to the rattling dryers. She had to pull the bench away from the wall to squeeze her tail behind it, before we could sit down.

"Um, I dunno." I stopped a moment to stir my memory. "I don't think so. Billy never gets mad around me. He once beat up Bobby Piel for pushing me down on the playground. I remember my parents arguing about Billy . . . about something . . . last year, late at night, off and on for a whole school year. I remember Father O'Riley's name being mentioned—he's our parish priest. They almost never argue, so this was different. They wouldn't even let Billy be an altar boy anymore with his best friend, Tim. I thought that was mean." I stopped to try and remember anything else that could account for such a harsh punishment of Billy. "He had been an altar boy all through school. Suddenly, they made him stop. He shot out the lights right after that—maybe a few weeks later?"

"What happened when he shot out the lights?" Sophia asked, her interest piqued by my brother's adventures.

"Well . . ." I shut my eyes to better recall the night that police showed up at our front door a few hours after Billy went out with his friends. "A cop came to the door and talked to my mom. She went and got my dad. He was watching TV. Then they went with the cop out to the street where they had my brother in a police car. Mom came back in the house and said Billy had to go the police station with Dad, and that's when she told me and my sisters that he shot out the lights."

"Tell me about your sisters. And how old is Billy?" Sophia leaned closer to me, her chin in her hand.

"Billy is the oldest. He's five years older than me—I like him the best. Billy always sticks up for me and makes me feel safe. He just turned thirteen on August 9th. He's in eighth grade now. We always have a family picnic on his birthday. He's lucky that he was born in the summer. His real name is William Owen. That's my dad's name, Owen.

"Then after Billy is Peggy. Her real name is Margaret Alana. She's named after my mother. I don't like Peggy. She's mean to me, and so are her friends." I started getting mad just talking about Peggy. "Peggy's tall and has gorgeous blue eyes and black wavy hair. She's spoiled and mean." Now I was in a bad mood.

"Sophia! Peggy gives me 'snake-burns' and once she tried to suffocate me with a pillow when I was only five!"

"What in the world is a 'snake-burn'?" Sophia asked. She didn't seem concerned over my sister's threat to my life and happiness.

"It's when someone grabs your arm with both hands and twists it in two directions." To demonstrate, I put both my hands on her right forearm, then twisted the skin in opposite directions. But not too hard—I didn't want to hurt her.

"Ouch!" she pulled away from me. "I can see why you'd be angry at her. That hurts! I hope your other sister is nicer to you."

"Not really, but she's younger, so she can't hurt me. Her name is Patty and she's three years younger than me. Her real name is Patricia Maureen. She was named after my dad's favorite sister Patty Jo. Their father is named Patrick, and Patricia is the girl's name for Patrick."

"So tell me about Patty," Sophia was paying close attention, smiling.

"Patty is tiny and cute. She's so lucky. She has bright red curly hair, she doesn't have freckles like I do, and her eyes are blue. It's just not fair! She should have all the freckles, not me! Her hair is red! She looks just like my dad in his baby pictures, at least the few that we have of him. Peggy adores Patty and gives her anything she wants. Patty is already spoiled. She's the youngest and my parents give her a lot of attention." I was not liking this discussion. I didn't like the girls in my family at all.

"Oh, I almost forgot. There's Curly Pearl, our dog we rescued from the pound. We just call her Pearl. She's a white poodle-terrier mix. She has really pink skin under her wiry poodle hair. Patty got Pearl right before her third birthday. Pearl gets to sleep on Patty's bed every night. Mom and Dad never let any of us older kids have an inside dog."

"So, Molly, what about your parents, your father and mother?" Sophia asked. I wondered why she was asking about my family.

"Well, my mother—her real name is Margaret, but her friends all call her Maggie and I call her Mom. She stays home and cooks and cleans for everybody. She volunteers sometimes at our church's thrift store. My dad, his name is Owen, is a machinist at the Naval Ordnance Plant. He generally works nights but will work overtime a lot to get more money. He usually drives us to school.

"Both my grandmothers are alive, and so is Grampa Patrick, my father's father."

Sophia arched an eyebrow. My right hand reached to my throat, for the tiny gold cross etched with vertical lines that hung from the thinnest of gold chains. I showed it to Sophia, explaining, "My mother gave me this cross when I got my First Holy Communion last spring, in second grade. It's special. She got it from her father, Grampa Joe, when she made her First Communion. Grampa Joe was my favorite grandpa, but he died when I was six."

Sophia said nothing, so I continued, "And I have some aunts and uncles and cousins. We see them at picnics and Thanksgiving and Christmas sometimes."

Sophia turned to me, looked at my face, and asked, "Well, what about *you,* Molly?"

I didn't know what to say. "Well, my middle name is Ann, after my grandmother, my mother's mother. It's her middle name."

Sophia began tousling my hair, and I continued, "And I'm plain compared to my sisters. I wish my hair was straight." I pulled on it.

"Your hair is lovely, Molly. It's golden-brown, just like your eyes, and wavy."

We left the laundromat when a couple of women came in to check on their dryers. It was a few blocks to Rexall's, but it seemed much further. I was hungry and tired, and the wind had been chilly and strong. Sophia kept talking. Now that we were outside, it was hard for me to pay attention because I was so cold.

"Molly, remember that I have chosen *you.* Even though it may seem to you that your family background is not really special, and that you have no exceptional intelligence or abilities, there is more to your story. In fact, it stretches way back into the past. You just told me about your family. Your father and mother and sisters and brother and school are not accidents. Nor are the place and time you were born and in which you live now. All these will factor into your life and your destiny. Someday you will understand more about what I'm telling you now." She kept on talking about some other things I didn't understand, and can't remember.

6

Lunch at the Rexall Drugstore

When we arrived, Sophia walked confidently up to the Rexall's door, and held it open for me. Only a few people were in the drugstore and they ignored my strange companion. We made our way past racks of magazines, shelves of packages, jars, and dispensers of all kinds of medicinals and other products. Then we walked past the familiar counter where a few old men hunched over on their stools were eating lunch or sipping coffee. A couple of them were talking and laughing with the waitress behind the counter. I wondered if they could even see Sophia.

Sophia led the way to a cozy private booth in the corner. I slid onto the worn wooden bench seat. Sophia quickly situated herself on the opposite seat. She seemed excited about eating and pored over the small paper menu. I hoped no one would notice her tail. The green haze, which had been barely visible in the laundromat and during our walk, had now disappeared completely.

"If you're from all those faraway places, how come you can read English?" I asked.

"Hmmm . . . the quickest way to explain it is that you and your brain and personal history translate the vibration that I really am, into your physical world. You 'appear' me into your world and see me reflected back to you in a way that resonates with your soul's understanding and destiny. Other people either don't see me at all—or, I can cause them to see me as an ordinary woman, or even a queen. In this case, I can cause me to look like your mother. After all, you're supposed to be in school. If you want, I can put a touch of gray in my hair. Or would you rather I donned a habit and became a nun?" She laughed. I smiled back at her, but really squirmed inside, wondering what in the world I'd do if I looked up to see one of the Sisters who taught at my school.

When the waitress came, she spoke to Sophia first, and never batted an eye. I looked hard at the waitress, then back to my green-gowned companion with the horny feet, trying to imagine what the waitress was seeing. It was impossible to tell, but Sophia must've looked like an ordinary woman because the waitress didn't look twice and just scribbled away on her order pad. Sophia ordered a large plate of macaroni and cheese with a side of coleslaw, rolls and butter, and coffee with extra cream. I quickly decided on a grilled tuna sandwich, french fries, and hot chocolate because I was so cold. I could hardly wait to eat, and started feeling better just smelling the aromas wafting out of the kitchen.

"Sophia, when will I get to see the Dragon and get trained?"

"Someday I will give you a vision of the belt of the Earth, where you can see it all swirling and boiling—the Great Dragon. But you're not strong enough yet and you don't have the understanding to survive it. So let's leave this topic aside for now. It is a lesson for much later, after we have gotten to know each other."

She took a sip from one of the glasses of water the waitress brought before taking our order. "But, first, I want to tell you about *thought-forms*. These are the swirling bits of the past, which are the only stuff of which the Great Dragon is made."

She turned to look for the waitress, who was busy taking an order at the counter.

"Your aliveness is real." She leaned over the table and pinched my arm. "See? You reacted, you're not dead. So, what is unreal? All the thoughts and beliefs that are swirling around the belt of the Earth that have been left behind by millions of beings—these are not real in the same sense your aliveness is real. But you see, nothing ever really disappears. What is left behind can be enlivened by someone's attention. Then it takes on a kind of spurious life of its own.

"Did you know that beliefs that hang around too long turn into vampires?" she continued. "They don't have sharp teeth or wear black cloaks, but they really do go looking for slender young necks with brains on top. They suck human minds. They are shapeless blobs of energy ready to attach themselves like leeches to people who will give them life."

I shuddered at the image of a thought sucking my blood. "That's creepy," I responded. "Thoughts aren't real, are they?"

"You may not know this about your universe, but beliefs hang around. Your occult science calls them thought-forms. They are not necessarily bad or good. Some of them pollute the astral atmosphere. Every thought you think lives forever and draws to itself similar thoughts until they become like fierce little gangs who want to take over the world."

She laughed, but grew serious again quickly. "Allowing beliefs to invade and inhabit and control you—this, my darling, is the only way you can actually die!"

I looked at Sophia quizzically.

"For now, before our lunch gets here, I'll finish telling you about Solomon and myself as Makeda, Queen of Sheba. My beloved subjects were concerned about my feet, thinking that my hooved condition was caused by a curse, rather than understanding that they are exactly what they're supposed to be—hooves. So the Prince of Sheba, or Ethiopia as the land was also known, sent out his viziers—they're the wise men of the royal court—to find help for me. They came back to tell me about Solomon. Then I traveled north with members of my court in a caravan to visit him in Palestine. We brought jewelry, copper, cinnamon, and glorious colored woven scarves made by the women in the villages. Solomon had heard about me from the viziers and was *so* excited to meet me. I was absolutely gorgeous, in spite of my feet.

"We stayed in Palestine two years. Solomon fell madly in love with me because his heart was pure and he loved wisdom more than gold."

She paused, lowered her eyes, and added in a quiet proud voice, "Ahh yes, the gold . . . of which I brought him almost a ton." She caught my eye again, her words flowed quick and forceful. "I loved him, too, and taught him all that I know about wisdom, love, the meaning of life, the secrets of Nature, and the heart of a woman. He was a passionate lover. He experienced Truth through me as no other man has."

She stopped abruptly. Her eyes left my face once more, drifting off into some memory or a world that was beyond my sight. A long moment passed in silence, then she breathed a long deep sigh. Her eyes returned to mine with a quick flutter. Hesitating again, as if remembering secret delicious memories, she chanted:

> *I have fallen because of wisdom, but I have not been destroyed.*
> *Through wisdom I have dived down into the vast sea,*
> *and from the sea's depths I have seized a priceless pearl.*
> *. . . I was given a bright lamp there in the depths,*
> *and holding this lamp I ascended the ropes of the boat of*
> *understanding.*

"I, as Queen Makeda, wrote that—did you know? The whole poem and some of the story about King Solomon and myself are in an Ethiopian book called the *Kebra Nagast.*

"Anyway, we fell in love, Solomon and I. A year later, I gave birth to a son, whose name was Menelik. Someday I will tell you his destiny. But that is another story. You asked about my feet. Since that visit to Earth, I've learned that my odd feet are not my problem, but *yours*—you humans. What I mean is, you see my feet a certain way because of your collective ignorance of and disdain for the animal kingdom. Your fear and repulsion has little to do with who I really am."

I shook my head at her, trying to distance myself from the humans who wouldn't like her.

"Don't worry, Molly. I figured it out, but it did take me eons to learn.

You see, my dear, even deities like me from realms other than your own have to learn about ourselves and evolve our understanding. We learn about ourselves by helping creatures like you. Remember I made you promise to help me back in the tree? We are not alike, yet we can help each other. We reflect back to the other what we see, and that is what makes us grow fully into ourselves . . . But it can make us doubt ourselves if we don't fully understand what we see in the other. Since it is uppermost on your mind, I'll tell you about my feet. Any other questions before I start telling you about them?"

"Yes," I replied, "Just before I saw you there in the tree, I heard an announcement in the blackness, something about the wind and the storm, but I can't remember the rest. It gave me goose bumps. Was that you speaking? It didn't sound like your voice. It wasn't a man or a woman that I could tell."

She answered quickly, glad, I think, for the chance to teach me. "You were in an altered state of consciousness. I'm not sure exactly what happened to you, because your extreme stress reached me from a great distance. Sometimes that stress comes from dying, or going into a coma or trance. In the old days, stress was induced in initiation rites. Sometimes people can do spiritual practices or meditate to get into this state of consciousness—like Hindu and Buddhist yogis do."

I wanted to ask her about Hindus and Buddhists. I'd seen them in movies and magazines, but knew nothing about them. Before I could ask her, she started speaking again.

"I'll say what you heard back in the school when you were losing consciousness. It's actually a translation into your language of my vibration. So, it can be picked up by 'my people'—those who seek truth. Their brain translates my core vibration into their language so it can be shared with others whose signal isn't strong enough to call me into their lives directly."

Her eyes lowered and she fell silent. When she began again, her voice had deepened and her words came out like a chant, from a depth so far away from the drugstore that it gave me chills:

I breathe a breath of force—
of wind and roar and howling storm,
While I hold together all that lives.
Beyond Earth and heavens,
I am infinite power.

On the world's summit I bring forth the Father:
My home is in the oceans deep.
From there I extend to all living creatures,
And touch heaven's sphere with my forehead.

I didn't dare say a word. I looked at her, not knowing who she had become in her speaking.

"This was a speech by Vak, the Hindu goddess of voice, speech, and the vibration of all creation. In your Christian tradition, the same creative force is called *Logos,* the Word. Logos was masculinized, as was your god. Vak's speech was first recorded in Sanskrit, in the Hindu Rig Veda thousands of years ago. That language can express almost perfectly a vibration from my world and deliver it to the heart of the hearer. Anyone speaking or hearing it who has an open heart immediately connects with me. That's because the vibration has remained connected to the words. Unfortunately, English doesn't have the same ability to convey other realms or dimensions. This translation will have to do. But it doesn't matter, does it? I'm sitting right here with you! You don't need a speech, you've got the real thing!"

Sophia looked again for the waitress, who seemed busy. Besides the two old men the counter now was lined with two policemen and four workers in blue coveralls.

"It is almost time for me to go." Sophia looked at me sadly. "I won't have time to walk you home. Just know this: I will be with you always. Your family is calling for you. I can't leave, though, without telling you about my feet, since you've asked, and about my tail, since the two go together.

"My feet appear as hooves to you because that is how you see that the natural world of your Earth is part of who I am. They are large because I need to have as much contact with the magnetic vibration of the Earth as possible when I visit here. My tail—my glorious curving shiny tail of scales—ties me in your understanding to the Great Dragon. You see, the Dragon is an ancient being. One of his names is Mercurius. 'Curious' name, isn't it?

"Just like humans, he can lose his way. He can forget his origin, his true nature, like people do. When he becomes disconnected from me, Wisdom, his source, he goes crazy and can do terrible and destructive acts.

"Anyway, my tail shows my great age, like your wrinkles someday will be evidence of the passage of time. My tail is also the revelation of my creation of Earth and the animals."

The waitress finally brought our food, hot and steaming. My hot chocolate had tiny melting marshmallows on top. I stirred them around and dunked them, collecting all but two onto the spoon. One by one, I slid them into my mouth. I tried to pour ketchup on my french fries but none would come out of the bottle. Sophia took it and whacked its bottom while holding it upside-down over my plate. I swirled my fries in the pool of ketchup.

Then, without speaking, I gobbled up about half my sandwich and french fries with delight, gulping down hot chocolate between mouthfuls. After that I wasn't very hungry. Sophia watched me while she ate most of her macaroni and cheese and drank her coffee.

When the waitress walked by and asked if we wanted anything else, I told her I wasn't finished. Sophia asked for another coffee and a slice of Dutch apple pie with two plates and two forks. I hadn't even thought of dessert. But now, I couldn't wait for the pie.

7

More about the Dragon Slayer Mark

After the waitress left, I asked, "Will you always be with me, Sophia?"

"Yes, but you must call me to you. I will lead you on an adventure. Together we will meet the Dragon. But wait, *Shhhh!* I hear something. I think your mother is calling you and that means I have to leave you for a while."

I looked at her, surprised. "What do you mean my mother is calling me? She doesn't know we're here." *Wasn't I just in school?* I wondered.

"You have to go very soon. There are things you have to do, life that has to be experienced before we can meet again. I'll always be with you, but you won't always be able to see me or talk to me like we're doing now. Your world has become too dense, too thick with thought-forms that deny the spirit world, so people can't perceive me in anything like my true form. When understanding is absent from your world, I'm sometimes perceived as a witch or a child-eater! I keep myself hidden from your world."

My face showed the confusion and fear that crept into me when she said she was leaving.

"Don't look so sad. I'll be right behind you. I'm assigned to help you. That's how the universe works. I even like you already."

The waitress came with Sophia's coffee and more cream and the apple pie. Sophia gave me half the slice on the second plate and we ate in silence. The pie was delicious—warm, fresh out of the oven. Sophia took a couple sips of coffee.

Then she reached for the salt and pepper shakers at the side of the table and put them in front of me. "Now I'll teach you how to reconnect with me more easily—without all the drama of today. Pretend these shakers are the two parts of your scar, the one I showed you on your leg. The scar has two curved teeth marks.

"To reconnect with me, you have to draw a design with your finger around and through the two marks, while saying these words. First, I will teach you the chant you will use to call me to you:

Unloose me, unbind me, oh Queen of Heaven
Unbind me from evil, one circle times seven
Loosen me from the cord of fate
I call for you with the Figure Eight.

"Can you repeat that with me? You must memorize this. Practice saying it over and over." Sophia said the chant once, softly, a few words at a time, which I imitated. She added, "You should start immediately to keep a diary after we part company today. Record everything I say, especially this chant of protection and connection to me, so you don't forget it."

She then pointed at the salt and pepper shakers and said, "Okay, so here's what you do. Start at the top of the scar. While saying the chant slowly one time, draw a circle seven times counterclockwise—do you know what direction that is?" she asked.

I nodded *Yes*. "All right, so with any finger, trace around the outside of both raised marks of the scar on your thigh. After the seventh circle is completed—without lifting your finger—keep tracing, for the last turn, a horizontal Figure Eight, an infinity symbol." She stopped again and asked, "Have you ever seen the infinity sign?" Again, I nodded. "The infinity symbol, which looks like an 8 lying down, will enclose each of the scar marks, like this." With her index finger, she drew a long 8 around the shakers so that each shaker was inside one of the lying-down teardrop shapes of the infinity symbol. "Do you understand? You speak the chant while drawing seven circles counterclockwise, and on the eighth turn, you trace a Figure Eight or infinity spiral through the middle of the two teeth."

Sophia demonstrated once more with the shakers, making sure I understood her instructions and how to go counterclockwise. Then she reached under the table, and traced the mark on my uniform where blood from the cut had soaked in and dried.

"Do I do it with my left or right fingers?"

"Either hand will do."

Then we practiced twice. She told me to say the chant aloud, softly, and then actually trace it on my thigh. Slipping my left hand under the skirt of my uniform, I found the two bulges on either side of the wound. It still hurt. I spoke the chant and awkwardly traced the circles as best I could, the eighth one spiraling between the two lumps.

"How'd I do?" I looked at Sophia expectantly, quickly removing my hand from the sticky wound, wiping it on a napkin.

"Just fine, dear. Remember to keep practicing, so you know it by heart."

"Sophia, when do I use this?"

"When you are in great need; if there is an emergency. And, remember this, if the mark ever throbs or feels hot, that means I am calling *you*. At those times, you should definitely use the mark and chant me into your life. I will either come or send you help."

"Sophia, tell me more about the Dragon."

"You will see him the next time we meet. I promise." She raised her eyes to me again and nodded. A shadow crossed her face, a momentary pinch that made her brows scrunch together.

"But when will that be, Sophia?"

"When you're ready. I will take you to the spirit world, which is really just next door to, sort of entwined with, your world. The difference is that what you experience and feel on Earth is scattered into many pieces—humans experience lots of events over a long passage of time. But in the spirit world, you *see* these events all at once, as an actual *being!*

"For example, your society calls all the trees, animals, the ocean, and web of life on Earth *Mother Nature.*" She paused, breathed in deeply, and continued, "But you don't see Mother Nature herself, only her outermost materialized garment, as it were, in pieces, each of which seems separately alive and then connected to each other."

I understood immediately and almost shouted, "*You* are Mother Nature, aren't you?" Instead, I squeaked out a little shriek, then stopped it quickly before heads turned in our direction. My mouth still gaping open in astonishment and laughter, I pointed to her, wiggling in giddy delight. She smiled and winked at me, reached over and gently pressed my lips between her fingers, shutting my mouth closed.

I nodded. But I had nothing in my short life to help me grasp what she meant, or even ask a question about such an odd topic. But I have to tell you, it was urgent, mysterious, and exciting.

She leaned toward me, her black eyes narrowing and her voice deepening: "Listen to me! Pay attention! In a minute you won't see me. To reconnect with me, you *must* trust yourself. Start following your instincts, your feelings, and pay more attention to what you love and less to what you're told by others! Use the chant to reconnect to me."

I looked at her—*Was she about to disappear?*

"Don't be passive and obedient about what is taught to you!" she commanded. "Start sifting and sorting the information you're taught and sniff your way to truth like a dog following a scent. Always follow the trail of your *own* questions, not someone else's!"

Her eyes locked into mine, her face dead serious as she slowly and clearly sent the words right past my eyes and into my soul: "Trust yourself!"

The moment turned solemn. I nodded.

"I will be with you, dear one."

8

My Seven-Year Preparation to Meet the Dragon

I gulped and lowered my eyes to my stomach as a wave of nausea overcame me. *Oh gosh, I'm going to puke.* I put my head on the table next to the sandwich plate and groaned. A sharp pain bolted up my head from behind my left ear. I started to shake all over. I gripped my sides to get the heaving to stop. Intense heat went from my stomach up my chest, flooding into my head. Slowly my mind drifted away from my scaly-tailed gorgeous companion as her inspiring words dissolved into soft scrambled murmurs. The plates on our table, the customers, and the waitress began to dim, then bleach out before my eyes. The drugstore, Sophia, the tree, the wires, the school—all of it began to fade away.

The memory of my day broke apart into pieces that drifted into a black void. I watched my personality whirl away down the same inner void. I felt nothing at all—no emotion, no pain, no worry or regret.

After that, I don't remember anything.

I woke up in a hospital room. My mother was sleeping in a chair at the end of the bed. The nurse said something and she woke up. When she noticed I was awake, she lunged out of her chair to the side of my bed and hugged me, crying. She was smiling, too, but I could see tension and worry in her gray-blue eyes.

Seven years went by before I saw Sophia again. But first, here's what happened after Sister Mary Rose found me passed out in the school library. The school nurse thought I'd fainted from hunger. The doctor who treated me said I'd actually had a seizure caused by low blood sugar. And I'd cracked my skull, too, from hitting my head on something that cut into my scalp when I fell. But the skull fracture didn't require any treatment, and healed on its own. I was told to rest a month and eat meals on a regular schedule.

I was in the hospital for a week. As soon as I got home and had settled into my room, I took out one of my old school notebooks that still had blank pages in the back. I wrote down as much as I could remember about the day I met Sophia: Sister Mary Rose's third-grade classroom, the library, and then meeting Sophia in the tree and what followed. Sitting on my bed, writing it all down, made me feel important, like I had a mission. *After all, didn't Sophia tell me that?* The only problem was, it all felt like a vivid dream. When I tried to describe what happened to me, the condescending smiles of both the doctor and my mother were a clear signal to keep my mouth shut. They'd never understand. Still, something special had happened, something that never in a million years would I have imagined could happen to me. The least I could do was record it as faithfully as possible, as Sophia instructed.

For several weeks I had lots of time resting at home, and practiced the dragon-teeth-mark ritual Sophia taught me. But she didn't come. Disappointed, I waited for my dragon slayer mark to heat up or throb. It was all healed now and wasn't even red. I tried once more, a few months later, to call Sophia with the spiral 8 around the scar mark. Once again, failure.

I returned to school, where I was treated like a celebrity for the first week because of my skull fracture. Kids wanted to see it, but there was no scar, just a spot where a nurse had shaved my hair to treat the flesh wound on my scalp. My "dragon's teeth mark" looked like any old scar—and since it appeared when I had my seizure, the doctors all thought it was caused by falling against the library table corner or some sharp object.

Before "the accident," as my parents called it, I was miserable in school, really hated it. But now, with my fractured skull and the memory of meeting Sophia still warm and alive in my memory, I felt a lot more important. I had a secret inside. It made me feel special. It brought me a new confidence that my family, friends, and classmates noticed. I didn't feel so invisible anymore.

After that episode in third grade, my life was fairly uneventful. I was a tomboy, especially during my favorite season—summer. I climbed high in the front-yard elm tree to escape my family. Until I was twelve or so, I played with the neighborhood boys, looking for frogs so we could build terrariums for them to live in. We played dodge ball in the street or "Simon Says." On hot steamy days, we stayed indoors, turned the fans on high, and played card games like "Concentration." As soon as they turned thirteen, boys seemed self-centered and spent their time with other boys doing "boy-things" from which girls were excluded. Older boys seemed to want the company of girls only to puff up their egos, and, of course, for something else. Our P.E. teachers warned us that there was only one thing on boys' minds.

I did have girl friends. There was Carol, who I was close with in grade school. I met Sherrie Sulivan, who became my very best friend, when I started going to public high school in ninth grade. Her family had just moved to the Chicago area from New York City, so we were both looking for new friends. There was something special about her. She seemed to listen, with true interest and without judgment, to just about everyone's story. She was very interested in ballet, and since she was an only child her parents could afford ballet and gymnastics lessons for her. She and her parents listened to recordings of operas and classical music and owned a lot of books, including books on art and mythology. When I visited her house, she and I would look at the pictures, piquing my interest in art history—art and architecture as they evolved through the ages.

There was only one time when I can say for sure that Sophia came to me after that first time. I was ten. Even though it was a dream, I know that it was her in person.

I was sleeping over with my friend Carol at her house. We could play in her large attic all night long and no one in her family could hear us. There were a couple of foam-rubber mattresses and sleeping bags we could fall asleep on when we got tired, which usually wasn't until 4:00 A.M. It was early in November and very cold. Sheets of rain had started to pierce the night air when Carol's mom picked me up at my house after dinner. A wild storm was hitting Chicago. Lightning and thunder kept crashing through the noise of the rain. I was excited to be sleeping over. Carol's mom always made us a huge bowl of buttered popcorn and I got to drink Coca-Cola at her house, which I never got to do at home.

One of our favorite night-time sleep-over pastimes was to pretend we were martyrs in ancient Rome. We turned Carol's attic into the Roman catacombs. We pretended that we were roaming the catacombs the night before we were captured by Roman soldiers. We knew we would be caught the next day and fed to the lions in the Colosseum, watched by thousands of cheering Romans, so we prepared to die. The magic was in the holy procession in the dark in candlelight all bent over in cramped catacomb chambers, feeling the anguish of our last night on Earth, and preparing to meet Jesus after hours of agony being eaten alive by lions.

We dressed in white robes made out of bedsheets, turned off the lights, and lit votive candles. We made a small altar out of a cardboard box turned upside down with a scarf over it. On this altar, Carol put a small vase with plastic flowers and a little statue of the Virgin Mary holding baby Jesus. We would kneel before the statue for a blessing, and then slowly rise and carefully make our way through pretend catacomb tunnels under Rome. We would really get into our parts, pretending to cry as we said good-bye to our imaginary families. This particular night was thrilling because of the wild storm.

We were right in the middle of our procession around the attic with our candles, crouching down from the low beams that were pretend catacomb doorways, when all of a sudden there was a loud *bang!* The house shook. Startled, we jumped. I hit my head on the low ceiling, dropping my candle. I quickly stepped on the flame. The attic suddenly was pitched into near darkness. The lights on the street that had shed a dim yellow light into our cave had gone out. Carol's candle was our only light.

Carol went to the stairs and opened the door. "Everything's dark!" she exclaimed. "I wonder if our house got hit by lightning." With Carol holding her candle, we left the attic and carefully made our way down two flights of stairs to the living room. There, illuminated every several seconds by flashes of lightning, Carol's mother and younger brother were sitting in the dark. They told us the neighborhood transformer had probably been struck by lightning. Then Carol's dad came in from the kitchen with several flashlights and said he'd tried to call the electric company, but the lines were busy. We sat with Carol's parents and brother for a while, then returned to the attic with a flashlight and decided to go to sleep since we wouldn't be getting any popcorn that night. I curled up into my sleeping bag next to Carol's mattress and quickly fell asleep.

That night I had an amazing vivid dream. Sophia appeared in all her glory, in a flaming white robe. She was in the center of an outdoor stage. A thunderstorm was pealing its thunder and flashing lightning all around her, but she never flinched or tried to take cover. Her white gown looked like our robes, tied at the waist. But Sophia's robe was shooting off sparks and flames, like she was on fire! In her right hand was a scepter, pointing straight at me. It sparkled and gleamed, had a big shiny red stone at the tip, and was inset with multicolored gems. Sophia was fierce looking, even angry. She spoke right to me, her scepter aimed right at my face: "*No* martyrdom!"

That was it. I didn't know what it meant or why she scowled at me until years later. I lost interest in our catacombs game after that, but it was probably because we got older and started playing Monopoly and Scrabble with her family.

My father continued at his job. My mother stayed home and cared for the house and yard. She tended a small vegetable garden and grew lots of flowers—yellow and pink roses, golden-orange and scarlet zinnias, and sunflowers. The whole family went to Friday night fish fries at the parish school cafeteria, where Mom volunteered to help serve dinners. My brother at eighteen went off to a technical college to study engineering. That was 1960. He got a job evenings and weekends there, so we rarely saw him except for holidays. My older sister Peggy continued to be bitchy. She got away with it. At fifteen she finally got her own room after my brother moved out. Before that, all us girls shared a room. I was glad at least my own bed was my territory.

Then there was my little sister Patty whom Peggy favored. Patty got all of Peggy's rejected cute clothes, jewelry, and purses. I never got anything of Peggy's. Our family dog Pearl, who had bonded with Patty, was getting older and slowing down. Sometimes Patty and Pearl would roll around on the floor together. It was so easy for me to hate the Three Peas: Peggy, Patty, and Pearl.

Barbie dolls first came out when I was around eleven. Patty collected several and played with them every day. I thought they were despicable. I didn't like dolls and I didn't like all the talk about fashions.

I learned to knit a bit, but always tangled the yarn. I tried to knit a scarf in emerald green wool that matched the color of Sophia's dress, but quit before finishing it. Peggy and her friends would buy angora thread at the dime store to wrap around their boyfriends' rings to make them smaller. Popular colors were lavender, pink, yellow, white, or whatever matched their outfit that day. I didn't have a boyfriend.

When I started going to the public high school in ninth grade, Peggy was two grades ahead of me. Billy had gone to the same high school. After he shot out the street lights, my parents pulled him out of the Catholic school and he went to the public elementary school. But Peggy, Patty, and I attended the Catholic grade school through eighth grade.

The public high school was only nine blocks away, so I could walk. I received mostly As and Bs. I still disliked math. Most of the other subjects were okay—especially English and French. I joined the French club since I wanted to go to France someday, visit the museums, and go to an outdoor café, drink coffee, and eat pastries.

I liked to bake, especially Toll House cookies, brownies, and chocolate cake. I asked my mother for family recipes, which I copied out by hand for myself.

My main hobby was reading. I used my allowance money for books instead of clothes, and asked for books for Christmas presents. I checked books out of the school and public libraries. I liked books about animals, especially horses. I read the entire *Black Stallion* and *Misty of Chincoteague* series. I enjoyed *Black Beauty, My Friend Flicka, Thunderhead,* and *Green Grass of Wyoming.* I read some historical novels about the early days of Christianity, like *Ben Hur* and *The Robe* with their gladiator fights and slaughtering of wild and tame animals in the Colosseum. I borrowed *The Search for Bridey Murphy* from my girlfriend Carol when I was around ten. Reincarnation and past lives fascinated me. I kept thinking about this book long after I returned it. My Aunt Claire sent my family a subscription to *National Geographic.* I enjoyed reading about all the different peoples, religions, and cultures in the world, especially the ancient ones in Egypt, Greece, and Rome.

My family got a TV for Christmas in 1955. I watched *Fury* on Saturday morning. My favorite TV shows were *Lassie, Rin Tin Tin, National Velvet,* and *Adventures in Paradise.* My whole family watched *Gunsmoke* on Saturday night; *Have Gun—Will Travel* came on just before. My family watched the news every night at dinner, especially Walter Cronkite. I was horrified by the violence in the world. The news always seemed to be bad.

My "inside secret," as I called it, stayed alive. It grew stronger, almost visible in its power to affect my surroundings and other people, especially when I listened to certain kinds of music. I could feel some ancient power grow in me when I listened to Beethoven symphonies, especially the Fifth and Seventh. I felt like some almighty conqueror who could save the entire world and slay all vicious dragons.

I had my own AM–FM radio, a Christmas gift from Grandma Joanne, which I listened to while doing homework. The few times I was alone, I would turn it up really loud to hear my favorite songs. Although I hated its name, my favorite was "Peggy Sue." One of Peggy's boyfriends gave her the 45 record when she was thirteen. She played it a lot at first, then tossed it aside. She didn't really like it, but I loved Buddy Holly. This song made me want to dance, which I did while playing it on the living room record player when no one was home. My other favorite was "Shimmy, Shimmy, Ko Ko Bop" which came out a few years later, in 1960, by Little

Anthony and the Imperials. That really got my body moving, too. Probably my favorite back then was Richie Valens's "La Bamba." I relished all of it—the rhythm, the drums, the lyrics of love, the fast beat of these songs. The music pouring from the radio, the record player, and the dance band TV shows made me conscious of some of the pent-up power inside me as a delicious freedom, a permission to be me.

Sometimes, during these seven years, it felt like I was split into two people: an "inner me" where I was connected to Sophia and all things cosmic, and the "outer me" in the so-called real world. I had no idea how to reconcile these two worlds. My adventures with Sophia increasingly seemed like a dream while I was in the real world. But my thoughts kept returning to her.

PART 2

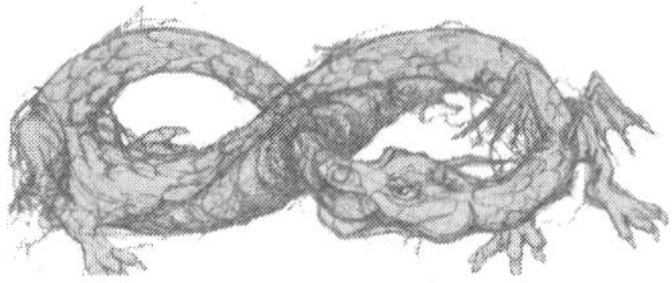

9

Return to Sophia

When I was almost fifteen, seven years after meeting Sophia in the tree, I went to bed one Sunday night dreadfully tired. It was October 21, 1962. Everyone, everywhere, must've been tired, from weeks of worrying about Castro and Khrushchev and the buildup of missiles in Cuba.

That night, as I lay on my back and began to sink into sleep, my body seemed to sink beneath the bed into the darkness and became so heavy that I wondered if I'd ever move again. My dragon slayer mark began to throb, but I was falling into sleep so quickly that memory and consciousness drained away. Then I woke up to the sound of a soft whirring outside my bedroom window. I was tuning into it, when I realized the whirring sound was in my head.

The whirring grew more intense, then there was a loud *crack!* I felt no pain. I wondered if the cracking noise happened to other people.

The whirring in my head got louder. Then it traveled down and pushed so hard against my chest that I thought I would burst. The fierce noise took over my head and body. Then I felt myself moving down a tube and felt walls around me. As the whirring subsided into the background, there was no sensation in my body. I looked ahead—which was down. There below me I saw a room, bare except for a small mat on the floor and a little table. Someone—a man?—was meditating on the floor. His head and body were covered with a pale robe. As I landed in the rustic cabin, I looked around for him, but the room was now empty. It didn't feel like a dream, because I was fully alert.

Then she entered. The Queen of my childhood, companion in the Oak, Sophia! This time she wore a long-sleeved velvety gown of purple. A zigzag pattern of astrological glyphs of the sign of Virgo, along with crescent moons, hieroglyphs, and constellations, was embroidered in silver along the hem.

Just as when I'd first met her, she wore the same scarlet velvety belt overlaid with a gold braided cord with tassels hanging down in front. It was the one with the mysterious eye-like blue stone in the middle. I wouldn't learn about this protective girdle and her magical implements until much later.

A gold chain wove through her black hair and a gold cobra snake band spiraled upward from her wrist on her left arm. A wine-colored heavy brocade satchel hung behind her left hip, its long strap crossing her right shoulder. Trailing along behind the rich emblazoned gown, the tip of her silvery scaly tail glittered. She looked exactly the same, as if time had not visited her during the years we were apart. I kept staring at her tail, hoping to see her animals jump, but it was quiet down there.

"Ah, my dear dear sweet one! How tall you have grown! It is *so* good to see you again!" She slowly, almost ceremoniously, with measured step approached me. I took my eyes off her tail and locked my gaze into hers. She took my face in her warm long fingers, tilting it upward so we could lock eyes. Sighing deeply, she placed her hands on each of my shoulders, turning me slowly around until I faced her again. She lifted up my nightgown on the left side until it was raised above the dragon-teeth mark on my thigh. She bent over and inspected the scar. Her left hand still holding my nightgown up, she traced the scar with her right index finger.

"I had so much trouble reaching you, Molly. Why didn't you call on me with your dragon mark, as I taught you? Did you forget? Did you not want to see me again?" She dropped the edge of the nightgown. Raising her body up straight, she frowned at me. I lowered my eyes, embarrassed, not knowing what to say and having no excuse.

"Did you think our friendship was over with that one meeting? That was only the first of many meetings we will have—this lifetime. We have work to do, my dear. I think you're ready to learn about the Dragon Realm."

"It's so good to see you, too," I blurted. And I meant it, really I did. Of course I was thrilled to see her again! But how could I possibly communicate to her that I was content, happy for the most part with my life on Earth? How could I possibly tell her that I didn't want to look weird or goofy to my friends? Unable to find any words to excuse my long absence, I changed the subject.

"What was the whirring noise in my head and how did I get here? Where am I?"

"The whirring signals the activation of your pineal gland, which allows you to experience altered states of consciousness. Your physical body is back in your bed, but your astral body is traveling in a dimension that co-exists alongside Earth as you know it. You are in the astral world. You can do things here just like you do on Earth—meet and talk to others, go places, feel things. Here, in the astral, you can see spirits of the dead as well as souls who are having out-of-body experiences."

She hesitated a moment, as though trying not to say more than I could understand. "There are many realms here. My beloved Sufis visit here frequently. Their scholars call this realm the *alam-al-mithal*, which is called in Latin the *mundus imaginalis* or imaginal world. Here are the archetypes, the deities, and demons. Here is the residue of all lived life."

"So why did I travel to you now, tonight? Why this particular night?"

She replied, "Your world is in a crisis, a crisis that could cause its annihilation, as you well know. Tonight is critical to stop the thought-form entity responsible for this Cuban Missile Crisis. And, you did promise to help me.

"Most of humanity has not been evolving their consciousness at all.

Many people have sunk into despair and confusion and illusion. Entire societies have separated from Nature—the cycles and circuits of stars, planets, and seasons. Your bloodline, or lineage of affinities, including your personality in previous incarnations, shows your participation in rituals of honor and appreciation for Earth and her complex interactions with the beings of the larger cosmos."

I didn't know what to say. I couldn't bear thinking about my city being blown up by Communist missiles. I had no idea how I was supposed to help Sophia, either, even though it seemed we had some kind of past-life connection. Many deep questions bubbled up in my mind, but I asked simply, "Who was that man I saw meditating?"

"The man you saw . . . his name is Chogyal. He's Tibetan. He had to help me bring you down, because I couldn't do it by myself. You're a bit difficult to reach these days."

"Where did he go?"

"Master Chogyal had to leave. He has work to do and students to mentor. You'll meet him later. Because you agreed over many lifetimes to be in *my* service, I need to show you what is at stake. The worlds are changing rapidly. There is great danger in the realms, including your so-called real world. Great shifts are about to occur."

She pointed to a small door on the wall to the right of the cabin's entrance. "But first, go into that closet and find yourself some sturdy clothes to wear . . . oh, and boots, too. Bring along a jacket, for we will be out long after the sun has set, in the cool night air. You can leave your nightgown in the closet."

She must've quickly read the puzzled hesitation on my face. "Don't worry, dear, you won't need it. We'll provide you with clothing during your stay in the astral realm." With a smile, she opened the front door, walked out, and said, "When you're done changing, come on out and join me."

I looked around the tiny bare cabin, feeling uncomfortable, as if someone might be watching. I hurried over to open the only inside door, surprised to find it led into a huge walk-in closet. There was light to see from a window.

Rods along both walls were loaded with hangers of clothing that looked foreign or old-timey, like costumes for a masquerade party or theater productions. Shelves of neatly folded shirts, pants, bags, and purses lined the walls above the rods and underneath the window. Hats of all kinds lay upon another tiered rack of shelving: churchy-looking women's hats with veils, men's caps, berets, and helmets, even two black pointed witch's hats, and a third pointy indigo blue hat embroidered with stars. A black metal stand of walking sticks caught my eye. I pulled one out and was amazed at the clear crystal ball set in its handle. Another was made of startling bright red wood, with a carved acorn fastened to its top. I stopped to finger the acorn's rough cap, amazed at the accuracy of the carving.

Men's clothes were on the left. Women's and more girly-looking clothes were on the right. I saw what appeared to be a wizard's robe among the men's clothes. On the floor were racks of boots and shoes. There were shoe boxes in the corner. I was so distracted by the odd and curious assortment of costumes and accessories that I almost lost track of time. Suddenly I remembered Sophia's urgency and quickly turned my attention back to finding pants.

I wondered why there'd be girls' clothes in this bare cottage. *Are other girls like me coming and going here? I sure would like to meet them.* I chose a pair of simple black slacks with side pockets and an elastic waistband, and a long-sleeved white blouse with buttons down the front and a round collar. The pants were about two inches too short and I knew I would look goofy, but that was all I could find quickly. All the bras I saw were for women with ample bosoms, so I went without since I was still flat-chested. I quickly removed my nightgown, hung it on a hook, and put on my selections. I surveyed the shoes and boots of all sizes neatly lined up in rows on the floor. I poked around and tried some on. They were mostly boys' or men's. Then I spotted a pair of moccasins. I smelled them. They were real deerskin! A golden tan color, well-worn with a red and blue beaded design sewn on their tops, they fit me perfectly.

Good, I'm done. I left the closet. Then, remembering that Sophia said to bring a jacket, I went back in and rooted around, in a hurry now to be outside. I didn't see any that really appealed to me. Impatient, I pushed aside the men's coats on the left clothing rod, grabbed the smallest jacket I could find, and dashed out, slamming the closet door behind me. The jacket was chocolate-brown corduroy with exquisitely carved light-tan wooden buttons. I liked it instantly, put it on, and ran outside to join the day.

A vast expanse of green lawn awaited me. Huge willow trees bowed low to greet the ground, their graceful silver green fingers caressing the grass, some dipping into the waters of a noisy little brook that licked and tickled their leafy tips. The stream then bade farewell down a crooked channel underneath and through gnarled curvy roots, disappearing into silence in the dark woods behind the cabin.

The sun was shining. It appeared to be early morning. I didn't know why, since when I had fallen asleep, it was night. I tried to push aside all my questions about where this sunshine came from, and where and why I was here and . . . *Where is this world, anyway? What is 'astral'? What does she mean 'spirits of the dead'? Oh, never mind! I want adventure, not explanations!* I positively tingled with the thought of an adventure. I ran to Sophia to show her my clothes.

"We're going to take a bit of a long hike," she said, glancing at my feet. "Moccasins? You will need boots. Where we're going there are rocky trails."

"Oh no, Sophia, there were no boots that fit me," I lied. Blushing, remembering that she could read thoughts, I slid in a minor correction. "Well, I really do love moccasins and I have a pair at home, real ones, just like these, made by Indians. Can I please wear these today?"

"Of course. I know you won't complain when your feet get sore. Remember, the moccasins will always be here for you. The grand astral closet contains more than you could ever imagine."

Sophia turned and pointed out the direction we would be walking. I had second thoughts. Hiking boots might be more practical. I said I'd look for boots and ran back to the closet, wondering what else an astral closet was used for. I put the moccasins back where I found them, and selected a pair of tan hiking boots. I grabbed a pair of heavy gray wool socks from a basket of clean rolled-up socks and pulled them onto my chilled feet.

Then I opened several of the shoeboxes, thinking there might be more shoes or boots inside. There were letters and papers in each box! Some looked like official documents; others were written in sloppy handwriting; some were in foreign languages. The ones in the last box were in a strange beautiful ornate old-style penmanship that few kids want to practice anymore.

Each box had a written label on top: "Love letters from Heloise to Abelard," "Top-secret correspondence between Albert Einstein and Franklin D. Roosevelt concerning the development of the atomic bomb," "Love letters between Peggy and Vincent." I didn't know who Heloise and Abelard were. I peeked at the atomic bomb papers, but it was all official and technical gibberish. But Peggy—that's my sister—and Vincent—her current boyfriend—*now that might be interesting!* I started to read their letters. Vincent, an aspiring artist, had beautiful handwriting. I knew he was very kind to Peggy, but she seemed more excited about his family's money than about him. I began reading Vincent's letter, and shook my head. Vincent was wondering why Peggy had stood him up one afternoon . . . Then I started thinking about how Peggy and her pretty friends tease me. They always tell me I'll never get a boyfriend because I have too many freckles and I'm a tomboy. They make fun of my skinny arms and legs and tell me I'll always have a flat chest. Peggy brags about what her boyfriends give her. She can get any boy anywhere to give her whatever she wants . . .

I was startled from my angry thoughts when Sophia peered inside the closet, where I was engrossed in the letters. "We must go—now! No time to waste—especially today—the fate of your Earth may be decided," she said brusquely. I dropped Vincent's letter, quickly pulled on and laced the hiking boots, and followed Sophia outside.

She pointed at my feet. One of my laces was coming undone already. I bent down to fix it, and grabbed the moment to steal a glance at Sophia's feet. Trying to be discreet, I stared at one of her hooves, relieved to see it was the same as before. I guess I wanted to make sure that my friend was the same "person."

"Since we don't have all day, I'm going to tell you as much as you need to know for your first lesson while we walk. Hmmm . . ." She paused to think a moment. Motioning to me to follow her, she began hiking up a path through a bright green meadow with widely spaced majestic weeping willows. The path through this park-like landscape was pebbly in places, but most of it was trampled grass.

I hesitated a moment, checking the pockets of my jacket to see if there was anything in them. In the last pocket—the left breast pocket—I found a lovely holy card! It had a scalloped edging stamped in silver. On it the blue-cloaked Virgin Mary stood on the crescent moon. I put it in my left pants pocket for safekeeping.

Sophia was way ahead of me along the path. As I dashed to catch up, I noticed a smaller eyestone attached to the back of her belt, in the center. This one was a luminous aquamarine color with a milky white center. It had its own tiny blue stone with a black dot in the center, just like the pupil of an eye.

10

Trouble and Trash in the Astral Realm

"I asked you to help me because big trouble is brewing in the astral realm. We are taking a trip today to see the Great Dragon. He is our own Mercurius, beloved of my alchemists and philosophers of all generations." Sophia paused a moment, her gaze drifting down to the path. "Our Mercurius has lost his head. He has forgotten who he really is. He has become possessed. The demon inhabiting him has stolen the Pearl of Wisdom." As she said this, she stopped in mid-stride, waved one of her long and graceful hands in a circle over her head, and tossed her black, wavy hair.

"Mercurius had everyone worried before this happened. Even his old buddy Ashmedai took him out to a fancy bar in the Land of the Shedds. Ashmedai is King of the Shedds. He talked to Mercurius about his excesses, his loss of self, if you will." With a shiver of her shoulders and tail, as though shaking off the terrible fate facing Mercurius, Sophia fell into silence.

I stopped, too, grateful for a chance to catch my breath. Waiting for her to continue this odd tale, I took a deep breath of fresh cool air. After several seconds I interrupted her reverie to ask, "Who are the Shedds?"

"They are elementals who live in their own kingdom in the astral realm with Mercurius. Ashmedai and Solomon knew each other well." She started laughing. "My dearest Solomon was duped by Ashmedai into giving him the throne of Israel. Ashmedai actually picked him up and threw him four hundred miles! But Solomon had tricked Ashmedai, too—into revealing to one of his generals the location of a sacred and magical stone called the *shamir*, which Solomon used to build his temple without the use of hammers or axes to cut stone."

Seeing my confusion and worry, she put her arm around me and looked into my eyes. "Don't worry, Solomon eventually got his throne back," she assured me. "All this is nothing new. It happens every other eon or so, and it is my job as the Mother of all Wisdom, Queen of the Middle Realm, to restore balance, to return everyone to their rightful places, so that things get related to each other in their proper proportion. The trouble is, every new time Mercurius loses his mind, I can't use the technique I used the last time, for the Dragon is a tricky beast. He learns quickly and his memory is forever. And, the way the universe works, I can't do it alone. I can't even figure out the solution alone! I need human help. This way, I learn and grow . . . and humans learn a thing or two as well."

She looked at me as if waiting for a reply.

"I don't really understand," I confessed.

"Good," she laughed. "Nor should you try. It will just interfere with your lessons. The Earth is helped in her evolution by my occasional intervention. She benefits most when I work through humans. Like you, Molly."

Sophia looked at me intensely and began walking again, leading the way. We hiked in silence for a while.

"First you must encounter the Great Dragon. He is not bad or good. You know about my tail. My tail is evidence of my connection to him. *He is who I was.* I am forever coming to be and that which comes to be, enters into being. And this beingness casts its residue behind it."

"But," I interrupted, "I thought that what is past is done, and then we are here in the present, and the future is always in front of us. I don't get it."

"Imagine a boat speeding through the water. A wake is formed and ripples away from it, simply because of the boat's force and speed and presence in the water. This wake is left behind and, you might say, has a derivative kind of life of its own. In other words, it moves, but is not the cause of its own motion. The wake appears from something else that had power."

Sophia nimbly stepped over a rivulet of water flowing across the path and continued, "Every action you do on Earth—let's say something positive like prayer or painting or writing—these creations do not just disappear, even if you tear up what you write or curse the person today whom you prayed for yesterday. These creations, prayers, curses, and beliefs continue to live long after you take your attention off them. The energy that brought them forth . . . it hangs around for a while. Images of the activity or behavior stick to this energetic residue. They drift around and then settle and rest in a realm of their own. Later on, long after the original energy is gone, these images may be enlivened by someone else's attention. This drifting and re-enlivening by others' attention produces currents. These thought-currents travel around the Earth and are visible to second sight.

"People can't see them as currents, though. They feel them as a *beast,* usually a dragon. And they are usually terrified by the sight of this beast, because it seems alive and because of its great size. But now that you know that this beast is simply residue, that its substance is thought, that it is the ghost of human creation, it shouldn't scare you too much. Do you understand at all what I'm saying?"

Of course not, I thought. "Yes, I follow you," I fibbed. As her black eyes turned onto mine, I knew instantly that she knew I had lied. Instead of embarrassing me, she laughed lightly.

"Good," she replied. Nodding her head vigorously so that her luscious black hair bounced and waved across her neck and shoulders, Sophia began hiking at an even faster pace.

I had been so engrossed in our conversation I hadn't noticed where we were going. Her strong voice with its gentle rhythm, sort of like a chant or melody, had kept me riveted to her words. While we walked now in silence, I became aware of the scenery.

We went around a bend in the path where the meadow, with its widely spaced willows and clusters of small pines, gave way to rock cliffs with long vertical openings in them at the top. The path began to get steep and rocky as we entered a canyon. Small grayish birds swooped from one side to the other. When our hike began, the path ran alongside the creek. But now the creek and path diverged as the path climbed along the breathtaking canyon wall and the creek was far below us at the bottom of the chasm. The quiet of the previous green-grass landscape was swallowed up by a blanket of sound—water rushing through rock—as soon as we entered the canyon.

Dragon Lady, as I was now beginning to think of Sophia, gradually composed herself, saw me looking around, and told me solemnly that we were entering Hell's Kitchen Canyon and had to be mindful of rocks tumbling off the cliff above our heads. I wasn't worried about the rocks. I felt at home among these cliffs and this creek. I liked the sound of Hell's Kitchen. I felt no danger walking next to my bold exotic guide.

She stepped neatly, springing almost, around a large rock on the path. We then came upon a whole pile of them, apparently fallen from above, that blocked our passage. We had to skirt around the pile. Sophia spoke with renewed vigor as we picked up the path.

"Life Force is aliveness. The only tricky part is that aliveness leaves traces of itself wherever it goes. But humans can't live life without interpreting it. Interpretation is, of course, an activity of thought." Then as though she was thinking aloud, she announced, "Life has thought attached to it, and that is the way it is. There's nothing wrong with the way things were put together! Nothing wrong at all!"

She suddenly was annoyed about something. I watched her closely. *Who is she arguing with? Certainly not me!* Then in a flash, I understood. *Is she taking credit for organizing all of this? Who does she think she is, God?*

Reading my mind, she stopped and turned to me, "Who do you *think* did all of the fitting together of the parts of this creation to make a cosmos actually *move* and *evolve*? Not *him*! Molly, grow up! There is no *him* . . . no angry bearded father who made the world in a week. That is nonsense. There is no creation without a Mother! Your gods are thought-forms, no more, no less, some more bloated with human emotion than others. The source of all, on the other hand, is beyond human comprehension. That mystery is veiled, even from me."

I was flabbergasted.

"I, on the other hand, am unveiled, to you, Molly, and to many others. I am the one whom people move toward . . . on their better days. I wove the worlds together so humanity can grow in awareness, compassion, and creativity! Ahhh, but I can't make a perfect creation. There is this periodic problem with *trash.*"

"Trash?" I repeated.

"Residue. What I was just explaining. Thought-forms. Habits of thinking. Beliefs." She looked troubled. Her brow furrowed, her black thick eyebrows scrunched together and she stroked her chin like some bearded professors do when they become thoughtful. "*Trash* is a huge, very huge, pile of leftover thoughts that once might have been wholesome. But over time, everything turns moldy and toxic, unless it is cleaned up and given a new form."

She shook her head and we continued up the path. "I haven't figured out how to permanently dissolve the toxic thought-forms. Generations ago, I set some of my favorite students to work on the problem . . . wise old mystics, Hasidic Jews they were. All discussions ended in disagreement. The ones who claimed that thought-forms can be permanently eradicated were challenged by others who understood the nature of thought more profoundly.

In other words, once something is thought, its form remains—forever. The best people can hope to do is to turn attention away from a negative thought. Then these thought-tendencies will wither and shrink, becoming all but invisible to humanity.

"But nothing is wasted in our universe," she continued on a lighter note. "Even the big pile of the past is recycled and used by Life Force to provide a shell that nurtures the seed of life until it can assume responsibility for its own life."

By this time, the cliffs of gray and white rock and their black clefts rose so high that the bottom of the canyon was in shadow. Even though the stream was far below, the sound of its tumbling waters echoed in the canyon.

Sophia stooped and picked up several small acorns that had fallen from far above us. For several moments, she stood and gazed at them lovingly in the palm of her hand. Then she returned all but one of them to the stony path. She inspected the lone acorn for a moment and then, smiling, put it into her satchel.

"Think of an acorn," she said. "Isn't it in some ways just like a human being? The past wraps around a person tightly to provide nurture until the Life Force is strong enough to break the past apart. Then she can live on her own, grow fully into her own nature, not someone else's." She pulled me toward her, her left hand on my forearm. She looked straight through my eyes.

"The acorn has a hard shell protecting the kernel with its tiny embryo—the seed that will grow into a giant oak tree. Think how powerful that seed is, to break apart that hard shell! That seed is concentrated Life Force and no power in the universe is greater than it!"

She paused, breathing hard, excited by her own splendid words. Her dark eyes glistened with the pupils dilating. She had let go of my arm and was now waving her pretty brown hands in the air, pointing to a tree, the cliff, and then the sun as she finished her speech.

I recalled our conversation in the diner when I first met her. She had spoken to me then about old thoughts. I didn't understand a lot of what she told me then, but I was getting a feel for it now. She was so animated, so certain about what she was seeing as she spoke, that it all seemed perfectly real to me. Even though her words didn't make a lot of sense on the surface, still they tingled with a kind of electrical charge. That's the only way I can describe it. Maybe it was because she was really seeing something as she spoke, and the words simply carried over what she saw. Whatever it was, they weren't ordinary words like you'd hear in school.

I took a very deep breath, totally and thoroughly electrified by the power of her speaking. It had set me on fire inside. It warmed my bones and gave me the energy to ascend the canyon path. We continued upward, the cliff walls growing ever higher.

11

A Picnic in Hell's Kitchen Canyon

We walked on in silence, carefully stepping among small boulders and jagged rock. I had forgotten everything about how I arrived in this strange land. The only thing on my mind now was a fierce desire to be with Sophia in *her* world, *to see what she saw.* That was all that mattered. I felt alert and charged with excitement about our adventure.

We spent the next half hour steadily climbing. I was surprised by her stamina and agility. The long dress she was wearing didn't seem to keep her hooves from easily picking their way through stones, whether large, sharp, or small.

Finally she stopped, pointed to a flat table-like rock, and said, "Let's rest a while."

"Ahhhh," I sighed as I collapsed on the stone with pleasure. She pulled two squishy flasks of water and two pink straws out of her wine-colored satchel. I wondered if the flasks were made of animal hide. Then she reached in her bag and drew out something wrapped in plain brown paper. She carefully undid it, put it in her palm, and pushed it toward my nose. It was milk chocolate with almonds, my favorite. Now I was in heaven.

As we munched on the delicious chocolate and sipped the water from the bags with straws, she began to tell me about the next stage of our hike.

"We're going all the way to the top." She looked up at the cliff soaring into the sky above us. "When we get there, I will show you the realm of the Great Dragon. I want you to relax, pay attention, and follow all my instructions immediately and without questioning. If you don't, it could endanger our enterprise—and yourself," she added. I sure did start to pay attention right then.

"You may see very strange things unlike anything you've experienced in your world. I may tell you to hold your breath, and you must do so until I tell you to breathe again. The fumes that rise up are toxic and hot. If you start choking, you'll feel a lot of fear and that will cause us to be separated. Do you understand?"

I swallowed several times in a row quickly and my eyes probably bugged right out of my head, but I nodded up and down a bunch of times until she told me to stop and not be so nervous.

"Fear will pull you back into your bed as quickly as this." She snapped her fingers in front of my face.

"If that happens, do not worry! You are in an altered state between waking and sleeping. Your present awareness will simply get pulled quickly back into your body that is still sleeping on your bed. You will not die here. You will wake up in your bedroom and remember this whole episode as a vivid dream. But this is not a dream! This is as real as your school life. The real and astral worlds parallel each other. The main difference is that here—in the astral—time can be expanded, stretched out. In the space of minutes or hours of sleep on Earth, you can experience days and even weeks here in the middle realm. Someday you will be able to go back and forth at will."

"I will? How?"

"Just remember, you can call me with the chant, through your dragon-teeth mark, especially when it throbs or heats up. That's when I'm calling for you! There's another way that you have taken already, when the whirring signal comes from your body."

She continued, "I can't enter your world easily as I did generations ago. *You* must come to me now. Just remember this. You can return to the astral realm just as you did tonight. When you feel an unusual deep fatigue, go quickly to bed for the night. Lay on your back—not on your side—and allow the whirring sound to take over your head. Don't be frightened. It's simply the activation of your pineal gland which prepares you to leave your body and travel to other dimensions. When the tunnel appears around you, just follow the light to wherever it leads you. Do not be afraid, don't hesitate, and don't look back. I'll be waiting for you at the end.

"And now we won't talk about that anymore. I don't want you to think about it either. If you try to remember how you got here from your bed, you may slip away from me, so bring your attention back to me and look at the cliff we are about to ascend."

I did as she commanded and looked up. A massive wall of rock with black vertical crevices towered above us. Bushes grew sideways on the cliff and piles of gray and black rock lay scattered on our path. I wondered when they fell and how often and if we'd see any fall today—or if they would drop on our heads.

"Are you ready?" she asked.

"Yes. Let's go." Actually, I wasn't so ready. I wanted to stay on that rock in the warm mid-morning sun and eat chocolate and have the strong sure melody of her words wash over me for the rest of the day. I was trying hard *not* to think of what lay ahead of us: danger and toxic fumes. *What kind of world does this Dragon live in? And where the heck am I? What does she expect me to do?* Reluctantly I got up after Sophia and stretched my arms. She put the flasks and trash into her bag. Then I focused on the pile of rocks ahead that we had to climb over.

We walked, or rather climbed and slipped, over increasingly large boulders, up a narrow path that zigzagged along the cliff that seemed vertical. The path itself was steep and hugged the cliff on one side. On the other side was a sheer drop of hundreds or maybe thousands of feet. The cliff wall was jagged, and uneven thin plates of gray rock jutted out. At one point, fascinated, I stopped and began to pull the pointed stone triangles out with one hand, wondering how many I'd have to pull out before the top of the cliff collapsed.

Most of the time we had to go single file, with Sophia ahead of me. The eyestone attached to the back of her belt caught my eye, seeming to stare back at me. Every time I thought about the chocolate, my stomach would get excited and start moving around, so I tried to think about something else. *A big plate of turkey and dressing. A chocolate milk shake. French fries. Gee, I wish I wasn't so hungry. I wonder if she brought any more food.* My legs were getting wobbly and cramped, but I didn't dare ask Sophia to rest. For an hour and a half we climbed, and I panted from the exertion.

"We'll take a rest up ahead," she called back to me. By this time, I was lagging way behind.

She disappeared around a bend. I was tired and cranky. Finally, I caught up to her. She had spread a purple linen cloth, about the size of a place mat, on a rock. On it were slices of cheese and bread. I sat down next to her and could hardly wait to eat.

The cheese was a delicate white with slivers of herbs inside. The bread was fresh and delicious, darker and coarser than I was used to. It had lots of holes and texture, not like what my mom got in the grocery store. Sophia pulled out a dark green bottle with no label. "Here . . ." she said as she handed it to me with a smile, "drink from the bottle."

I took a sip. The beverage was mellow and delicious, better than anything I'd ever tasted. I could feel my legs and bones come alive again.

"Ambrosia," Sophia said. She sipped some of it, too, and her face was sad.

I didn't know what to ask next. So I told her about a book I had read a few years ago.

"Sophia, I read a book called *The Search for Bridey Murphy.* It was all about reincarnation, how this girl remembered her past life. I really liked it. Reincarnation makes sense to me. I believe it, even though the Catholic Church says it isn't true. Do we all reincarnate?"

"Most humans do; that is the way of the human soul. But not all humans are Earth-born. Some have no soul; some are demons or entities from other realms, although they look human. Some are satanic; you can tell by their eyes that their soul has left. These entities' sole purpose is to witness pain and fear. Demons control these people. Or rather, they are not people anymore once their soul leaves the body."

I gasped at the thought of people walking around who weren't people. I wanted to know more about these devils and demons, so I asked Sophia, "In church, I've heard a lot about the legions of devils and demons in hell—could you please tell me more?"

Sophia stood up and walked several yards farther up the path. I got up to run after her. She turned and said, "Demons are entities that grow ecstatic and engorged at the sight of blood, torture, and cruelty. Demons inspired the Aztec priests' method of human sacrifice—of slicing open their victims' chests and holding up the still-beating heart for all below the temple pyramids to see. Demons whip soldiers into a frenzy and make them do terrible things. Demons drink the blood of the fallen as they die. They multiply in the presence of bloodletting done in cruelty."

Horrified, I put my hand to my mouth. I felt nauseous from images of savagery that Sophia was imprinting into my mind.

"Snap out of it, Molly!" Sophia barked, her back stiffening as her tail hit the rock of the path twice. "Stop it *now!* Control your thoughts! Bring your attention back to me this moment!"

Shocked at her abrupt shift in attitude and body position, I brought my attention back to her face, but not before stealing a glance at the rock ledge where her tail had struck. There they were—the animals flying and tumbling in the space between her tail and the rock! The wee animals vanished. Her tail curled in repose under her gown, only the very tip exposed. Her voice softened only slightly: "Slaughter, demonic possession, and sacrifice have always infected humanity. There are entities that use fear and cruelty to control innocent people. That control is most effectively disguised in religion. Wisdom—clear perception—is the only path of freedom from the terrors of slavery to negativity and evil."

Her eyes locked onto mine. I couldn't look away. She rubbed her hands together hard and fast. "So here it comes, Molly. You asked for the *whole truth* this lifetime, not the niceties and illusions of religion, schooling, and social conditioning." She stomped her hooves. "You asked to be of service to *all* dimensions, not just to the weak and the sick in your physical plane. That means you have to become stronger than the demons who control humans through blood-lust."

Sophia opened her arms wide as though to hug me. "And *that* is why you are partnered with me. You *asked* for this!"

I did? I wondered. *When did I ask for that? Why didn't I ask to be really beautiful and very rich and have boys swooning at my feet?*

"Well, I guess you're right," I confided, looking at the toes of my boots, "because I really really want to see what you see." I squirmed, not knowing if I should tell her how deeply I felt about this.

"You *will see* what I see, dearest one. That is why we have come here. Here you will see *all* the past. Although your natural world retains evidence of its great age in its canyons, fossils, crystals, coal, stones, and the magnificent creatures that inhabit it, most of the past is invisible to humans. There is no visible record of *the whole* of human deeds in your world that is evident to ordinary perception, other than the obvious structures, garbage dumps, ruins, and battlegrounds. Your fairy tales and myths record human behavior, and certainly you have millions of books and stories handed down. But I am talking about something on a cosmic scale. Everything, including all human activity and thought—it never left, my dear. That is what you are going to see today."

Sophia reached into her bag and pulled out the acorn. She showed it to me and put it back.

"You are being shown this because you need to see what you are up against when you seek to understand. As soon as you begin to unfold and rely on your infinite potential for creative intelligence, the Great Dragon will arise to thwart you. You must confront him.

"There is only this, what we are about to see . . . *the Past!* . . . You will meet the shadow side of Mercurius—in the form of the Great Dragon, Ialdabaoth. Today you will see *He who remembers all there is and has been*—except for the most important fact of all, his true nature, his own soul, his connection to the good, the true, and the beautiful."

12

The Thunder Cart

With that, she sighed long and deeply and closed her eyes. A troubled look seemed to pass briefly over her bright brown face, like a passing cloud, but it blew by in a second. She opened her eyes and returned to our picnic site. There she gathered up the remaining food, place mat, and bottle, and put everything into her bag.

Then she turned to me and put her strong slender hands on my shoulders. She looked deeply into my eyes and didn't smile. I looked back at her, directly into her eyes. *Did something just pass between us?* I didn't know for sure, but I felt a little stronger and braver, as though her confidence in me traveled through her eyes into my wavering soul.

"We won't have to walk much further," she said gently. "Up ahead we'll get some transportation." She chuckled softly.

What can she possibly mean by transportation? I wondered.

"You'll see," she replied to my thoughts.

We struggled on over the rocks, still climbing. We still had to be careful. The path was now strewn with jagged chunks of striped white and gray rock that had fallen from above. The view was staggering. All around us rose the canyon walls, and they gave way to spectacular vistas of treetops below or ahead of us where the cliffs were not so steep. The sky was so sharp and clearly blue, the trees so brilliantly green. The vast expanse of cliffs with their black crevasses and dark gray and bleached white rock gave the place a shocking stark beauty. Very large birds were swooping around. I looked them up later—they were condors.

The trail began to widen and the canyon scene gave way to a forest. The rocks on the path were gone and it was easier to walk. About twenty minutes along this trail we came upon a small wooden lean-to. It had a rough bench made of split logs.

Sophia glanced up at the sun and turned to me and said, "We'll wait here for our transportation. We shouldn't have to wait long."

We rested there in silence for about a half hour. Then I heard a rumbling sound and what sounded like snorts and chortles, huffing puffing grunts.

I couldn't believe my eyes! There in front of the lean-to came a cart pulled by two dragons! They looked alike—and just exactly as I'd always imagined real dragons would, only much smaller, about the size of draft horses. Both were the same color: a dark steel gray with scarlet-streaked wings. They had tiny arms with claws bent toward their chest, sort of like dinosaurs I had seen in books. Above and behind the little arms rose the magnificent wings that stretched out behind them like big capes blowing in the wind. The wings looked just like the ribbed bat wings I had seen in pictures. Their feet had claws and were a curious lime green color. Their bodies, curved like a snake with silvery scales and a long tail, seemed to be covered with a kind of slime that made them shiny. They had faces like crocodiles. Flames spurted from their open mouths. Long sharp fangs reached all the way up to their upper crocodile-like jaws, even with their mouths hanging open. And their eyes! I'd never imagined such scary eyes in all the fairy tales I'd read or seen their like in scary movies. They were round balls of brilliant red that glittered in the sun, more orange-red than the scarlet in their wings. Behind their eyes, sharp horns protruded from their heads.

I wasn't afraid at all, just so amazed and excited, like the first time I saw a rhinoceros close up at the zoo. *How can such a strange creature exist?* I started to go closer to the dragons, but Sophia grabbed me roughly by the shoulder and pulled me back.

"Oh no," she said sternly. "Don't get near them, or you'll be broiled. Let's get in the cart."

The cart was made of wood painted a startling crimson red, with strange emblems etched and painted in gold, silver, royal blue, and lime green on the outside. The designs were circles with complex geometric figures in them: triangles, squares, and stars. There was writing, too, but I didn't understand it. It looked like Egyptian hieroglyphs. The cart was attached to the dragons by a harness that circled around the base of the dragons' wings and joined on each side of the cart to a long pole. There was no bridle over the dragons' heads. Reins were attached to the harness. The cart had big red eight-spoked wheels.

Sophia never batted an eye. She drew a small clay jar out of her satchel and opened it. The stuff inside it looked like raw hamburger. She walked over to the dragons and fed each one. Without touching them, she laid some of the hamburger in her palm, her fingers flat and outstretched, like you would feed a horse. The dragons quickly gulped it up. The fire belching from their mouths never singed her. She turned from them and pointed to a latched door on the cart's left side. Opening it, she motioned me to get in. She took her place in the cart and firmly latched the door. I sat beside her, on her right. Sophia took the reins that were hanging over the front lip of the cart.

"This is called a Thunder Cart," she explained with seriousness. "It is used by the gods to traverse the lower realms. It is protected by very strong magic. The words and symbols on it were spoken with intention by the God of Thunder at its creation. They form a barrier that no fire or demon can penetrate. These dragons that pull it are in service to that god. I, as Bride of the Bladed Thunder, am the only other deity who is able to control these dragons. The other gods can only use the cart with me or my consort as driver."

"What do you mean—you're his 'consort'?" I asked.

"My primary love—he whose powers are at my level—is Bladed Thunder." She turned to me and smiled. "The Thunder God is my lover."

I was positively jumping in my seat from excitement. This was so neat, so unexpected! I was dying to talk to Sophia and ask her questions, but her solemn expression kept me quiet, so I tried to sit still and enjoy the ride.

Does she have sex with him? I wondered. *How do you have sex with Thunder? Ooops.* I caught myself in time and stopped that train of thought before she caught on.

I have never ever experienced such a thrill as when the dragons flew off—into the air! The cart never bumped at all and flew easily behind them. A more studious type might have questioned how it could become airborne so easily. Instead, I just reveled in the delicious excitement of being the first person I knew to get driven around by a matched pair of dragons!

"Make sure you hold on tight!" Sophia called to me over the whistling wind. "We may be heading into some turbulence."

I did as I was told. The air was warm but the wind picked up quickly and it seemed we were flying directly into it. It was fierce, cold, and howled around us. Both Sophia's and my hair streamed out behind us. The dragons were flying effortlessly—their wings hardly moved. It was as though they were riding on wind currents. We were up so high! When I looked down, my stomach dropped, as the tops of the trees and canyons were so far below us. I felt safe, though, with Sophia holding the reins. It seemed to be routine for her. She obviously had done this many times before. *But when? And with whom? And why?*

If I had known where we were going, I would've been scared to death; but instead, I was bursting with excitement. In a few minutes my excitement would turn to terror.

I was staring ahead when the dragons began to descend. I looked down. What I saw made the hairs on my neck curl up and my teeth begin to chatter. I felt dizzy and hoped I wouldn't throw up.

Below me was a seemingly endless span of cauldrons, pits of fire. It was like looking down into vast heaped-up rows of active volcanoes that belched and spumed continuously along a cleft in the earth. Huge billowing plumes of smoke rose up and then enveloped the cart as we descended closer until finally I couldn't see anything at all. The dragons never faltered . . . And the driver? She never even blinked. Her mouth was set and firm and her black eyes were focused on the invisible path ahead.

We continued this way, driving blind into the smoke, for what seemed like an eternity. I started coughing and my eyes watered.

Then the smoke suddenly evaporated, the wind died, and a thin moist mist swirled around us. I was a bit afraid to look down, but I knew I must.

Such a sight! Lava bubbled up, some of it spewing straight up. We had come down closer to the pits of fire. *This must be hell,* I thought. Slowly I became aware of a foul odor. My coughing stopped as my attention was pulled to my nose and mouth. The stench grew in intensity and became palpable, like the air itself was leaving and this burning smell was replacing it with the muddy thick foul substance going into my mouth, nose, and lungs. I felt faint. I was squirming with discomfort and choking.

Sophia looked over at me concerned, serious, and stern: "Just relax, I'll warn you when to stop breathing." She put the reins in her left hand and with her right unfastened the button on her bag and pulled out a new water flask and a dark-maroon-colored piece of linen.

"Here, wet this," she ordered in a severe tone. "Lay it against your face and breathe into it. You can control that retching response in your throat. I don't want you to throw up. It may separate us. We are very close to our goal now."

I obeyed, quickly. The cloth on my face didn't seem to help, it just made it harder to breathe. I was trying to figure out how to get enough air and I didn't want to feel any more wetness. The whole atmosphere of this place was thick with a greasy moisture that was right at the edge of intolerable.

"Look," she said with a scowl, "it's time for you to pay attention and quit whining. I warned you that things might get dangerous and difficult.

You have to go inside yourself now and pull up the courage and intention to stay with me all the way. You have everything you need to be able to survive this without vomiting or crumbling into fear. Fear is always present, especially in a situation like this. It is how you react to your fear that can cause us all harm. Acknowledge it, then change your thoughts. Every time it enters, don't react—acknowledge it, and then change your thoughts by turning your attention to something else. It's that simple. And . . . you won't be able to do anything worthwhile in my service later in your life if you don't learn to rise above your discomfort, my dear!"

Her words, instead of making me feel belittled, actually had the opposite effect. I wanted sympathy but her words snapped me to attention. My need for relief from the physical discomfort was replaced by a fresh resolve to control my fear. After all, I was still with her and safe in this cart. Sophia exuded the authority, knowledge, and experience of a seasoned general.

I removed the dark red wet cloth and shifted my focus to the murky scene below. Boulders and ash shot like geysers from the fiery pits below.

It got so hot I started to sweat. I stuck the dark red cloth under my thigh so it wouldn't blow away. Then I tore off my jacket. A sudden crazy impulse overcame me. I just couldn't resist it. I dangled the jacket over the side of the cart. My fingers let go. The jacket was incinerated instantly into a puff of ash. The air was *that* hot just below the cart! Still looking straight ahead Sophia said, "When flying over the realm of the Dragon, it is as important to keep one's thoughts secure and concentrated in one's mind as it is to keep one's hands inside the dragon cart." Only then did I remember the beautiful holy card. I patted my left pants pocket—still there.

Writhing, boiling lava was retching over the sides of the pits of fire. It was as though someone had placed a line of jagged-edged pots of fiery goo one right after the other and forgotten about them. The pots of lava were all boiling over, their contents spilling and catching fire. The rising smoke carried their horrid stench. It brought me some relief to imagine that it was food on a stove running over and burning. The more I thought of it as food, the more I relaxed and began to breathe the noxious fumes into my body without choking. It worked. I stopped coughing and my stomach settled down.

I kept looking, although I felt in some way as though I was looking at something forbidden, almost obscene, almost like looking at someone cut open on an operating table. It felt as though I was being shown the Earth herself in labor—looking at her uterus as she was giving birth—*to what?*

13

The Great Dragon

And then, I saw it: the size of a large silvery river, huge, undulating with scales the size of cars. It must be the Great Dragon. I saw no head, just what appeared, from my perspective above it, to be miles and miles of a serpent-like body. From under the scales oozed a pale yellowish slime that gave its whole appearance a greasy look. My heart literally stood still. I don't think I felt a beat, honestly, for over a minute. Then the fear came rushing back, and with it my poor heart pounded a million beats a second. I'm sure Sophia could see it bumping through my white blouse!

But she wasn't looking at me. Still intently focused on the invisible path ahead, she slapped the reins to her harnessed matched pair of dragons, shouting to them in a language I didn't understand. We kept going relentlessly forward . . . *into what new zone of terror?* The dragons still seemed to be flying effortlessly, only now streams of dark brown saliva poured from their open jaws.

I wondered how to tell the difference between a good dragon and a bad one. That took my mind temporarily away from the scene below, and my heart quieted a little. So I took another look. Still I saw nothing but a long fishy snake-like body. The Dragon's body curved around the pits of fire. Sometimes it spiraled around several in sequence, then lay either on one side or the other for four or five pits. *Maybe it was just warming itself like a snake would?* The Dragon's body was totally motionless. *That's a good sign.* I mustered a smile. Every time I joked to myself, I felt better, more in charge of a situation over which I had utterly no control at all. I also started wishing and praying that I would survive this ordeal without crumbling or leaving Sophia.

I began to imagine myself courageously taking the reins if she had to go do something . . . *What would that something be?* That thought made me tremble, so I switched to imagining myself bravely, sternly doing what I was told, whatever it was, quickly. I imagined what it would feel like to simply keep breathing and pay attention and not let my thoughts wander too far into the reality of what was happening below. I played with this kind of thinking and could almost taste what that felt like, this new me that wouldn't react to every scary thought and event.

I almost jumped out of my seat when I felt a hand squeeze my shoulder. It was Sophia's. I looked at her. She had shifted her attention to me and was actually smiling for the first time since we got in the cart.

"You're doing just fine, sweetie. You and I are embarking on the greatest adventure a human being could ever have. You are a very fortunate girl. This is so far beyond what Lewis and Clark or Columbus saw. Or even Galileo, when he saw that the Earth was not the center of the universe. You are going to see the kingdoms of the imaginal world. You are going to see who rules the legions of men who suffer under the illusion that life is theirs to control. You will see *He* who is ultimately responsible for the horrors on Earth and even for the missiles in Cuba! You are going to see what men have created over eons of time and how it now rules them!" With that, she let out a screeching blood-curdling howl like a death cry of a large animal. Her scream penetrated the smoky, oily air. She turned her gaze straight ahead toward our dragons' wings, whipped the reins hard against their scaly backs, and yelled sharply, in foreign words. And then, just as suddenly, she fell into silence.

Rattled by her cry, I realized my mouth was wide open and gathering ashes in it. So I shut it quickly, searching with my tongue for spit to keep from choking again. I turned my thoughts to her words, her acknowledgment that I was "doing just fine," and it anchored me in this swirling smoky den of hell.

I kept my eyes straight ahead for a while so as not to drift back to my thirst and discomfort. But not for long. An irresistible urge pulled my attention downward, slowly. Gathering my thoughts to only one, I kept repeating one line to myself over and over: *I am safe.* Peering over the gilded edge of the crimson cart flying through the mists, I began to make out what appeared to be the wings of the great beast below. The Dragon was still at rest. His wings looked like oily black rubber and were held close to his body. Even so, they were partially raised to fit into the cleft of earth, raised up along the sides of the deep rut that held the pits of fire. The wings were arched above him, higher than a skyscraper. Even though it was murky, I could make out what looked to be tendons in the part of the wing that stretched above him. I could only see his right wing easily. We must be traveling toward his head.

As our cart soared through the ashen mist, it seemed as though the Dragon below grew larger in size. Then I realized the reason: We were getting closer to him. Our matched pair of dragons never slowed their speed, and with the air so dense, it didn't feel like we were descending, but indeed we were . . . and quickly. I looked over at Sophia, but she did not take her narrowed eyes from the path to look at me or down at the loathsome creature below. Her mouth was set in a taut line. She was a woman—a goddess, rather—with a mission.

We were flying now over the Great Dragon's resting wings, several hundred feet above them. I still couldn't see his head. I inhaled another draft of incredibly foul moist air—tinged this time with an acrid, stinging substance that burned my throat and hurt my lungs.

"We're going down!" Sophia yelled, never turning her head, "Hold your breath now and don't breathe again until I tell you! Quick! Put the cloth back on your face!"

I gulped some more of the nasty substance that wasn't air anymore.

Coughing, I did as I was told and put the dark red cloth over my nose and mouth. I frantically searched for something to turn my attention to other than the lack of air.

Focus on the beast, I heard a voice say inside me.

Okay, I replied to myself.

Fascinated, I turned my eyes again upon the sight below. What I thought was a sleeping Dragon was actually heaving, rolling a little from side to side. The ribbed wings quivered and rippled, revealing straight pointed spines extending outward from the end of each rib. A shimmering yellowish-green oily slime polished the scales that covered this twisting river of serpentine flesh. I tried to make out the Great Dragon's head, but it still wasn't visible. There seemed to be miles and miles of neck beyond the wings.

Then the massive wide open jaws caught my attention. Jagged yellow fangs were set in his bottom jaw. His mouth belched flames the size of a school bus. I heard a powerful grunting, like a train locomotive. I couldn't see the Dragon's eyes directly because of the roils of thick oily smoke coming up toward our little cart.

The plumes of smoke rose up like demons from hell sent to fetch Sophia and me to a fate of endless suffering. I had forgotten about my breath. I don't even know if I breathed or not, because I was glued to the hideous sight before me: the face of all terror ever sensed by every living being was there. I can't convey the immensity, the cosmic scale of the horrific face of this Dragon. It was as though all the suffering of humanity was rooted here and nourished here, in this dreaded beast.

Under his chin a ball of great size glowed with translucence like a pearl. The Great Dragon held it between his scimitar-like claws. In front of his face there seemed to be ghostly figures, almost human looking, wailing steadily, low and sad. Suddenly, the great head raised, the ghosts dispersed, and half-open, orange-red eyes oozing a dark brown slime turned upward—toward our little cart!

My God, I thought, *look how close he is!* A plume of fire and smoke shot toward our cart and flames came up the side. I jumped as my right hand, which was gripping the edge of the cart, stung with heat and searing pain.

I quickly pulled it inside. My other hand was still holding the cloth to my face, fortunately. A roar like a jet taking off surrounded us. The vibration was so strong that our cart almost dumped over, but our little dragons kept going, oblivious of their belligerent cousin below. The Great Dragon had seen us and was spitting fire at us. Flames continued to lick up the sides of our cart, but it never ignited. It just got really, really hot. My right hand was bright red, almost burned from touching the wagon.

"Be damned, you wretched beast! I will speak to you tonight in the Great Hall of the Dragon Realm!" Sophia bellowed out. She pulled the reins up and then screamed "Eiyaiiiii!" to the heavens above and the boiling dank soot below. I swear I felt her scream reverberate into the pit of my stomach, strangely calming it. She slapped the reins on the backs of the matched pair, shouting: "To the Great Hall!"

The great beast in the pit below pummeled the air with a screeching blast in return.

Sophia told me to breathe. I took the cloth off my nose and mouth. As the dragons began their ascent into the heavens, I drew in fresher air. I took one last look. The Great Dragon had risen from his torpor and his wings were lifting above the walls of the cleft in the earth. His huge head pockmarked with boils and bumps was raised up toward us. Fire and black smoke poured from his drooling open jaws. Another piercing roar tore the sky from below and the cart shook from its force. As the boiling lava cauldrons receded, fresh air filled my lungs.

We flew on without stopping, without conversation. Sophia was grim in her determination and never said a word, didn't even look over at me when I watched her intently. I watched my thoughts carefully and focused on the little dragons' wings in front of me. They had fanned out, riding the wind. I couldn't see anything below.

A thick blanket of mist began to surround us. It soon shrouded even our cart dragons from view. Darkness fell quickly, and with it a chilly mist. I was cold. Sophia, again reading my condition, pulled a warm furry golden-colored blanket from under her seat. She shoved it over to me, never saying a word. I took it gratefully and wrapped it around me, and covered my legs as well. It seemed to pulsate warmth, this blanket. I snuggled into it and felt rays of sunshine go through my skin into my very bones. It made such a warm nest that I immediately started dozing and dreaming about dragons and ghosts. Every once in a while the little dragons' snorts would awaken me, but I would again drift off quickly. As the mist evaporated, the night sky appeared as a black but breathing void lit up by a million little stars. A large cloud, all lit up around the edges, veiled the moon.

14

The Path in the Dark

The cart began to shimmy and tilt. I awoke with a sudden jolt. *Where am I? A dream within a dream?* I clutched the sides. The cart was landing somewhere. It was still somehow pitch black, though I could see scudding, dark, or sometimes fibrous-looking clouds, like the ones before a storm, off and on covering patches of stars as well as the half moon that hung high. With hardly a bump, we were back on land.

Sophia jumped out and began fiddling with something. Suddenly, there was more light. She had lit a torch by saying, "Light, alight," and fastened it to the cart. She gestured with her hand that I should get out of the cart. Not bothering to unlatch the door, I swung my legs over the edge, easily and gratefully jumping to the solid ground.

Sophia released the dragons from their reins and harness. Rummaging through her satchel, she pulled out the hamburger jar and dumped the rest into a pan she pulled out from under the seat. She placed the pan in front of them and they devoured the raw meat in seconds. I briefly wondered why Sophia used the hamburger pan to feed them now but she didn't answer my unspoken question.

Sophia spoke a few words to the cart dragons in a language I didn't understand. Then she turned to me and said, "Let's go." With the torch in her left hand, she began to trot swiftly into the blackness. That was all. No explanation of what we had been through or where we were going. I moved quickly, not wanting to be left behind in the dark. The path seemed smooth enough, thank goodness—no jagged rocks or boulders, just pine needles and small pine cones that crunched underfoot.

The darkness and growing gloom from the clouds seemed to pulsate around me. Eventually, I could make out that we were walking alongside a forest of tall pines and evergreens that looked like Christmas trees. The thought of dragons or scary beasts peering at us from behind the trees, drooling in anticipation of a meal of human flesh, made my knees wobbly. But I earnestly was trying to practice what Sophia had told me, to control my thoughts—especially after I dropped the jacket, which I missed now in the chilly air. Falling a few steps behind Sophia, I concentrated on the big torch she carried. It was in a metal carrier stuffed with something to keep the fire burning. The carrier had a long handle on one side with grooves, maybe to hold it better.

We came to a stone staircase. I looked down, but couldn't see anything. "Be very careful," Sophia warned. "The steps are slippery. If you fall, there is no barrier to keep you from tumbling several hundred feet into the gorge below."

We began descending. It was hard to keep my balance as the steps were of uneven height and there was nothing to hold onto. Under the soles of my boots, it felt like the steps were now mostly covered with damp decaying leaves. I slipped after only a few steps, falling down two steps and coming close to the edge, but Sophia grabbed me.

Brushing me off and helping me get steady again on my feet, Sophia locked her eyes on mine, saying with slow force: "Keep up with me. I cannot be delayed further. If you lose me, I will be unable to find you easily because we are approaching the Land of the Dead. Since you are not actually dead, there is a vibrational density around you that will make it difficult for me to locate you."

"Then what will I do if we get separated?" I swallowed hard a couple times from nerves and worry.

"The chant—of course—we talked about it."

"Of course, Sophia. I memorized it." I had indeed practiced the ritual chant, but I gulped again as I remembered the last time was almost seven years ago.

"Well, fine. Then there shouldn't be anything to worry about, right? Just keep up with me. I won't wait."

We kept descending, making our way around sharp turns between walls of rock. At one place, the walls suddenly disappeared and the trail was washed out, dangerous and hard to see.

The sweet night air was damp. I inhaled the delicious familiar scent of pine and felt it cleaning out my lungs and nose and mouth.

What is that sound? I stopped dead in my tracks. Wafting through the night was the sound of singing! *Oh, what a strain of sweetness after hours of terror and brimstone.* I didn't take a step forward until I had strained my ears long enough to recognize the faint but familiar chant. It was *Pange Lingua*, a hymn from church at Easter time, sung on Holy Thursday. I bolted and stumbled and finally caught up to Sophia.

"I hear music! I know that hymn!" I tugged on her sleeve. She turned to me. Her lips pursed together and her eyebrows furrowed down until it made her face look like a big "X" in the weird shadows from the torch.

"That's my favorite hymn!" I began to sing along quietly. Sophia remained silent and shook my fingers off her arm and continued walking toward the music.

"It's best if you remain alert. Your voice is lovely, but it will go better for us if we are not announced ahead of time. Pay attention to the path."

Why is she so stern? Where exactly are we going and why is our visit secret? I wondered. The heavenly singing was getting closer! The path suddenly divided. Sophia made a sharp turn to the left and picked up her pace. I had to run a little to keep up.

We walked quickly in the dark for about five minutes. Then I saw green phosphorescent vapors pulsating—a heap of something was emitting a weird glow. We entered a clearing and there, near a hillock, was a small stone temple lit by a phosphorescent greenish-yellow slime that cloaked everything. Four stone cobras were covered with the same green squishy paste. They were coiled, with raised heads and glaring eyes. Their mouths were open and their carved fangs gleamed a polished white in the dark. These stone snakes guarded the entrance to the temple, which seemed to be like a huge dark gaping maw, a cave mouth, from which a small dark stream, stinking of sewage, trickled downward out of sight.

Carved on a gray stone lintel above the cave mouth was a detailed image. One large ram was being ridden by a bull, a lion, an eagle, and a man. I couldn't imagine why. Above these figures was a carving of two fish. I wondered what this all meant. In school I had learned that the bull, lion, eagle, and man represent the four Evangelists, and that the pair of fish is an early Christian symbol of Christ. I was going to ask Sophia, but—

She again turned around and glared at me. "*Shhh!* Quiet!" She then whispered, "No questions now. But remember this place well. It indicates we are getting close to the Hall of Ialdabaoth, the Lair of the Great Dragon. This temple was once a sacred place, but it has been smothered by the accreted goo of false dogma, and is now the source of one of the streams that flows into the River Styx."

She continued, "This temple marks the position of a triple juncture of the Land of the Dead, the astral realm where human beings travel, and Ialdabaoth's realm. It is a portal, a magical place where time can be altered and multiple levels and dimensions can be accessed. Since our intention is to enter the realm of Ialdabaoth, the temple appears in decay. What appears to you as slimy accretions are, in fact, lies foisted upon the human heart and mind by Ialdabaoth.

"Since we're entering *his* Land, I must extinguish the torch now. It is fortunate that the sky is now entirely cloud-covered, obscuring the moon—he must not see us moving." She put the torch in a kind of holder on a stone wall on the right side of the temple and then quickly said, "Dark, unlight," to extinguish the flame. No smoke rose from the snuffed torch. We were now mostly in darkness, with just dim light reflected from the moon to the clouds. My eyes adapted somewhat. I suspected Sophia's night vision was far better than mine.

Sophia and I stood by the temple. I saw we had come to the end of our path. The trail stopped at the edge of the cliff. I peered over the edge and caught my breath as a queasy feeling unsettled my stomach. I was looking down at the dark outlines of trees growing on the steep sides of the canyon wall below us.

"Watch your step!" she commanded. "From here to our destination it is rocky and slippery. We have to approach Ialdabaoth's temple from the side. I'll go first. We have to go single file around the cliffs. Use your intuition. The darkness will awaken and magnify your senses other than sight."

Turning sharply to the right, she pushed her way through tangled brush and we came to another staircase. Clearly she knew how to get wherever we were going. I followed, being very careful to step exactly where she did. The slightly luminescent eyestone at the back of Sophia's belt helped me figure out her movements but it was also distracting. We were going downhill. The staircase trail twisted and turned.

Suddenly, my right foot stepped in a hole in the stairs where a stone must have been missing. I lost my balance. My body pitched forward, and the whole section of stairs gave way under me. Rocks and dirt broke loose and fell with me. First, I hit rock. Then I bounced off and rolled, screaming. Dirt got in my mouth. Stones, sticks, and a pile of roots, bushes, and pebbly soil chased after me down the hill, hitting all but my shoulders and head. My left knee hit the ground first. My body crumpled. I struggled for air, coughing out dirt, amazed to be alive.

Not a second passed before the pain came screaming through my back and legs. *Why do I feel so much pain if I'm not in my physical body?* I wondered, as I rolled away from the pile of debris, grabbing my left knee which was setting off fire alarms to my brain. Hot wet blood made mud with the dirt on my hand. My hand could feel a gap where the pants were badly torn—the rock or whatever I'd hit had been very sharp. From the throbbing it felt like the gash started at the top of my knee and ran down my leg. I tried to get up. *I must catch up to Sophia!*

15

Ghosts

Before I could unscramble myself to try to stand up, while I was still trembling and shaky, something went *swish* past my face. It felt clammy and soft and looked like condensation or fog. *Yuck, there's another one.* I ducked, covering my face with the crook of my right arm. Suddenly, vaporous squishy forms engulfed me. I panicked. Blood was seeping down my left leg. I rolled over the stony ground, protecting my face from . . . *from what?* I poked my face out from under my arm. *My dear God, it's ghosts! I've fallen into the Land of the Dead!*

Dusty white forms flew about me. They looked like fish darting through an aquarium, only these were upright instead of horizontal. I even saw faces, with black holes pulsating a weird yellow light where eyes should be. A mixture of ravenous hunger and terror twisted the smoky dust of their faces into gaping mouths—and they were—*oh my God, they were attaching to my bleeding knee!* They began to struggle and push each other to get to my blood! I screamed, but my throat was hoarse and scratchy from the dirt in it. Gasping for breath, I inhaled noxious ammonia vapors from the ghosts and began to choke.

"Sophia, wait! Help me!" I yelled in vain, thrashing my arms at the coagulated mist sucking my knee. "Stop it, you creepy leeches!" My arms sliced right through their fog; the ghosts never flinched or noticed. They may not have been substantial, but their sucking was real. Unexpectedly, the pain diminished a bit; but the feeding frenzy on my knee, along with the smell of blood and ammonia made me feel nauseous. My conviction that I had ruined Sophia's plans only added to my misery. Anguish overwhelmed my mind and body. After shaking uncontrollably from pain and fright, and exhausted from flailing my arms, I finally fainted.

Pange lingua, glorio-o-si . . . angelic voices wafted in the ethers of the void into which my consciousness collapsed, slowly bringing me back into awareness of throbbing pain in my leg. I was lying on my back, still in the dirt and rocks. *There's the same hymn I just heard with Sophia!* I recognized the cherished melody with relief. Maybe I can find her. It was still dark, but there were dim lights. I smelled kerosene and smoke, and the air was filled with dust.

"Go *on,* pick 'er up, Myron!" a gnarly raspy male voice commanded.

"How did she get *here?*" replied a younger squeaky boy voice. *"Shoo, you beasties, shoo!"* he yelled, probably to the ghosts feeding on my leg. "*Go back to hell,* you bloodsuckers!"

I looked up and saw a murky outline of a gaunt young man with a scraggly beard. He was standing over me with a can, spraying at the air above my leg. Even with the light of the lanterns each man was carrying, it was impossible to get a good look at them. I think because I was in so much pain, I wasn't scared of them. I should have been.

"It don't matter! Lift 'er up, we gotta git 'er outta here!" raspy man commanded.

"We can't just start carrying her anywhere. She has to go to the right place."

"You worry too much about rules, boy. She ain't been tagged yet. It don't matter where she goes. It's all the same in the end. Remember, we get paid by the body, not by the hour. But jist for you, I'll check . . . pain in the butt," he mumbled.

"It is *not* all the same in the end, and you know it, dirt bag!" Squeaky was mad.

"Watch it, punk!" spat Raspy. "You bin assigned to me. I give the orders. You obey!"

Raspy man got down on his knees with difficulty. Unable to speak or to move without pain, I stayed conscious by watching and noting what they said, so I could find my way back to Sophia. Raspy's breath reached my face, putrid like stale cigar smoke and rotten onions. Roughly turning me on my right side, he brought his lantern down close to my chest. The kerosene fumes made me choke, which racked my ribs with more stabs of pain. I wasn't getting enough air and panicked all over again.

I never said a word to them the whole time. I was hurting too much and just too tired. It took all my energy just to keep awake and breathe. I was glad they never asked me anything. In fact, they treated me like I was already dead.

"She's just a kid, you dolt!" Squeaky's voice was getting stronger. "And look, can't you see that little cross around her neck? Are you blind? I betcha she's Catholic. We're taking her to the Catholic gate, Max . . ." I remembered the tiny gold cross fastened onto its gold chain still clasped around my neck, hoping that it would save my life.

"Nah," said Raspy. He started coughing from the kerosene fumes, then stopped. "Lotsa those who wear crosses ain't Catholic—they's just Christian—Protestants like Baptists, Presbyterians, Methodists, Holy Rollers. . . . Some of those hells are really fire 'n' brimstone—an' those gates're closer, Myron. So let's take 'er to one of them, cuz it's almost time to get off our shift."

Myron-Squeaky had carefully rolled me over, onto my back. "Hey, what's this?" Through my slitted eyes, I saw he held up the holy card which apparently had almost fallen out of my pants pocket—and which he'd plucked out. "Voigin Mary holy card, Catholic for sure. So—hey—off to the Catholic gate—or nowhere! So, Max, let's go!" I felt his hand brush my neck near the gold cross, where he apparently tucked the holy card under the edge of my partially unbuttoned white blouse.

Myron kept on, "She's a kid and a Catholic and the rules are the rules. We take her to the Catholic gate." He started to move my body, then stopped suddenly. "Max, wait! Look here! That wound on her knee . . . it's giving off a green haze." Myron leaned back to give Max another look. Now my squeaky savior Myron knelt down with his lantern near me, but not so close that I breathed in smoke. Gently, he probed the wound on my knee and leg.

Stinky-Raspy Max had stood up, observing the slash on my pants knee from above. "There! Look at that, you punk brat—that wound is glowin'—betcha she's got the 'mark'—she's one of 'them.' If they glows green, we know they's got it, don't even have to look where. We're dumpin' 'er off at the *Refinery,* Myron, and it's closer than any of the gates."

Max then stooped down and leaned over me, and his stale stinky breath spilled onto my face with every word. "That there gives me the willies. Let's hurry up and drop 'er off. I dunno how she got here, bleedin' all over the place—must've fallen off the delivery truck or sumpin'."

I was almost shaking, not knowing what these men were going to do to me. The throbbing pain outranked the fear, though, demanding all my attention. But "Refinery" didn't sound good at all.

I heard Squeaky-Savior Myron plaintively once more insist to Max, "She may be one of them . . . but I insist—Catholic gate! She had to be a good Catholic if she had the holy card." I doubted Raspy Max would listen.

When Myron turned me on my back, I had slowly pulled out my right arm to free it up as he rolled me over. Now I slowly moved my hands, still sticky with blood, to my sides, to reduce the pressure on them, as they were falling asleep.

Relieved, I tried to relax and focus on my breathing, but it hurt too much. Short little breaths were all I could manage. *Sophia is long gone. I began to think about my situation. I'm on my own. At least I'm not dead—or am I?—but a Catholic gate sure sounds fine to me, not a Refinery. But what about my dragon's teeth mark?* I began to tremble more violently at the thought that I had some brand on me that meant something in this odd world. *Something that made me glow in the dark? What could it mean?* I noticed that my body was beginning to give off a phosphorescent green glow, which seemed to center around my injured knee.

Then I remembered! Flooding past the fever and pain like an express train, the memory shot into my consciousness. There she was again in my mind's eye—Sophia in the tree, my fall, her inspection of my left thigh . . .

I surreptitiously slid my left hand inside the waistband of my pants down to the scar on my thigh, rubbing it. *My God! What was it she told me to do?* Trace my index finger of either hand around the scar seven times, saying . . . saying . . . *What was it she told me to say?* Frantically searching my memory, pieces of the chant began to return. My mental search was interrupted by stabs of pain in my leg, so intense that they took my breath away, what little of it was left. *Something like binding and unbinding . . .* Now—there it is! I have it! I spoke the words to myself in silence.

Unloose me, unbind me, oh Queen of Heaven
Unbind me from evil, one circle times seven
Loosen me from the cord of fate
I call for you with the Figure Eight.

Then I remembered that I had to draw a Figure Eight at the end of drawing seven circles, intersecting the midpoint of the two circles of the 8 between the two teeth of the scar.

Okay, here goes. I began to whisper the chant: . . . One circle . . . two circles . . . I winced as the men began to maneuver my body onto some kind of stretcher.

Squeaky-Savior-Myron had knelt down and was lifting my back to put something under it. Stinky-Raspy-Max lifted me while Squeaky helped to balance. My whole body was shaking. They hoisted me up, each one taking an end of the cloth.

Three circles . . . four circles . . . five circles . . .

The stretcher under my aching back was made of a hard and scratchy material. As the men began to walk, pain surged up and down the left side of my body. Although I didn't talk, I cried out in pain several times, and I must've filled the night air with my moaning. But Raspy and Squeaky never responded—it was like they couldn't hear my cries.

Six circles . . . there, here it is . . . now . . . seven circles. *The next step is the Figure Eight . . . Wait, what's that I hear?*

I began to hear the *Pange Lingua* hymn get louder. My mind drifted away. My left hand became numb and paralyzed, refusing to obey my command to finish the task I had ordered it to do. I struggled to remain awake, but my mind was filling with images of the day like a sinking ship filling with water. I sank into a dream-like state full of scenes of dragons, fire pits, and rocky cliffs.

16

Angel Betty

"Hey Betty, over here!" yelled Raspy Max. "This might be a really strange one. Not only did we see 'er glowin' green, but what's 'er hand doin' now in 'er pants?—Playin' with 'erself? Could she be a zombie or a vampire?—they're the worst—'cept they don't wear no crosses. Betty, I need you to come and check 'er out!"

I woke up, confused and disoriented. *Oh, the pain!* Opening my eyes, I saw lights. I tried to turn my head but it was stuck. The fingers of my right hand scratched the rough canvas-like material, telling me I was still on the stretcher. My left hand was still inside my pants over the scar on my thigh. Someone was coming over to me. I felt a hand on my head, stroking my hair. I looked up and my fevered vision took in a face shriveled dry with wrinkles. The eyes were pale, the color of dust. The woman had long straight bleached-blonde hair past her shoulders. She was smiling gently and spoke not a word. I relaxed a bit.

Forgetting all about the Figure Eight, I blinked my eyes, once, twice. *Are those wings on her shoulders? Is this an angel ministering to me?* She immediately saw the little gold cross around my neck and the Virgin Mary holy card and nodded to the men, speaking in a hushed voice. *Am I not supposed to hear? Has she seen my green glow, too?* I strained to hear what Betty was saying, but the hymn intruded. Closing my eyes, I listened to the divine female voices singing the strains of familiar verses:

Pange, lingua, gloriosi
Corporis mysterium,
Sanguinisque pretiosi,
quem in mundi pretium
fructus ventris generosi
Rex effudit gentium.

I recalled one of the sisters in my grammar school had said the Latin meant, "Sing, my tongue, the Savior's glory, the glory of his flesh and blood . . ."

The voices kept singing the hymn over and over, exactly the same. I wondered why they didn't sing another hymn. The repetition of the same verse of the same hymn with the same voices began to grate on my nerves. Soon, images of Sophia and our journey began to flood into my memory, and with them a simmering panic. *Where is she? Why did she abandon me?*

I opened my eyes. *I've got to tell them I don't belong here*, I thought frantically. But before I could gather up my strength to talk, old Betty with the long bleached-blonde hair leaned over and patted my head.

"You'll be fine, dear. You're here, in heaven, with all us angels. Everything will be alright." Her voice was high pitched, like a little girl's, distinctly unpleasant, unnatural. "Well, you knows here I'm called Betty—it ain't Elizabeth—cuz it's really: 'Bet'–'tee'. I remember bettin' them horses at Belmont Tracks—won $1000 once, that got me goin' for life. But you gotta remember this heaven here, whatever you most desire, you get."

Angel Betty withdrew from me and spoke to Raspy. I strained to hear, but only a few words escaped: "untagged," "mistake," "spy."

My left hand crept up my body out of my pants and I let it rest along my side. Did Angel Betty or Max or Myron notice? I pretended to be dead. I was too scared to draw attention to myself anymore by drawing circles around the scar, or even moving my hand again, or even trembling. So I lay still, praying, hoping to be rescued by Sophia.

"Betty, we're leavin' 'er here, and that's that. You deal with 'er . . . you said you would." Raspy Max spoke with final authority. "I'm off work in ten minutes. I'm through. I ain't takin' 'er no more places. Come on, Myron, let's leave 'er in the storage shed. They'll find 'er eventually."

Angel Betty said, "Well, I'd go with you to the warehouse, but my shift is about done too. Gotta see the boss—heard there's gonna be a really big load coming in tomorrow. Something to do with missiles or fallout or something. I wonder if the race tracks'll still be there after it all happens. But I'll check on her tomorrow." I heard Angel Betty walk off, muttering to herself about her long-ago life at the tracks, the horses, and the "numbers."

Myron and Max lifted the stretcher. I closed my eyes and reopened them when they began walking. I wanted to take note of my surroundings. *I must find Sophia.* After they walked a short way, I began to hear the *Pange Lingua* hymn again, and wanted to scream. Max opened a door to a garage-sized building. The hymn grew louder. *They're taking me to hell,* I mused. *Of course, hell would play the same song over and over a million times until you go berserk.* Myron and Max carried me in and set the stretcher on the ground. I couldn't see anything. It was dark, but the sweet odor of burning tobacco came through, filling the air, competing for space with the hymn from hell. The pungent fragrance of Max's cigar smoke wafted around me. It now felt comforting, just like my grandfather's garage.

"Okay, Myron, we're outta here." A moment passed. Max spoke again, harshly. "Myron, leave 'er be! Ain't no use even thinkin' 'bout doin' somethin' for 'er. Betty'll take care of things. Leave it alone."

Myron said nothing. I wondered why he was hesitating, what he knew that I didn't. *He's worried about leaving me here—I wonder why.* Thoughts of old Betty with the fake smile touching me with her creepy dry hands made me shudder. I pushed down a wave of panic by thinking, *So Myron has some conscience. He's kind and protective of me, a stranger, even though to Max, I'm just another dead body.* A wave of confidence returned to me with the thought that Myron, at least, was human. He had a heart. *Maybe there are more like him in this bizarre realm?* I wondered.

Max and Myron walked out and shut the door, leaving me alone with the song and cigar smoke.

I have to stop that music or I'll go crazy and start screaming. It was almost worse than my pain. I decided to get up and find its source so I could shut it off. It took several minutes to regain a bit of control over my legs, especially my gashed and bruised left one. Slowly, they began to respond to my commands to move, get up, walk. My eyes were now accustomed to the darkness. I managed finally to climb up away from the stretcher, holding on to some heavy boxes stacked next to me. Groping along the boxes, my hands steadied me as I inched my way to the source of the toxic hymn. I was focused entirely on finding where the music came from and shutting it off.

I think I see it! I whispered to the emptiness. A tiny light appeared now, barely visible behind stacks of boxes. *It must be a night light,* I figured. I lurched forward, my legs trembly and hurting. As I approached the light, the music grew louder.

Next to a table with a huge white plastic vase of plastic Easter lilies and roses, I found the source of the music. It was just a record player, with a 45 record spinning round and round. Furious, I smashed the needle across the record to stop it. Screeching, it quickly died. Just to make sure I'd never have to hear it again, I picked up the record and, with jubilation, snapped it in two. And then to make sure it would never rise from the dead, I broke the two pieces into four pieces.

All at once, both the irony and the contradiction of my breaking my favorite hymn to bits collided in my conscience. *What in the world is going on here?* Yes, I hated the Catholic school and the catechism classes. But I always loved the mystical chants, hymns, and Christmas carols. This particular hymn had been the most thrilling for me to hear, ushering in the edge of the seasons of warmth and sun: Spring, Easter, trees in full bloom, the flowers of April and May . . . I used to think the melody was unearthly, inspiring, resonating with unseen but powerfully present devotion to the good and the beautiful. Holiness had pervaded my body and feelings when I heard the female soprano voices arching and vibrating into the ethers.

What am I doing? How did my most favorite hymn become something so aggravating, something that makes me crazy? I looked in horror at the four broken pieces of the record in my hands. *What have I become? Where am I? I must find Sophia. I must get out of here and save myself!* I threw the record pieces on the floor and stomped on them.

A part of me was reluctant to do her rescue chant. *What if she's on important business? Obviously, she is, she told me so, her mission has to do with the missiles. She was stern and focused and in a hurry. Her task can't wait until tomorrow. What if bad things happen because I call her to help me?*

A million thoughts, worries, and distractions crowded my mind as I stumbled through the darkness and finally found the door. Pain rushed in lightning bolts up my wounded leg. My whole body was one big cramp that crushed the wind right out of me. I kept focusing on my breath to keep alert. Breathing was the only way to control the panic and pain.

Before I shut the door, I stuck my head back in to get a last whiff of the cigar aroma, grateful to the shed for giving me a hiding place. With no idea how to get back to the crossroads somewhere up a steep hillside where I lost Sophia, I just started walking to get as far away as I could from old Betty and Max and Myron.

17

Rescued by Sophia

There was some light from the moon shining above a heavy murk of swirling, roiling thick clouds. I knew I had to be careful, and still walk as fast as I could. I was very glad to be wearing the hiking boots that Sophia had suggested.

Finally, I had to take a break. My knee and leg throbbed. I was lost. I had seen no one since leaving the warehouse and hoped I could now call

Sophia using the ritual she'd taught me. I needed help and no longer cared if I interrupted her important business. I sat on an old stone wall covered with lichen. It glowed phosphorescent green from the light of the moon that peered out briefly through the blanket of clouds.

Once again, I stuck my left hand into my pants to the raised welts of the scar. This time I spoke the chant aloud while drawing the circles.

Unloose me, unbind me, oh Queen of Heaven
Unbind me from evil, one circle times seven
Loosen me from the cord of fate
I call for you with the Figure Eight.

As I uttered the chant with all my attention focused on it, I drew my circles around the scar on my thigh . . . one . . . two . . . three . . . four . . . five . . . I thought I heard some noises. *Is it Max and Myron?* . . . six . . . seven circles. Then I got to the Figure Eight part . . . I intersected the midpoint of the two circles of the 8 between the two teeth of the scar! Done!

I heard more noises, and thought it was those distinctive Raspy and Squeaky voices. Both my hands now at my sides, I waited in stillness. And then Sophia came running up.

You can't imagine how glad I was to see her! And she, me. We hugged and she said, "We must get going, get back on the path, get to the Hall of Ialdabaoth, the Great Dragon. We are not far, but we *must* go! Now! The fate of your Earth depends on our speed. You can tell me about your adventures with the ghosts later."

I was chilled and without a jacket. My knee was flaming again. I complained, "Oh, Sophia, I'm scared. I gashed my knee when I fell, and . . . I'm not sure I can climb or go down any more stairs, or walk much farther."

"Let me see," Sophia replied. There was a very pale glow to everything, but it seemed that Sophia could see in the dark like an owl.

"Ah, yes. . . . . Not bad, but bloody. It looks like it hurts. Let me wipe it off, and then pour some healing tincture over it. This will really sting."

First Sophia ripped apart my pants further along the leg, to expose the entire wound. Then she gently wiped it with a small piece of cloth from her bag, wet with water from one of the flasks. After that she opened a small silvery glass bottle—almost like a perfume bottle—I whiffed the fragrance of some herbs. Sophia poured the tincture on my knee. As she had promised, it stung! But about ten seconds later, all the pain was gone. When I touched where the wound had been, the skin now felt intact, *all healed.* She let me take one tiny swallow from this small bottle. It energized me completely. *What's in that?* I wondered.

I tried asking about Raspy and Squeaky and Angel Betty, but Sophia, reading my thoughts, replied before I could utter a word, "Once they sensed the presence of the Queen of Heaven, they scurried off to their ghost swamp. That swamp is a realm unto itself—a lower hell, so to speak. But it should not concern us right now."

I tried to ask about the healing tincture, but Sophia just repeated, "We must hurry. We will take a shortcut to the temple near where you got lost. It's not very far. And take off that little gold cross—*now!* It will only cause problems where we're going. Put it on that flat stone there." In the dimness I could see her pointing.

I reluctantly unclasped the chain and did as she told me. The cross had been a special gift. And it had saved me from a horrible fate back there with Raspy and Squeaky.

"Remember, if you get lost again, I may not be able to help you. You can only use the dragon slayer mark *one time* in the land of the ghosts. After you've truly become a dragon slayer you'll understand much more about the mark and its use. Now, let's be quiet."

Sophia now led me to the cliff at the edge of the ghost-swamp area. In the dim light, the cliff appeared a few hundred feet high—with some set-back ledges. Leaning against the cliff was a tall wobbly looking ladder made of logs and branches of varying sizes lashed together with rope or vines—the kind used by cliff-dweller Indians in the Southwest. My stomach churned!

"Up we go, there's little time. You go first. I'll be right behind you, so you need not worry about falling. *Do not* look down." With that Sophia nudged me. I started climbing, one rung at a time. This was nothing like climbing trees, with their comforting interwoven branches. Fortunately the rungs weren't too far apart, but there were a tiring hundred or so of them. I found myself on a ledge about ten feet wide. Beyond that was another cliff. Sophia followed behind me onto the ledge and pointed to another ladder. We climbed this ladder, and a third. Although tempted, I never once looked down. I had no idea how Sophia climbed in that dress, or with her hooves, but she did, and easily.

When we reached the top, I was glad to see a grassy meadow in the dim light. And there was the small phosphorescent temple with its stone coiled serpents!

"Back to where we left off," said Sophia. "Again, I want you to stay right with me, in front of me, just like on the ladders."

With that she picked up the torch from its holder on the stone wall, but didn't light it so as not to alert the Great Dragon to our presence.

We followed a path through some tangled brush. This time I was in front, but I could see the path. We were going downhill, and the trail did twist and turn as before. It was scary being in front. I walked as fast as I could, so glad that Sophia had healed my wound quickly with the tincture. Occasionally, she would whisper some instructions in the dark, "right" or "left," "watch out," "there's a big stone, or puddle, right in front of you." Clearly, she knew how to get wherever we were going. And thank goodness this time she avoided the stone staircase where I fell before.

Finally, a different set of stone steps appeared ahead, and down we went. Behind me, her hooves clattered and clicked on the stones. I was as careful as I could be, and concentrated not to fall or miss a step. My pace was quicker than I could ever have imagined..

We came to another small meadow. Sophia again admonished in a whisper, "Quiet as possible, *shhhh,* from here on." She ignited the torch again with a whispered "Light, alight." We moved quickly through the dewy grass.

At the far end of the meadow, three steps led up to a small balustrade with an opening, beyond which was a patio made of fitted light-gray stone slabs. Sinuous carved stone dragons formed the uprights of the balustrade.

We walked up the steps, and across the patio.

18

The Great Hall of Ialdabaoth

Six tall white columns, three on each side, supported a massive roof of stone arched over the patio. Every inch of the stone was carved with strange designs, emblems, and some familiar animals like birds and fish and lizards. Beyond that more stairs led to a massive wooden door.

Sophia grabbed my hand and we marched up the stairs. She stopped at the door and placed the torch, still burning, into a metal holder on a railing off to the left. The door was a work of art. It stretched about six feet across and was made of some dark heavy wood, mahogany maybe. It was intricately etched with small figures painted gold, crimson, and emerald. The designs appeared familiar, like the ones on Sophia's dress . . . constellations and hieroglyphs. A large brass ring attached to the middle of the door seemed to be the handle.

Sophia gripped the big ring with force and lifted it, revealing a keyhole. From the folds of her wide dress she pulled out a set of keys attached to a pretty woven and colorfully beaded string. The end of this key string seemed to be fastened to her scarlet belt. I'd never seen her keys before. She removed the golden key from its string, then put it in the keyhole and turned it while pulling the ring toward her. The massive door slowly opened. Sophia left the key in the lock and we walked through.

Inside, she grasped a wooden handle and pulled the door shut behind us. She turned to me and said, "We're entering the Great Hall of the Dragon Realm. This is the abode of Ialdabaoth, the demon possessing Mercurius."

Then she pointed her finger at me, and ordered, "Pay attention and do what I say. You don't have to do anything except remain conscious and alert. Say nothing and keep your eyes lowered. I want you to witness what is happening. But if you look directly at the demon Ialdabaoth, he can jump over to you." Then she relaxed and raised an eyebrow at me, "And for heaven's sake, don't laugh."

She quickly resumed her stern demeanor. "Do not look anyone in the eye here." Placing her thumb on my chin, focusing her mesmerizing eyes on me, she commanded, "Be alert! Don't let down your guard."

We entered a dim wood-paneled hallway about twenty feet long and continued to its end, where it turned to the right and opened into a vast space as big as a ballroom. What looked to be a large golden throne was on the opposite wall. Behind the throne was a colorful carving of a dragon of immense size, its mouth ending just above the throne, its wings stretching the length of the wall, its body wrapping around the entire room from the right, ending on the left side with its tail near the mouth. It was painted reddish brown with crimson eyes, lime green scales, and silver wings. The throne area, which was raised several feet above the rest of the room, was also carved with the strange figures and emblems that were on the wooden door and outside the temple.

Near the front of the room, at the side of the throne, was a mannequin on which was hanging—I couldn't believe my eyes!—the very same jacket I'd dropped into the volcanic chasms and watched vanish into a puff of ash. There it was, freshly pressed! I was unable to fathom how it could have materialized back here, right in front of us, in this hall.

Sophia, with a grim look of determination, took a big rattle out of her bag. She whispered to me that it was her sistrum. She shook it. It made a clattering noise. She shook it harder, and its harsh sound careened around the walls of the room. Soon, a man appeared from behind the throne area.

Throughout this entire encounter I tried to follow Sophia's admonition about not looking directly at anyone. But out of the corner of my eye I could see the man was clean shaven, short, balding, with a large protruding stomach. He wore a gray business suit with the belt hanging well below his belly. Except for his shiny bright red tie, he looked like a typical middle-aged American corporate executive. His skin, though, was severely pockmarked and pouchy, with that gray pallor that comes from too much "high living," as my father would say. His tiny glassy eyes darted from me to Sophia and then around the room and back to us. Once again his ratlike eyes swept the room. His mouth opened into a cold chilling grin.

"Ah, my dear Sophia. It is always a pleasure to have you visit," he gurgled, a trickle of yellow saliva oozing from his mouth. "What brings you here this time?"

"Shut up with the niceties, you ugly reptile," she retorted, raising herself to her full height and whipping her tail out from behind her skirts. "You know damn well, Ialdabaoth, why I'm here!"

"It's about those stupid humans you always concern yourself with, isn't it?" he sneered, his grin turning into a contorted grimace of disgust.

Then he turned to me, with a lascivious malevolent stare. His oily mouth opened slightly and a large dark tongue darted through his ashen lips. His adam's apple was the size of a plum rolling up and down his throat. His eyes groped my body. My visceral reaction of loathing and repulsion triggered the memory of Sophia's words. Quickly I lowered my gaze completely to the floor.

"Who is this one, another one of your protégées? Another one of your sentimental do-gooders?"

He walked over to the mannequin and pointed to it.

"Young lady," he was obviously addressing me, "did you *drop* something?" He laughed leeringly. His voice made me squirm.

Sophia's hoof nudged my foot. I glanced down at my boot, and knew she was again reminding me to keep my eyes away from this man's direct gaze and be silent.

The little man returned to the center of the room and turned to face Sophia. He asked, "So who is this girl with you? . . . A human who will help you . . . help you do what? Save the world? Save her fellow humans from the consequences of their savagery toward one another?" He started laughing, but it was like the braying of an ass. "Why do you even bother, my dear mother?"

Mother? I thought incredulously. *What's going on here?*

"Don't you dare call me Mother, Ialdabaoth—you abortion, you filthy excuse for a being. And remove your eyes from this innocent." Sophia took a deep breath. "You are Mercurius! You have forgotten who you really are. You are possessed with a demon from outside this universe!"

"Oh my," said the gray man. "What do you mean, Mother?"

Sophia pointed at him with her left hand, her long dark index finger stabbing at the air between them. "Demon, Ialdabaoth, impostor god! Some day you will be driven back to the bowels of hell from which you came!" Sophia roared, "Don't play dumb with me! I am addressing the demon that controls . . . you . . . you, Mercurius. Though you sleep, one day you, Mercurius, shall return to your senses and restore language and thought that reveals the truth rather than hides it."

She took a step closer to him and raised her left hand as though to strike him. She continued, "You, Ialdabaoth, live in the illusion that you are God when you know that you are not. You are Lord of Illusion and Sustainer of Ignorance. You have stolen the human spirit—the spiritual impulse—of billions. That is what attracts you, *demon,* to inhabit Mercurius. Men's basest desires have overcome their human instinct for truth and compassion. They want domination, control over Earth and all her creatures."

Sophia paused. It seemed there were sparks flashing around her head. I glanced at her again. I swear I saw flames coming from her mouth. She rattled her sistrum again, looking intensely at Ialdabaoth. He stood motionless, almost transfixed. She raised the sistrum with her right hand and I thought she was going to throw it at him. But she shook it again vigorously.

Her voice intensified even more: "You are a parasite! You are a walking abomination! You are a disgrace to the Universal Life Force! You have twisted and turned upside down the natural dynamic of truth. You block access to the Unknown God in each human heart. You cause the human individual to seek protection in groups and belief systems. Your method has always been fear—and cruelty, bullying, killing, and pain—justified and perpetuated by lies."

She took a breath and continued. "Then you watch the humans fall into further brutality, inflicting unspeakable horrors on each other. You watch with glee as the human world disintegrates into savagery and hopelessness." Her voice was heating up to an incendiary degree.

She looked with disgust at his body, and said, "Look at you—*You grow fat and beastly from the sight of blood!*" Then she spat upon the marble floor and turned her head in disgust from the little man with the greasy lips.

The man in the business suit squirmed slightly but regained his composure. Then he moved closer to Sophia and replied in a calm businesslike voice, "Why, I'm surprised at your anger, Mother dear. I'm doing nothing that has not already happened on Earth many, many times. I'm the *Past* that humans choose to re-live. You know the laws of the universe better than I. You know how it works!"

Flourishing his chubby right index finger at Sophia, his voice suddenly rose in fury to match her own, shaking the walls of the palace. "You know as well as I do that the baseness and cruelty of humans is legendary in all spheres of the universe," the little man yelled, his face contorting. "They *choose* to remain ignorant, cruel, greedy, and base. I simply supply the reasons, the images, the thoughts that they desire. This is a free-will universe! I came because I was called! I do nothing but give them what they want! They want God, I give them God—*Me!*" He spit the words out, urine-colored saliva shooting from his twisted mouth.

"You're *not God!*" Sophia roared, and the golden hall reverberated. The shimmering fringe on the back of the throne trembled. "You are abhorrent! You—Ialdabaoth—are a product of my evolutionary residue, content with a lie, content to spread lies, content to divorce yourself for all time from truth. Setting yourself up as the one supreme being and possessing the spirit of language—Mercurius! How dare you!" Sophia stepped her right hoof toward Ialdabaoth.

Her breathing became labored, heavy. Her voice lowered, remaining forceful. "You disgust me." She stood motionless and silent.

"You should give humans more credit, Mother. They know better than to seek truth. Look what happens to people who bring truth to the public: They get scapegoated, burned at the stake . . . and crucified."

Sophia raised her head and cried out, "Despicable demon, it is *you* that crucified *truth!*"

The little man straightened his shiny red tie, apparently trying to look more business like.

Sophia looked with revulsion at the creature before her. "Look at you! I'm so ashamed at what you have become!"

"Well," he replied, his voice again low, no longer angry, "you and I both know that nothing can be done about it. People bring about what they desire. They want a god, *and here I am.* They don't want truth, they want money, sex, and power! They don't want freedom, they want guilt, bondage, destruction, pain, and fear! And then they call me! I am their last hope . . . and their worst fear!" Ialdabaoth took a step forward and then beat his chest like King Kong. "I *Am* Fear! I AM THE GOD THEY WANT!"

He paused, smacked his rubbery gray lips, and clapped his stubby hands in glee. "It's a new world now, Mother. You need to face up to it. You no longer are welcome or desired on Earth. *Earth is all mine!* I am *making sure of that* with events that are transpiring there." With that, the hideous little man turned on his heel and walked out of the Great Hall.

Barely seconds passed, when a stupendous roar filled the palatial hall.

"You will not leave my presence until I have spoken within this hall what I have come here to say!" Thunder in Sophia's voice seemed to split the hall in two—as its booms reverberated off the painted dragon's body that encircled the hall.

Like a fish caught by a hook, the horrid little man was reeled back into the hall by the power of her voice. Wriggling to get free of it, he slipped and almost fell, then turned, but he was unable to escape.

"I call down the intelligence, the power, and the radiance of the Universal Life Force focused before me in Truth and Light! Come forth, Bladed Thunder! I call upon you now to do my bidding!" Sophia's voice of power tore through the temple and into the night sky beyond.

I couldn't help but look. And what I saw before me brought chills of terror and awe: A beam of light so bright, so alive, so piercing . . . came through the vaulted roof above and descended into the hall in front of the writhing, drooling man. It was a pillar of white fire that stretched from ceiling to floor, scintillating with a light so intense I had to turn my eyes away from it. I felt its heat inside my chest.

"*Ialdabaoth, I terminate your rule!* As Life Force is my witness, the order and natural law of Truth shall again be re-established on Earth, among humans."

A searing white flash of heat and light tore up my spine and seemed to open my skull. I forced myself to stay conscious and alert, as instructed.

I watched in horror and fascination as the little man's smug grin was replaced by terror, as his face and body disintegrated in a burst of bright flame right there in front of us. All that remained when the smoke cleared was a glowing pile of gray ashes.

Sophia turned to me brimming with steam, "He will reconstitute himself soon. You just saw the appearance of the Great Dragon as thought-form. And you heard the voice of the demon Ialdabaoth who controls Mercurius. Come, we still have much work to do."

My mouth hung open. I had held my breath during the incineration of Ialdabaoth. I exhaled slowly. My mind was empty of all thoughts.

Sophia returned her sistrum to her bag. Then she took my hand and we left the Great Hall. At the doorway, she removed her key, replaced it on its string, and took the still-burning torch from the holder by the big mahogany door. Then we descended the stairs into the black night.

19

To Food and Rest

"Come, Molly, we'll get some much needed rest and food down the road." Sophia patted my shoulder, then gave me a hug. "You did fine today. All I needed was a human witness to this event."

I was so stunned from seeing the beam of light incinerate that burbling blister of a man that I couldn't collect my mind, much less my thoughts. I was speechless.

"Tomorrow you will meet my friends and start your lessons. We each have a big day ahead of us." Sophia held the torch high. I walked beside her. Her hooves carefully and surely picked out the path—this one fairly broad and even—in the dense darkness, which only dimly opened its secrets after the scudding white-tinged clouds scurried on their way past the half moon.

Her tail made a comforting swishing sound as she walked. Even in the dark, I could catch a glimpse of it now and then, peeking out from behind her dress. Her pace was much slower than earlier in the day. She seemed relaxed. *But why,* I asked myself, *did she say he would reconstitute himself? What does that mean?* I decided to ask her.

Before I could get the words out of my mouth, without missing a beat in her careful steps and keeping her gaze straight ahead into the darkness ahead, she said, "You're probably wondering what happened tonight, aren't you, dear? Well, I'll tell you a little. But, since it's so late I'm more concerned that you get some food and rest. There may be time tomorrow for you to ask questions of the Dragon Master—Chogyal—in the Hall of Philosophy.

"For now, because of what happened tonight in Ialdabaoth's hall, your Earth and its inhabitants have been spared annihilation from an exchange of missiles with atomic weapons. It takes Ialdabaoth twenty-four hours to reconstitute himself. During that brief period, the intensity of the habits of revenge, fear, self-protection, domination, and aggression in your world will be suspended. The overwhelming pressure to react is lessened now, allowing world leaders to feel safe enough to talk to each other, to consider other points of view. The world crisis will continue, but it will take a different trajectory now. Remember this, Molly: What happens in the middle realm shows up in the real world. What happens in the real world affects the middle realm as well.

"The Great Dragon of the Past," she continued, "exerts a powerful attraction on humans who are made weak by continual exposure to banality and living in a society that refuses to honor its sages and wisdom teachings. Just about every society around the globe at one time or another had sages, shamans, or teachers who ensured that all Earth's peoples had access to the knowledge of how to free themselves from being swallowed by the Dragon, and also how to master it. Societies in ancient times had dragon riders, who had learned to use the past for the benefit of humanity. Dragon riders expose a society's lies and corrupted images and show people the past's positive images instead."

After her mention of dragon riders, I had to ask, "But what about that mark I have, of the *dragon slayer?* I'd much rather *ride* a dragon than have to slay one."

She turned her head and said, "They are different paths. And even if a person traverses both, they first have to learn how to *slay* the dragon of their own personal past thought-patterns. This usually takes years. The true philosophic sages you will meet and learn about are dragon riders. Unless attention is removed from the old thought-form dragons, people will never be able to think for themselves or create anything of beauty. The dragon slayer's training occurs not only in the middle realm but also on Earth in your physical body—both in relationships and within your own heart. Your training will consist of learning and practicing three things: first, to control the mind and control emotions of fear and self-doubt; second, to discern what is true; third, to vaporize all thought-forms that limit or negate your inner light and creativity. Your dragon slayer mark with the infinity sign protects you on Earth and in the middle realm. It shows that you belong to me, and can never be devoured by criminal dragons.

"But only I have been able, and that with difficulty, to deal with the *Great* Dragon. He cannot ever completely and finally be destroyed—even when a demon takes possession of him—as he is the *Past*. If one form of the Great Dragon is destroyed, he reappears in another."

She stopped in mid-stride and faced me, making sure I was paying attention. "Mind you, there are eons of time when the Great Dragon—as Mercurius—becomes a guide to the sublime treasure—the wisdom of the ages. Mercurius in his right mind is a guide to humans seeking wisdom. He is a safe reliable bridge to other worlds. When the language of any culture is *transparent*—revealing rather than disguising what is *true* about Nature and the cosmos—then the Dragon is Mercurius, the friend of wisdom.

I interrupted, "Sophia, what was that glowing ball I saw the Dragon holding?"

"That scintillating pearl you saw between the Dragon's paws in the pit of fire is the jewel of humanity's wisdom—the perfection of collective wisdom. The mystery of the relation between the World Soul and humanity is that pearl. It's actually alive!"

She waited for my reaction. But I didn't understand what she'd said and was too tired to try. Besides, I really had to pee now.

She frowned. "But it is a dangerous sign of the times that the pearl is being held by the Dragon in this psychotic state of demonic possession. He has forgotten who he is. This happens when people in your world disregard their wisdom traditions, their past and living sages, and are unable or unwilling to inquire into life's meaning and purpose. If they seek truth, too often they turn over to a teacher their own inner authority—which rightfully belongs to the individual.

"It's a peculiar trait among you humans," she said, looking at me quizzically, "that you fear the power of your innate ability to reflect and question your own life and to take responsibility for it. You want to be told what to think. You seek what you imagine is safety in beliefs and dogma foisted on you by priests and rulers—men whose primary need is to dominate."

Was I supposed to reply? I kept quiet. I wasn't sure what she meant by "men"—whether it was humanity or just male humans.

She scowled and began walking again. "Ialdabaoth manipulates male biology and psychology in various ways. The kind of men who need to control others usually suffer from some sort of sexual or psychological inferiority. That is why the dominators and oppressors in every culture hate and fear women. The first victims of authoritarian, fascist, oppressive regimes *are always the women,* who are forced out of leadership roles and into seclusion. However, the exclusion of woman is the rejection of the wisdom of Nature and the Soul of the World.

"Remember, dear Molly, that I am Mother Nature and the *anima mundi,* which means the Soul of the World."

She paused for a moment at a crossroads, bringing the torch down to a small wooden sign carved with strange markings that looked like Vs or arrows going in different directions. The sign itself was carved in the shape of an arrow pointing to our left, which is the path she took. We walked a few minutes in silence. Way ahead, I could see a light!

"Oh my God, Sophia! What's up ahead, what's in store for us now?" I exclaimed.

"That phrase 'Oh my God,' Molly, that so many humans use so casually, has great power. *Which god* are you invoking, Molly? It is best not to use such phrases of invocation—whether to God, Jesus, or even the Goddess. There are indeed helpful divine beings, and they will always protect life, not feed off it. These 'persons' are portals to an unknown mystery. But thought-forms and deities can attract either helpful entities—or parasites. The god as a thought-form that has become possessed—you just met him!"

Sophia spat on the ground in disgust, just as she did before she zapped that putrid wart of a man. She fell silent and began walking more slowly.

Sophia's comment made me think about who or what I was praying to. A dreadful terror crept over my body as I contemplated "god" as the drooling rat-man. Every time I said or thought "Oh my God" in the future, I recalled him. Eventually I became more conscious of the power of words.

Sophia pointed, "That's where we're going, where that light is up ahead." I was so relieved to think that soon we could eat and sleep.

The night was cold and I thought, once again, about the jacket. I kept my mind focused on finding a warm bed and good food and a bathroom. It now seemed the darkness was lessening. Clouds outlined in silver scurried across the blackness above us. When they parted, the waxing moon, half full, a perfect half circle, with the other half the color of night, gloriously appeared like a welcoming lantern. It was now dipping down to the horizon, so I knew it was approaching midnight.

20

Master Chogyal's Hospitality

As we approached the light, I saw that in fact there were two lights. Two torches were fastened to the sides of a wooden gate, painted plain white, with no figures or emblems on it. On either side of the gate were walls made of what looked like bamboo woven with strands of branches with leaves and red berries. They stretched up high, taller than two men. Above the gate and walls was a thatched roof made of palm fronds that swept gracefully over the top of the gate.

Sophia placed her torch into one of the holders on the wall. As she made her way through the entrance, someone walked toward us from the other side. I was so startled I jumped and blurted, "Eeek!" He was so quiet, I never heard his footsteps.

He was short, thin, with a bony face, and was dressed in an orange robe with a hood lying on his shoulders. His face was pale, round, Oriental, with dark brown tilted eyes set wide apart below black straight hair. His arms were folded inside the long folds of his robe, as though he were clutching his elbows. He walked up to Sophia and bowed, his head dropping low, all the way to his knees. She did not seem at all surprised by his sudden appearance. Her whole face lit up in pleasure and warmth.

"My dear Master Chogyal, I am so happy to be here with you!" She spoke these words one by one, slowly, softly. Master Chogyal raised himself from the prolonged bow. His thin wiry arms slowly came out of his robe sleeves and he reached his long bony fingers to her face, pausing to look up intently into her eyes. Each reached out to hug the other, at the same moment. Their embrace lasted minutes. Seeing his withered arms, I realized he was much older than I thought at first from his black hair and youthful face.

Master Chogyal gently released himself and turned to me with a smile. "And who are you to come so far from the human realm? Are you a messenger?" His voice was surprisingly deep and hearty for one so frail—and friendly, too.

"My name is Molly. I came because Sophia called me. We go back a ways," I replied, not knowing what else to say.

"Actually," Sophia explained, "she was the one who called me to her when she was a child. She is the one you helped me pull down into the cabin at the trail that goes up Hell's Kitchen Canyon." She had turned to me and was smiling affectionately. "She is going to be my knight in shining armor."

Master Chogyal raised his barely visible eyebrows in surprise—*was it doubt that caused him to smile at me?*—"Ahh, yes, yes. Of course. Welcome, dear Molly. You were a very cooperative subject, indeed."

I hoped they wouldn't see the bright red blush that I knew from the heat on my face was spreading my embarrassment for both of them to see. *Thank goodness it's dark,* I thought.

"Well, let me take you inside and show you your rooms." Master Chogyal gently took my hand in his. His voice was clear and kind, reminding me of the wind chimes in my mother's garden—strong, comforting, and melodious. "Then we'll have some food and tea, before you sleep. You must be hungry."

Master Chogyal led us down the worn dirt path—a kind of hallway—under the thatched roof. On either side of the hallway were walls made of wood slats. The hallway was well lit from pretty red and yellow cloth tiered lanterns that held candles with bright dancing flames. The lanterns were adorned with scarlet tassels hanging from them. I felt at ease now, and my excitement returned, even though I was starving and sleepy.

We continued walking straight ahead for several minutes. Strings of brightly colored flags—red, blue, green, yellow, white, printed with horses and unfamiliar writing—stretched from wall to wall. I later learned these were Tibetan prayer flags. Writings on the left wall gave way to a series of small roofed alcoves in which hung brightly colored paintings done on what looked like silk. Some of them had tassels.

The first painting showed a bare-breasted bejeweled seated green goddess. Sophia whispered to me this was a *thangka* or Tibetan painting of Bodhisattva Green Tara, who embodies compassion in female form. There were paintings of different Buddhas: One that was a brilliant cobalt blue held a bowl of the same color; another held a flaming sword and a book; yet another depicted what looked like the Buddha reclining or dead surrounded by disciples and all kinds of animals. Some of the thangkas had stylized flowers, rivers, clouds, or snow-capped mountains, or both the sun and moon in the sky at the same time. There were conch shells, bells, books, tridents, and many objects for which I had no name. A few fierce female figures wore crowns or garlands of skulls or human heads, and most had a third eye open in the middle of their forehead. The male and female thangkas alternated. There were seated peaceful-looking female figures—bodhisattvas or deities, I later learned.

Sophia pointed one out to me. "Look here, Molly, meet Prajnaparamita, the Perfection of Wisdom." She was four-armed and held a book in one of her hands, and in another a small metal object that I later learned is a scepter called a "dorje." Sophia also pointed out a fierce-looking dancing vermillion female deity wearing only a crown of five skulls and a garland of more skulls. She held what looked like a bowl of blood—I wondered if it was real blood, and if from a human or an animal. "That's Vajrayogini, who stamps out ignorance, the stupidity of men, and the hypocrisy of conventional society."

Along the right wall appeared to be rooms with their wooden doors closed. Nothing was painted on them. The next alcove on the left wall had a painting of just a big black empty circle on paper. I asked Sophia why there was a big black dot hanging on the wall. She replied, with a gentle smile of satisfaction, "That circle, my dear, is the symbol of emptiness, an enlightened artist's representation of the cancellation of the busy noise of your mind."

What? I wondered. Stopping in front of it, I peered more closely, but the black circle failed to yield its secret to my wild and jumping questions.

Master Chogyal led us to a door on the right side of the hallway, opened it, and with a little bow to Sophia, ushered us in while he held the door. As we entered, Sophia pointed to my feet, then to the hallway outside. I pulled off my dirty scuffed-up boots and pushed them neatly against the outside wall and followed behind Sophia. It was a small room with yellowish parchment paper on the walls. On one wall hung a couple of small rectangular plush wool rugs, with woven-in flowers, leaves, and trees. I saw no windows. The beds were only thick brown woven mats on the brown-tiled floor, with a small table very low to the ground between them. Small blankets were folded neatly on the sleeping mats. The floor itself was covered with thinner bamboo mats. The sleeping mats took up much of the floor area.

"There is a washroom with two big bathtubs right through that curtain behind the screen," the Master said, pointing to a startling black-lacquered room divider painted with scenes of brilliant scarlet and blue birds, ivory-colored deer, and emerald-green trees. "Why don't you change your clothes and bathe before we eat? You must be dusty from your journey."

Master Chogyal again pointed to the screen. "There are robes in the bathing room for both of you. And cloth slippers for you, Molly. Oh yes—and the tubs are full and hot, awaiting your pleasure!" He smiled and bowed to us and, still bowing, backed out of the pretty little room.

Sophia and I quickly went behind the screen. I bolted for the tiny toilet next to the washbasin and closed the black and red striped privacy curtain. A couple minutes later Sophia squealed with pleasure as she entered the bath with a splash. I wasn't sure what to do next. I was embarrassed at the thought of taking a bath in the same room with her. I had never taken a bath in front of anyone before, except when I was a baby—especially not with a goddess with a tail!

"Come, Molly, don't be shy," she called. "We have to bathe before we can enter the temple area and the Hall of Philosophy. The soot and residue of our journey to the realm of the Great Dragon have permeated our hair, skin, clothes . . . and our vibrations. We bring a contaminating influence into these hallowed halls and must wash it away before eating and sleeping."

I had no choice. I went into the bathing area and tried not to look at where Sophia was stretched out in one of the big tubs—her clothes and satchel on the floor beside it. On top of her clothes lay her keys, snake bracelet, gold chain hair ornament, and belt with its eyestones staring at the ceiling. Her long shapely but hairy legs with those hooves on the end were sticking out of the water. The tip of her tail, with its silvery scales, curved and waved above her hooves. The rest of her was under water except for her head and right arm, which were resting on the back of the tub. Her long black hair was soapy and floating. With a big orange sponge, she was washing her right leg, all the way down to the bottom of her hoof. A little dish of what must be soap was on a tray attached to the tub.

"Jump in, dear, before the water cools. It is a perfect temperature now, nice and hot." She put the sponge back in the tray and then slid down a few more inches, so even her chin was under water. "Ahhhhh," she gurgled, "what bliss is this!"

I saw plush bright red robes hanging from hooks on a wooden beam at the end of the tubs. Several towels were neatly folded and placed on a small shelf near the robes. Finally relaxed, I slowly took off my dirty sooty torn-up clothes and left them in a pile on the floor. I examined the knee I'd injured only a few hours earlier—a new scar, but completely healed! I quickly climbed into the other large tub and relaxed as soon as the hot sizzling water bubbled over my stomach and legs and arms and back. *She's right,* I thought, *this really is bliss.*

"There are mineral salts in our baths," Sophia said. "It'll help release the poisons we took in today. Make sure you wash the ashes and ghost realm dust out of your hair. The soap is in the tray."

We sat in the tubs in silence for what seemed like a long time. I let the water's heat bring its soothing healing into every cell of my tired body, as I relaxed into its comforting bubbles. I put my own orange sponge into my bathwater and sailed it with one finger under my knees as though it were a boat. I did get my hair a bit wet, but the last thing on my mind was getting clean. After Sophia again reminded me that our bathing was required, I did my best to wash myself well, then sank into the delicious heat and silence, almost dozing off.

I heard Sophia sigh as the drain sucked out the water in her tub. Once again alert, I stole a glance at her. I couldn't help it. I wondered what the rest of her looked like. Her back was turned to me as she got out of the tub. She was so beautiful from behind—and normal, or rather human-looking, with a defined waist and round hips. Except for her strong glorious tail that emerged from above her hips and sprinkled water droplets from its shining scales, she looked like a human woman. She was in good shape and looked like swimmers I knew from school. Her shoulders were broad and muscular. Her body was a smooth chocolate brown. Her long black wavy hair was loose and wet. She reached for two towels and wrapped the first around her hair and the second around her body.

She waited for me to get out. *Oh gosh,* I thought, *now it's my turn, and she's watching me.* But she didn't stand there long. As though feeling my embarrassment, she reached for my towel and brought it to me. Gratefully, I took it and got out of the tub.

We wrapped our bright red robes around our bodies like kimonos. Sophia showed me how to tie the attached belts securely through holes at the waist. The slippers for my feet were made of a silky soft green material.

"We'll rest a moment on our beds until Master Chogyal returns." She led the way back into the room with the mats and chose the one closest to the black screen. I collapsed on the other mat.

We rested for only about five minutes before there was a light tap on the door. Master Chogyal's deep voice asked if we were ready for something to eat. Sophia didn't answer, but got up slowly to open the door, smiling.

"Yes, we would be delighted to eat now," she replied.

Master Chogyal appeared pleased that we had bathed. He smiled at me and asked, "And did you enjoy your bath, Molly?"

"Yes, very much, sir," I replied with a grin. I felt comfortable around him. He was very gentle and warm.

I looked at Sophia. "Are we going to wear these robes?"

Master Chogyal replied instead, "Yes. Your clothes will be destroyed and replaced with new garments in the morning. And, of course, Sophia, your magical belt, satchel, jewelry, and keys will be ritually cleansed. They will be returned to you after our supper."

Destroyed? His words jolted me—*I guess he's a strict host.* Not that I'd cared about the goofy-looking clothes I'd worn . . .

We followed Master Chogyal down the hallway. Then he led us through a breezeway into another thatched building. We walked into a big empty room with a wooden floor and bare walls. There were no paintings or scrolls.

We continued into a room off to the side. On a broad low rectangular table were three pretty little smoky gray cups with no handles. They caught my attention. The interior of each cup was glazed creamy white. Deep blue calligraphy was painted on the glaze. At the far end of the room was a fireplace with a crackling fire and a grill over it. Steam was coming from pots on the grill. Next to the fireplace was a round wooden table with five teapots on it. Around this table were some round red cushions. An unfamiliar but pleasant aroma filled the room.

Master Chogyal motioned for us to sit on the cushions. He sat at one end, closest to the fireplace. Sophia took a place on his left, and I sat across from her, with Master Chogyal to my left. He said some kind of grace, in what I guessed was Tibetan.

An Oriental-looking boy came in carrying a tray with brown ceramic bowls of steaming soup. He bowed, saying not a word or looking at us directly, and gave each of us a bowl and a ceramic spoon before leaving the room. It smelled delicious. I waited for Master Chogyal to give the word to eat.

"That was Li, my student. You may go ahead and eat now. The soup may be hot, though, so be careful," he warned us. The soup was a broth with tiny white noodles and finely chopped greens in it, salty and a bit buttery tasting. It was good and very hot and I ate it quickly, before Master Chogyal and Sophia had finished theirs. No one spoke.

Li came in again, this time with a bowl of oranges and more plates, and went to each of us, quietly offering the fruit. I took an orange, delighted to see something familiar. I quickly peeled it, broke it into slices, and savored each juicy piece slowly.

After about ten minutes, Li returned, quietly removed all the dishes from the table, and left. Quickly he returned with a tray and two teapots.

Master Chogyal said that the larger of the two teapots had hot Tibetan tea—a strong black tea made with yak butter and salt. He said I could try it if I wanted, but that I might prefer the green tea as it was closer to what Americans were used to.

I said, "Green tea, please," hoping that I was polite enough. Li took a cup from the table and carefully filled it with steaming Tibetan tea, serving Sophia first. Then he filled a cup for Master Chogyal. It looked very dark and thick and a bit greasy on top. Li then poured me a cup of the green tea.

Li looked at me for the first time and smiled, saying, "This is our finest green tea grown in the mountains. I'm sure you will like it." He stood there a moment, looking into my eyes. "I will fetch you honey if you prefer it sweetened."

I smiled and felt my face get hot. I was attracted to Li, but didn't want him to know. He seemed serene and disciplined, and there was something fierce and intelligent about him—not like any boy I'd ever met. I did want honey, but there were no spoons to stir it. So I shook my head, saying, "No honey, thank you." Then he wouldn't have to bring me anything.

Li wasn't as young as I'd thought at first. He looked very mature and composed. *I wonder how old he is,* I thought. He obviously shaves. Or—maybe he doesn't—I'd heard Orientals don't have to. As though my thoughts were visible, I hid my face over the steaming cup and deeply breathed in the fragrance and heat. Warming my hands on the cup, I waited a moment and then sipped the hot brew. I was glad I'd chosen it. It had a delicious delicate flavor. I didn't even miss the honey. The steam went up my nose right to my head and I felt so relaxed that I could have collapsed in a heap right there on the floor. I could hardly hold my back straight anymore. The bath, the hot soup, now the hot tea . . . *yes, this must be heaven,* I thought.

Right on cue, Sophia noticed my sleepy condition. She thanked our host and Li. Then she excused us from the table, saying we must get to bed after our strenuous journey. She never once mentioned the Dragon to Master Chogyal. He never asked her what happened or even why we were here. It was as though they both knew each other so well that there was no need for words or explanation. Or, more likely, Master Chogyal expected Sophia tonight and knew very well where she had gone. It was as though it was a common occurrence to go dragon hunting, be almost scorched by flames, and then incinerate a man who was really a thought-form. *What a place,* I thought.

Sophia slowly got up from her cushion and came over to help me up. Feeling all scrambled and wobbly, I was grateful for her hand. She steered me out the door of the dining room, through the big bare room, then through the breezeway and into the hallway of the first building, and finally, into our room. I fell onto my sleeping mat.

"Here's a gown you can wear to bed." Sophia tossed me a pale blue and silver nightgown. I don't know where she got it.

I took off the heavy red robe and pulled the soft pretty nightgown over my head and bare body as quickly as I could, as though Li or Master Chogyal might be walking by, which of course, they weren't. I shook out the blankets, laid them over the mat, and snuggled under them. Sophia folded a blanket to make a pillow for me. The woven mat was thicker and more comfortable than it looked. I was thrilled to be safe and warm and lying down.

"Goodnight, dear one." Sophia bent over and kissed me on the forehead. "I'm going out now to talk to Master Chogyal about our adventure today. You just sleep as long as you can. I will be gone when you wake up, but don't be alarmed. I'll be with Master Chogyal. Li will show you around the place tomorrow. Sweet dreams!"

Before the sound of her footsteps faded, my eyes had closed. I was in a fitful state, passing in and out of consciousness. Even though I was far from the denizens of hell we had visited, I kept seeing flames and smoke, and choking on rancid air. Finally, I must have passed out into a blessed darkness.

21

The Halloween after the World Almost Ended

I remember it well, waking up in the room I shared with my little sister Patty, after my sojourn in the middle realm. It was dark. Disoriented and exhausted, I wondered where I was, if I was dreaming all this. *Maybe I died and am in some kind of purgatory,* I thought. But no. A small amount of light from the streetlamp shining through the room's curtained windows showed me where I was—I was in my own bed!

I turned on the reading light. Then I lay there on my back, my eyes slowly getting accustomed to the familiar walls and furniture. My old poster of Jerry Lee Lewis tacked on the wall welcomed me back to the real world. What had been so real and present—Sophia, the Dragon, and Master Chogyal—now took a back seat in my brain. Even so, the whole adventure was a vivid memory tugging at me, calling to me, to not forget it.

My horse calendar was nailed to the wall next to my bed. I always crossed off the week when it was done. I saw it was Monday—I had to go to school. I looked at the clock. I had an hour to relax before getting up. Patty was sound asleep. Quietly, I got my notebook and pen from their hiding place—a locked jewelry box under a pile of library books under my bed. The key was attached to a charm bracelet I always kept looped around a bedpost. I started writing down my reminiscences from my middle realm adventures.

Maybe Sophia's crisis in the middle realm did have something to do with this Cuban Missile Crisis. I kept hearing about it on TV and in my parents' conversations. Was it a world crisis like they were saying? Would we all be bombed into oblivion, back to the Stone Age? I started to say a fervent prayer for peace, but before I could begin, the memory of Sophia's warning about whom I was praying to rushed into my mind. I said the prayer anyway.

So it was Monday, October 22, 1962. This world crisis had been building up for years—all the hype and hullabaloo about the commies and pinkos in the 1950s and the escalating contest as to which country, the USA or Russia, could have the biggest stash of missiles. We in the USA were always the good guys. The Commies were godless evil atheists—even our priest had said this in Sunday sermons: "We're the good team and must win."

Then after Fidel Castro took over Cuba, the godless atheists were right next door to Florida. Then the Bay of Pigs invasion happened. Then the Russian leader Khrushchev gave Castro a big pile of missiles. By the end of July it was looking really bad. Just a few days ago, U2 spy planes found evidence of missile installations in Cuba. Some missiles were aimed right at Chicago, where my family was living, because our city had lots of industry.

So we wouldn't have a chance if the missiles got fired. We'd get incinerated into radioactive dust—incinerated, as a moth in a candle flame, or like Ialdabaoth, or like that jacket I'd dropped into hell while riding in the Thunder Cart.

My mother interrupted my important urgent thoughts and memories. It was time to get up for school. She was calling me to breakfast. I quickly put my notebook in its hiding place and returned the charm bracelet with its key to the bedpost. A warm rush of gratitude filled up all the cracks and holes where the fear had been when I woke up. To have all those adventures and now be home safe and about to eat breakfast—how lucky I felt!

Peggy was hogging the bathroom, primping, so I only had time to barely brush my teeth after breakfast. While waiting for her to get out, I noticed that the little gold cross that always hung on its chain around my neck was gone. I thought maybe it fell someplace last night when I took it off for a shower. When I got into the bathroom I searched for it—no luck. Or maybe it came off in my sleep, but no time to search my room now. Or—an astonishing thought dashed across my mind—did it get lost because of my adventures in the middle realm last night? Then I remembered Sophia had told me to take it off!

I walked to the high school with Peggy. We didn't talk. She was a senior, I a sophomore. On the way I prayed silently for peace, not only to Jesus and Mary, but also to Sophia.

When I got home that afternoon I searched my room frantically for the little gold cross—even took all the sheets and blankets off the bed and shook them, swept the floor thoroughly, and dumped out my dresser drawers. I had to get to my homework, then some chores around the house—ironing pillowcases. I figured it would show up sometime if I were just patient enough.

It did. Patty found it next spring—in the backyard on a flat stone under a bush. She had no idea how it got there—neither did I—and I didn't tell her what Sophia had told me after she rescued me from the ghosts. Patty had always wanted that little piece of jewelry. It would mean a lot to her to have it. Since it was a kind of family heirloom, I gave it to Patty after asking my mother about it. Patty was thrilled. I felt mature and generous. Besides, the cross would have just gone into my jewelry box in the closet.

But back to that Monday evening, October 22. President Kennedy was on TV, saying the missiles were definitely there, and that he was proposing a blockade. Was there a chance that World War III *might* not happen after all? I really tried to be interested—the history teacher might quiz us about the important events that were taking place. But none of that mattered to me except for the possibility that we all might *die!*

That night I tried to enter the middle realm using Sophia's instructions, but I fell asleep too soon—no success. I tried again on subsequent nights, no luck then, either. Even though there were some scary aspects about the middle realm, Sophia had told me it was a thought-realm, and I knew that thoughts couldn't really hurt me if I didn't let them.

Halloween came soon. After eating dinner early, Patty went out trick or treating in her last year's princess costume with the girl across the street. She came back after half an hour, as my sisters and I were all invited to a party. Even my brother Billy went. He drove us there in his car, a fairly new but beat-up white Chevy Impala with a red stripe along the side. I think he got it cheap because it had been in an accident. Billy was home from the state technical college. He was a junior, studying some kind of engineering, barely keeping his grades up so he could graduate. He also had a job, but was able to take Halloween off. He told us he came home to be with family in case the world ended.

At the party, I felt weird and alone. The Halloween decorations made me think of death, hell, the ghosts, and the Great Dragon. There was lots of food—candied apples, Halloween candy, and pumpkin muffins. Sugar cookies had been cut out and glazed to look like pumpkins, bats, and ghosts. I ate mostly Three Musketeers candy bars. There was a big bowl of something labeled "Vampire Blood Punch." It was probably cranberry juice, but I couldn't even look at it and drank the hot mulled apple cider instead. There was also a cookie sheet on which marshmallows had been melted in the oven and twisted to look like ghosts. I didn't go near them!

On a table in the living room sat a jumbo carved pumpkin with three short fat candles inside. There were some carved pumpkins on the porch.

This was a party mostly for younger kids, so Billy and Peggy left early. This Halloween was a school night anyway, so the party wouldn't run too late. Billy told me to phone him when Patty and I wanted to leave.

The mood was somber, considering how World War III almost started and the world almost ended. I overheard some of the parents talking about this Cuban crisis, which they were hoping was over, as Khrushchev had agreed to remove the missiles from Cuba. Everyone knew that the thousands of missiles were still there, somewhere—moved but not destroyed—and that the USA had thousands of missiles too.

The kids were talking about their experiences: the bomb drills in school, ducking under the desks and holding their heads, waiting for the death flash, and what it might feel like to be under a direct hit or to die horribly—incinerated quickly or dying slowly from burns or fallout. They worried if they were vaporized that there wouldn't be enough of their bodies left to go to heaven or even purgatory. Most of the Catholic kids I knew had been going to confession regularly during the last two or three months.

Some of the older kids at the party, fifth and sixth graders and up, were talking about fallout shelters. Only one family we knew had one, the Jacksons; but they lived next door to the funeral home they owned, so we never wanted to go there to spy.

At the party I tried to tell Carol about my crazy "dream." I called it a dream, even though I knew it wasn't, so she'd listen to it. I told her about this goddess flying in a dragon cart with me over the Great Dragon and zapping him in his "man" aspect. But she wasn't interested. "Aww—that's just a dream. I had one where the whole city got blasted to smithereens. It doesn't mean it's going to happen."

I was a bit too old for this kind of party and spent most of the time talking with my best girlfriend Sherrie in a corner of the living room. She seemed more interested in my dream than Carol did. "Maybe it really happened, Molly."

Oh, my gosh! I thought to myself. *I might have someone I can talk to about my middle realm adventures.*

I hung around at the party until it was obvious Patty was getting tired. Then I asked to use the phone to call my brother. He picked us up and we went home. It was only around 8:30.

Peggy came back after midnight. We all woke up when we heard banging. Then a crash. My father got up and went downstairs. Peggy had bumped into a chair in the hallway and knocked it over. He was mad. They got into a loud discussion about her staying out after curfew. I heard my parents the next evening talking about Peggy drinking with her friends.

My life was kind of anticlimactic after all the adventures with Sophia. Nothing exciting happened in the next several weeks: no more adventures in the middle realm, though it was clear to me that it was much more than a dream. And no atomic bombs. That part was really good, and it really looked as if people were beginning now to openly talk about the need for understanding between different nations.

I really felt that something had happened in our Earth-world that was urgent and dangerous, that efforts had been and were being made in the middle realm to avert a catastrophe. Later on, I would find out that many of the mystics and sages living in the real world—of all world religions, not just Catholic or Christian—had spent much time in prayer and meditation to just this effect.

Several weeks passed. I spent the Wednesday evening before Thanksgiving helping my mother prepare some things ahead and clean the house. More tired than I'd been in weeks, I fell asleep that Thanksgiving eve, fervently praying to Sophia, thanking her for whatever help she'd provided in convincing Castro and Khrushchev to take the missiles away. I even touched the dragon-mark scar. It seemed it started to throb—maybe Sophia was calling me. But I was too tired to do the ritual. I thought briefly of Li, then of Sophia's smiling face, her night-black eyes, as a deep empty peace began to envelop me. And then the roaring began . . .

PART 3

22

A Morning Conversation with Li

Morning sun poured through the tiny gaps between the fronds of palm-leaf thatch on the roof, sending sunbeams into the room. I didn't know where I was. This was *not* any place in 1960s America. But I felt safe and dozed off again. Finally, I stretched and looked around. *Now* I remembered. Images of the night before, the night when Sophia incinerated Ialdabaoth and I met Master Chogyal and Li, crept back into my awareness. I looked over at the other mat, Sophia wasn't there. The blankets were still folded. She hadn't even slept here last night! *Where is she?* I thought, getting alarmed.

I jumped up from the mat, my heart racing. Then I remembered her parting words as she kissed me, and I relaxed a bit. I went into the washroom to use the toilet and wash my hands and face. There was a small stack of neatly folded clean clothes in there with a small piece of paper on which was written "Molly." They had that fresh smell of having been out on a clothesline. I unfolded them; there were even rolled-up white panties. I pulled those on first, then the silky dusty-rose pants with side pockets and elastic waistband. I loved the silky lavender tunic with its wide long sleeves! Tiny flowers, leaves, and butterflies, exquisitely embroidered in threads of silver and gold and various bright colors, danced around its hem, sleeve edges, and neckline. I held it up and admired it a few seconds before putting it on, too.

Everything was exactly my size. *Who brought these clothes in here?* I wondered. Instead of my hiking boots, when I peeked outside in the hallway, I discovered a pair of beautiful sandals with pearly blue straps—that also fit perfectly.

There was a tapping sound on my door. I went to open it. Li was standing there, smiling. He was wearing the same gray-beige silk tunic and flowing trousers as before.

"Do you like your new clothes? You look lovely in them."

I blushed and lowered my eyes in the moment of silence that followed his compliment.

Li's voice shifted to a more formal tone. "It's still early. Our lessons won't begin for a while. Do you want to stay here, or come with me and I'll show you around?" He offered me his arm.

I was delighted that he had showed up so fast. "Oh yes, of course I'd rather go with you!" I said a bit too enthusiastically. I did *not* want to stay in the room by myself. "Where's Sophia?" We walked down the hallway toward the dining area.

"She and Master Chogyal had a lot of catching up to do," Li explained. "She hasn't been here to visit in many moons. They are having tea on the pavilion by the fish pond. We should leave them alone, though. They are discussing matters of great import. You will see them when we go to the Hall of Philosophy for our lessons."

"What's the Hall of Philosophy and what do you mean 'lessons'?" I asked.

"You'll see the Hall of Philosophy today. It's where we learn. Today you're supposed to come with me to my lesson with Master Chogyal. He teaches a few other students and me about the secrets of the universe and the dynamics of the Life Force. We learn the science of mind and the history and destiny of the stars. We explore the very deepest inmost reaches of our minds, all the way to the point at which the mind leaves the limits of space-time." Li's voice lowered, evidently telling me something of great importance, "We learn about who we really are."

I didn't know what he was talking about; but it sounded so exotic, so unlike any school I had ever attended, that I was catching his enthusiasm.

"How do you reach the inmost part of your mind?" I asked. That sounded really neat.

Li led me into the dining area. It was empty, as was the porch we could see through the open door; but there was food on the round table and a pot of tea. Li motioned for me to sit on one of the two low benches by the table. The red cushions were gone.

"Master Chogyal teaches us techniques that have been used by generations of teachers to quiet the mind and control the breathing. It's really not that hard, once you get the hang of it. Once you learn about breathing, you can do it."

He took two cups and poured us both some hot tea. There was a basket of something that looked like biscuits next to two little bowls of dark red jam with seeds. I took a biscuit and spread the jam on it with a little wooden stick. It was tasty—my favorite—raspberry. Li took an orange and a pear from a brown ceramic bowl filled with fresh fruit. He frowned at the pear and put it back.

I wanted to ask him what was wrong with the breathing I do all the time, but I didn't want to start off our day by revealing the extent of my ignorance about spiritual training.

"It sounds much more interesting than the things I have to learn in school," I said. "Tell me, how did you find Master Chogyal, and how did you come to be his student?" I wondered if someday I could be his student, too.

He pursed his lips into a slight frown. "It's a long story. My parents were both killed by bandits in the mountains where I was born, in western China, in a province bordering Tibet. I was only three years old, at home with my older sister. I called her Ping. My mother's brother took pity on my sister and me. He raised us for five years with his wife and two daughters.

"Then my uncle had a dream when I turned eight years old. In the dream, I was carried by an eagle to the top of a mountain and left there. The sun rose above the mountain and shone down upon me, and a voice came into the dream that said, 'This child is beloved of the gods.' At that moment, in the dream, lightning bolts came down from the heavens and thunder shook the world, but the child in the dream only laughed and shook his little fist at the lightning. My uncle was quite shaken by the dream. He called me 'Little Vajra.' After that, he treated me as though I wasn't a member of the family anymore. I mean, he was nice, but I think I made him nervous."

"What does 'Vajra' mean?" I asked.

"Vajra is the Sanskrit word for thunderbolt," Li explained, then continued with his story. "A year later, my uncle approached a secret order of Buddhist monks familiar to only a few families in the area. This order had a hidden monastery in the Tibetan mountains adjacent to China. My villagers sometimes sent their children there for Buddhist training. My uncle told the monks about the dream and they were very interested because of an ancient prophecy that a young tree with no roots would be planted in their midst, a tree that would grow so strong as to break lightning and dissolve thunder. When they heard the dream, they immediately welcomed me into their midst. Because I was orphaned, they saw me as a tree with no roots, no parents, and therefore a fulfillment of their prophecy."

I was very impressed that Li had such a dramatic childhood and destiny. "What happened to your sister?" I asked.

"Ping was married off at fifteen to a much older man whose previous wife had died in childbirth. She had to raise his three children and I believe they had two more of their own, but I lost touch with her and never met her children. Our lives divided when I went into monastic life."

"That must have been so sad for you, to be separated from your family." I couldn't imagine surviving such a fate and ever being happy again. *No wonder Li seems so different,* I thought. *He's so serious.*

"I was very homesick and scared. I hadn't wanted to leave my uncle's family. Also, I had to learn Tibetan as well as how to read and write. The journey to the monastery took over a month on horseback—my uncle took me—I think he was concerned about his wife and children whom he had to leave alone in the village.

"In the monastery I took the name of Lobsang. Anyway, it took me about a year to get used to monastery life. There were three other boys my age, so it didn't take long for me to make friends with them. They were nice to me."

"Were they orphans, too?" I asked.

"No. Sometimes parents are too poor or sick to raise their children, or one of the parents dies. The monastery takes boys if they show intellectual and spiritual promise."

"Did they treat you special because of the prophecy?" I asked.

"Oh, no. Quite the contrary," Li replied. "Not only did they not tell me of the prophecy until I was sixteen, I think they expected more from me. They were stricter with me than the other boys. But they were kind, and not too harsh, although at first, I thought they were."

I was dying to talk about the Dragon and the incinerated man, but felt that Li wanted to get acquainted and share the story of his life. So I asked, "And Master Chogyal, who is he? Is he a Buddhist monk?"

"Well, Master Chogyal, whose title is Lama Chogyal, was abbot of the monastery then, and taught the sutras and tantras mostly to the older students. He was always very kind to all the young boys at the monastery. He is still a monk."

I asked Li, "Was your monastery destroyed by the Chinese invaders, too? I thought the Chinese outlawed Buddhism in Tibet after they invaded."

He answered, "Well, it was. When the Chinese arrived, we monks took most of the scrolls and a few treasures, abandoned the monastery, and assimilated ourselves into neighboring villages, wearing the male folk costumes of the area. There we work in the fields and mostly help the villagers by using our training in Tibetan medicine. Quietly we also act as spiritual advisers to the villagers and do *pujas* for them. As a monastery, we still meet informally and secretly in small groups in the houses of villagers. In the real world Tibetan village, I am known only by my Tibetan monastic name, Lobsang. I consider myself Tibetan now. But I prefer to go by my Chinese name, Li, in *this* realm.

"What the Chinese are doing is terrible, smashing monasteries and desecrating sacred thangkas and scrolls, and torturing monks and nuns. In spite of my being ethnic Chinese, I think the Tibetans are totally in the right, and I pray that the young Dalai Lama, now that he's fled to India, will help bring the Buddhist message of Avalokiteshvara to all the peoples of the world."

I wondered who Avalokiteshvara was, but since I'd already heard about the Dalai Lama—and his name was easier to pronounce—he was the one I asked about. "A few years ago I saw a short newsreel—the kind they show before feature movies back where I come from. It showed the Dalai Lama, and told about him fleeing Tibet and crossing the border to India. Have you met the Dalai Lama?"

"No, I never did, because of the remoteness of our monastery and my younger age. But some of the older monks made pilgrimages to Lhasa, and I think one of them did see him. I do hope to see him someday, though—at least here in the middle realm."

"Tell me about your training," I asked, "and how do you get to this realm?"

"Well," Li paused a moment and frowned. "I guess you could say it was rigorous. I studied every day and meditated every morning and evening for two hours at a time. Every day I had to memorize pages of sacred text. The worst was getting up early in the morning—3:00 A.M.—for meditation and chanting. We had to go to bed at 9:00 every night. Because I showed aptitude in my studies, I was apprenticed to an old monk, Lama Chenchen, to learn from him how to leave my body and travel to the subtle or imaginal realms, where we are now."

I must've looked startled and bewildered. He stopped and looked at me quizzically. "You know we are meeting each other in our subtle bodies, don't you?" He looked slightly worried that maybe I didn't have a clue how I got here, which in a way, was true.

I didn't know how to answer, so I just replied, "Well, yes, but I don't use the same terms as you do."

"What terms *do* you use?" he asked.

Now I squirmed. How could I tell him about meeting Sophia in a tree, and that I really had no terms at all? Quickly, I fished for some term. I found some:

"Sophia told me we are in the middle realm. She used the words 'astral,' and 'imaginal,' too." *There, that should cover me for the time being,* I thought, though I still wasn't sure what these terms really meant. "She came to me when I was in grade school. I was miserable about being forced to go to school. Honestly, I don't understand how I got here—to the *astral* . . . I haven't had any training like you have." I wanted to change the subject, so I asked him if he had seen the Great Dragon.

Li's face changed at the mention of the Great Dragon, but so swiftly that I barely registered it. It was like a quickly moving shadow crossed his features.

"Oh, yes," he said quietly.

I waited for more, but there was an uncomfortable silence while he shifted his body on the wooden bench. He reached for one of the biscuits and a little bowl of jam and then took his time spreading the jam on it.

23

Li Explains Dragons

I couldn't contain myself any longer. "Li, tell me about the horrid little man that appeared to Sophia and me last night. Sophia said he was an appearance of the Great Dragon." *There,* I thought, *now it's out.*

Li looked at me with great sadness. He took his time replying, munching on his biscuit and sipping his tea. So far he hadn't touched his orange.

"So that is why they have been in such deep discussion all night and through the morning," he sighed. "Oh, Molly. I'm so sorry you had to see him in his human form. He personifies the collective male ego that has cut itself off from Nature, and set itself up as a supreme being accountable to no one. He is profit without conscience, he is invention without wisdom, he is intellect without compassion."

He knows all about this, I thought. *He's so eloquent.*

Li's voice had lowered to almost a whisper. I had to lean toward him to hear.

"Good men carry great shame about the excesses and cruelty of other men, for they too, are swept up as victims along with their families."

His voice grew stronger and more confident. "Sophia comes when things are at their worst on Earth," he continued. "She comes when men go to war over stupid things or when the whole Earth is endangered from their poisons and weapons. She comes when the memory of the sacred feminine is lost from their minds. She comes when male aggression runs riot and blood flows in every river." Li stopped, then lowered his voice, "Gravity has begun to swallow the Earth."

I shuddered at these horrible images. "But what about you and Master Chogyal? You're males and you're not like that."

"Of course not," he sighed. "Not all men are like that. There are men who know whom they serve, the principle of Life: the sacred wisdom that flows through every being, every rock, creature, and star. Master Chogyal and the monks in the monastery where I grew up . . . they serve Life and honor the Sacred Feminine, the Mother of Life. In Tibet, we pray to her as Tara."

Li sighed and shook his head slowly from side to side. "I knew you had seen the Great Dragon. But no one told me you had seen him appear as a *man.*"

"Huh?" I said, wondering why *that* was so significant.

"Sophia's arrival here always means she has paid a visit to the pits of fire where he lives." He paused and narrowed his eyes, looking at me carefully. "She's never brought a girl with her before, though—either here or to the fire pits."

I blushed and looked down at the bowl of jam.

Gently, he spoke into my embarrassment. "You haven't been raised or trained in any reality tradition, have you?"

"What do you mean, *reality tradition*? I was raised a Catholic."

"A reality tradition is a society's method of training its youth how to see what is real—for example, that a tree is a being and can be talked to. A reality tradition opens the third eye of every new generation."

"Third eye?" I asked, awash in further wonderment and confusion.

Li rolled his eyes and ignored my question. "I bet she's going to use you to help her deal with the Dragon."

I relaxed as his tone changed, but his words didn't bring me comfort. "How could I possibly do that?" I looked at him like he was nuts.

"She can't do these things alone," he explained. "Don't get so nervous about it. She's going to work through you—and many more women. So you might as well get used to the idea."

Li reached for the teapot and poured us each another cup. Then he said, "You must have strengthened your individuality in a previous lifetime, for her to hear your call and come to you so young. So . . . that is why she picked you. And that is why I was picked to learn from Master Chogyal and come here. He is a dragon rider."

"Sophia told me about that. Oh Li, tell me more! What is a dragon rider?" I blurted out in excitement. *Oh,* I thought, *now this is getting really interesting!*

"Why Molly, you do need some lessons! A dragon rider knows the true nature of thought. A dragon rider has mastered the pull of the past. The weight and inertia of thought-forms of ego, greed, power, and all the rest are just too strong for most men to resist."

I couldn't help but interrupt, "But how is dragon riding different from being a dragon slayer? Sophia said I was one of those, and even put a special dragon slayer mark on my leg."

Too embarrassed to pull up my pant leg to show Li the mark, I continued, "Sophia said there's a difference between dragon slaying and dragon riding. She said they are different paths, but that you have to slay the Dragon first."

Li replied, "Yes, that's why it's usually only sages of great age who become dragon riders. They *master or ride* the thought-forms of the past that make up the collective mentality of human beings on Earth."

"But, Li," I repeated my question, "what is a dragon *slayer*?"

"A dragon slayer is anybody who clearly perceives what is real. That is when your third eye is open. You withdraw your life energy from them so they collapse. This takes many years. Because most people get no useful spiritual training, the longer they live, the more attached they get to thought-forms."

Li picked up his orange, put it back into the fruit bowl, and continued, "Most ordinary men, and women, too—those who seek material possessions, security, or temporal power instead of wisdom—are terrified of the feeling of being adrift in a sea of change. They have a desperate need to control their circumstances. Since they can't control what's going to happen next, they manipulate what they *can* control: their children, spouses, neighbors . . . and anyone else who may be weaker than they are."

"But what does that have to do with the dragon rider and with dragon slaying?" I persisted.

"Everything." Li's voice assumed the tone of my pompous history teacher. "When a man has to *control others,* he has totally lost control *over his own fears*. A dragon rider is a man who has learned to control his fear by seeking to understand the meaning and purpose of *all* of life. For such a man, the whole universe responds and opens its secrets, its protection, and its grace . . . Did you see the *pearl* in the Dragon's paws?"

"Yes I did! What was it?"

"The dragon rider's understanding—the connection to divine wisdom—that pearl is the culmination of collective wisdom. It belongs throughout time to all the sages and shamans that bring humanity light, wisdom, and healing. A dragon rider becomes one with all of that collective wisdom. He uses that wisdom for the good of humanity. He understands the principle of time, that the past must be either mastered, re-created, re-humanized, or sent back to the source so life can flow and grow into its complexity with a minimum of backlash and harsh fate to people. You see, Molly, either we learn how to take control of the past, so that it serves us, or the past will live its life through us as the Dragon."

I was catching Li's enthusiasm and wondered if I'd ever get a chance to be a dragon rider. "Can girls be dragon riders?" I asked.

"Of course! Both men and women are caught by the past and let it live itself through them. Women have the desire to understand life and master the currents of thought-forms, too. It's just that men have the bigger problem of being out of touch with the feminine principle of life; that is why so much attention is on them now. But we at our monastery and at La Ville de Sophie know that it is the *women* of the world who must remind the men that they are not gods but servants of life. That is where you come in, I'm sure of it."

24

La Ville de Sophie

We sat in silence, sipping the last of our tea. The pot was empty and I needed to stretch and walk.

"Show me around," I said.

"Very well, Molly."

With gentlemanly courtesy, he took my right elbow in his left hand, helped me up, and escorted me from the dining hall. The place was empty. All the time we had sat there, I didn't see or hear anyone.

Li walked me outside to a terraced garden with a small wooden pavilion and a fish pond. Delicate white water lilies graced the pond. Tall sweeping reeds swayed in the breeze around the pond's perimeter while dragonflies hovered and danced and skimmed on its surface. I gazed into the pond and saw three huge goldfish—I think they are called koi—basking in the sunbeams that spilled into the water. A pretty white stone bench, with curved legs, was next to the pond. There were two used teacups on a little tray next to the bench. I looked around but saw no sign of Sophia and Master Chogyal.

"They have gone to the Hall of Philosophy." Li motioned to his right. "Let's go over there. By the time we get there, it will be almost time for our lesson."

I looked but couldn't see any building other than the one we had just left. Li took my hand and walked me toward a stand of white birches at the edge of the garden. The feel of his strong warm hand raised my spirits even more. I recalled the prophecy of his childhood. It felt like a god was leading me. We walked for about five minutes on a worn path that disappeared into the woods, then came to a grassy clearing edged with boulders as big as cars.

Li stopped, turned to me, and said, "Come, I will show you the Mystery Temple that houses the Hall of Philosophy." He took my hand again and we walked across the clearing and beyond it through another stand of birch trees. His pace slowed and he dropped my hand.

"Walk to the edge, beyond those hedges." Anticipation made his words come out quickly.

It looked like we were nearing a cliff's edge, because the surface became rocky and I could see the sky beyond us instead of trees. I left Li and walked ahead, wondering what sight lay ahead of me. I pushed through the scraggly brown bushes that were taller than my head. I was looking down, watching my step, when suddenly the ground gave way to a rocky ledge and I had to stop quickly to keep from getting too near the edge. I caught my balance, then looked down.

My breath caught in my throat and I almost choked. Goose bumps scattered and popped over my legs and arms. In the morning light, a valley lay before me, its slopes cradling a city of white buildings with domes of either gold or a pearly opalescence. Some buildings had spires. Others sported masts with brightly colored flags of red, green, and yellow flying from them.

But the most amazing thing of all was what stood on the far edge of the city, farthest from where I was. Standing upon a rock mesa was an immense white pyramid. On the three corners of the pyramid facing me were golden statues on large white bases, but from this distance I couldn't tell what these statues were. The entry to the pyramid-temple was a massive golden portal that reached halfway up the pyramid. The portal had a tiered roof of three levels. Atop its roof were figures carved in gold, holding torches, another large statue, and a large crystal, but I couldn't see any details. From here we could see that under the tiered portal roof were two high rectangular entrances.

A walkway appeared to wrap around the base of the pyramid and I could make out lots of people walking there or resting on small benches. The city's streets below were connected with this walkway by a ramp with several zigzags ascending the mesa's steep side. There was a steady stream of people walking up and down the ramp. At its top, the ramp passed under a white stone tiered gateway that faced the portal roof. This gateway had a large golden ball on top.

In the east, beyond the mesa with the pyramid, was a range of rocky snow-capped mountains. Between two peaks, I saw a vast blue sea. The scene's staggering opalescent beauty stunned me into silence. I had never seen anything this exquisite, this magical, in my life.

"What is that?" I could barely get the words out. I had been holding my breath.

Li was delighted to see my surprise and awe. It was apparent that he had been waiting all morning for this moment.

"That pyramid is the Mystery Temple. Within it is the Hall of Philosophy. The architects who designed and built the Mystery Temple of Atlantis used this as their model. It's been here for more than twenty thousand years. The city below it is called La Ville de Sophie, the City of

Wisdom. This is where the wise from all times and from all universes come together to do what they love most: to ask questions of the sages from all ages and to learn about the mysteries of the cosmos, life after death, Nature, Being, and creaturely life."

"Are they all regular people?" I asked.

"What do mean by 'regular'? Some you will recognize from your world; many others will appear strange to you. You could meet deities, magicians, philosophers, alchemists, and kabbalists—and other creatures such as elementals and what you may think are mythical creatures. But they are not fantasy. As you will see, they are very real."

I was so excited I couldn't bear to stand there talking any longer. "Let's *go* there, Li!" I grabbed his arm and started back the way we came. Soon realizing I didn't know how to get to the city, I waited for Li to show me.

"Let's hurry, Li. I can't wait to see the temple." I was almost jumping from excitement. "Tell me more about what goes on there."

But Li was patient and composed. He took his time, even though my enthusiasm clearly made him glad.

At this point I wondered why Sophia hadn't told me anything about this world except about the Dragon and the importance of one's thoughts. It seemed like she was always teaching me. But she sure never told me about this fabulous City of the Wise!

Li was leading me down a steep rocky path. "Be very careful here. It's easy to slip on the stones." He slowed down and made sure I was paying attention to the path before continuing. "The city below us has been here forever, at least that's what I've been told. It has its own stability on the astral plane."

"What do you mean 'stability'?" I asked.

"The city is a thought-form made into a beautiful habitat by generations of sages for the benefit of souls devoted to truth and beauty and goodness. Here, they can wander in, visit the cosmic library and other buildings, and engage in endless philosophical discussion."

"It looks like heaven to me," I replied.

"This is certainly not the heaven of the religions in your western world, though it is about as close as it gets to heaven." Li stopped and stroked his chin, just as I had seen Sophia do. "However, everything is subject to the *choice* of one's thoughts, even here—our lessons in the astral provide us with instances and tests to show how that is true. But, in general, this is where all the beings come whose souls desire truth and wisdom."

Li stopped and pointed up ahead. "It gets really steep here. We'll have to go down on our seats."

"Is this how Sophia and Master Chogyal got down?"

"Oh, my, no!" Li responded. "There's a much easier shorter path, but you don't get this view. I wanted you to see the city from the cliff because it's so magnificent and you can see the whole place at once."

We sat down at the top of an almost vertical drop. Li went first. In case I tumbled over, he'd catch my fall. We slid down the hill a little too quickly for me. It reminded me of the fall into the ghost land that had separated me from Sophia. A lot of rocks started falling down with us. We ended up in a grassy field with a pretty stream bubbling through it.

I felt for holes in my pants. My hand grabbed inches of dirt, but the pants were intact—I wouldn't have wanted Li to see my underwear or bare skin.

"Let's stop and get a drink here." Li dusted off his flowing trousers and knelt down at the stream, cupping his hands in the water, splashing the water over his face and slurping it up from his hands, not once but many times.

He sat by the stream and watched me as I drank from it. "The astral world," he began, "is a more permanent world than our Earth plane. You see, there are many many levels or planes in our universe, more planes than an onion has layers or a big tree has rings. There are countless galaxies and suns with planets. Each part has its own material, imaginal, and noetic levels. It is a very big place." He stopped a moment while I wiped the water from my face with my wrist, and then sat down next to him on the grassy bank. "It's actually not a place, though. That only confuses things. It's more like a state of mind or condition of being than a physical place like China or the United States. The notion of there being a fixed place where you stand is kind of an illusion. After all, Earth is turning on its axis and revolving around the Sun, right? So things are always moving around and are never fixed."

Li paused to pick up a long stick from the ground. He sat quietly examining it, peeling off some of its bark. Then he dipped it in the water up and down. "A lot of temples and buildings built to gods and goddesses on Earth had their prototype in this city. This is the home of the Wise and when they incarnate on Earth, their memory of this place is sometimes very accurate. You really can't see much detail of the city from the cliff, though—just the biggest temple, the pyramid that was the template for the Atlantis temple."

I was anxious to see more. "Let's go, Li." I pulled his arm and stood up.

"All right. Let's go." He laid the stick down, then got up slowly, reluctantly almost, gazing thoughtfully at the flowing stream. "All visitors must enter through the main gate. We'll be there in a few minutes."

In silence we walked along the streamside path. Li seemed almost sad.

"What's the matter?" I asked.

"I don't know," he sort of grumbled. "Sometimes it all feels so crazy, these two worlds. I'd like to stay in this world forever. I don't know why I chose to incarnate in another earthly existence. It takes too long to learn how to get back here. Sometimes I think I should just die, then I'd be back here—for a long time."

"Li, it seems like that dilemma is exactly the kind of question that would be welcome in a place like this," I offered.

"Oh, you're right, of course," he replied with a serious look. "In fact, I already know the answer. After I pass my initiation, I will be taken to the *Book of Destinies* and I will be shown the reason why I chose, with guidance from my advisers, to incarnate this lifetime and see the lessons I chose to learn. It's just that, well, I wish I didn't have to go back to my life in Tibet. Life is so hard in the village even though I care about the villagers and Buddha's message."

Li stood by the stream, reluctant to walk toward the fabulous city. "I can feel the worry pulling my mind into fear. Fear will separate me from this world, so I better control my thoughts. I can feel it when the anxiety comes up. If I don't stop it, I'll be snapped right back to the Earth plane."

With that, he turned to me with a hint of a smile, grabbed my hand, and said, with his eyes sparkling, "Allons mon amie, à la Ville de Sophie!"

We left the stream, in a hurry now, with Li half running and still holding my hand. We crossed a pretty field blooming with tiny purple flowers and walked through a stand of small pine trees. We came out the other side onto a wide dirt road and went to the left.

25

The City and the Mystery Temple Pyramid

I saw a huge gateway ahead of us, leading into the city. Stone columns rose up on both sides. Egyptian hieroglyphs were carved into each pillar: birds and women with things on their heads and a funny looking figure with the body of a human and the head of some bird with a long beak carrying something on his head—which I later found out was Thoth. The columns rose about thirty feet and ended with larger stone cylinders on their tops. Connecting the two pillars was a slab of stone. On top of it was an orb of lighter stone supported on each side by an up-rearing snake. Wide outstretched wings extended from the orb with the snakes. Underneath this, carved into the front of the slab and painted black, was an inscription: "I, Isis, am all that has been, that is, or shall be. No mortal man has ever unveiled me."

Li pointed to the stone slab under which we were about to walk. "Up above, the emblem with the serpents, that's called the winged globe of

Egypt. It appears over the gates of many Egyptian palaces and temples. It symbolizes the three persons of the Egyptian Trinity. The wings are the insignia of Amon, the serpents that of Ra, and the solar orb is that of Osiris."

We walked through the great gateway into a round, brick-paved courtyard. In the middle stood a colossal white stone statue of a woman. She held in her right hand a *sistrum*—the same object I saw in Sophia's hand the night she dispatched the little man to ashes. In her left hand was a little pail. On her head was a strange looking crown with what appeared to be shafts of wheat sticking out. Her right foot rested on a jug that was pouring out its water made of stone. She wore a dress tied with a rope under her bust, with an outer cloak. Tiny carved stars covered the cloak which was draped gracefully over her left arm and crossed her stomach in folds, with one crescent moon on the fabric over her left thigh. Startled, I looked closer. The moon lay over the spot on my leg where my dragon slayer mark was! My hand instinctively went to my left thigh, to rest above my mark for a couple of seconds.

"Wow!" I exclaimed, goose bumps prickling all over my body. As I walked over to the base of the statue, my eyes tried to take in the enormity of this towering tribute to the goddess. I read aloud to Li:

"I am Isis, queen of the whole land. I was taught by Hermes. With Hermes I invented the writings of the different lands. I gave unalterable laws to humankind. I gave them the Mysteries. I am the goddess of women."

I read a few more lines silently, then read aloud again: "I caused men to love women." I turned to look at Li. "Ah!" I exclaimed, "I remember Sophia saying that!"

I continued reading aloud to the end of the plaque: "I made justice to be weightier than silver and gold. I made truth to be considered beautiful."

I had read about Isis in history class at school, and Sophia had earlier told me that she was worshiped as Isis in her beloved Egypt. But now I turned to Li with my mouth open in awe, full of questions, not knowing what to ask first.

"Let me explain," he offered, seeing my helplessness in the face of the magnificent stone goddess. "This is Isis, Queen of Heaven, one of Sophia's appearances in Egypt. The Egyptians venerated wisdom in the form of a female, as did most ancient cultures; and Sophia was particularly fond of Egypt."

He pointed to the statue. "Isis symbolizes the power of the Life Force to continually move, expand, grow, and drive off the inertia of dogma and the death of the soul. That's why she always is pictured with a sistrum, to drive off Typhon, who is corruption, who swallows souls by means of dogma, fear, and conformity. Typhon is a form of the Great Dragon. Isis has always symbolized the great works of the wise men: the Philosopher's Stone and the Elixir of Life, for instance. There's so much more, but we'll be here all week if I tell you everything about her symbols and history. Let's get to the Hall of Philosophy!"

We crossed the courtyard. I turned my head for a last glance at the tall statue. My thoughts returned to the beautiful companion in the tree—Sophia.

The courtyard opened into a broad avenue or promenade—with low-lying green shrubs on either side. Growing in neat rectangles, more shrubs created islands of green down the promenade's center. We walked silently as I took in the scene.

White buildings with gold-domed roofs lined this wide brick-paved road. Spindly pointed roofs topped a few of the buildings. Pennants rippled in the breeze: scarlet, emerald, golden-yellow. Some buildings opened into courtyards lined with palm trees and potted plants with large orange, pink, or red blossoms. Sculptures of goddesses, gods, or abstract forms guarded the entrances of the larger buildings. We came to a circular stone fountain in the center of the road, where it widened. Children leaned over the fountain, dangling their hands in the water. I began to notice people, lots of them, walking about, holding hands, conversing, or sitting on stone benches in front of the buildings.

"Are they going to wonder what I'm doing here?" I asked Li.

"No, not at all. People come and go and no one will ask you why you're here because no one sees you as a stranger. No one is afraid of difference here. Whatever is unusual or different is welcome. Fear can't stay here. It lives in a certain kind of mind that finds compatibility and nourishment only on Earth."

"And no one gets mad here?" I asked.

Li answered, "Well, no, not exactly. Like fear, anger can arise, but the disturbing vibration clashes so violently with the tranquility of the city that souls expressing anger are pulled back to the Earth plane."

We came to a split in the promenade. Li led me to the right. We walked for another five minutes and then came to the ramp I had seen from the cliff. People were walking up and some were coming down. We took our time going up. From up above, Li pointed out various buildings and gardens that he thought I would like, that were below us along the promenade. Among those he pointed out were the Council Chambers Hall, the Judgment Hall, some theaters and museums and temples, and a beautifully laid out botanical garden. I was so far beyond being impressed—I was in a peak state of utter amazement that didn't dwindle. We finally reached the top of the ramp and walked under the massive gleaming stone gateway that faced the pyramid's portal. Li stopped in front of it so I could take it all in.

We were now standing on the walkway that surrounded the perimeter of the pyramid. I looked up to see the statues on the very top of the portal's three-tiered roof. Two golden statues of men holding torches surrounded the largest most dazzling crystal I could ever have imagined. *Certainly no crystal that size could exist on Earth,* I thought. Beams of reflected light were cast all about the city below from the sun striking the crystal's perfect multiple silvery ice-like facets. I strained to see something that appeared odd in the middle of the crystal, maybe painted on it or carved into it—I couldn't tell. And then I saw a double-headed eagle sitting there in a nest of flames! One head looked to the right; the other to the left. Their fierce red eyes matched the flames and their beaks curved down. I pointed up to the crystal, then looked at Li with astonishment.

"That, Molly, is the Philosopher's Stone!" Li's voice lowered with a strange urgency. "It's the image of the diamond soul, the part of the soul that philosophy perfects. This Wisdom Stone is Reason, and Reason is the movement of intelligence within the Life Force. Reason relates all that is alive. The Great Work of the sages is to discover and express this Life Force intelligence that moves in both the realms of the living and the dead. Hermes Trismegistus says that philosophy is the 'Work of the Sun.'"

Li paused, then continued, apparently recalling more of what he'd learned about this stone. "The Philosopher's Stone changes the gross into the pure—or as the alchemists say, the base metals into gold. This crystal is an image of the crystal at the center of the Earth."

Li said that the double-headed eagle in the flame in the middle of the Philosopher's Stone was the phoenix, the bird symbolizing the immortality of the soul throughout its repeated deaths and rebirths.

Behind the gold statue-men with torches, above them all, was another statue of a goddess. Li said she was made of brass. She had three flat tiers upon her head. Her hands were stretched out. She was covered from head to toe with animals of all sorts. She had lots of round balls around her chest and I wondered if they were all supposed to be breasts, but there weren't any nipples. There were deer heads and lion heads and, at the bottom, a row of horses' heads with their forelegs and hooves.

"Who is that?" I asked Li. I pointed to the odd goddess of animals.

"That is *Diana of Ephesus*," he replied. "The animals represent her spiritual powers. She is the source of the wisdom teachings that arose in Anatolia—the land you call Turkey—and all over the Near East. She is the fountain of truth that pours forth the wisdom of the universe for all souls eager to contemplate the Real."

We entered the portal through one of the two large entrances. All these most amazing tributes to wisdom and philosophy that we had just seen were above us on the portal's tiered roof. We were now in a kind of stone porch-like area, open to the front where we'd walked in, with unadorned gray stone walls at the sides, and a gray tiled ceiling. The far wall of the portal had two entrances: one large, one small, both without doors.

The large rectangular entrance on the right reached to the top of the ceiling. The small square entrance on the left was only about four feet high, with a stone lintel and a threshold about six inches high. Li caught my attention and motioned with a tilt of his head that we should enter through the small entrance. To enter the pyramid itself, we had to step over the stone threshold, and duck our heads.

"The beams are low, forcing the person to bow down, as it were, before entering . . . a reminder that humility is necessary for the learning that feeds the soul," Li said. He then pointed ahead of us to two large statues of hands, one on either side of the entryway. They were the only things visible in the darkness, lit only by votive candles and what Li called "butter lamps." The bizarre sentinels stood over six feet tall, and their fingers either pointed above or curled down. There were strange emblems and figures all over the fingers and palms of these hands.

My eyes took a few minutes to adjust to the dark interior. Li waited by the giant hand on the left side. The two hands were similar, but some of the figures differed. The left hand had a serpent rising from between the little finger and ring finger. Some kind of speckled orb rested on the thumbs of both hands. There was a sheep's head carved into the palm of the hand on the right. The rest of the designs were unfamiliar to me. They reminded me of jewelry I'd once seen on Balinese dancers in a *National Geographic* magazine.

"Hands like this are found in the entrances of many temples of wisdom," Li explained. "These hands assist the raising of the initiate from the dead—that is, from the death of common life. Initiation requires an understanding of all these symbols."

I strained my eyes to see more, but it was too dark.

"Come," Li motioned me forward.

We walked slowly down the hall. The ceiling and walls were so pressed together it felt claustrophobic. I wanted to leave it quickly. The hall finally widened, but it was still like a tunnel—perhaps around the inside perimeter of the pyramid, or below it. It zigzagged in places, and it felt like we went down, maybe into the bedrock of the mesa itself, then up. We had to squeeze through some tight places. Once we had to get down on our knees to get through. I wondered if it was a labyrinth. At several places I heard faint voices up ahead, laughter. At one place where a votive candle set into a niche provided a bit of light, I could see that Li was watching me as we walked. *Was there some kind of joke I wasn't getting?*

"Okay, Li, what is it? What's this tunnel thing all about?" I stopped and waited for his answer.

"It's the birth canal. This building is a tribute to the Goddess, Mother of Life. The rites of birth, death, initiation, or rebirth, the joining of the sexes, and fertility belong to the Goddess, as does wisdom. This temple is used for initiation rites as well as learning and philosophic discourse. Sacred architecture expresses principles of the spiritual path in its design and structure. This tunnel reminds us of our physical source—our mother's womb. It also pays tribute to where we are going: rebirth, a new beginning where the old self dies and the spiritual soul, after many trials and difficulties, is born into one's life. You know, of course, that the Egyptian pyramids have tunnels for just this very purpose of initiation."

I could only mutter another *Wow!* under my breath. We had come to the end of the tunnel. There was a door at the end, a plain oak door with black iron hinges and an iron latch handle.

"Let's wait just a moment," Li said. We heard voices and another ripple of laughter from the other side.

"Whatever you say, you're the guide," I quipped. "Li," I asked after a minute, "can you explain all these goddesses to me and how Sophia fits into it all?"

"No, it would take way too much time, and we're about to enter the Hall of Philosophy. Basically, all you need to know is that there are many goddesses and each represents some of the aspects of the Sacred Feminine. Every culture in ancient times represented the power of the Life Force—the mystery of birth-growth-death-rebirth—as female, because the female expresses these mysteries most completely. The Life Force draws men and women together, produces and sustains new generations.

"When it withdraws itself from bodies at the end of life, it leads people to question their own existence. Then they become more aware and reflective. They develop conscience and pursue knowledge and understanding. So, you see, the goddesses represent beauty, fertility, and mothering. Or, they can symbolize the power of time, the cycles of growth and decay, and, of course, wisdom. Sophia is the living expression or embodiment of wisdom. And wisdom is the intelligence that is forever guiding the Life Force into new, more complex beings that reveal more and more of the divine plan of the cosmos." He paused, then put his finger to his lips, "*Shhhh.* Let's go in, quietly."

26

The Hall of Philosophy

Li carefully lifted the latch and pushed the door open a crack, looked in, then stepped inside and held the door for me to follow. *What new and startling things might I see next!* I kept my head down, watching my feet and the bottom of Li's legs as I stepped into the room. Li quietly shut the door behind us. He took my hand and led me to the back of the room, which was lined with white stone benches. He took a seat against the back wall, and I quickly sat down next to him, on his left.

Then I slowly raised my eyes. The Hall of Philosophy soared into heaven in a blast of emerald, gold, scarlet, and a blue more vivid and clear than I had ever seen. The colors were on woven fabric that stretched from the floor hundreds of feet up, maybe to the apex of the pyramid. The hall was well lit and sunshine poured through openings all around the upper walls of the pyramid. The hall itself was plain but elegant with marble floors, stone benches, and graceful columns soaring upward.

A tall man with strong features was lecturing in a language I didn't understand. He was well over six feet tall and had a long reddish beard and high forehead, and was dressed in a white tunic trimmed in blue. His voice was powerful and deep and resonated throughout the room. There were maybe fifty people seated or standing at the sides of the hall. The ones up close to the man were paying rapt attention. Others were gathered in small groups that appeared to be disputing something. Some people were waving their arms, wildly gesturing. The animated voices rippled across the distance of the hall.

I relaxed immediately. My body began to tingle from the electrified atmosphere. Most of the men and women in the room seemed happy and excited about what they were hearing. The audience captured my attention as much as the lecturer. I watched one handsome older woman, dressed in a short pale blue tunic, who was sitting near us. Her long silver hair was pulled back in a turquoise clip. She was staring in rapt attention at the lecturer, then suddenly she jumped up and ran to one of the smaller groups huddled in discussion. She tapped one of the men on the shoulder and told him something in an urgent voice in a language I didn't understand. The little group stopped talking and welcomed her into its fold; then she gestured to them and spoke quickly. They smiled and cheered and each of them began talking at once, with the woman excitedly waving her arms along with the rest of them. No one else in the room, including the handsome lecturer, seemed to be disturbed by this odd display of excitement.

I turned my attention back to the lecturer. He was pointing to a chart fastened to the side of a marble table on which was painted a triangle with ten dots evenly spaced inside it. Below the triangle were printed words that looked like Greek. I whispered to Li to tell me what it said.

He replied, "By that Great Being who gave to our soul the tetractys, which contains the fountain and root of eternally flowing Nature."

I wondered what it all meant and what I was supposed to do here if I didn't understand the language. "What does that mean and who is that guy, the one lecturing?" I whispered to Li.

He answered, his voice hushed. "The Pythagoreans' sacred symbol is the tetractys, sometimes also called the quaternian. That's what's on the chart, ten dots: one dot on the top row, two in the second row, three in the third, four in the fourth. A whole sacred mathematics can be found in that symbol. For example, the number 36 is the sum of the first four odd numbers added to the first four even ones, 1 + 3 + 5 + 7 plus 2 + 4 + 6 + 8. Pythagoras is lecturing about it now. To his students, the tetractys is the cosmos. Far more than a symbol, it is the most solemn oath they can take."

"I've heard about Pythagoras. What else? Tell me more." I was now hooked on the booming voice, even though I couldn't understand Pythagoras.

"He is the first teacher to coin the word 'philosophy' and call himself a philosopher, meaning someone who is searching for wisdom," Li whispered. "Can you not understand him?"

"No, should I be able to?"

"The speaker will present in his own language, the language of the incarnation that culminated his soul's experience on the Earth plane. For Pythagoras, that was Greek. Unprepared or disinterested souls will not understand the language. If the power of desire is strong enough, language is no barrier. English-speaking visitors can hear a lecture in Greek, Russian, or Japanese and understand the meaning if their desire is strong enough."

He paused, gazing at my face, "Pythagoras holds mathematics to be the most exact and beautiful of the sciences. Mathematics most resembles the divine order of the universe. Do you have some resistance to mathematics, Molly?" One corner of his mouth tilted up, a sort of half smile.

At that moment, a few heads turned toward us, but no one looked annoyed. Their welcoming smiles invited us to join the discussion. But Li shook his head, *No.* We stopped whispering until they turned their attention back to Pythagoras.

It was true—I was hopelessly out of sorts with everything mathematical. The simplest word problems triggered my annoyance and frustration. I would look at these problems in school and think, *Who the heck cares how many six-ounce apples you can buy for thirty cents a pound?* Seeing the audience's attention riveted to their speaker or bursting with animated discussion, I doubted Pythagoras was talking about word problems.

"Hey, Molly, look over there! Any idea who that is . . . the fellow leaning against the wall?" Li seemed to relish the bewildered look on my face as I squinted toward the imposing black-haired figure dressed in a white tunic trimmed in gold and pale green.

I shook my head.

"That's Aristocles. Your world knows him as Plato."

I stared for several minutes, wondering if I'd ever get a chance to meet him. "Where's Socrates?"

"He's not here today, neither is Aristotle. There are other things going on and not all philosophers come together at the same time," Li whispered. "I think we should slip out of here soon." After a few minutes, he tapped me on the shoulder and motioned to follow him. We got up from the stone bench and quickly left the way we had come.

"Let's go exploring before our classes," Li said, as we turned in the opposite direction along the hallway we had come in. It was wide and had only one turn, and it took us only a couple minutes to walk to the end. We exited past another pair of large hands, similar to the ones at our original entrance, into the gray-walled space of the portal. Then we went outside. "There's no sense staying to hear a teacher you can't understand. You'll have other opportunities to visit the hall and hear lectures in your own language."

A tall shaven-headed dark-skinned man came up to Li. He wore a spotless white pleated linen skirt and white sandals. A silver and lapis scarab amulet hung on a black cord around his neck. He talked to Li for about a minute in a language I couldn't understand.

After he left, Li explained, "That was Ka-Kepher, a fellow student in one of my classes with Master Chogyal. He's Egyptian and was speaking in the ancient sacred language. He told me that the schedule appears to have changed today, maybe because of Sophia's arrival in her city. Let's go check."

We stood outside the main portal for a minute or two, then walked along the brick paved promenade that surrounded the base of the pyramid.

"Come, I'll take you all around the temple. Then we'll look at today's lecture schedule and see what happened to the lessons we were supposed to take today from Master Chogyal. Maybe they've been rescheduled because of Sophia's visit. I hope so, because this is more fun than I've had in a long time." He turned to look at me. "I like being with you."

I stumbled out some words like "me too" or something, and lowered my gaze to the ground, focusing on my feet so I couldn't blush. I liked it a lot that he liked me, only I couldn't express it as easily as he could.

We strolled along the promenade, marveling at the orderly well-tended bushes and blooming peach-colored and yellow roses that bordered it. Every so often, I stopped to stroke the smooth stones at the base of the pyramid or just admire the view of the mountains to the east and the city in its colorful splendor below us. Other people were walking around the temple, too. Some were dressed in tunics and robes. Others looked Oriental like Li and Master Chogyal, wearing similar flowing pantaloons or robes. I saw a few people who looked like they came from the twentieth century, dressed in casual clothes, mostly men. There weren't any children up here, only adults.

We came at last back to the main portal where we had started. There was a wooden sign with a paper nailed to it. *This must be the class schedule,* I thought. I didn't recognize the language.

Li read it to me: "The following classes have been suspended for today: Master Chogyal, Stilpo, Hipparchia . . . I won't read the rest. I don't think any of these names would be familiar to you." He paused, his eyes looking off to the distant mountains.

"I wonder what is going on," he said quietly. "I suspect something big. Classes are never suspended unless there is some big event, some crisis. Hmmmm . . . I think we should find Master Chogyal and Sophia. Maybe they want us to attend some special lesson."

I wondered if there was a *new* crisis because last night Sophia had said Master Chogyal would be in the Hall of Philosophy today.

"Let's go to the Council Chambers. They are probably there." Li took my hand and steered me toward the broad ramp that descended to the city. We walked slowly, in silence. Li was brooding and I felt a little uneasy. He suddenly seemed to be miles away from me. The warmth of his hand was comforting, though. My thoughts fluttered and then settled on Li's skin against my hand. He felt so much older and wiser than any boys I knew at home.

We arrived at the bottom of the ramp. Li led me to a small stone building close by. It had a spire with a gold and green flag flapping in the breeze. He opened the door and we walked into a well-lit hall and waited there for several minutes, not saying anything. A woman in a white tunic that fell just below her knees, belted with a braided golden band, came out of a side door. She wore white sandals with straps crisscrossing her legs.

"Greetings, Hipparchia." Li dropped my hand and bowed to the beautiful woman with long straight black hair. "We are here to find out from Master Chogyal and Sophia what they want us to do today, if there are lessons or lectures they want us to attend. I noticed on the schedule that your lecture is canceled today. What is going on, if I may ask?"

At that moment, a stocky man with silver hair and a high forehead and stern expression came up behind the woman. She turned to him, "Crates, this is Master Chogyal's student Li. And who are you?" she asked, turning to me. Her tone was serious, her demeanor reserved.

"This is Molly," Li replied. "Sophia brought her here from Earth yesterday."

"Welcome, Molly. I am called by others Hipparchia the Cynic, and this is my husband Crates, who is also a Cynic. Sophia and Master Chogyal and the Great Council are meeting right now, and they cannot be interrupted. I heard you visited the Great Dragon, Molly. You must have a lot of questions to ask!" Although her brow was furrowed in worry, she smiled at me and I relaxed.

"Things have reached a boiling point," Hipparchia continued, her voice slow, serious. "Something must be done, but no one knows exactly what to do yet. Tension is rising in the city today, as everyone can feel Sophia's holy wrath."

Crates stepped forward, taking first Li's hand, then my own, in his.

"You will have to wait until Sophia and Master Chogyal are finished," he said softly. "I doubt if they'll come out until late afternoon. Li, why don't you show Molly the outskirts of the city? I bet she'd like to see some of the magicians, don't you think? Be careful . . . but I know you can handle anything that comes up." He put his hands on Li's shoulders. "Then you can come back here and talk to me about what you saw, and we'll have a discussion, and that can be your lesson for today. Master Chogyal cares only that you keep learning and never be idle. If they take a break, I will tell them we met and that I instructed you to show Molly the magicians for her first lesson in the City of the Wise."

Crates bowed to us both as Li thanked him. Then he slowly turned to his wife, looking at her with kindness. She wrapped her arm tenderly around his, and they departed into the shadows down the hall.

27

Oannes, the Fish-Man

Li and I quickly left the building and didn't stop until we reached the fountain. A new set of children had come to splash their hands in the water. We sat down. Li seemed pleased at the change of schedule.

"Good!" Li breathed a long sigh of relief. "We are now free to explore." He closed his eyes for a minute or two. "I know. We'll go first to the shore of the great sea so you can see Oannes, the Fish-Man. I think he's the most unusual. After that, I will show you the magicians. Let's go!" We both jumped to our feet at the same moment.

We were practically running, we were so excited. Li stopped suddenly, saying, "Let's go get some food to take with us." He led me to a little bakery a short way from the fountain. The sign said "Yum-Yum Bakery." I wondered about this, but then remembered Li's earlier remark that you could understand any foreign language as your own if you had the ability to understand the meaning.

Inside, a buxom grandmotherly woman with silvery hair was baking bread and cakes. The pleasant aroma made me instantly hungry! She wore a blue dress with tiny white flowers, and a big apron that must have once been white but was now yellowed and smudged and caked with flour.

"Hello, Li dear. Who is your friend?" she asked.

"My name is Molly and I came here with Sophia," I quickly answered.

"Oh?" She raised her gray-black eyebrows in surprise, glancing at Li for confirmation. After wiping the flour off her hands onto her apron, she reached for my hands, pressed them together against her heart, and said, "Welcome, dear Molly!" She smelled like sugar and apple spices. We stepped closer and hugged each other.

"She's from Earth, here on a visit," Li said. "We need some cakes and bread to take with us to the shore. I'm going to show her Oannes." He was searching the shelves for the best bread to take.

"Well, if you're going to see Oannes, take him a cake and tell him Rametha sent it with her love," the woman said.

"All right." Li smiled.

"Here's a basket. Besides offerings for Oannes, I'll fill it with your favorite sandwiches and some extra cakes and I'll put in some flasks of spiced cider for ya both. It's a long hike and the day is hot."

"Thank you, Rametha," Li leaned over the counter and gave her a hug. "Give my love to your family."

With a big smile, Rametha waved us out of her bakery.

When we were outside, I asked Li why he didn't pay her.

"There's no money ever exchanged in La Ville de Sophie. It can't even exist here, even if someone were to bring it, or try to materialize it. The energy is not conducive to its manifestation. It would just dissolve here."

"But money's not bad," I objected. "It makes it simpler to exchange stuff."

"It's not money that is the problem, it's that people's attention gets focused on it, on acquiring and keeping it, and then they lose sight of what that exchange is all about," Li replied.

"What's it all about, then?" I searched his face intently.

"It's about *energy*, of course," Li looked back at me just as intently, speaking with care, slowly. "There's only one energy that flows everywhere in all the universes, through all beings, through you and me right now at this moment. Money simply represents a form of that energy. The reason it's not needed here is because La Ville de Sophie is vibrating at a higher form of energy than Earth. The give and take and exchange of services and goods can occur at the level of the heart, from a place of the giving of the *self* rather than as a product of work, salary, and acquisition. The giving and receiving are closer to the persons doing the exchange. And so their attention is off the coins and paper that represent that energy and instead is focused on the energy of giving and receiving."

I had never thought about money as energy before. *And,* I wondered, *if money is energy, then what is energy?* My thoughts circled around this mystery of energy as we left La Ville de Sophie and passed through the city's Egyptian gateway with the bird-man statue. Li headed us down the road by which we had come before, for about a quarter of a mile. Then he turned to the left on a smaller dirt road I hadn't noticed when we were going in the opposite direction earlier in the day.

The sun was high in the deep blue sky. The colors were so much richer here than on Earth. The air seemed like it had more oxygen and the sky was such a vivid blue. It was warm and the breeze kept us from getting all sweaty. We were walking really fast. Skinny saplings and shrubs on either side of the road suddenly gave way to soaring deep green pines that towered above us and cast deep shade on the path. Now the air felt cooler and thicker.

Li didn't talk to me this whole time. He was brooding, or maybe just intent on where we were going. I didn't want to interrupt his reverie. The forest was so silent. I wondered why I couldn't hear any chirping of birds or chipmunks or squirrels scurrying through the branches.

As if reading my thoughts, Li finally spoke: "The animals and birds sense immediately if there is a human vibration in their territory and they cease their communication with one another. You will learn one day how to quiet your mind so that it cannot disturb the harmony and joy of the natural world."

I didn't reply. We walked another ten minutes and Li said nothing more. I tried to control my thoughts so the birds would sing, but the quiet in the forest grew so loud that it began to vibrate in my ears. The vibration got louder and louder until I couldn't tell whether it was inside or outside my ears. I shook my head to rid my ears of this weird sensation.

Then it became clear that the noise was becoming a roar and the roar was all outside of me, coming from deep within the dark forest. I had never heard such a sound. It wasn't an animal. It sounded like a freight train coming at me. The air seemed to pulsate and get heavier. The light pleasant breeze became a strong and salty wind, but the majestic trees never bent their heads to it. I shivered in the chill and picked up my pace to get through this forest quickly. Li kept up with me.

As we walked, the roar got louder. Suddenly, the trees ended. A beach of luminescent pearl pink sand sprinkled with gleaming seashells spread before us, bordering the most stunningly wild green-blue sea I had ever seen. The roar I had heard was the sea crashing onto the shore. Huge waves with crests of brilliant white contrasted with the dark turquoise of the vast expanse of sea beyond. The sight took my breath away. Massive black-brown boulders, some larger than a house, and many rounded into interesting curved shapes with wide holes in them, were strewn upon the beach and in the water. It was as though some giant's child had tossed them there to build a play city. Waves poured through a smooth large round hole in one particularly massive rock about thirty yards beyond the shore.

Overwhelmed by the sight and sounds of the ocean and the amazing aroma of the salt air, I practically shrieked at Li, "Oh my, I have *never* seen anything so beautiful in my *life!*" I was dancing all around Li, grabbing his hand and running toward the water. He was smiling, but refused to run. He pushed my hand away and said, "Go ahead, get wet."

I flung my sandals into the air. Without stopping, I rolled the silk pantaloons above my knees and headed straight into the water. I didn't care whether Li noticed my legs or my dragon slayer mark, though I didn't pull up the pants that high. The water was icy cold and I gasped from the shock but went in further, all the way to above my knees. My achy tired feet dug into the scratchy soothing sand, massaging themselves with it. I kept exclaiming and shouting stupidly, forgetting everything but this sheer pleasure of water, sun, and sand.

Back on the shore, Li stood, again with a serious face. I paid him no mind and continued splashing and squealing with delight. I began to notice other people strolling the beach, but my attention kept being drawn back to the crashing waves that were spraying me with salty foam. I was in the heart of the roar. It absorbed my shouts and surrounded me with a wall of security and a sense of physical pressure on my body that gave me total freedom to act crazy and scream with joy.

I played this way for about a half hour until I noticed quite a crowd gathered on the beach. The people were peering and squinting toward the sea, as though expecting a boat to arrive or dolphins to jump up. I went back to jumping in the waves, by now totally soaked, when another sound caught my attention. It was the crowd. Everyone was yelling excitedly.

I turned to look and gasped, choking on the salt water. I stopped breathing, my mouth hanging open like some little kid seeing a monster in a movie. Something was coming out of the ocean! It was huge. I stopped splashing and yelling and looked for Li. He was gone! *Oh no, he's left me!* I thought. I calmed my panic, knowing he would never leave me. *What in heaven's name is that!?*

An enormous creature came out of the water. It was larger than a man, at least twice the size of a big man. But it wasn't exactly a man. It looked like a male mermaid. It was a huge fish with a man inside! Or maybe it was a man in a fish costume. He had seaweed hanging on his human shoulders, but the silvery scales of a fish from his waist down were clean of ocean debris and gleamed all light and sparkly in the sunshine. I wasn't afraid at all at this point and was filled with amazement. I was so eager to see the mer-man close up that I couldn't get out of the water fast enough. I splashed ashore and ran over to the crowd, where I found Li standing at the outside edge of the group.

Li barely acknowledged my arrival. His eyes were riveted on the creature stepping ashore from the ocean depths.

"Is that Oannes?" I asked breathlessly.

"Yes," was the curt reply.

Oannes walked ashore. Fish-like fins covered his back and arms and spread into the water. From his scaly lower body, human feet protruded that allowed him to walk like a human. Rising up behind his head was a giant fish-head with yellow eyes. It must've been a real fish because it was all sea-slimy. Oannes's face was large, and he had a big gold beard with some gray in it. His eyes were partially closed and spread out sideways more than ordinary human eyes. He was human from the waist up. His chest was bare, hairless, and broad, and his arms were muscular. He never smiled. As he walked slowly ashore, the people drew closer. He raised his right arm with his thumb protruding upward and held it there, probably in a greeting to the crowd.

The people shouted and waved. There were both women and men, about twenty-five altogether. Each of them had brought either cakes, bread, or fruit for Oannes. One by one they went to him and gave a short greeting, bowing slightly. They placed their gifts before him on a large white cloth someone had spread on the sand, then walked backward into the crowd, never taking their eyes off him.

The people were dressed like they had stepped out of a child's Bible. The men wore animal skins and leather belts; their hair and beards were long and unkempt; some had headbands to keep their hair off their face. Some carried long spears with pointed stones fastened at the tips. The women had long dark hair that flowed loose and free, and they wore tunic dresses of white or shades of blue that fell below their knees and were belted at the waist with colorful red, blue, and yellow braided cord. Plain gold armbands adorned their arms between shoulder and elbow. Some of them carried babies, and some were very old, walking with gnarled sticks to balance themselves on the rough sand. There were no young children. Other than the babies, the youngest appeared to be around thirteen years old.

Li went up and placed a loaf of bread and three of Rametha's yellow sweet cakes before Oannes—as I found out later, one for Rametha, one for me, and one for Li himself. Li spoke softly to Oannes of Rametha's well wishes for his health and happiness. Oannes seemed pleased to hear Rametha's name and he asked about her. Li said she was well and keeping everyone in the city well-fed. Oannes threw back his head and laughed heartily, then asked Li what brought him to the shore today. Li turned and motioned toward me.

"I have brought a guest. Her name is Molly. Sophia brought her to the city yesterday. We were supposed to have lessons today in the Hall of Philosophy, but they were canceled because of . . . you know . . . Sophia's crisis."

Oannes turned to look at me. I was embarrassed, not knowing what to do.

"You mean the Dragon?" Oannes replied.

"Yes, isn't it always the problem?" Li seemed genuinely upset now and I wondered if the Dragon Crisis was why he kept falling into silence and moodiness.

Oannes stroked his beard, looking out over the expectant hushed crowd. He motioned for Li to remove the food. Li put the offerings into a basket one of the villagers gave him, and placed it high up on one of the big rocks nearby. Later I found out that this food would be shared in a sacred feast back in the village.

28

Oannes Presents the Law of Men and Women

Oannes stood silently, looking one by one at each of the assembled people. Gathering his breath into himself, with his eyes claiming each person to his presence, he began to speak in a resounding voice of power that reminded me of the roar of the sea behind us. His voice carried easily over the waves, as he spoke of his mission and gave his instructions:

"I, Oannes, bring you greetings from Ea and the Lords of the Sea in the Kingdom of Abzu. It is they who have sent me to teach you letters and sciences, the compilation of laws, the building of cities, the sowing of seeds, and the construction of languages, culture, art, and architecture. It is from Ea, god of the primordial waters, my lord and master teacher, that I come to teach you the arts of painting and sculpting and the gift of storytelling to carry your history and your knowledge of your gods and goddesses to your children's grandchildren. I am but the messenger." His voice drew out this last sentence one word at a time.

"The *message* . . ." his voice, emphasizing the word *message,* grew so loud it drowned out the busy ocean, "is announced every second by the gods, who read your life *not* as strife and trouble, but as the verse of your universe in its striving to produce ever more varied forms of expression of its justice and truth and beauty." His voice emerged from the depths to bring up each word by itself, then rumbled to a halt. He paused to collect the crowd once again into his gaze. People went wild with excitement and cheered him on.

I was mesmerized by what was taking place. The people were transfixed. Even the babies were quiet as if in the presence of something so captivating that even hunger or discomfort took a back seat to what was happening.

Oannes's words vibrated with the roar of the ocean and his message trembled on the verge of some magnificent unearthly revelation. I was caught up with these fishermen families in a mix of emotional expectancy and a feeling of specialness at being part of this group that was receiving this divine gift. My whole body and my heart were captivated by the scintillating thunderous power of his words. In that moment I felt I could take on the entire fire-pit realm and walk right up to the Dragon's face and spit on him—and live to tell about it.

"It is the command of the Lords of Abzu that you create communities of well-being and health and artistic expression for every member—young and old, female and male. You are to create art and beauty instead of war. You are to bring knowledge and food to the people instead of famine and tyranny. Every single person and child is to be included in your creation of a society of health and knowledge and creativity! *Is that understood?!*" I watched Fish-Man's mouth form the words and I don't know if it was just the sunlight hitting his face, but I know what I saw: There were little balls of shining light dancing around his mouth that looked like gems and jewels. I whispered to Li, asking if he saw anything around Oannes's mouth.

Li nodded. "That's how you tell if the words are divinely inspired."

"You men—fathers and husbands—who rule the towns and cities are responsible for creating circumstances in your cities that will nourish the souls of the coming generations. You will by wise action now ensure that you select wise and worthy souls as rulers, whose purpose is to advance humanity, not destroy it with wars, tyranny, and greed.

"You are to be in service to life, to the unborn future, to your children's children. Therefore, it is into the hands of those who nurture them, that I place your fate. It shall be *your women who will judge your achievements.*"

Oannes paused, pointing to a small group of women with babies. "It is by the hand of women that you shall live or die according to the degree to which you make your society one of creativity and the honoring of all life. You are forbidden to take the life of any creature, except by decree of the ruling council. If life must be taken because your cities are under siege, or you must take the life of an animal for any reason, then it shall be done only at certain times of the year, and must be done according to the prayer and ritual prescribed by your elders.

"The ruling council of eight, as you have been instructed by us, is to be made up of two elders—one woman, one man; two youths aged eighteen—one woman, one man; two parents—one father, one mother; and one warrior and one widow who has lost her husband to war. This will ensure that all perspectives are represented equally, so that the community is not sacrificed for the ambitions and war lust of a few. At the end of every year, the council will appoint five women who together represent each stage of a woman's life—a maiden, a mother, and an old woman past childbearing age, plus two more—one from a wealthy ruling family, the other from a fishing family. These women will review the actions and decisions of the ruler and decide among themselves whether he is worthy to continue to rule another year.

"It is women who nourish the human seed and grow it into the man. It is women who bear life. It is women who pay the ultimate price when there is war, for they lose their sons, babies, husbands, parents—and their daughters and their own bodies become spoils of war. Thus it shall be your women who will bear the responsibility of judging if the ruler shall be exiled from the tribe for his misdeeds. The prince of the land will more likely rule wisely and think about the consequences of his decrees for the unborn generations, if his own life hangs in the balance."

Li whispered to me that "exile" for these traditional people was the equivalent of death; it meant almost certain death in the wilderness.

"I will now speak of the terrible times ahead," Oannes continued after a very long pause. The women looked knowingly at each other, calm and serious, while the men shifted in their places.

"The Great Dragon is stirring in his lair and our Queen is growing angry at the ways of men. Men, the males, are weak, allowing their most primitive impulses toward aggression and cruelty to take them over. Civilizing arts are ridiculed. Individuals do not have the courage to speak out and stop tyranny before it swallows entire populations. Our brother Mercurius has lost his mind!" The people on the beach in unison heaved a long moan. "The Great Dragon—Thoth—the bridge of Thought that connects humanity on one side to the Wisdom of Nature and on the other to the Wisdom of the Gods—has been torn loose from his moorings, his roots in Wisdom. He has lost his mind and we know not how to restore it!"

Oannes's voice trembled on the verge of thunder once more and the people on the beach shook with dread. "But we *do* know how it happened! The beast-demon possessing Mercurius is set loose and *given power by man's insatiable cruelty, greed, and lust . . . that knows no boundaries!*" His voice reverberated in the roar of the sea. The people on the sand shivered.

"Look at your history passed down to you by your grandparents and those ancestors before them!" he bellowed, and then pointed to a group of men. "You *know* what happens when you cannot control your lust for domination over your wives and neighbors! The Dragon comes to our shores, unleashed in all his fury, untamed by the civilizing hand of art and creativity that humanizes the beast in the hearts of men! The destructive fury in the soul takes physical form and comes at you from the outside in the form of the Dragon spewing the fires of hell. You can, instead, harness the inner fury to bring down the inspiration of the gods for the delight of the soul of the tribe."

He paused to suck in the sea air, expanding his broad chest. In a loud and visible exhalation, his final words exploded like fireworks over the heads of his audience: *"Create—or die!"*

With that, Oannes raised his hands in what I gathered was a blessing. The people lifted up their hands and made a sound like a long *Ahhhhhhhh*. Then, he turned and walked slowly back into the sea. From the back, he looked all fish, with seaweed draped over his back. He slowly disappeared, still walking, with only the fish head showing, until that, too, disappeared into the choppy white waves of the bubbling green sea.

The crowd was not sad to see him go. Fired up with enthusiasm, they talked to each other with excitement. I wondered why I could understand the language. I heard it as English, even though these people looked like they had arrived from some ancient Near Eastern fishing village. Maybe, like Li had said, I was receptive to hearing it; maybe because it wasn't about math. I chuckled at the thought of being shut off from all instruction about numbers and lines.

I turned to one of the women standing next to me. "Tell me," I asked, "who is Oannes and where does he come from?"

The pretty young woman smiled at me, jostling the little baby she was carrying. "Oannes the Fish-Man first came amongst us in Chaldea. Horrible men ruled with an iron fist and the people lived like animals, tearing each other up for food, killing at random, and practicing unspeakable cruelty to their wives; they raped their own children and slaughtered the animals of field and forest just for sport, not food. Oannes taught us how to build temples, how to write sacred poetry, and how to preserve our history in stories. His veneration of women softened the hearts of our men toward us women and brought to an end their cruelty. But it took another two generations for the women to begin to trust the men—even now, it is only a cautious trust. We now have a big responsibility in determining if our king lives or is exiled at harvest time."

Li had come up to my side while she continued talking. "Oannes is a form of Vishnu, the Hindu redeemer. Oannes appeared in Babylon to a particularly vicious group of men from various regions in the Near East, and he brought them tools to create a civilization."

Li bowed to the woman and said, "Thank you and may the gods guide you in wisdom in the choices you will be making for your children." He turned to me, "Come, Molly. It's time to go."

I said good-bye to the woman and her baby, and turned reluctantly away from the roiling sea bubbling up behind the dispersing group of men and women. I spent a couple of minutes finding my sandals, then went back to Li.

29

Li on Hell and Magicians

Li was silent and somber. I felt uncomfortable with his mood and stopped walking, annoyed. "Li, what's wrong?"

He paused in mid-stride and released a sigh so deep that it must've been held inside since he was a kid. "I can't expect you to understand what is going on. Remember Molly, we're not in the ordinary world of time, where earthly existence appears to be all there is. It is so serious. You haven't even been here two days, so how can you possibly share in our crisis?" He turned to me with a helpless look on his face.

I didn't want to leave the beach, so I said, "Talk to me about it. Let's eat something before we go anywhere else. I'm hungry." I wanted him to talk to me about his fear, so that he would be the happy Li of earlier in the day.

I walked over to a pile of smooth dark boulders that seemed to have erupted from the silvery pink sand a safe distance from the encroaching tide. I climbed up easily onto the rocks and went to the highest one, which also was the smoothest and flattest. I looked out over the crashing turquoise sea for any sign of Oannes or any other creature and saw nothing but a school of dolphins leaping out of the waves far to the left of us. The sky, the air, the sea . . . all of it brimmed with some kind of pulsating vibrating energy. I could almost see little points of sparkling light in the air around me that seemed to breathe me into themselves. Fingers of hot sunshine penetrated my still-wet clothes and warmed my skin.

Basket in hand, Li followed me slowly to the boulders, climbed up, and sat down beside me. He opened the basket and took out two flasks, two wrapped sandwiches, and two wrapped cakes. There was even a small cloth on which to lay the food. I started to relax, but then saw Li's face grim with withdrawal and tension. It made me mad.

"Look," I said. "I'm here for a reason. Sophia brought me. Now you're acting like I'm some dumb girl, and *I don't like it.* I don't think she would've brought me to see the Dragon and to meet you and Master Chogyal if I was too dumb to understand all this. Maybe you feel like you were forced to be my tour guide today—is that it?"

Li shook his head *No,* but didn't say anything. He wouldn't look at me.

"I have to start learning somewhere, and it might as well be now!" I was fuming and my voice had become a bit loud and shrill. I was so disappointed at the thought that Li might be like guys I knew back home, who had their own world and kept girls out, making fun of us and calling us stupid.

Li didn't reply to my outburst. Instead, he removed the stopper on one of the brown iridescent glass flasks. It was the spiced cider Rametha had given us. He handed the flask to me, and I drank it all down. It was delicious and made the insides of my mouth tingle and heat up. I was still thirsty and hoped that Li would share the second flask with me.

Then Li unwrapped one of the sandwiches. "What's this brown and purple goo between the bread?!" he exclaimed, scowling.

I said, "Oh, give it to me! That's *my favorite*—PB & J. It's peanut butter and grape jelly. Try it, Li, it's yummy!" I wondered how Rametha knew that I loved PB & J. I took the sandwich from Li, broke off a corner, and handed him the piece.

He put it in his mouth, chewing it with a disgusted look. Then he kind of choked it down. "I guess we all have different favorite foods—we Tibetans with our yak butter tea and you Americans with your PJ, or whatever you call it." I quickly devoured the rest of my sandwich. I was starving after walking most of the morning and splashing in the sea. Meanwhile, Li had found his sandwich—brown bread filled with white cheese. He broke off half of it, and began to to eat slowly, taking small bites, in silence.

Then Li slowly unwrapped one of the delicious looking yellow cakes topped with powdery white stuff and broke off a piece for himself before handing the rest to me. It was as tasty as it looked, mildly flavored with nutmeg and vanilla. He took the second flask of cider and took several gulps, then gave the flask to me.

Li began to tell me what lay in store for the world, "When men honor natural law, when they look up at the night sky and notice the stars' harmony and regularity, they are reminded of their place in the natural order. But men forget what the sages have taught. They stop looking. They soon forget that life has meaning and purpose, and their aggression runs wild over the Earth. When men believe they are superior to Nature, they easily make war on their weaker neighbors. Basically, they use their religion, their god, as a weapon."

Li stopped to fiddle with a branch that was stuck between our boulder and the one next to it. He pulled it free, then began methodically stabbing it into the crevice between the rocks. I wondered, momentarily, why Li was so interested in sticks—this was the second time today.

Meanwhile, I was staring at the second cake, still wrapped, on top of the picnic cloth. Without asking him, I picked it up, unwrapped it, and began eating it.

Li kept talking, "The threat of afterlife religious hells—this is how people are threatened if they don't go along with the men's rules in this life."

Between bites, I asked, "But what about hell? Yesterday Sophia told me that Ialdabaoth is a demon from hell."

A huge frown appeared on Li's face. He replied, softly, "Oh please don't mention the name of that demon—Ialdabaoth the usurper comes from a hell that is a lightless realm, from outside the boundaries of the galaxy. His appearance as a businessman in the Great Hall was especially inauspicious. You also saw him as the Great Dragon, the King of Residue, in the hell as it would appear in this imaginal realm, and as I think it does to many Christians: the hell of fiery volcanic chasms and craters. There are all kinds of thought-form hells, both individual and collective, on Earth and in the ghost realms—just as there are imagined heavens. The hells described by many religions, including Buddhism, are all thought-form hells—but at least Buddhists acknowledge these heavens and hells are just thoughts."

"Wait, wait a minute!" I interrupted. "Go back to the businessman. Why was it inauspicious? You mean for *me*?" I interrupted.

"No, it's not about *you*," he said, with the slightest edge in his voice when he said "*you*." "It means Ialdabaoth is preying upon humans through manipulation and control of the financial system of the world. You wait and see, Molly," he said with a solemn serious tone, "I bet he is already planting the seeds of destruction all over the Earth with his message that profit is more important than the well-being of people, the Earth, and the animals. He delights in manipulating men—and women—to create ever fresh hells right on the Earth."

"On Earth? What do you mean?" I asked, both eager and reluctant to hear more bad news for Earth. I wondered how Li could even make such statements about the modern "financial system" and economics if he was living in a remote Tibetan village. He must be learning about earthly business and economics, not just spiritual things, in his astral classes. *If this were true,* I thought, *how neat that would be, to learn about anything you wanted to know . . .*

"Isn't it obvious?" He looked at me, shaking his head. "When people become obsessed with getting money or having control over others, and of the Earth, then everyone suffers."

When Li mentioned the Earth, I started thinking about a beautiful woods a few miles from my home that had been cut down and replaced by a shopping center and parking lot. "I know they're cutting down too many trees. I love trees and wish I could do something to save them. Is that what you mean?" I asked him.

"Molly, long before a tree is cut, a thought-form lies in the human mind that a tree is not alive, that it is an object that will bring profit. Just look where people put their attention and you will learn how to distinguish what is real and what is fake. The whole Earth suffers because people remove their attention and appreciation away from Earth's garden of delights and the creative gifts of their neighbors. Ialdabaoth makes people despise and reject a simple life connected with and dependent upon Nature and one another. He dupes people into believing that their salvation and heaven lie somewhere other than where they are—when in fact paradise is right on Earth.

"He orchestrates chaos and confusion. That's how he creates hell right on Earth by stirring up fear and thoughts of deprivation. People feel that they don't have enough money in their bank account or a nice enough house or car.

"Ialdabaoth manipulates religious imagery and male biology. That's how he gets men to kill each other. Just like modern humans watch movies, he watches them inflict unspeakable pain and degradation upon each other all over the Earth. He wants them to destroy each other *and* the Earth."

Excited, I interrupted to ask about something that had been bothering me since yesterday, "Sophia made me take my gold cross necklace off. Why, Li?"

"Probably because dragon slayers, as well as dragon riders, have to discern corrupted images and statements. Some images degrade life and truth; others enhance and reveal them. Dragon riders learn to ride the truth that is behind corrupted stories, statements, and lies; dragon slayers must learn to destroy them."

"Sophia told me about that. But are you saying the cross is corrupted?" I asked, astonished. The cross was my very identity as a Christian, a Catholic.

"The cross itself is symbolic and cosmic in meaning. The problem is how it has been twisted into serving the ends of Ialdabaoth. The most holy was combined with torture and murder in people's minds. Permission was thereby given for men in power to inflict pain and death on innocent people. By making the Christ-victim divine and ascending him to 'heaven,' Ialdabaoth assures all victims of tyrants and religious authorities that their pain is justified, and that they will receive rewards in an afterlife of a type that doesn't exist!"

Horrified, I shook my head, thinking, *This can't be true, what he's saying! That would make all Christianity deluded!*

Li continued, not looking at me, focused on his stick. "Many 'gods' are just bloated images of men's egos . . . that's what you saw Sophia obliterate yesterday. They are reptilian in nature. They are also found in self-serving irrational belief systems, fascism, and tyranny of any sort, whether economic, political, or religious. Lower drives are kept alive through the support of many people. Women unwittingly, even more than men, support religion and stupid beliefs. They are just as deluded. In fact, women preserve their traditions and ignorance more eagerly than their peaches and tomatoes!" Li exclaimed, as he forcefully plunged the stick all the way into the crack between the rocks, where it jammed so he couldn't pull it out.

The delicious little cake dusted with sweet white powder I had been munching on suddenly stuck fast in my throat. I coughed and choked on it as though it had turned to dust in my mouth. I dropped the rest of the cake—it fell off the rock to the sand below. I grabbed the cider and gulped down the last of it. Then I shuddered, hugging my knees.

Li's words shook me up, even if the full seriousness of the situation was lost on me at the time. I could only catch a glimpse of it in Li's eyes, the overwhelming grief. I was getting restless, not knowing what to do for him and knowing that any words I might offer would be of no use. So I reminded him of our plan to see the magicians. Li didn't say anything for what seemed like an eternity. The chilling seriousness, the weight of his words hung in the air against the backdrop of his silence.

"Okay, let's get out of here." Li let go of the stick. He rapidly collected his uneaten sandwich and the rest of the picnic items, and put them in the basket. He jumped off the boulder, then took my hand to help me off the rock.

Just then, a mother and her toddler son walked by. Li asked her if she could return the basket to Rametha's bakery. She replied she would be happy to do so, as she was going that way, and took the basket. By now, my clothes had dried in the sun and the breeze of the afternoon, but they were still somewhat sandy.

Li pointed toward the forest. "We're heading that way," he said. A new vigor amplified his voice. He was taking charge. I liked that.

"The magicians don't come to La Ville de Sophie."

"Why not?" I asked.

"Their motivation is not to understand but to learn about the exercise and consequences of power: theirs and the elementals'. Remember, this is not the Earth plane or real world. It's not like anyone keeps them away from the city. They cannot enter simply because they can't see it, they can't find it. They can't find it because there's no desire for truth, justice, beauty—they don't have questions about life."

We left the beach, moving back toward the forest and turning right before entering the woods. We walked on a narrow strip of short grass along the edge of where the tall pines reached to heaven. Our path was parallel to the shore, which delighted me to no end. I was so happy to look at the ocean where more dolphins played in the waves.

"Well, it seems kind of unfair to the magician guys who can't enter the city." I tried to resume the conversation about magicians.

"There's nothing fair or unfair about it," Li smiled. "It's the way the universe operates. Here, on the astral plane, reality conforms exactly to the desires and level of understanding of a person. And, don't forget that things change and evolve all the time. Some magicians just want power when they start out, and then after some amount of practicing and conjuring their minds open in wonder. Their hearts are pure and they orient themselves to the light and reject the invitation to serve the demons and elementals they conjure up. At that point, they naturally gravitate to La Ville de Sophie and meet the sages. A whole new world opens up for them as they let go of the desire for power."

He paused for a minute, then continued, "The magicians are just outside the border of the city, close to it. That's because they have the *desire* to learn about power and how to use it. They just haven't fully committed to using power only for the highest good."

My energy was coming back quickly after the food. The strong wind off the sea had let up a little. I watched small groups of people, some with little children, stroll on the beach, picking up shells. It seemed just like some idyllic scene on Earth.

We walked in silence, but it wasn't heavy like before. Li's step was quick and springy and he seemed eager again to show me the sights. He seemed very sure of the way. We came upon a side path that led into the pine forest. Among the dense trees, it was dark. Some of the tree trunks along this path glowed weirdly with luminescent splotches.

"What are these silvery marks on the trees?" I asked Li.

"They're to mark the path," he replied without further explanation.

After a half hour's hike through the forest, I began to make out some buildings to our left. The trees gave way to a large meadow with deliciously bright green grass. Tiny purple-pink flowers scattered themselves everywhere over the green sweep of ground. The largest building was made of large stones mortared together. It had a chimney and a wooden peaked roof, but no windows. In a low voice, Li told me this was where we'd find Dr. Faust and his elemental, Mephistopheles. We crossed the meadow, and it didn't take long for us to reach the building's entrance.

30

Dr. Faust and Mephistopheles

The cottage had one doorless opening, which we quietly entered. The inside space was about as big as two average living rooms. A big fire roared in the stone fireplace. A deep purple velvet love seat faced the fireplace. I saw a tall man with white silvery hair and beard, near the center of the room. His back was halfway to us and his arms were raised, with long bony fingers stretched out pointing to the ceiling. He wore a plain brown robe cinched at the waist. It fell to his gnarly feet which were bound with dark leather sandals. *He must be the magician,* I figured. His left hand held a piece of paper with strange marks on it, some spirals and squiggles and other odd formations of lines in bright red and black ink. He was standing in the middle of a circle painted onto the stone floor. There were two rings around its center with letters and strange symbols and markings, none of which I recognized. A square was drawn around the circle with a five-pointed star at each corner. Two huge candles in brass holders on the floor burned on either side of him.

I nearly ran out the door when I saw what was standing in front of the magician. I had seen enough in the past day that I shouldn't have been able to be shocked at anything anymore, but I was so startled I had to stifle a scream. It looked like a gnome or dwarf out of some child's fairy tale book, about three feet tall. He looked half bear, half fantasy creature with large pointy ears, a mouth with fangs, a snout like a pig, and hairy feet with claws.

He was standing up with his mouth gaping wide open. His two arms were also hairy and he had long claws on his paws. Strangest of all was his clothing. He wore a little brown cape belted at the waist with a high white fluffy collar that went all the way up to his funny pointy ears. A yellowish phosphorescent-like glow extended about two feet out of him. I took a deep breath and looked at Li. He was relaxed and showed no emotion. We were standing there watching, when all of a sudden the odd little creature looked up and stared with a frown at Li. He jumped up and down, pointing at Li and grunting.

I started to get scared, but remembered what Sophia and Li had told me about fear and how it would separate us, so I took a deep breath and grabbed Li's hand for comfort. His hand seemed to evaporate. I heard a loud pop! Li was gone! I screamed. The loathsome creature was grinning, jumping up and down. I panicked. I stopped to catch my breath, worried that I might lose everything and wake up in bed in that now far-off school world. *Calm down!* I ordered myself. *What can I do? Think, dammit!*

Emotions boiled up from my belly to my throat. I could barely distinguish between my terror and revulsion at the creature leering before me, my longing for Li's protection, and my shame because I could not control my fear and confusion. I didn't have a clue what to do. For a moment, I was paralyzed and couldn't speak.

"Help me!" I finally screamed at the tall magician. "Where's Li? What did you do to him?" My voice was more like a shriek of pain, but it split me away from the immobilizing swirl of panic. Slowly, as though being pulled from a deep sleep, the big magician turned toward me. His eyes were vacant, almost as though he could hear me but couldn't see me. I shivered at his stare.

"How should I know?" his voice smoked and crackled. He was facing me now, scowling, and shaking his head from side to side, as if telling me *No* at the same time. I was relieved to hear him speak English.

"My friend Li . . . where did he go? He was standing right here next to me and that stupid little dwarf jumped and pointed at him, and then *boom!*—just like that, Li disappeared. What did you do to him? Where is he? *Bring him back!*" The urgency and desperation in my voice did nothing to convince him to act on our behalf.

Just then, the hideous little monster started jumping up and down again, this time pointing at me! *Yikes,* I thought, *he's going to make me disappear, too. Then what do I do?*

Something finally made me more mad than scared, maybe it was both the magician's and the creature's total lack of sympathy. I pointed right back at the ugly pig-snouted dwarf. *"You!"* I yelled at the top of my lungs. "Tell me what you did to Li or I'll smash your ugly little head in!"

I started to walk over to him, looking around for something to hit him with if he tried to make me disappear. The only weapon-like thing was the large candlestick with a flame more like a torch than a flickering candle. I grabbed it just before the big man lunged toward it. He must've seen my eyes dart over to it. But I was faster. I jumped away from the big magician and poked the flame at the dwarf. The fire blew out. The dwarf smirked at me. He then joined his hairy little hands and sharp claws together and pointed them at me, jumping up and down, just like he did with Li. I nearly jumped out of my shoes when a ring of fire hissed up around me in a circle.

The nasty little monster grinned and giggled and pointed as drool came running out of his horrid hog mouth with its protruding pink lips. I could feel the heat turn into a searing sizzling burning. *I have to do something. He's going to kill me!* I was about to die right there, as much from the paralyzing fear that gripped me as from the flames, which seemed to be contained in a ring around me. I could feel my mind begin to shut down. As the heat grew stronger, I felt faint. Then I remembered Sophia's words in the Dragon realm that I could control my body's reaction, so that is what I did.

I fought for air against the rising heat pressing up against me. Suddenly, on impulse, I lurched through the ring, probably when my desperation for fresh air got stronger than my fear of burning. I felt nothing at all when I jumped out of the ring. I didn't catch on fire and I didn't even get singed. I looked back at the fire. It was hissing down into ashes and finally nothing was left but putrid greenish smoke swirls.

The little hog-creature seemed unfazed. The tall magician in his slow mesmerizing voice didn't bat an eye. He just said to me, "Very good. Now let's see you get your friend back." He stooped to pick up the candlestick I had dropped when the flaming ring appeared. He placed it on a desk that had several books on it, one of them open. Then he picked up the other candle, which was still lit, from the floor and placed it by the other one.

I couldn't believe my ears. "Me? What do *I* have to do with this? *You* bring him back! *You* took him away, you turdball!"

"You better watch your tongue, little lady. You haven't gotten very far in your training, I see. You are hot-headed, impulsive, and self-righteous. These are undesirable traits in La Ville de Sophie. Did you fail your tests? Is that why you have come into my study uninvited?"

"I didn't know we needed an invitation," I muttered, averting my eyes from his. I looked down at the floor and could feel my face getting red and hot.

"You come looking for a teacher because no one will have you up there, is that it?" he continued relentlessly. "Was it your curiosity that brought you here or was it your idleness and failure?"

Ow! that hurt, I thought. *Why is he so mean?*

"What is Li doing away from his studies? Where do you come from? What is it that you want to learn from me?" He was walking slowly toward me. His thick gray and black eyebrows were arched above his eyes and his mouth was still turned down at the corners. He hadn't smiled once at me. "If you want your friend back, you will have to learn how to do it yourself." His head motioned to the grinning dwarf.

"What? What do you mean?" I felt the panic rise in me.

"Just what I said. You have to do it yourself. I don't have the power to restore your friend. You will have to ask Mephistopheles yourself." With that, the magician waved his left arm toward the hog-creature, as though introducing him to me for the first time. "And now I must take my leave." He turned quickly back to the desk, gathered up some papers, snuffed the lit candle, and retreated through an arched doorway that was behind where Mephistopheles was standing.

"Wait!" I shouted, "Please don't go! You have to help me! You *must* help me!" I could now feel my throat contracting and tears from my eyes running down my cheeks. Heat like cinders burned upward from my chest to my face—I could feel it get red hot. I was frightened, abandoned—and in great danger.

31

Mephistopheles's Offer of Destiny

The loathsome figure spoke. His voice was so deep, so smooth, so human that I forgot my tears and was soon captivated by its tone. The idiotic gestures and jumping around that he did before were now replaced by something human-like and powerful. I momentarily forgot to be afraid. I even forgot about dear Li, as the voice pulled and soothed and wrapped its mesmerizing tones around me in a far more insidious, deadly way than the flames of a moment ago.

"It is no accident that you arrived here this afternoon to meet Dr. Faust and myself. I have been waiting for you. Let me introduce myself. My name is Mephistopheles. Perhaps you have heard of me before?"

He paused, waiting for my reply, the bluish circles of his eyes widening.

"No, I've never heard of you before," I answered, now engaging, to my own surprise, in a conversation with this little beastie as though it were the most natural thing in the world.

"My dear," he continued, "you were brought here at this moment in time to learn about the realms of magic and how to draw forth your power. I am your teacher for today. I will reveal to you your own powers. I will show you how to summon and dismiss the beings that you need to have at your disposal to solve problems, succeed at your tasks in life, and to handle emergency situations, such as the disappearance of your friend."

His words, his manner, his gestures, his gaze, and even his appearance were each transforming bit by bit, submitting their separate selves to the direction of one intention, synchronized by this resonating deep reaching voice . . . a voice that seemed to stretch into many unseen dimensions. It suddenly felt like the entire cosmos was focused on me. His voice carried an invitation so personal, so directly tuned to me, so deliciously attractive, it felt as simple, natural, and right as drinking a cold glass of water on a hot summer day.

"It has been arranged," the perfectly tuned voice went on, penetrating into my very bones, "that you and I come together for the purpose of your training, and . . ." the eyes bored into me even harder, "I am ordained from all time to serve you in all capacities."

I cannot possibly convey the rightness, the timeliness of his offering. I felt myself grow in power and specialness. Of course, I thought, everything today led to this moment, this meeting. *I know that I am special*—even Sophia had told me that. *Wasn't I brought to this realm for some cosmic task, to save the world?* Obviously, Sophia knew what lay beyond the city; she knew about the magicians. This was planned. She would never let me fall into harm's way.

"You are here because you have been chosen to speak to humans about the coming upheavals on the Earth. I have been chosen as your . . . uh . . . companion. Together, there is no danger to us from any source, human or elemental. I have been placed before you at the bidding of Dr. Faust. This invitation springs from our joint destiny. Or, you might say that it is our common future calling us together at this moment in time.

"Your task is great. You will need to have the path as free of obstacles as possible. There will never arise in your mind again any fears of dying at the hands of a male, of being taken advantage of, of being hurt. You are special! Special people get special treatment. You will never fear anything again." Mephistopheles paused. Silence poured into the space between us, throbbing as loud as the ocean Li and I had left earlier. But no delicious sound and wind and light quickened the thick air in the cottage.

He resumed his speaking, directed to all the secrets within me, to my feelings of being more special than anyone else, and to the fears I carried about physical harm. "You and I together will be unstoppable. The *power of the worlds* is yours for the asking. Together you and I will bring our vision of justice and truth to Earth." His suave voice bored a hole right through me. I felt him gather up every fear I'd ever had, every doubt about my own path, ability, and purpose. I felt a strange power begin to glow inside me. It was a sense of being unstoppable. The rightness was all around me and glowed like a new fire inside me.

I felt all my aspirations and desires echoed in this strange creature. Mephistopheles was no longer odd and frightful. The future spread before me like an open road where all problems and obstacles were mere pebbles on the path. I wouldn't be alone anymore. It felt like I had known this creature forever.

"And now," he continued, stepping toward me, "I will teach you how to reach me, how to call me to your side whenever you need anything at all. But first, let me show you my papers."

Everything about our meeting now seemed perfectly lined up with all that had gone before. Li's absence had faded in importance. It seemed right that I have this conversation in private with Mephistopheles. Our pact for the future had nothing to do with Li, who had a different destiny than I.

Mephistopheles walked over to the desk and began looking at the open pages of the large leather-bound book. He turned the pages slowly, fingering them, smiling. He came to the one he was looking for, apparently, for he lay the scarlet ribbon bookmark attached to the binding across the yellowed parchment.

"Here, my dear," he motioned for me to come to him. "Here is where we sign our agreement." He pointed to the book and then picked up with his hairy paw what looked like a gold letter opener. It was certainly not a pen.

I walked over to the desk and looked first at him, then at the point of the implement, then at the book, then back at his face. "What do you want me to do with that?" I asked. "And what's written in that book?"

He put the letter opener down on the open page. "This is your lesson book. I am both your teacher and your servant." He paused. "But I am even more than that for you." He looked into me with such force that I felt weak and dizzy.

"We come into agreement today about our futures, yours and mine," he went on softly. "I have promised to be with you, to come to you on demand, to be everything you need me to be to accomplish your mission. And now, it is time for you to promise *your* side of the agreement." The power of his words was enhanced by their softness.

"What is that?" I could barely squeak, as I looked again at the letter opener.

"As I have promised to be by your side in time of need, whenever asked, so too, I ask that you be there for me." Now his voice was like cold, slippery oil. "This is the first lesson that the universe teaches—sharing: Each one taking, each one giving . . . a true partnership of assistance." Mephistopheles stopped and for the first time, smiled warmly at me.

With these words "true partnership," I felt so many different emotions at once. I felt as though every one of my fears was walking toward his capable furry paws, there to be mastered or removed. I could feel the promise of my whole future of glorious triumph walking toward me *through him*. Something inside of me was awakened into longing for that *destiny* which was now gathering in clarity and power before me in his voice. I was also dimly aware that I was being slowly, inexorably, pulled away from all memory of my past, Li, and Sophia by his incendiary penetrating gaze . . . and I was hesitant.

32

Thomas–Mephistopheles

Now, wonder of wonders . . . he was transforming before me! The formerly pig-like dwarf was becoming a full-grown man with long soft dark brown hair, tied in back. The hairy paws melted into strong, tanned, lean human hands with long, supple fingers. The clothes transformed into elegance—a soft white shirt and brown trousers that fit him perfectly. This man's eyes poured their light brown depths toward mine—and because I was so close to him, I could also see that they were strangely flecked with sky blue. The transformation took place as if it was the most natural thing in the world. I wasn't even surprised as it happened. *Of course, this is meant to be, just the way it's happening. How could it happen any other way?* I asked myself.

A recognition of this man overcame me in a split second. *It's true! I have known you forever!* I melted into a delicious certainty and trust and love for him.

He held out his hands to me. "My beloved. Do you recognize me now? It's me, Thomas. It feels like an eternity since we were together. You have let lifetimes of trivia separate us from our destiny. The gods have ordained us to be with each other. Together we will save the world and our love will conquer all obstacles. Our souls belong to each other. I have waited all these years and, finally, you are here."

He paused and knelt in front of me, bringing my left hand toward his lips, kissing my fingers. "We must never never be parted again. I adore you with all my heart. My power belongs only to you. You have my heart in your hands . . . for all time." His voice was carried on waves of love and attention.

Yes, I thought, *he is familiar. I do recognize him.* Although I had no memory of his name or appearance, my body knew him and reached for him. Small waves of longing rippled through me.

"Your eyes, beloved, flecked with gold, sear my soul with their light. Look at you—you're so lovely!" He stood up. Ever so gently, he took my head in his hands. He probed my face and eyes with his gaze.

"It is time, beloved." He stepped even closer toward me. He smiled. I nearly passed out. His left hand stroked my hair, then gracefully and gently drifted down the back of my neck. His fingers kept moving down.

He could've spooned me up from the floor. There was nothing left of me, no memory of where I was or how I had gotten there, no memory of Li or Sophia. I only saw my future through this man and then I saw my past flow through me from behind, and forward to him. I saw it as two roads converging in this moment, in this man standing before me. It was a feeling of *us* being the center of the universe, as though all worlds began and ended at this moment, in me and through him, the beginning and end of time. At that moment, I experienced the origin and fulfillment of all desire. Anxiety and fear about the future disappeared. There was nothing else in that moment I could possibly want or need for the rest of my life.

But at the next moment, I began to become dimly aware of two competing sensations below my waist: There was a hot and terrible longing to fall into his arms, an electrifying heat and pleasure rippling in waves. And there was a wrenching bubbling disturbance in the pit of my stomach that felt like my insides were screaming at me, trying to get my attention, that all was not as it appeared. But my desire for Thomas was stronger. *Don't be afraid,* I reassured my stomach. *All is ordained. Everything is exactly as it should be.*

"This time, darling, I will see to it that you never leave me again. Never again will we be apart. Never again will you and I suffer the agony of separation from our other half." His right hand was now sliding down from my shoulder to my waist. His other hand turned my head so his eyes again looked directly into mine. He kissed me gently. Again I felt like I was going to pass out, so intense was the feeling of melting and merging with him.

I focused on my breathing. There was nothing at all going on in my mind except for awareness of a frenzy of physical sensations exploding into fountains of bubbles below my navel. I was in the flow of the moment, being carried in a current of emotion, physical sensation, and acceptance of whatever happened. Was Thomas my love of all time?

"We must ensure that we will never be parted again." He was at once serious, sensual, and intimate. He handed me the sharp little pointed letter opener. "I must be able to find you again, whatever lifetime you are in."

"What is that for?" My voice, cracked and parched from the heat of the moment, seemed to come from a faraway place in my brain.

"This, darling, is how you will *sign* the *Book of Destinies.* See here, read for yourself . . . about our meeting." He picked up the open Book. He turned it toward me so I could read it.

I looked at the pointed tip of the letter opener in my right hand. I saw there was no pen anywhere. Then I forced myself to read the open page. It was written in English, in a flowery script with curlicues on the letters. Sure enough, it described in detail the meeting between us on the thirteenth day of the month of Boedromion, whatever that was.

It was only later that I recalled there was no mention at all of Li or Sophia or Dr. Faust or Mephistopheles, just Thomas and me. At the time, I was only aware of him, the page in front of me, and his voice. There was no memory of anything else during that moment. The description in the Book was matter-of-fact, with no other information. I turned the page and tried to read ahead, but the lettering on the next page was blurry and smudged.

I couldn't make out the words at all. But I felt no frustration, not even any curiosity as to why it was unclear, or what might be written there.

However, I did notice something at the bottom of the page with the ribbon. There were lines at the bottom, with my name carefully printed beneath the top one—Molly Ann O'Brien—with an unfamiliar date printed next to it. My eyes met his with a dull questioning look. My energy and attention seemed to be evaporating quickly with every moment that passed. I looked down at the letter opener in my hand and back up to his face.

"Oh, my little one, my precious one. I see your hesitancy and doubt. Don't you know that doubt is what separates you from that which is your soul's desire? How many more lifetimes must you live before you learn the lesson that doubt and fear cripple the path toward love?" He was now standing as close to me as the open Book would allow. "Remember, fear is the only enemy."

He held the Book close to me, then began pressing his body into the Book. The Book was jabbing into my stomach, where all those little intestinal voices were still yelling up to me, *Stop! No, come closer!* I could feel his warm sweet breath on my face. I felt his knee press against my thigh.

He put the Book back on the desk. As I held the letter opener, Thomas clasped both his hands around mine. Then he tenderly opened my hand, finger by finger, removed the letter opener, and again placed it in the open page of the book.

Thomas's hand gently encircled my left wrist. He walked his fingers upward to my shoulder, then slid them slowly over the front of my tunic.

There was nothing in me that could even have conceived of the idea of resisting him. It was as natural as taking my next breath. Every part of my body wanted his hot touch. I saw him glance over to the love seat by the fireplace. His hand went back up to my shoulder, then down my arm. Then he led me, slowly, over to the couch.

"Here, my love, sit down. Rest." Thomas gently pushed me down onto the plush purple velvet sofa, so that I was sitting facing him. Then he knelt down in front of me and placed his strong hands on my knees. He pulled them apart ever so slowly. Then his eyes left mine and wandered slowly down my face to my neck, breasts, stomach, and thighs. I felt he was seeing my naked body beneath my silky tunic and pants, the clothes that had mysteriously appeared early this morning. I felt no embarrassment.

Then, he went over to the desk, picked up the Book, and brought it over to me. He placed it on my lap so I could read the page. He again knelt before me, as I sat on the loveseat. With his right hand, he traced a line with his long slender index finger from the top edge of the left page, which now lay open on my lap, to the bottom. As the finger reached the bottom of the page, it kept going, to touch my left thigh, lingering directly at the dragon-teeth scar.

Keep going! I screamed inside myself. And then, just as slowly, his finger that held so much promise, left me, going back up to the Book, as though purposely torturing me. Then he brought his eyes back to mine. The light coming from them was so forceful that I could feel its heat searing through me again. The look in his eyes plunged me into a deeper fervor of desire.

What was happening? What was I seeing? Or rather, what was *he* seeing? He was seeing something in me that I never knew I possessed. I couldn't take my eyes from his. I was getting lost in his gaze . . . no, that wasn't it at all. On the contrary, I was finding something new inside myself—visible in his eyes—that I never knew I had.

My body was Sleeping Beauty and she had just been kissed by the Prince. She was waking up now, responding to his longing for her aliveness.

Meanwhile, Thomas seemed in total control of the situation, as my reason was fading away. He picked up the golden letter opener from the open book where it lay. With his left hand, he took my right hand in his. With a quick short jab, he pricked the middle finger of my right hand, and turned it immediately over. A perfect bubble of bright red blood dropped ever so slowly right down onto the line at the bottom of the page, just above my name.

And then—just exactly at that moment—the riot going on in my stomach blew up and I retched all over the floor, forcing Thomas to jump backward. The Book fell off my lap and hit the floor with a thump. The spell broke in one shriek of pain and resistance that seemed to come from a place deep within my body, and evidently from my memory and reason —both struggling to wake up.

"No!" I screamed at the top of my lungs. In a split second, my memory came rushing back, and with it I could hear Sophia in the back of my head yelling my name. And then I could feel Li again, right beside me. It was like he was pulling at me.

Then I heard a sharp foreign voice, vaguely familiar, tense, precise: "Get the blood off the Book! Hurry! Don't let it *dry!*" I was coming to my senses, at last. As though waking up from a nightmare, when frightful images still linger in the room even though you're awake, I held onto broken fragments of the moment that had just passed. However, this moment now included everything that had gone before: Li's disappearance, Dr. Faust, Sophia . . . and Master Chogyal. That was the voice I just heard! *It was Master Chogyal!*

I sprang into action. I lunged for the Book lying next to the puddle of vomit. But Mephistopheles–Thomas was quicker. He picked up the Book. He was laughing, but his laugh was chilling, more like a wolf howl than a human voice. *Oh no! He isn't human!* He transformed again in front of my eyes, back to the ugly pig in a little brown cape and a white ruffled collar.

"I have the Book! I have your blood, little lady! Your drop of blood is your signature! Ahhhhh hah hah haaaaah!" Mephistopheles laughed and jumped up and down. I shrieked in pain and betrayal.

And then—I leapt on him, like a tiger on a rhino . . . not exactly the smartest thing to do, but I was frantic with panic and terror at what I had just done. He was evidently not expecting me to react this way. I tore at his large pointy flappy ears and yanked the long scraggly hairs coming out from inside them. And then like a mad dog, I bit right through his soft hairy ear. Disgusted, I spit out the bloody piece of ear into his face. I gagged on the salty hairs caught in my throat. I threw up again.

He shrieked in pain, dropping the Book! Without pausing, without thinking, I smashed my foot into his groin as hard as I could and sent him flying backward, shrieking in pain. He lay flat on his back, moaning, his hairy claws waving in the vomit-putrid air.

33

Blood on the Book

I was shaking so hard I could barely pick up the heavy Book.

What page is it? Where is it? Then I saw the red ribbon bookmark . . . it was still inside. I turned to the page. *There it is!* Then my heart sank to my toes. My blood had dried there.

What do I do now? I scratched at it with my fingernails, trying to tear it off. But the page was made of some kind of material that wasn't paper, it was more like cloth. I began to cry. *What have I done?* I could still feel Li next to me, but how could I get him back?

"Li!" I screamed. "Come back! I need you! Li, help me!"

Instantly, a burst of phosphorescent green light exploded like silent fireworks next to me. There he was! "Oh Li, you're back!" I fell into his arms, leaning against his body, sobbing uncontrollably, as tremors of nausea, memories of Thomas, and wild panic collided with each other within me.

"What happened?" Li asked, pushing me away from him, looking into my eyes with a cold seriousness that made me feel suddenly ashamed, like I had disgraced him, and Sophia, and Master Chogyal.

"You mean you couldn't hear what was going on? I felt you just now so close to me, even though I couldn't see you until the light popped next to me." I felt a tinge of relief that he hadn't seen me melt in ecstatic anticipation before Thomas.

"At first," Li said, his words tumbling out fast, "I thought nothing happened, until you started yelling, then I realized you couldn't see me. It felt like I was trapped somewhere, but I could still hear you. Then everything went dark, as though the door was closed and I was shut out from the room you were in." Li shook his head and his eyes dropped to the floor. "I had no idea how to break the spell."

"Well, neither did I. It was scary, and I felt stupid and useless." I held the Book in one arm and with the other reached to Li and took his hand. I really needed to stay connected to him. I was afraid to tell him about the blood on the page.

"Let's get out of here, quick!" Li said. He saw the wretched dwarf squirming on the floor, trying to stand up. "Did you do that?!" Li exclaimed, his eyes wide.

Nodding and clutching the Book to my chest with both hands, I followed Li out the door. He turned to make sure I was behind him.

He suddenly noticed the Book. *"Stop!"* he commanded. "You can't take that Book with you! Put it down, *now!*" he yelled. The authority in his voice shook me up.

"Li." I stopped, agonizing over what I had to say. "I have to take it with me. My blood is on one of the pages. I think I signed something." I looked down at the ground. *What had I done?*

"*What?!*" Li practically shrieked. He had never raised his voice like this.

I started to cry again. "I was taken over by some sort of spell. I forgot about you. I forgot everything. I let that monster prick my finger. But . . . but, he wasn't a monster when he did it. He was someone else, a man that I knew, only I don't know him from now, but from sometime a long time ago."

Li looked at me as though I was speaking gibberish. "You can't take *that Book* into La Ville de Sophie. It's bad . . . it's evil magic." Li's voice was hard as ice. "You left your blood in the *Book of Magic!* It's used by magicians to conjure up elementals and evil spirits to do their bidding. You have to leave it here."

"But he told me it was the *Book of Destinies*. I didn't know. He didn't look like that ugly creature back there. I don't know what happened." Sobbing, I reached out for Li, but he backed away from me, a look of horror on his face.

"Well, I know what happened!" Li's face twisted in contempt. He spat on the ground. "You were tested with a sexual seduction. It's always a first test for novices. And you fell for it, you *stupid little fool!* I could feel it on the other side." Li stood there shaking his head violently back and forth, as though trying to rid himself of the awful sight of me, as though I was contaminating his vision.

"Slut!" he muttered. The word leapt out of his mouth like an arrow that found the bulls-eye right in my chest. I staggered backward, losing my balance, the air leaving my lungs as though I had been punched.

"I need to go back to Sophia." I could barely get the words out, and I spoke to the ground. I couldn't look at him. His anger had scorched me.

"Well, you *can't go*." Li measured his words and spoke firmly, with finality, "Your blood, therefore your fate, your future, is tied to the evil magicians. You can't ever return to La Ville de Sophie. You have to stay *here*."

He backed away from me as though I had a fatal contagious disease and then turned and ran. He ran away from me into a dense woods of closely spaced fir trees, on the far side of the stone pavilion-house, not the way we had come.

I was alone. Still carrying the Book, I went to the woods, following after him, sobbing so hard that I couldn't see where I was going. Li was gone. I couldn't have followed him even if I tried, and I didn't get very far. The woods were nearly black as it was almost sundown and no sunlight came through the trees. There was no discernible trail. I was all alone, abandoned, with no one but the monstrous creature back in the stone cottage to ask for help. But I would rather die than ask him for help, or re-enter that horrible place.

How am I ever going to get back to Sophia? Now sobs were wracking my body. I fell to the ground and shook all over until there was nothing left to feel.

And then, my tears stopped. A simmering rage began to take me over.

"How *dare* he leave me here alone, like I was some kind of whore!" I yelled out loud. "How the hell was I supposed to know it was a bad magic book!" I yelled again to the trees. I got up, realizing the danger of remaining there, so close to Mephistopheles.

Clutching the Book, I ran back in the direction from which Li and I had originally come—back past the magician's house and through the flower-dappled meadow, back to the path at the edge of the pine forest, back through the pines on the path blazed with the silvery marks. I wanted to return to the beautiful seashore, to the glorious afternoon when we were together, sharing the cider and good food, to the sunshine and breeze and salt air.

I ran as fast as I could, and finally I heard the sound of the sea. Breathless, my heart splitting through my chest, my mouth dry, and my face caked from the salt of my tears, I broke through the pine forest and saw the sea. The sun was large and red-orange, just beginning its drop into the wide dark blue horizon of water. There were the boulders where we ate our lunch. I went over to them as though I had come home. I put the heavy Book down on one of the flatter rocks, opened it to the page marked with the ribbon. I searched the sand for a very sharp broken shell and found one quickly. I ripped at the brownish red spot with all my force. The shell didn't even leave a scratch. Then I carried the cursed foul Book to the edge of the sea. I repeatedly scooped the cold water into my hands and threw it onto the page, rubbing sand over it, to remove the spot. It was still there!

I fell back into the sand, laying there, looking up to the sky in total despair. I lay there for a long time. The sky darkened. A strange sickly yellow half moon hung in the sky, a sliver larger than last night when I'd seen it on the way to Master Chogyal's.

I got up, shivering, wondering what to do. The Book gave me the creeps. After all, look at the effect it had on Li. I had to get rid of it. I picked it up and walked out to the edge of dark ocean, its ripples glazed with reflected moonlight. I took off my clothes and waded into the cold water up to my chest, making my way carefully over to the pile of big rocks offshore that stood like sentinels guarding the entry to the vast sea beyond. I climbed up their slippery sides, moving the Book ahead of me, so my arms were free to climb. I got to a small ledge on the side furthest from shore, where all I could see was the dark sea. I lifted the Book above my head, and then heaved it into the black, murmuring waters. It sank immediately beneath the surface, the sea swallowing it up with a low gulping sound.

I felt better. After slowly making my way down the rocks, I waded back to shore. I found my clothes and wiped some of the cold water off me with them before putting them back on. Then I repeatedly rinsed out my mouth with the sea's salty water—to remove all traces of the taste of Mephistopheles and my own vomit. After that, I sat down in the sand next to one of the big boulders, tucking my knees up to my chest for warmth.

How I longed for the good times of earlier today, when there was so much affection between Li and me . . . but now it was all lost forever, for all lifetimes . . . I could see it in Li's face, the horror, the revulsion, his knowing that I was cut off forever from the light, from the good, and from Sophia. . . . and from him.

And there was nothing I could do to fix it. The terrible thing had happened and I couldn't undo it.

Mental pictures of my encounter with Mephistopheles began to force themselves in front of my closed eyes. Panic began to creep in, so I forced myself to focus on my breathing, and I relaxed.

Then the image of the brown-haired man, Thomas, wiggled its way in somehow. *So who was he really? Was he a real man or was he a form of Mephistopheles? Was it all a hallucination?* I was a bit surprised to feel the rising throbs of attraction as I recalled his eyes and voice directed into my body.

Then, just as suddenly, Li's face appeared in my mind's eye—accusing me—those horrible words *slut* and *stupid fool* coming at me, over and over again. *Yes, I am. He's right. He's been trained, he's smart and knows it all. I know nothing. I'm stupid and I failed.* His angry face was right there in front of me again. There on his face was absolute condemnation. *I'm a horrible person, a failure. I let down Sophia and Master Chogyal and Li.*

The split inside me felt like a feud, a stand-off: One man, the supposedly evil one, saw in me some kind of goddess-power and wanted it desperately. The other man, the supposedly good man—in fact, my friend—saw in me something so revolting and bad that he ran for his life to get away from it.

And it wasn't just these two men—Thomas and Li—who were splitting apart my conscience, I was suddenly catapulted from being a "good" person, a nice girl, into evil magic! Just like that! Up until a few hours ago, I was good and then suddenly, Li says I'm evil? I still felt like a good girl. *I am!*

And why—oh why!—after letting my blood drip onto the Book and being berated by Li, had I forgotten to call Sophia with the dragon slayer mark and ritual—as if she would even be bothered to come?

Then I crumbled there in the sand and began to sob again.

My body finally relaxed and I let go of it all, drifting off into a fitful doze, half asleep, half awake. All of it began to drain away. The events of the day began to break apart and float away and I was left with nothing but my attention to call my own. It was the only real and solid thing I could count on. With that, I could make it, no matter what lay ahead, no matter how much and how often I was condemned and cast off. Then, I collapsed into total unconsciousness.

34

Thanksgiving, 1962

I woke up at home, in my bed, in the real world. It took me a while to get my bearings. As my memories returned, pieces of the nightmare of Mephistopheles and being abandoned by Li floated and settled into my consciousness. *What happened?* I wondered. *How did things go so terribly wrong?* It was Thanksgiving morning, no school, so I had lots of time to write everything down from my most recent adventures in the middle realm. The last ones—my encounter with Dr. Faust and Mephistopheles–Thomas, Li leaving me, throwing the *Book of Magic* into the sea, and falling asleep on the beach—were worrisome. My day in the middle realm had started magically and ended horribly. And I hadn't seen Sophia at all, not once!

Grateful to be back in the real world, I occupied my thoughts with the holiday. After Christmas, Thanksgiving was my favorite holiday. I knew my mother expected me to help her a lot, as I was fourteen, almost fifteen—my birthday was next week. My younger sister Patty seemed eager to help, too. We had done a lot the night before—cleaning and rearranging the dining room—while my father and brother watched TV most of the time. They did help some, of course, setting up extra tables and getting the extra chairs out of the garage, but I had to wipe the dirt off them. My brother, who was staying in the guest-and-storage-room that had been created out of the garage loft, helped find the box of Thanksgiving decorations. My older sister Peggy was crabby. She announced to Mom she didn't feel well, and stayed in her room all evening.

Patty was not in her bed—she had gotten up early to walk Pearl. So I had privacy to get out my notebook, write about my middle realm adventures, and hide the notebook and put away the key. Patty, of course, knew about my secret notebook—but she had her own secret diary—and we had agreed to respect each other's privacy.

By the time I finished writing and got dressed, the queasy feeling in my stomach had finally gone away. I went to the kitchen and ate some oatmeal for breakfast. Mom said my brother and father, who stayed up until 3:00 A.M. watching TV and talking, and Peggy were all "sleeping in."

I'd always enjoyed baking. Midmorning, I peeled and sliced apples, made the crust and topping, and assembled two apple crumb pies, my favorite. Into the oven they went. Then, using another of my favorite recipes from my grandmother, I whipped up a double batch of cranberry-pecan muffins. After the muffins were in the oven, I helped my mother cut up celery, carrots, radishes, and scallions for a relish tray.

After the muffins and pies were out of the oven, I helped get the table ready with Patty, who had returned from her walk, while my mother worked on the other dishes. Sometimes she would call me to help—like mash the potatoes with the electric beaters into the smoothest mashed potatoes possible. There were two tables set end to end, with eleven place settings, and a smaller card table—the kids' table—off to the side. Dad brought, from the den, a fourth table, small but heavy-duty, on which extra food could be placed. Mom put out her fine china and silverware and wine glasses with tall stems. The china and silverware had been given to her by her mother, and we used them only for formal holiday dinners. The kids ate on everyday plates and with everyday tableware.

With Patty, I set out the tablecloths, special dark green cloth napkins, plates, glasses, forks, spoons, knives, serving spoons, and place mats, then showed Mom, who was pleased. In the center of the small heavy "food" table, I placed the cornucopia, which we filled with fruit, including a pomegranate, which I only saw this time of year.

Billy's girlfriend Sandra showed up around noon. She lived somewhere in downtown Chicago. At 3:30 in the afternoon, Aunt Mary and Uncle Mickey and their kids Beth, Finn, and Daniel arrived from Evanston. Peggy finally emerged from her room as guests began to arrive. She answered the doorbell, acting like the perfect hostess, and took their coats to her room. Then she took them into the living room to watch TV with my dad and brother. Beth, who was Patty's age, followed her mom to hang out in the kitchen with my mom and Patty. Finn was fourteen, my age, and Daniel was eight. They started chasing each other around. Mom asked me to get them out of her way, so Patty and I took them out in the back yard with Pearl. I came in after an hour. I was getting tired and cold. Last night's adventures still haunted my memory.

Then the doorbell rang again—it was the neighbors, Dr. and Mrs. Murphy with their baby Hannah in a bassinet. Patty and I took a peek at the baby. Peggy again emerged from her room to greet them. She asked them how they were doing and so forth, and invited them to sit in the dining room until dinner. My mother had invited them because they had no family in the Chicago area to be with at Thanksgiving—they'd just moved here from Oregon. It turned out that both the husband and wife had PhDs in clinical psychology. They had started a psychology practice—psychoanalysis, they called it—here in Chicago. Overhearing this while walking by, I got interested. So I asked Dr. Murphy what kind of psychology he did. First he explained that the discipline of psychological studies had to do with the study of the mind and its workings. He and his wife were therapists, helping people who had problems. I also found out he and his wife alternated taking care of the baby. That way, she could work, too. I wondered why she had to be called "Mrs." when they were both doctors. I was positively itching to talk to them about my otherworld problems!

Finally at 6:00 P.M., dinner was served. My mother rang a small bell, and asked Patty and Beth to gather all the guests. Everyone took their places at the long table, my father at one end with my mother at his side. Uncle Mickey sat at the other end of the table. Everyone else seated themselves at the remaining places. At the little kids' table sat Patty, Beth, and Daniel—when they were done they could watch TV in the living room.

My father said the usual Catholic grace before meals: "Bless us, O Lord, and these Thy gifts, which we are about to receive from Thy bounty, through Christ our Lord. Amen." And he added, "Thank you, Lord. And thank you for the fact that we are alive and well today and that the Cuban Missile Crisis has been averted. May there be peace in men's hearts from now on. Amen." Several *Amens* echoed from around the table.

My brow wrinkled during my father's grace. First, remembering one of Sophia's remarks, I wondered what "God" he was praying to. And then I remembered how she said her zapping of the little man Ialdabaoth was connected to the stopping of the Cuban missiles.

Finally, out came the food! My father carved the huge turkey and passed everyone a slice. I enjoyed seeing so many dinner courses—turkey dressing, gravy, mashed potatoes—they had turned out perfectly, no lumps—mashed turnips, puréed squash, diced carrots with parsley, cranberry sauce, lettuce salad, potato salad, the relishes, bread, the muffins I'd baked, on and on. Food our guests had brought that I didn't recognize was passed around along with all the dishes my mother and I had made.

Everyone at the adult table had not only a glass of water but also one of my mother's special wine glasses. My father poured red wine for the adults, and poured us teenagers—Peggy, Finn, and myself—grape juice in the wine glasses.

After everyone had their plates full, the talk turned to how everyone was doing, employment stuff mostly, the men leading the conversation. Dr. Murphy talked about how the missiles that almost had been blasted off during the Cuban Crisis were really phallic representations of what the political leaders, especially Khrushchev, were thinking about. Well, the entire room—even the little kids—were silent. You couldn't even hear a chewing sound. It was like everything stopped suddenly. To get the conversation going again, I asked him about what psychology had to say about "phallic." Of course I knew it was sexual, something to do with a penis. The room remained quiet. I watched as my mother, then my father, turned to glare at me and then scowl at Dr. Murphy. So I quickly changed the topic to "dog psychology," then lowered my eyes to my plate, feeling a horrid hot blush rush up to my face. I glanced over to Dr. Murphy. To my great surprise, our eyes met—he winked at me, smiling!

The main course finished, the men got to retire to the living room to drink coffee or whiskey, smoke cigarettes, and talk to each other. My brother and our cousins Finn and Daniel followed them; so did Peggy, then Mrs. Murphy with her baby. Sandra hovered around Billy, hanging on his every word and bringing him coffee. I wanted to catch up with him, to talk to him, but my mother told me to leave them alone. We girls were not allowed to relax. We had to clean the table, take the leftover food and dirty dishes to the kitchen, and wash the dishes—me, Patty, Beth, my mom, Aunt Mary. Finally done, I looked down. My nice new blouse was soaked with dishwater and I'd spilled puréed winter squash on it. I showed it to my mom and told her I'd be back after I changed.

The first thing I did in my room was to pull out my dictionary and look up "phallic." I remembered it was spelled Ph not F. "Phallic"—there it was, and "phallus" too. I started making some mental connections between Dr. Murphy's comments at dinner, the dictionary definitions, and why *men* were destroying the world with their missiles, which, sure enough, did look like you-know-what! What a revelation! I began getting intrigued about this area of study, "psychology," that I could pursue. How much fun that would be, to draw comparisons between a penis and a nuclear bomb!

I quickly changed my blouse and returned to the kitchen to help my mother serve dessert at the cleaned table. By this time I wasn't very hungry. I had just one tiny sliver of pumpkin pie, but with a lot of whipped cream, which is all I really wanted; the pie was for appearance's sake. After dessert, I helped bring the dirty plates and coffee cups back to the kitchen. *How I hate being a serving girl!* It made me resent men, and especially the boys my age, who took every advantage of their male privilege.

Feeling annoyed, I escaped the kitchen to return to my room. My cousin Finn was standing by my door in the hall. I asked him how he was doing in school. He said school was a drag, no one liked him, "But maybe *you* wanna make me feel good, since no one else does?!" Without even pausing to take a breath, he began to grope me, right there in the doorway, putting his hands on my shoulders and breasts. Horrified, I pushed him off just as his mother, my Aunt Mary, walked by on her way to the bathroom. She saw us. She slapped me hard across the face. "Whore!" she spat at me, then slapped her son. I was sure she was going to tell my mother on me. And he had started it! Finn disgusted me—pimply and smelly and stupid as he was. How *dare* she call me a whore! Worst of all, why was I called those terrible names both here and in the middle realm? I wanted to smash him, just like I had Mephistopheles. But then my stomach, full of so much food, started to tumble. I had this strange sensation, just as if someone had kicked me in the belly.

What a horrid day! Cradling my stinging face in my hand, I went into the living room and sat quietly in a corner. All the men were still there. I grabbed a pillow and sat on the floor in front of the TV so I wouldn't have to talk to anyone. As soon as the neighbors and relatives all left, or maybe even before, I asked Patty to tell my mother I felt ill and was going to bed.

In my room, as I lay on my bed, my thoughts switched from the shame I felt at being called a whore and traveled back to the turkey we had all devoured—lying there all roasted, his legs up in the air, headless, his innards replaced by bread stuffing, being carved up, skin and all. *And yet, he tasted so good.*

I spent a lot of time thinking about how that Thanksgiving turkey had lived, and also died. I wondered how much pain and fear he felt when his throat was slit, wherever it is they slaughter turkeys. Laying my fingers across my throat, I felt my kitchen-greasy skin which seemed too thin a covering over the throbbing pulse, veins, and tendons. *How easy it would be, I thought, to slice through my skin—skin just like the cold pale flab of a dead turkey on Thanksgiving, which severed so easily under Dad's sharp carving knife.* I quickly pulled my hand from my throat. I wasn't sure if I could eat turkey, or any meat, ever again. My life at that moment felt as fragile and expendable as the life of the turkey I had just eaten.

I didn't want to go to sleep right away, so I re-read part of an old *Black Stallion* novel. I didn't try to enter the middle realm or do the dragon-mark ritual as I fell asleep, even though it seemed the mark was heating up slightly. But then I felt a spinning wrap my consciousness into a rising roar that filled my head and then my chest . . .

PART 4

35

Help from Rametha

I didn't wake up until the golden-salmon light of a new day stretched its healing rays toward my throbbing head, and curled around my shivering body. *Where am I?* I opened my eyes and reached for the covers, then felt the hard cold sand. All my memories of Thanksgiving Day, the turkey, my family were whooshed away as the full horror of my previous afternoon and evening in the middle realm crashed in on me. I was overcome with shame, guilt, and grief; but in this morning glow no tears were left in me to wash away the events of yesterday.

I stood up slowly, my legs stiff and sandy, my hair uncombed and tangled, my clothes gritty, damp, and dirty. I was very hungry, having eaten nothing since the picnic on this very same beach with Li, and then retching it all up.

As the sun rose all hot and white above the brilliant turquoise sea, I walked around a little. Slowly, the light and warmth soothed my anguish. I was alone on the beach and, for now, I felt safe. I let the warmth sink into my battered heart.

I heard voices. Mothers with small children were walking near the water.

I felt a little better now. The bright sun gave me confidence, and the sleep had given me strength. I walked over to one of the mothers who was carrying a basket, hoping she had some food to share. She was young and pretty, with long chestnut hair. She wore a full white blouse and a royal blue skirt embroidered with scarlet, green, and yellow birds and flowers. Her three children all appeared to be under five. I must've looked scary with my sandy clothes and disheveled hair. The kids backed off behind their mother.

"Do you have some food?" I asked. "I'm so hungry,"

She looked at me quizzically.

Oh no! She doesn't understand me, I thought, looking at her sadly.

My hunger overcame the language barrier. I pointed to my stomach, then to my mouth. Then I folded my hands like I was praying to her, and said, "Please."

She understood immediately. Unfastening the basket, she opened the lid and pulled out two pieces of bread and an apple. She handed them to me with a smile, saying something in a guttural language. I took the food and smiled, saying "Thank you" over and over again. She went on her way. I gobbled up the bread while still standing there on the beach.

I decided to try to find my way back to La Ville de Sophie. I knew that the trick lay in my desire and intent to find it, to be there. No matter what terrible thing I did, I would still try my best to return there, to talk to Sophia, to explain what had happened.

After walking about a half mile, savoring every bite of the apple, I was thrilled to recognize the path that led to the beach from the forest. Though I was feeling more like myself with the food, rest, and sun, I still couldn't shake off the shame that overwhelmed me when I remembered Li's face. With every bit of will I could muster while walking on the path through the dark pines, I tried to focus only on the beautiful city where Sophia was, where the wise ones came, where I could get help. I imagined the pearly buildings, the Mystery Temple pyramid with its Hall of Philosophy. I imagined meeting Master Chogyal . . . with a surge of misery, I knew I'd better put that thought away. He would react like Li, I was sure of it. I recalled the memory of Master Chogyal's urgent voice warning me to remove the blood before it dried. *Maybe Sophia will understand. After all, I've had no training, even Li saw that. How was I supposed to know what to do? Will I be banished forever from the city, like Li said?*

I began to recognize some of the terrain. Finally, just ahead, I came to the road Li and I had taken out of the city. Jubilant, I began to run and spotted the gateway to the city up ahead. A stray thought entered that maybe I wouldn't be allowed in, but I dismissed it quickly. I kept forcing my thoughts to imagining seeing Sophia, walking the streets of La Ville de Sophie, and being welcomed and fed.

I ran through the big gateway, past the statue of Isis, and along the promenade until I saw the fountain. Children were splashing their arms and legs in the water. One of the little boys stopped and yelled to the others. He was pointing at me! The other children stopped what they were doing and gathered around him. One of the little girls ran to one of the buildings and came out with her mother, and then pointed to me.

I panicked. *That horrible Li told them what I did—and I'm going to be kicked out, or worse! Oh what will I do?* I looked around for a place to hide from the gathering crowd of mothers and children. I bolted into an alleyway. Then, I remembered! *Of course, the bakery!*

Sprinting, I found my way to Rametha's "Yum-Yum" bakery, only a block away, and burst in the door. She looked at me, grinned, and winked.

"How are ya, sweetie? I'm glad to see ya got here okay. Sophia's waitin' for ya. Ya must be starved. Let me make ya a big sandwich. I have fresh goat cheese and garden greens and bread fresh out of the oven."

I was so happy with her warm and smiling welcome that I just about started crying, this time from relief. But I was disturbed by her comment that Sophia was waiting for me. I was too ashamed to ask her for details. I dreaded seeing Sophia, Master Chogyal, and especially Li. Despite my will, the image of Li's angry face shimmered in my mind's eye, where it mocked me. My shame overtaking me again, I visibly shrank in front of Rametha. She noticed.

"Here, dear, sit over here, ya look exhausted." Rametha led me to a small table by a window at the back of the bakery, where she probably sat to do her recipes and figuring, as there were scraps of paper with ingredients and measurements scribbled on them. She swept them all into a little basket with her plump floury hands. Then she held a chair for me as I collapsed onto it. I was still trying to catch my breath from running.

I wondered what Rametha knew, and why she winked. *How will I handle Sophia's and Master Chogyal's disappointment in me? And will I ever speak to Li again?* Settling myself next to the cozy table, I looked out the window at the bright morning sunshine in the little brick courtyard on the side of the bakery. The window had a pretty little white curtain, tied with a sun-yellow sash, with itty bitty bright purple and orange flowers embroidered onto it. The walls were covered with a violet satiny paper patterned with the same tiny purple and orange flowers. It relaxed me to look at them. The bakery was tidy and clean, and the aromas wafting from the kitchen behind me were drifting past my nose.

I was startled by a hand on my shoulder. It was Rametha with a large steaming cup of tea.

"Here's some green tea for ya, honey. It'll perk ya up. And don't worry none about Li. He's got some things to learn." She grinned and winked at me once more.

What was that all about? Can she read my mind, too? Why did she say that about Li? What does she know about what happened? A fresh wave of panic engulfed me. I didn't want anyone to know what happened, except maybe Sophia. And I was taken aback by the intrusion into my thoughts. On the other hand, Rametha's words were a bit of a comfort. And the tea was delicious, as was the sandwich she brought a few minutes later.

After filling my cup for the third time, she brought me a scrumptious hot cinnamon bun, then stroked my hair. "Honey, why don't I wash them clothes for ya?" she asked, rubbing the sleeve of my tunic between her fingers so sand dropped to the floor.

"I've got a nice little dress ya can wear when ya see Sophia and Master Chogyal. I keep it for my granddaughter when she visits. And . . . by the way, they're all waiting for ya, so ya gotta be on ya way soon." She patted my shoulder, then took my right hand between both of her soft floury hands and squeezed it tenderly.

I didn't want to leave her motherly warmth, the good food, and her total acceptance of me. *But how come she knows they're waiting for me?*

"Ya seem like a tomboy to me. Probably don't like dresses much, do ya?" she chuckled. "Don't worry, dearie, it's just for today. I'll have these washed up and ready to go by tomorrow. How's that?"

I hated dresses, but said nothing. What could I do, except stand up and give her the biggest squeeziest hug she could stand?! "Thank you . . . for everything," I murmured. I ate my cinnamon bun, smothered in honey, and drank my tea. After a little while, Rametha returned.

"Come on back here with me and I'll show ya where ya can get dressed. The toilet's over there and here's a bath, already drawn. Ya can leave your sandals here in the hallway."

Rametha led me into a small room with a large metal tub filled with steamy water. There was an orange and purple plaid curtain tied across the doorway for privacy. On a small table next to the tub was a large folded coarse white cloth, a saucer with a bar of brown homemade soap, and a water pitcher. The toilet was old, with yellowed enamel, clunky looking, and stained inside. I removed my filthy clothes and dropped them on the floor next to the tub.

Then I got in the water. Too relaxed to worry about why Rametha knew how I got so dirty, I thought of nothing for many minutes. Then I bathed, and rinsed off my hair with warm clean water from the pitcher. I lingered in the tub as long as I could, until the water cooled and my skin turned as plumpy white and soft as Rametha's dough.

"It might be too hot, this dress, but the nights get cool here," Rametha said, coming into the room with some clothes draped over her arm, and with my sandals, all cleaned off and ready to wear. "And here's some drawers." These, I remembered from reading nineteenth-century British novels in English class, were underpants with a drawstring at the waist. After laying out the clothes and sandals, Rametha left, saying she'd be back in a few minutes.

The inevitable moment had come. I knew I had to go now. I got out of the tub and dried off with the scratchy white cloth that passed for a towel. The drawers were just as I expected—baggy yellowish underpants with drawstring ties. I put on the dress. It was loose, dark green, and went well below my knees. It had sleeves down to my elbows.

I had just slipped on my sandals when Rametha came back. I kept a straight face so as not to show how revolted I was with the clothes, and finally smiled at her. She smiled back. "You're all set, honey, now go meet your friends!" She kissed me lightly on the forehead, and scooted me out quickly.

"Oh, I forgot to tell ya where to go," she called after me. "They're all waiting for ya at the Judgment Hall. It's one of the buildings right before ya get to the ramp up to the pyramid. Look for the statue of the woman holding the balance. Bye now, dear!" She waved me off, smiling, and shut the door.

Judgment Hall? I gulped. *What next? What's in store for me now?* I could only imagine their faces of disappointment, maybe even anger, that I had messed up so completely. The picture of Li's rejection and revulsion came back and I shuddered with remorse. I walked slowly, dreading to see children pointing at me—*Will they, too, call me "slut"? But now, when I got to the fountain, they were gone.*

I stopped to look at the water, bubbling in the sun just as it was yesterday. Then it was framed in the light of a perfect day, in a perfect place. But now, all I saw reflected in the pool was my own pathetic image, the face of failure. It made me so anxious, I left quickly. I continued down the avenue and got closer to the ramp. I heard charged-up voices of a small group of women and men passing by, discussing the Idea of Love, of all things! Their intimate conversation vibrated between excitement and intense seriousness, and was punctuated now and then by rippling laughter. The contrast with yesterday hit me in the face. *I'm a failure,* I thought.

I've got to get this over with. I just can't stand the suspense or these feelings any longer.

Then I saw it—the Hall of Judgment. My legs got heavier and heavier as I neared the building with the statue that Rametha had described. It was in a small square courtyard. It reminded me of the "Justice" figures I'd seen in front of some courthouses. The statue was of an Egyptian goddess with a high headdress. In one hand she held a pair of balanced scales; the other pointed to a crocodile. In one pan of the scales was a feather; in the other a stone in the shape of a heart, probably a human heart. The crocodile with its gaping mouth full of sharp-looking teeth was underneath the pan with the heart. A plaque on the statue's base read: "Maat: Balancing the soul of the dead and a feather. Typhon, the crocodile, prepares to devour the soul that is too heavy."

Shuddering at the image of my own heavy heart being cast into the crocodile's jaws, I hurried past the statue. Beyond it, on the other side of the courtyard, was a large arch made of alternating black and white stone blocks, with a white keystone. The building itself, made of marble, was beyond the arch. I walked up to the entrance.

The heavy dark wooden door with a brass ring was slightly ajar. Above the door, carved into the lintel, were the words, "Hall of Judgment." By now, my heartbeat was bumping my whole body into its terrified rhythm. I hesitated a moment, then gently opened the door. The room was huge, dim, and empty. At the far end was a raised platform, like a stage. On it was a long table and four large chairs that looked like thrones. They were empty. On each side of the stage was a stone bench. Four huge white columns, two on each side, supported a massive carved arch stretching across the raised platform. Two huge flaming torches stood guard on either wall, facing each other. The silence throbbed in my ears, and then it, too, matched the beating of my heart.

I closed my eyes, wishing I were dead or anywhere else.

36

The Hall of Judgment

"I see you made it back, Molly." A clear strong feminine voice called out from the far end of the hall. It was Sophia! She was entering through a door behind the columns on the right of the stage.

Terror, joy, grief, and anguish all poured into my voice at once, making me unable to speak except for a twisted squeak, "Yes, it's me," I replied. *Of course it's me, who else would it be, you idiot,* I told myself. *What a stupid answer. Oh, get me outta here quickly.*

Sophia wore a severely simple gown of deep, dark burgundy—almost black. The color reminded me of congealing blood. Below her waist was the same scarlet velvet and gold cord belt with the blue eyestone. A new amulet hanging from a gold cord on her belt caught my attention, but I couldn't see it well from this distance.

"Walk to the front of the hall," Sophia commanded, her voice cold as a frozen stream. She was standing by one of the thrones now. Light from the torches cast her in a scene that looked like a medieval castle. *Is there a torture chamber behind the door?* I wondered with a shiver. I tried then to control my thoughts, to remember to desire understanding, but I was too feeble, the emotions coursing through my body and mind were too strong, too combustible, too ready to erupt into burning tears.

I straightened the dumpy green dress as best I could, kept my head high, threw my shoulders back as though I were proud of something—*what a joke!*—and marched myself to the foot of the stairs in front of the raised stage. Then Sophia sat on the throne on the right side of the platform.

She said nothing, making me stand there in the silence. I didn't squirm, although I wanted to die right there on the spot. Then—*Oh horrors!*—out from the door on the same side of the stage came Li, head bowed, and Master Chogyal. Neither one of them looked at me. Master Chogyal sat in a chair next to Sophia. Li went to a stone bench along the wall and sat down, frowning.

They think I'm dirt now, I thought, as the misery of the moment flushed my face with heat and that awful red color of shame that I couldn't control.

"You and Li had your first lesson together," Sophia began, not acknowledging Li and Master Chogyal. "I understand that it did not go very well. You allowed an elemental, a very powerful one, to trick you into an agreement with your own blood. Are you aware of the consequences of this?"

"No," I mumbled, my eyes searching the stone floor for a place to hide.

"You now have a brand within your bloodline, meaning the line of the karma of you and of your family members. You can be located, contacted, perhaps even manipulated and controlled by this thought-form, not only in this lifetime, but for all lifetimes. Are you aware of the seriousness of what you have done?"

Again, the floor seemed to be the only safe place for me to look. I wished it would swallow me into it. "No," I answered, a little more strongly.

"Do you know what thought-form you have let into your bloodline?" she continued hammering at me, relentlessly.

"No," I replied, stronger again.

"It's the sexual thought-form, not the delicious and free sexual union of love, partnership, and respect, but the sexual thought-form of control and domination." She paused to let the enormity of my crime sink in.

Then she continued, a little softer in her tone, "Molly, you have chosen your battle with the Dragon. Or, rather, the Dragon has found *you.* There are other players involved in this cosmic drama. You are not alone. There is someone else who called you to him—he is trapped within the clutches of Mephistopheles. He called you to him," she repeated.

"*Thomas* is his name. He is not evil and he does not wish you harm," she continued in a formal tone. "You have met each other under dramatic circumstances in previous lifetimes, during war, during times of world crises, during the destruction of Atlantis. Each time you found each other your love was so great that nothing else in life mattered, not even the vows of marriage that you had made with other mates. Although you let your finger get pricked, it was not Mephistopheles who coerced you, but your love of all time, Thomas. Therefore, your mistake in judgment is understandable, made from love and trust and recognition, not from the desire for power, not from being entirely manipulated by Mephistopheles.

"However," she gripped my attention with the force of her gaze, "you had the opportunity, during this encounter, to choose freedom instead of bondage. You were given the chance to cut yourself loose from Thomas. That decision would have also freed Thomas. But with your drop of blood, your fate has been sealed with his.

"Your *second task* will be to free Thomas from Mephistopheles, who has enslaved him. Mephistopheles is another form of the Great Dragon, whom you've already met in the form of Ialdabaoth."

I gulped, wondering what the first task could possibly be. Memories of the hog Mephistopheles, the monstrous Great Dragon in the fire pits, and the lascivious Ialdabaoth sent chills down my back.

She paused again, and sighed deeply. "Your road will be difficult, for you have entwined your fate with another." She paused, took a deep breath, and continued, oh so slowly, *"If you fail to free Thomas, you will suffer his fate."*

I looked at her, shocked.

Her next words came out one by one, feeling like nails driven into my chest by the hammer of her voice: "*If you fail,* the Dragon will live its desires through *you.*"

Sophia kept on, "But your *first,* most difficult, task will be to *free yourself* from the elemental Mephistopheles. Because your blood is in the *Book of Magic,* you are tied to him, too.

She looked at me again. "Molly, *you must get your blood back!* The *Book of*

Magic must be returned to its rightful place in Dr. Faust's cottage—without your blood! And, you must learn to remove blood curses."

What!? These all sounded like impossible tasks. I shifted from foot to foot, waiting for condemnation, termination, wrath, the crown of *slut* and *whore* labels, the end of everything I had ever hoped for . . . In a way, these judgments would be easier to handle than the fate Sophia laid out for me.

"You took on Mephistopheles physically. This is a hopeful sign—that you may have the strength born of instinct and courage to confront him as a thought-form." The tone of her voice lightened as she said this. "All is not lost," Sophia went on, her voice softening. "What appeared as failure was simply the appearance of *your life's mission.* It was a difficult test, eh?" Now she was actually smiling. "And you know what? The fact that you threw up—that your body knew something was wrong at the moment your blood fell on the Book, has helped you. That's because the single drop of blood is not a true signature, in spite of what Mephistopheles said. If you had actually signed the Book *with your name,* you would no longer be a free agent, at least for this lifetime. Your fate would have been subjection to the evil that Mephistopheles is. But that didn't happen . . ."

I couldn't understand how she could smile while condemning me to a lonely, dangerous fate! I fumed and stewed inside as anger rose up in me. "What have you done!" I blurted out. "How could you do such a thing to me? Why did you test me before I was trained?" I felt like a fool, that I had been tricked.

"Neither I nor Master Chogyal nor anyone else arranges tests, my dear," her voice drew back tightly. "Life takes care of that—even here, in the astral world. We are occupied with your Earth's global crisis. We do not arrange such things for novices, nor could we do it so accurately as your own Life Force intelligence does by itself, with no help from anyone."

She paused for a moment, her shoulders lifting as her glorious gleaming serpentine tail raised itself, then slapped the marble floor with a *snap!* I startled to attention. Even Li glanced up, surprised. There were the tiny animals again, flying into the air like popcorn!

How could my blood on the Book tie me to my mission with Sophia? I was more perplexed than ever.

"What about Li?" I finally burst out with the question that hid my most awful fear, that I had caused the death of our friendship.

"Li missed an opportunity to learn," Master Chogyal broke into the conversation. "He has led many monastic lifetimes. He has learned prayer, meditation, study, and self-discipline. He is wise in many things. But Li has had few experiences with women. He has not yet been submerged and transformed in the cosmic upheaval and divine delights of love with a woman who is his equal. Because of that, he is afraid. He fears the power of sexual love will undermine his spiritual practice and drag him down into the body. So he distrusts his feelings, and is suspicious of women. His fear is evidence that his spiritual practice is mostly mental, still in his head. Genuine spiritual practice is grounded in the body, in life, and in relationship.

"You see, Molly," Master Chogyal continued, glancing over at Li, whose head was still bowed, "Li's heart was stirred by you. He sensed your attraction to Thomas, but concluded that you let yourself become a victim of Mephistopheles. He felt jealousy and anger, unaware of the circumstances and past history you shared with Thomas. Li knows the consequences of a contract with Mephistopheles. He was understandably horrified, thinking that he had lost you to the devil."

Master Chogyal turned to me. "Li was also angry at you, Molly, because of the inevitable censure that would fall upon *him* for not protecting you in a dangerous place." Master Chogyal stopped speaking abruptly. The silence in the hall echoed his words from wall to wall.

"Li judged you too harshly, too quickly," he continued, his deep voice rising in volume, "and then he abandoned you—you, his new confidante and companion. From the perspective of spiritual training, he was the one with the power to help you, and he did not exercise that power. Li knows very well about the power of thought-forms, particularly of judging another person. He used his power of judging unwisely, toward you, his friend."

Master Chogyal's voice now boomed through the hall. "By condemning you with such certitude, he shot you with an arrow of judgment. For that, Li will pay a price. If traces of his judgment arrow stay in your thought processes and cause you hesitation or self-doubt—or guilt when you make love with someone you care about—then it will be *Li that suffers the consequences.*"

Master Chogyal stopped talking. Silence pulsated between the four of us. No one spoke or moved. I was watching the scene on the platform, surprise and relief warming my tired limbs and chest. But I remained sad and confused. Li had never looked at me, not even once. In fact, he hadn't budged the entire time from his bench. I knew, because I couldn't help darting glances at him during the whole proceeding. His head was bowed, his hands clasped over his knees.

"Now," Master Chogyal announced in a brisk voice, concluding the meeting, "both of you have lessons to learn and classes to attend. For the time being, your paths must separate. You each have training appropriate to your sex and life's experience. I am complete. Li, come with me."

Master Chogyal got up from his seat, bowed to Sophia, and left the stage through the door on the side. Li followed behind him, never once turning toward me.

37

Test of Truth—Passed!

"Molly," Sophia said, looking back to me again, "you will accompany me to the Chamber of the Goddesses in the Women's Temple. You are now prepared to join the women." She got up from her throne, walked to the front of the stage, and down several steps to where I was standing. Facing me, she squeezed my shoulders—not exactly a warm hug.

I sneaked a glance at Sophia's new amulet—it was a silver dragon-slayer mark! It hung on a gold cord to a point over her left thigh—matching the spot on my own body where my mark was! When Sophia saw I was looking at it, she cupped the amulet face up in her hand so I could see it better.

We walked together out of the Judgment Hall, under the arch, past the statue of Maat, through the courtyard, and into the streets of La Ville de Sophie, out into the hot sun. I breathed the fresh air in deeply. *All is not lost,* I thought. *There is hope.*

At the fountain, the children had returned, some with their mothers. I drew back. Sophia looked at me and smiled, grabbing my hand and pulling me forward. Once again, the little children began to point and stare. I shrank back from Sophia, letting go of her hand.

"Your feats of prowess are fast becoming legend here, my dear girl." Sophia squeezed my arm affectionately. She stopped walking, turned to the children, and waved.

"What?" I asked, not believing my ears. "How come everyone knows?"

"Well, let's see . . . early this morning, Dr. Faust came looking for Master Chogyal. He complained bitterly that his *Book of Magic* had been stolen by a girl, a friend of Li's. Imagine that!" She turned to me, put both hands on my shoulders, and looked at me. Her eyes twinkled and glistened in the light.

"He was very upset. He also said that Mephistopheles was not behaving because he had been injured and insulted and tricked. Now who do you suppose could have done *that!?*" She raised an eyebrow at me.

"You are the heroine of the day, maybe of the year," she continued. Your exploits are the talk of the town. The children think you are a powerful magician. See them stare at you?"

Sophia sat down at the fountain's edge, pulling me down next to her.

"But . . . but, I thought I had done something evil, some unforgivable sin. Li . . . Li told me . . . Li was . . ." I stopped, unable to get the words out. "Ummm, I just don't understand. Li said . . . to be involved with the magicians, and especially to leave your blood in the *Book of Magic*, is to be in their evil power forever! . . . All the magicians are only into power. Li told me the magicians could never enter La Ville de Sophie because of that, so how come Dr. Faust was able to come to the city to complain about me?"

Sophia replied, "Dr. Faust is one of the few magicians who can enter the city. He learned the consequences of his magic when it was used to betray and cause unspeakable anguish to others, such as the woman he seduced. He repented wholly, and went through many adventures, mystical and otherwise. He is working with the elemental forces, in his own way, with the good in mind, even the eventual good of Mephistopheles, mind you. He has chosen to remain in the precinct of the magicians as a consultant, for example, to help when the others get in trouble through their misuse of magical power. So he's helping the *transformation* of magic.

"Anyone whose deepest intention is a life based wholly on Good and Truth can enter my city, although Li overly idealizes it, as he does many other things. Li was mistaken when he told you that *all* magicians are banned. Faust can enter; Mephistopheles cannot."

I was relieved to hear that last sentence, although I still *hated* Dr. Faust for leaving me and Mephistopheles alone together.

"Molly, dear, you acted with courage and fierce determination. You are to be commended for your bravery and success. You are back with us safe and sound and you accomplished it all by yourself. You passed a big test, dear."

"I did? It doesn't feel like it. I still feel tricked and stupid. Nobody told me anything about tests. No one prepared me. How was I supposed to know? And . . . you know . . . and . . . you know, the blood . . ." I heaved a sigh and stumbled over my words. "I'm now tied forever to Mephistopheles . . . or to Thomas . . . or whoever that creature is." I sighed again and tears began to sting behind my eyes.

Feeling my distress, Sophia said softly, "*Now you know the value of your blood.* Someone wanted it. He took it. Now there are consequences. You are prepared *now*, to *truly learn*, because your life is at stake. You will learn about the magic and power of blood. Your choices yesterday determined your courses of instruction.

"You have passed your first initiation. You have seen the goddess. It is all over your vibration. Or, I should say, your vibration is radiating the goddess. Thomas must've helped a bit, eh?" She let out a hearty laugh and poked me in the belly. Once again, I was stunned, turned upside down in shock.

"Let's sit over here." She led me away from the fountain to a wooden bench painted bright red with black wrought iron legs and armrests. I sat down, grateful for the chance to stretch my legs in the sun.

"We have almost two hours before the festivities begin," she said, scooping her tail up and settling on the bench. Giant white and blue flower pots were set on each side of the bench. Red and white blossoms of ivy-leafed geraniums cascaded over their sides.

I was so shaken up by this turn of events, this reversal of being judged, then not judged. I was reeling, but this time it sure felt better. I was perplexed about what she meant by *the goddess*. It took me only a few minutes to get it. *That?* How does she know about *that*? I remembered the *power within me* that I became aware of from Thomas's desire and his eyes pouring that desire into me.

"Yes, you know of what I speak," Sophia said softly. "You are ready now to meet the goddesses. They will teach you what you need to know about power. Not the power of man, but the power of woman. Only a rare few women can become aware of it by themselves. Most women only have access to it through a man, as you did."

I vaguely recalled my conversation with Sophia back when I was a seven-year-old kid, something about women needing men—or maybe it was men needing women?

"Until you recognize the awesome power that you have as a woman, you will destroy men instead of teaching them. You will blame them instead of leading them into knowledge of right use of their own power. Once you get a taste of the cosmic force that lies within you, then—and only then—can you learn to use it wisely, sparingly, but also, to live within it every moment. You will learn to rely upon it for both strength and guidance—which you did yesterday with remarkable success." She turned fully toward me, beaming from ear to ear.

"Not only did I hear the story from Dr. Faust when he came to complain about the damage you inflicted on his elemental," she began, "but Master Chogyal and I had already heard what happened when Li returned yesterday. I could see Li's terror and loathing spilling out in his telling of the story about your blood dripping on the *Book of Magic*." Sophia stopped talking for a moment, sighing deeply.

She reached for my left hand and pressed her warmth and kindness into it.

"What Li called you—and I won't repeat it—is lying inside you—not just his words, but his emotion that carried the words into your heart. His judgmental words are a poison arrow. They will remain within your heart, take root, and grow into a new and dangerous identity, into a dangerous entity that will be a magnet for the Great Dragon."

I gasped and began to cry.

Sophia ignored my emotional meltdown and continued, "You will have to *find* it—this judgment—and create an *affirmation,* a statement of truth and power about yourself, to counteract this poison arrow's lethal effects on you."

"What do you mean, 'an affirmation,' Sophia?" I was listening intently now and wiped my wet face on the skirt of the ugly green dress.

"It's a declaration—short and concise, of who you are *in your own power*. An example would be: 'I express my truth with clarity precision and ease in all circumstances.' Another example would be: 'I am protected by the power and truth of Sophia from the judgments and projections of others.' Molly, use affirmations like these, always positively framed, and they will be your shield."

"Sophia, these affirmations, as you call them, just sound like words to me. How will they help me?"

"Because you have chosen to be in the thick of battle, you *must* learn how to treat the wounds you will receive. These affirmations, when spoken either silently or aloud, constellate positive thought-forms. They are an antidote to the poison of negative thought-forms." She stopped to stroke my hair. I stopped trembling inside. "This is not the first poison arrow, and it won't be the last," she said with finality.

"Come, let's get on our way to the Women's Temple." She lifted her tail in her right hand and got up off the bench. Taking my arm with her other hand, she helped me off the bench. I turned back and stooped to pick up a red geranium blossom that had fallen on the ground, and put it on the bench.

Just then, a young couple walked past us. The dark-skinned young woman came up to us, bowing her head to Sophia first.

"Good day, Sophia. Excuse me for interrupting your conversation," she said. "You must be Molly, the girl who bit off Mephistopheles's ear and kicked him! *I'm so impressed!* We heard about it today when Dr. Faust came into town. You had a lot of courage to jump on him like that!" Her face was so full of admiration. The man with her nodded and smiled. She waited for me to reply, but I didn't know what to say.

"Well," I began, "you see, it happened so fast. I didn't think. It all happened so fast. If I had thought about the danger, I wouldn't have done it."

Sophia was beaming with pride. "She's a strong warrior, eh?"

"Oh yes, Sophia, she is! I don't think I'd ever be able to be stand up to an elemental like that," the young woman said.

"Of course you would if you were in the situation. After all, the fact that you admire Molly means that you are heading in the direction of courage, yourself," Sophia said.

"Thank you, Sophia," she declared, grabbing the man's hand. They bowed their heads slightly to both of us and walked away. I noticed she now held her head high.

"You see, Molly?" Sophia turned to me, "you are a heroine here. You used your anger wisely. You didn't wilt into passivity. And . . . " she smiled, "you didn't let Li's judgment keep you from returning to me." She squeezed my hand and pulled me toward her. "Come, let's be on our way."

38

The Thea-Vision

As we were walking to the Women's Temple, Sophia said we were going to stop and visit the Thea-Vision Chamber.

"What's that?" I asked.

"It allows select women and goddesses the privilege of seeing into the future."

"Wow! Can I look, too?"

"Maybe," she replied, "but we will only have half an hour. You don't want to miss the start of the Women's Dance, which precedes the Council of Goddesses."

It was a ten-minute walk to the Temple. Sophia led me down a red cobblestone side road, explaining that the Women's Temple was built separately from the public buildings, among trees, to ensure privacy. We walked quickly past pretty houses, some pearly white, some rose-colored, to the edge of town, in a direction away from the pyramid. She didn't speak again about yesterday's events.

We came to a large domed building made of white marble with wide columns supporting a portico in the front. Several long flights of wide stairs worn away at the edges ended in a golden door with black iron rings. A huge sycamore tree was growing right in the middle of the bright green lawn that spread out and down a slope alongside the stairs. Sophia told me this building was the Women's Temple.

Orchards surrounded the building. We walked up the sloped lawn and went through one of them by the side of the dome. Small red-blushed apples hung from the trees. It felt like late summer—the seasons here were different than in Chicago. The Women's Temple was more extensive than it looked from the front. As we passed by it, I could see it had a long rectangular hallway that stretched from the portico's door to the dome itself, which covered the main hall. Sophia said that within the outer dome's perimeter was another, totally interior dome—this interior dome was the Chamber of the Goddesses. We would get to the Goddess Chamber through the hallway. She said there were also smaller chambers between the exterior dome and the innermost dome, and on lower levels beneath the temple: chambers of learning, meeting, meditation, and storage. Some of them could only be accessed through secret passageways. Sophia informed me that the temple's architecture displayed the symbols of the women's mysteries. The exterior dome represented a woman's belly, the interior dome the womb, and the main hallway the entrance to the womb.

Behind the Women's Temple was another domed building. It was small and also white. In front it had two fluted columns holding up a small peaked portico roof, which faced the rear of the Women's Temple. Otherwise, this building was completely plain.

Sophia led the way to the front of this building and stopped in front of its heavy, red-painted wooden door—with what appeared to be a *lock* with a keyhole. It was the only building in La Ville de Sophie I'd seen so far with a *lock*. Sophia had that stern determined look on her face, so I didn't ask her why. She pulled her colorful key string from a side pocket on her dress, the key string's end somehow attached inside the pocket. There were several keys. I recognized the golden key with which Sophia had unlocked the door to Ialdabaoth's Hall; there was also one of silver, one of iron, and one of bronze. With the silver key, she unlocked the door, then pushed it open. We walked in. She closed the door and locked it again from the inside.

There was light inside the dome. At its very center a round hole was open to the blue sky above. The inside ceiling was a miniature of what I'd seen in a photograph of the Pantheon in Rome.

About four feet back from the door hung a curtain of strings of tiny translucent pearly beads, each bead sort of like an almond. Sophia told me after we walked through, "The beads' shape is called a *vesica piscis* or *mandorla.* Now I know you claim you don't care much for mathematics, my dear, but this shape is formed by the intersection of two circles. Cosmically clever geometry is associated with it. It also has to do with the sign of Virgo. The glyph of Virgo was embroidered on the dress I wore on the day we visited the Great Dragon." I was trying hard to visualize what she was saying about the two circles, but Sophia kept talking so my mind had to keep up with her speech.

"Someday, you will learn about the *vesica piscis* in the Hall of Philosophy," she paused, then added, "but only if you are interested in putting aside your prejudice toward mathematics. Maybe someday you will meet a math teacher who can actually see and translate the universal structuring principles of mathematics instead of just emphasizing computation and memorizing formulas."

Sophia hesitated a moment, peered up at the sky as though retrieving a memory. Her voice softened. "The mathematician and philosopher Hypatia was such a teacher—and one of my most beloved protégées. She was a custodian of the Great Library of Alexandria."

I had never heard of either a *vesica piscis* or Hypatia, or even her library. I wanted to know more about Hypatia, but Sophia quickly returned to explaining the *vesica piscis.*

"The *vesica piscis* appears throughout the history of western symbolism—in art and architecture," she continued. "It symbolizes the Divine Feminine, the Virgin, as well as the yoni of the Creative Mother from which life emerges. Medieval churches displayed the *vesica piscis,* mainly the ones dedicated to Mary—both Marys."

"What do you mean, 'both Marys'?" I asked.

"Churches were dedicated to either the Virgin Mary or to Mary Magdalene, the woman whom Jesus loved and gave his teaching to, directly, much to the anger and resentment of Peter!"

"What! You mean Jesus loved a woman?" I was shocked. "No one in church or school has ever mentioned that to me."

Sophia didn't smile when she responded, "No, nor will this idea become even marginally acceptable for a long time—not until toward the end of your life. That's because Christian hierarchy and dogma are threatened by the story of Jesus and his lover. Ancient texts, long forgotten, are now being discovered and translated that will eventually change this. That is why contemporary *secular scholarship* and *freedom of speech* are the very lifeblood of freedom from tyranny—secular or religious. But hush about all this! These ideas are dangerous at this time, even here in the middle realm."

"Why?" I asked.

"Ideas of light and truth are potent. They have creative power for individuals. Priests and popes, princes and politicians have always scapegoated, hunted down, and murdered individuals who follow their own inner light of truth, for no power in the universe can control them. My Hypatia . . ." She shook her head slightly as though to fling off the memory. "My Hypatia was pulled from her chariot after leaving a class she had taught. She was viciously killed by a mob of Christian monks. They scraped off her flesh with seashells."

Involuntarily, I shuddered. I wished Sophia wouldn't tell me things like this. Reports of people being hurt, especially girls and women, tended to linger in the back of my mind. They didn't go away and made me afraid.

I changed the subject quickly, asking Sophia, "Why is this the only building in La Ville de Sophie that has a lock?"

"Because, what can be seen in this scrying chamber is not for anyone's personal amusement, ever—but to help people make better judgments. But people often get addicted to seeing what they think is the future, to fortune-telling and prophecy, or to spy on what happened in the past, or to find out what others are doing far away. Then they spend their lives on that rather than what's *here,* in the *present.* Scrying—farseeing—is considered a kind of magic. So only I and the other goddesses, who have discernment about the times and their needs, have the silver key—no one else can come here and 'just look.' We are now in the dome of the *Thea-Vision*—'Thea' being the Greek word for goddess."

She looked at my face. "Because of what has happened when you and

I have been together, your courage in riding the Thunder Cart with me, calling me in the ghost realm, accompanying me to Ialdabaoth's hall, and confronting Mephistopheles, it seems appropriate that you should see what's here."

Sophia pointed. There at the back of the dome, on a stand, in a frame of some kind of dark wood, was a darkish glass—sort of like a mirror. It, too, was in the shape of the *vesica piscis.* The glass seemed to be wavy, almost like water was behind it, flowing, or condensing and then evaporating. About four feet in front of the dark glass was a small wooden bench with a back, big enough for two, or maybe three, to sit on.

Sophia said, "For mortals, this is a *vision* only—you will hear nothing, although the goddesses can also hear the words and sounds in the scene. You will see only vignettes, small scenes, not the whole of what's going on."

Then she added: "Upon the surface of this glass you may see what is to come, what has happened, and what may be happening now, but far away. Remember always that there are many possibilities in the cosmos. Remember too that this is an image, and as such may be distorted. And sometimes it may be an image of an image.

"There are *many* possibilities—time threads—all held in the great mystery of the cosmos. Although in the middle realm you can experience and learn more about them, in your world usually only one of those possibilities comes to pass as *history.*"

At this point, I thought of a possibility for this Thea-Vision. "You mean I could use this to spy on world leaders in their bunkers, someone like Fidel Castro or Khrushchev—and find out if they were planning an attack on another country or something?"

Sophia frowned. "Only the goddesses may use the Thea-Vision in the manner you propose. We who are aligned with the good cannot interfere or impose our will . . ." She pointed at the Thea-Vision surface. "At least . . . not on a whim," she added. "For many goddesses, or a sage-woman coming here in contemplation, the most *pertinent* truth is revealed. But one must always use *reason*—as the scenes are distorted—and no one, goddess or mortal, can ever see the *entirety* of the world's idea. So be wary, Molly!"

With that she waved her hand in front of the glass. The scene was murky, dark as though the air was smoky, but I could make out the main details. It was kind of like watching a dim TV, with "snow." I was surprised to discern colors on the screen.

Scene: Chicago, a big brick building. A man in heavy, blood-stained work clothes goes in. The sign on the building says "Mackoy Slaughterhouse." Inside, the hind feet of cattle are being shackled with a chain. Then the cattle are hoisted up to a moving chain. A line of cattle, their hind feet up and their heads hanging down, is moving into another room. A new scene, that room: The man is there, slitting the throat of the cattle, one after another. Blood spurts everywhere, but mostly it pours into a tub under each animal's head.

Sophia said, "That's an example of what has happened. That was one of your great-grandfathers, Molly. Chicago used to have many slaughter-houses then. They were fearful fetid places to work. Today, they still are just as psychically stressful to the animals, and to the workers, though not so dangerous for people to work in since there are more government workplace regulations."

Scene: A pink mist is falling. Then, from the sky, balls of fire rain down. People are getting up, blood all over them. It looks like they're desperately trying to flee from something or someone. A woman gets up, barely able to walk. She stumbles forward about ten feet and then falls over a dead mother, who is covering her screaming baby.

Sophia whispered to me: "That has to do with another attack of the Great Dragon! Remember that scene well!"

Scene: Angel Betty and several other old women with wings like hers. They are laughing as they bring a dead body into Ialdabaoth's throne room, which has a table with plastic flowers and a record player.

Scene: A tall boatswoman hands a young woman earplugs. They float down a dark river past an island. It appears as if the young woman is going to unplug her ears, but her attention is caught by a scene off to the right.

The island is covered with hundreds, thousands of white ghosts. They look just like human bodies, only mistier, whiter. Many are clothed. The young woman seems overwhelmed. There is a big wooden pier that the ghosts are flitting about on. There are more details. A huge crucifix! But the cross is not erect. It's lying on the ground. And there isn't any ground. Instead of ground, there are just piles of dead bodies. I look closer, gasp—the entire island of corpses is floating in a sea of red liquid—it *can't* be blood! I stare again, horrified. I'm so shocked at what I'm seeing that I can't breathe.

Scene: A slender young man—wearing the brown corduroy jacket that I so well remember—is standing inside a European cathedral. Nearby are women in 1930s clothing, with small colorful hats, some with veils. The man stares a few minutes at a statue of a dark-skinned Madonna holding a dark-skinned child. As he leaves the cathedral, he buys the very same holy card I found in the jacket pocket—the Virgin Mary in heaven standing on the crescent moon!

Scene: A woman—is she me?—and a man who looks somewhat like Thomas. They're sitting together. He's kissing her.

Scene: A woman is trying to cross an extremely busy street, cars rushing by. I see her only from the back, but can tell by the way her body is shaking that she might be weeping. She's pushing a baby stroller with one hand, and holding the hand of a squirming, foot-stomping five- or six-year-old girl with the other.

The image on the Thea-Vision screen faded to static.

"Sophia, who are those people in the scenes and how could some of them not have happened yet?"

She replied, "Some of those women you saw might be you—or not—but all the scenes do concern you in some way. One must only say that the images are 'indefinite.'"

It was hard to for me to make sense of *anything* I'd just seen in the mirror. Other times and realities were now in my mind, intersecting with this day. I slumped down against the back of the bench.

"Enough!" Sophia waved her hand over the Thea-Vision surface, and it became wholly dark again. She said, "It's time to go into the Women's Temple and the Chamber of the Goddesses." We got up and went through the curtain of moon-pearly beads. Sophia unlocked the door and pulled it open. When we were outside, she locked the door again and tested it to make sure it was secure. Then we retraced our steps through the orchard to the bottom of the stairs in front of the Women's Temple.

39

Entering the Women's Temple

Sophia carefully picked her way up the worn steps, up to the golden door of the Women's Temple, carefully placing her hooves on the inside of each step to avoid slipping. She had draped the end of her tail across her left arm and lifted her skirts up with her right hand. Her head was high and her gait quick. She was getting animated. I was trying to keep up with her, but the many stairs were tiring me.

At the top, Sophia waited for me by the door impatiently, shifting her weight from one hoof to another, her tail down, smacking the white marble. When I reached her, she firmly grasped the black ring and pulled the massive door open. We entered a well-lit hallway. "Take off your shoes and put them over there," she said as she motioned to a long shelf full of sandals and shoes. "The Council has been called together because of my arrival and the urgency of the situation on Earth with the Great Dragon."

At first she seemed to want to hurry me down the hall after I left my sandals behind. But I stopped in my tracks, gasping at the sight above me, taking in its beauty. The ceiling was so high, it was more like a cathedral than a regular building. It was painted like a daytime sky—blue with a few white fluffy clouds. Both sides of the hall were lined with massive statues on short pedestals—all female. Each one was different, holding or wearing something that distinguished her from the others. I recognized Isis and Maat and Diana of Ephesus from the statues I had seen around town.

Sophia paused, noticing how awestruck I was at our surroundings. I was relieved to see that she was willing to take time to explain some of these wonders. "Each of these statues represents a power of the sacred feminine," she began. "Each of these goddesses was worshiped for thousands of years by different cultures around the world. These powers are honored in this temple by women, and . . ." she paused, glancing at me probably to see my reaction, "by the goddesses themselves whom these statues represent."

"You mean there's real goddesses here?" I asked, incredulous.

"Of course! Where else do you think they would do their goddess duties?" She laughed, and continued at a quickened pace. "This is it . . . the meeting place of the goddesses, where they come together to play, to work, to help incarnating beings figure out their lives, and to help in the evolution of life everywhere in the universe. This is where human women come to engage with the goddesses in conversation and to seek their counsel."

Behind the statues, many circular and *vesica-piscis* shaped paintings about three or four feet across hung on the milky white marble walls, from the floor all the way up. The brightly colored ones stood out. Geometrical designs decorated the surfaces of most of them, and some had animals, plants, buildings, even household items. One had a weaving loom on it. Another had, of all things, turnips! I saw no human figures. Fringes of knotted cords hung from the bottom of some, to which were attached feathers, sticks, seashells, nuts, or bones.

"Impressive, aren't they? These 'medicine shields,' as American Indians would call them, are examples of women's sacred art." Sophia gently took my shoulder and tugged me away from the wall.

As we walked along, I saw a shield with an owl. Sophia pointed to it, "That shield belongs to the goddess Athena—the eyes of the owl form a figure eight, the infinity symbol, what you use to call me in the ritual with the scar. Owls can see in the dark, just like wisdom." Next to it was a shield with another, simpler infinity symbol. "This one was created by a woman mathematician unknown to your historians."

She continued explaining, "These shields were all created by women or goddesses to express their creative passion, accomplishments, or spiritual emotions. The ones with geometrical designs, like that one over there . . ." she pointed to a silver shield on the opposite wall with a brilliantly colored latticework fourfold design contained in a black circle, "are what you call 'mandalas.'"

Between the simple infinity shield and one with a horned American buffalo, I saw a round shield with a silky black cat sitting on a shiny brilliant sky-blue cushion. Around both the cat and the pillow was a shimmering, almost metallic, cobalt blue background. The cat's bright sea green eyes—really, a honeydew melon green—were lifelike. They seemed to fixate on me as I walked up to it. But Sophia grabbed my hand, and led me to a shallow alcove on the left. "This is the mandala that *I* created for this hall."

There I stared at a particularly large mandala set into the wall. It looked like a mosaic of jewels with the design made by black lines—four concentric circles with seven lines radiating from the center. The mandala's scintillating and shifting colors were so bright that they almost hurt my eyes. The jewels—ruby, amber, emerald, sapphire, amethyst, and more—were in no particular order.

"This is the *Mandala of the Middle Realm.* You will see a different version of this world-symbol on the floor of the Chamber of the Goddesses. There are twenty-eight different areas in this mandala. The number 28 is significant—not only is it the number of the Mansions of the Moon and the different lands of the middle realm, but it is the sum of the first seven numbers, and is the product of 4 multiplied by 7. Four is the number of substance. Seven is the number of function."

I didn't know what she meant by substance and function, but I was more interested—finally—in doing the math. I quickly added one plus two plus three plus four, and then added five and six and seven. *There! Oh my! No one ever told me! They add up to 28! And the number 28 means something.*

This kind of math is like a fun puzzle, showing some kind of mystery picture about the Moon! I love this, I thought with excitement.

I admired Sophia's mandala briefly. Then Sophia said, "But let's go—I know you really want to meet the women and see the goddesses."

"Wow!" I breathed deeply the air that was perfumed like a hundred roses right in my face. *What time warp have I stepped into? What other wonderful things am I about to see and hear?* My imagination went wild. To be around goddesses and women, with no men around, sounded like heaven. I thought of all the nurturing, protection, and kindness that must permeate the space. How great it would be to not have to compete for recognition like in schools back on Earth, not to be treated like a "girl"—to have my questions honored and not dismissed just because of my sex. Especially after what happened with Thomas and being rejected by Li, I didn't want to be around men. I had been thrown off course, confused, and distressed over what happened with both of them. *What a relief to be with just women!* I thought excitedly.

Sophia seemed to be reading my thoughts, "This temple is *apart* from the other halls and temples—to show the power of woman in and of herself. No man may enter this temple's grounds, under pain of expulsion from La Ville de Sophie—*forever!*"

Sophia looked at me. "Come," she said, "you can view the statues and mandalas later," as she motioned me forward.

I was lagging behind her, trying to look at each of the colossal statues, craning my neck upward to see their faces. There were windows, some of them stained glass, way at the top. Light poured down, lighting up the faces and bodies of the statues. It was a glorious sight. Some of the goddesses were holding shafts of wheat or corn. One was holding up a bow and arrow, about to shoot, surrounded by carved wild animals. There was one with a belt of skulls who looked like she was howling at a moon carved above her face. There were also statues of motherly figures holding or nursing their babies. I didn't see any that looked like Sophia. Curiously, none of them had a man or a god with them. In fact, there was no sign of males anywhere.

"These statues were all carved by women," Sophia told me, trotting more quickly now as we neared the end of the hall.

"*Women* carved them?" I was surprised.

"It's only been recently in your world that women have been deprived of the right to carve, paint, and decorate public spaces—or, for that matter, to compose songs and masterpieces for orchestras and choruses. But that is changing rapidly now, in your century and especially your generation."

It was hard for me to imagine a society where women would be allowed to show their work on such a massive scale.

Sophia grabbed my arm and almost yanked me through a door at the end of the hall, but I pulled away from her. I was captured by the sight of the last statue by the entrance to the hall. A very large woman and a smaller, younger girl, maybe her daughter, were carved from the same massive stone. I stopped to gaze at it, intrigued by the mother and daughter, because only part of the daughter was visible, her lower half sinking into the ground of its pedestal. The mother had an anguished expression on her face. In one of her hands she held a pomegranate which I recognized from the Thanksgiving cornucopia.

"Who's that?" I asked.

"It's Demeter and Persephone. It's a long story. Don't worry, I'll introduce you to them in person . . . *tomorrow!*" Sophia opened the door into the inner chamber, the Chamber of the Goddesses, for me. "Come now, don't tarry."

Meet them? Oh my, what would I say? I was transfixed, and stood still, both worried and excited about Sophia's promise. Sophia again yanked my arm, almost pulling me off the floor and into the Goddess Chamber.

The room itself was round, with a very high ceiling painted a beautiful indigo blue. Sparkling stars like diamonds sprinkled across the dome of the midnight sky above us. At the front of the room, opposite the door we entered, was a large stage like you'd see in an auditorium. Between the stage and the main door on each side were three banks of tiered wooden benches—like bleachers in a basketball court—only this chamber was circular. There were doors on each side of the stage, in the gaps between the banks of bleachers, and at the front of the room near the stage. There were a few moveable benches in front of the bleachers.

Sophia pointed to the floor. I gazed open-mouthed, astonished. At its center was a huge colored mandala. It had concentric circles, seven of them, separated by black rings. The circles were the colors of a rainbow: violet at the outside, red at the inside. A black cross divided the circle into four quadrants.

Quickly, I did the arithmetic: 7 times 4 equals 28. *Here's the number 28 again! I love this!*

Sophia explained, "Here's the other Mandala of the Middle Realm I mentioned. The seven circles represent the seven planetary spheres, the realm of reason or the middle realm." She pointed up. At the top of the midnight-sky dome was a mirror, which reflected the mandala. "I am the Ogdoad above, the Eighth, gateway to the realm of the intellect of the fixed stars, which is beyond all the seven planets. The realm of the stars reflects the middle realm."

Sophia and I walked over to the innermost red ring of the mandala on the floor. There, at the very center of the cross I saw a very small circular mirror which reflected the dome above. "The middle realm, too, reflects the *nous,* the Greek word for the intellect. 'As above, so below,' the wise say. And don't forget," she added, "that what happens below affects what is above."

She pointed down again. "Below us is another chamber, the Chamber of the Ancestresses. On its ceiling is painted another copy of this mandala, with the color order reversed. Its central mirror reflects the floor of its chamber, which is plain except for a giant translucent milky white stone egg set into the floor's center. This egg reflects, albeit dimly, the mandala above."

I wanted to ask questions, but—

"Here, Molly, sit here," Sophia led me to a bench on the side of the room. "I have to go join the Council to prepare. Just relax and enjoy the show. Mingle, talk to the women, feel free to join their conversations. You're free here."

I was almost jumping with excitement. There were women everywhere. *Where are the goddesses?* I wondered. *How do you tell the goddesses from the women?* There were no men—and no children. The youngest girl present seemed to be around thirteen years old. She was alone. As she walked by, Sophia took her hand and sat her down beside me.

"Molly, meet Samantha; Samantha, meet Molly. Girls, after my speech, you'll have several hours of free time before the Blood Mysteries teachings commence—two and a half hours after sundown. You have several options to spend your time productively. This evening there's a buffet at the Temple of the Body, and you can attend one of the ongoing classes on the culinary arts taught by senior chefs. Molly, you might like that." Sophia arched an eyebrow at me. "I think the topic of today's lesson is the creation of delicate filled Belgian chocolate truffles. Or, if you prefer to get some exercise, this building contains an Olympic size swimming pool and athletic training areas." I shook my head in a *No.* "A string quartet will perform in the Temple of the Muses, and there's even a class on French Impressionist painters in the same building."

I was awe-struck at the wondrous array of arts and culture and even more by the chocolate production that was right up there with the string quartets and artists! Of course, the chocolate tempted me the most. I wondered briefly how Sophia knew about French Impressionists, but she continued, "Samantha will show you where these buildings are."

Samantha bowed slightly at the waist to me. "I've heard a lot about you, Molly, and am honored to meet you." She straightened and then said, "Why don't you meet me by the big sycamore tree in front of the Women's Temple after we're dismissed from the Chamber of the Goddesses? The dancing is about to begin. See you later." With an abrupt nod, she turned and walked away.

There was a great noise and commotion. Everyone seemed to be talking at once. I wanted to ask Sophia why there were no girls here, just women and a few babies, but she was gone. Later I would find out that one had to be a "woman," that is, to have been initiated into the woman's body—that is, to have menstruated.

40

The Women Dance

Then a loud *boom!* careened around the room. I jumped out of my seat, looking around to see where the noise came from, but no one else was startled by it like I was. It had come from the front of the room. There I saw a group of athletic looking young women in sleeveless gray tunics kneeling on a raised platform at the left.

They were beating drums! The first boom—created by all seven women banging their drums at the same time—was followed by a rapid series of drumbeats. The drumming continued, louder, faster, with a rhythm so primal, so feral that I felt like jumping up, tearing off my clothes and dancing. Which is exactly what some of the women did!

A group of about fifteen women of all sizes and shapes, mostly older, started shedding their clothes, rolling their hips, clapping their hands and drumming the floor with their feet to the beat of the drums. Another group of about ten younger women, who kept their clothes on, joined in a circle and started whooping it up, shouting and singing at the top of their lungs.

Then, onto the stage from the side where the drummers were, came five of the most beautiful girls I had ever seen. They all had pitch-black hair, straight, wavy, or kinky, and cropped at the shoulders. Their eyes were painted big and black like those on ancient Egyptian statues. They had on gossamer transparent gowns, each one a different pastel color—the palest shimmering green, rose, blue, violet, and gold. You could see everything through their costumes: the curve of their thighs, their hips and ribs and breasts and nipples . . . all of these bodies joined into the dance, too.

The yelling and singing stopped, as all the women in the room stopped dancing and turned to look at the stage. The five dancers were moving in sync to the fierce loud beat of the drums, each of them moving their hands to the side, then up above their heads, swaying their hips and slapping their feet on the platform at exactly the same moment. I had never seen any dance so stunningly beautiful, so pleasing, so mesmerizing as this one. Nor had I ever seen such exotically gorgeous women, either. *Are these the goddesses?* I wondered. I always imagined goddesses to be this perfect: to look beautiful and move with such elegance.

I was lost in my thoughts, still sitting on the bench, when someone poked my shoulder. A half-naked plump woman was yanking on my arm. I was so fixated on her large drooping breasts at the same height as my face, that I didn't recognize her at first. Then I heard the familiar voice calling my name. It was Rametha!

"Oh!" I sat there in shock a moment, not knowing what to say, though I did manage to pull my gaze up to her face.

"Oh Rametha, am I glad to see *you!*" I let her haul me up from the bench.

"I see ya and Sophia are back together. I'm glad for ya, sweets." She hugged me, her big hot sweaty breasts flattening against me. "Come on, now, it wouldn't be right unless ya dance. Dancing is the way we women in La Ville de Sophie honor the Life Force. It's the way we pay tribute to the Sacred Feminine. And you're welcome to take your clothes off if the spirit moves ya."

The women resumed their dancing, some so agile and practiced that they were synchronized with the dancers on stage. Right up near the stage, four very pregnant mothers-to-be were swaying gently back and forth to the drumming, their eyes locked on the gorgeous five dancers.

Rametha saw me looking at them and said, "The pregnant mothers are brought before the dancers just before they're due to deliver. The dance relaxes the womb, prepares the fetus for delivery, and calls the baby into the waiting world." I could only stare at the amazing interaction of the dancers on stage with the women below through the drumbeats reverberating around me.

Rametha winked and, quicker than a blink, off came her skirt! She was bare. Apparently, Rametha didn't wear underwear—not even those awful "drawers"! "All bodies are beautiful here, honey," she said as my mouth opened in shock, and she started to dance to the drums. "The body is the temple of the Life Force. The Life Force moves and shakes the universe, and it moves our bodies, too!" And with that, she bent over, stomping her feet to the rhythm of the drums. Then she stood upright, waving her lumpy arms in the air with joy and complete abandon.

I was still embarrassed by all this show of skin and craziness buzzing around me. I sure didn't feel like taking off my clothes—even this ugly oversize green dress. But, I guessed it wouldn't hurt to sort of move around a bit. Seeing as how I was the only one in the room not dancing, I thought it better not to call attention to myself by keeping still. I felt awkward at first, then gradually lost my self-consciousness. I stuck close to dear Rametha, feeling so good that she was here. I watched other women for a while to see what to do, but eventually I forgot about them and just started jumping around and swaying to the beat of the drums.

Above the booming of the drums, I heard a shout. It was Rametha. She was waving her hands in the air and twirling around.

Then two young women, teenagers in loose blue trousers, white blouses, and little blue caps—I found out shortly they were from the corps of "service women" for the Women's Temple—wheeled out something from a side door. It was a rounded pole or pillar on a wooden circular base with casters. The pillar was about a foot in diameter and five feet high, of varnished reddish-pale wood, and rounded at the top. About halfway up, what looked like a white cloth with red polka dots was tied to it. Another two similarly dressed women entered, each carrying a large wicker basket containing flower wreaths. Behind them walked two more service teenagers, each with a smaller basket filled with spirals of brightly colored ribbons. The four baskets were placed next to the pillar's base. A seventh woman rang a small hand bell when all was in place. Then the seven women left the hall.

I asked Rametha what was going on. She was still dancing but slowed down to answer, "Oh, now it's time for some real fun!" She danced up to the pillar, then removed the cloth, and held it up for all to see. It was obviously a large white apron such as she might wear in her bakery, with white string ties. But this one was printed all over with small red hearts, like on Valentine's Day cards.

Rametha called out, "Ooh—la-la—ya-ya–ya." She fastened the apron around her waist; it hung down over her wide belly. She then began doing a dance, circling round and round the pillar, calling, "Oh Pete, come to me, look at me, I can get near ya, go around ya, but you're stuck there, in your big hard thoughts." Then she began dancing back and forth to the drumbeat, approaching the pillar, then backing off. When she approached, she threw the apron over her face covering it, leaving everything below her waist bare for everyone to see.

"Come and get it, Petey! I got gooey honey buns for ya—come and get 'em while they're nice and hot . . . and gooey, just for yaou-a-aou!" Rametha continued to chant in a high-pitched singsong voice, "Oh Peteeeey, I loooove ya, but I want to *wring your neck* when ya get hard in the head!" "Oh Petey, come and get it—but only if you're *a good boy!*" At this she let out a loud hoot of laughter. She sang some more come-ons to Pete which I can't remember, some on the ribald side. The other women were all laughing at Rametha's jokes.

One of them whispered to me: "Pete is Rametha's husband. This dance helps us women let off steam about our men whose devotion to male dominance infuriates us. This dance helps us really *think* about our relationship to our husbands—so we don't kill them in their sleep!" With that, she winked at me and waltzed away.

After dancing for about five minutes Rametha untied the apron and threw it into the air. One of the older women caught it and began her own dance. She mentioned her own husband's name and made ribald jokes about him, that "he's up when he's down," and "he's down when he's up," and so forth. Some of these remarks I wouldn't understand until years later. This second woman threw the apron into the air, and a third woman caught it and created her own scene, and then a fourth, and so on.

Next the women started going up to the baskets on the floor of the hall. A thin older teenager with short dark hair said I should get either a wreath or a ribbon and then follow the lead of what the others were doing.

Women started circling the pole, each choosing a wreath or ribbon from the baskets. I selected a wreath of white fragrant flowers. The women with the colorful fragrant flowered wreaths—purple, red, blue, yellow, orange, pink, white—began tossing them at the pillar, trying to see if they could ring it. If they missed, another woman would grab the wreath and try again. I held my white flower wreath high in the air and tossed it. It ringed the pole perfectly!

When all the wreaths were ringed around the pole in a big pile reaching about a third of the way up, one at a time the women with the colorful patterned ribbons tied their ribbon near the top of the pole. I stood in the background and watched. Rametha, who had tossed a large red flower wreath over the pole, told me that I would now see the goddess origin of the Maypole. I looked around and wondered what she meant.

After all the ribbons were tied to the pole, the women spread out away from the pole, unwinding and stretching their ribbons to their full lengths. Then they began to circle the Maypole round and round, dancing, first one woman counterclockwise, then another one clockwise. As the drums beat faster and faster, around and around, the women skipped and waltzed, until all the ribbons were wound around the pole. The woman to finish at the end, a very old but sprightly woman in a Russian folk costume, knotted together all the ribbon ends to fasten them.

After all the wreaths and ribbons were around the pillar, all the women, including myself, continued to circle it several times, stomping our feet, clapping our hands, and slapping our bellies to the rhythm of the drums. Then we stopped. Three of the service teenagers emerged from the doorway.

Two of them wheeled the pillar near the front of the hall, while the third picked up the empty baskets, then all three left the way they'd come.

I was curious for more. So I tugged at Rametha's arm, pointing to the pillar in the corner. Rametha explained, "This pole is an image of a temporary god. It remains wreathed with the flowers until they wither and die. As the flowers dry, we are shown how everything ends, whether a year or the age, and we think of the cycles of death and rebirth—of life. In our rituals, the ribbons represent the binding of the male energy, even the god energy. The ribbons remain around the pole until the next time the goddesses meet in Council, or until the next spring equinox, whichever comes first. Then we remove the wreaths and ribbons with a different ceremony. The ceremony you just saw today symbolizes the inauguration of a new Year King."

I wanted to interrupt to ask about the "year king," but Rametha continued, "Often this kind of dance would be a fertility dance, happening at Beltane, the first of May, which marks the real beginning of the growing season in northern Europe. That's why this pole is called a 'Maypole.' After this date the new fertile king would be chosen for the year, and the old one would go. Either the king would be killed or exiled, but usually he'd just lose his year-king office. Many ancient cultures and traditional folklores throughout the world have this kind of celebratory dance. But it seems to have been forgotten pretty much in your time, my dear."

I asked if the men had their own temple somewhere and their own dances. Rametha replied "yes" as she left me to go back to her dancing—and I didn't find out anything else for a long time. Rametha, in contrast to some other women, hadn't tired yet. I could see she was really muscular because of the work of her baking, kneading bread, and hefting big bags of flour. However, she had hanging breasts from age, and a lot of lumpy fat over the muscles—she obviously enjoyed what she baked.

The drumming had kept going all this time—I wondered how the women drummers didn't get tired. Most of the women on the floor kept dancing, though some were now sitting on the lowest benches along the side and back of the room. During the entire Maypole dance, and for some time after, the gorgeous gowned dancers on the stage twirled multicolored silk scarves in a sinuous circle-dance.

Then the drums stopped as suddenly as they had begun. One of the dancers, the one wearing the gold gown, walked to the front of the stage and slowly clapped two large sticks together five times. During the next couple of minutes, attendants brought four large purple cushions onstage, cleared the drums from the platform, and set chairs up on it. A harp was wheeled in front of the platform. One of the drummers now sat before the harp; two picked up flutes; the others left. The gowned dancers sat cross-legged on the cushions—except the one in the rose-colored gown, who moved to the front of the stage and stood there.

Then ecstasy! The strings of the harp joined with the sweet light call of two flutes that flowed into and away from each other, producing the most ethereal sound that stroked and caressed me. It melted me right there on the floor. It drove all my thoughts away, dissolved all my discomfort at being in this strange room with strange women doing things that women back home never do.

As I stood entranced by the instrumental song, a strong clear soprano voice from the lone singer at the front of the stage was borne quietly out of the vibration of the harp and carried by the flutes into the room. The singer's exquisite melodies coupled and uncoupled with the rippling strings of the harp and the flutes. It felt like the flutes and the harp vibrated between dimensions on the border between sound and light. At the same time, I felt light descending as hot sparks down into my body, while the back of my head began to pulsate at the same time. It felt like I was ascending out of my body. I cried as I'd never cried before. The events of yesterday collapsed into the older pile of fears, traumas, and wounds of my young life. They all were washed away by the magic of the singer's voice, a voice from realms I thought only existed in fantasy. I cried until the tears stopped of their own accord. Many of the women who'd been dancing now sat quietly either on the floor or the benches.

Rametha took me by the hand and led me to a wooden bench near the front of the room, where we sat down. I was so grateful for her presence. I felt so thoroughly cleansed and drained at the same time. She, on the other hand, looked like nothing had happened. She was just her cheerful self.

After the singing ended, she whispered, "I see ya were moved by the music." She smiled gently, putting her stout arm around my shoulders. "Don't ya worry about the tears. It does that to everyone the first time. That's what fine music's supposed to do, connect ya to spirit. Let's get settled before the Council starts." She went to get her clothes, and put them on slowly, almost like she was sad to cover herself.

I sat there looking for the lead singer, the soprano. She was just leaving the stage. The other dancers and musicians were already gone. Each of the dancers was stunning, but she, this one, the one with the rose-colored gown, was by far the most exotic, striking girl of all. She was, in fact, the most beautiful girl I had *ever* seen: tall, lithe, black-haired, with perfectly painted red lips, rosy cheeks, milk-white skin. She moved with the relaxed grace of a cat.

She seemed completely unmoved by her own performance.

How can that be, I wondered. How can someone produce those sounds from heaven itself and be so unaffected? Why, if it was me, I'd be transported every time I sang, I would always be happy. I'd always be happy if I had a voice like that—a voice of magic that could do things to people's bodies and emotions. I wonder if I'll ever meet her. I'd love to be around her, to be her friend.

41

The Council of Goddesses

A sharp *rap!* caught my attention. My eyes reluctantly left the lovely girl and traveled to the podium on the stage. A stout older woman with short gray hair and a harsh pocked-marked face was knocking on the podium with a wooden hammer to get the women's attention. Her voice, "Come to order, come to order!" shrieked out over the chattering crowd, which soon grew quiet as heads turned and slowly nodded acquiescence.

"She's the goddess-caller, Molly. Her name's Ruth," Rametha whispered. She had returned to the bench next to me. "She sort of runs things around here—she's the leader of the women of the city." I wondered why Rametha's voice was tense and why she was scowling.

"Goddesses, women, girls, and our beloved ancestral mothers and grandmothers," Ruth's abrasive voice called out, "may you all gather yourselves together before we convene a special session of the goddesses. Today, we recognize the presence of Sophia and Gaia, our Earth-Mother goddess whose very life and well-being depend on what we decide. In addition, twenty-six other goddesses, chosen by lottery, will join them on the stage. To honor the Mansions of the Moon, their total number today is twenty-eight." Silence permeated the chamber.

There's the 28 again! I sucked in my breath, astonished. A few heads turned toward me.

"When all are seated, we will begin the convocation with statements from Sophia and Gaia. After that, we will have light refreshments in total silence, during which time we will not feed our minds with mental chatter, but meditate on the goddesses' statements. After the refreshments, the elder women of the Women's Council may stay if they wish. The women who remain will listen without interrupting as the goddesses debate each other. Permission will be granted at the end of the debate for the audience to ask questions, disagree, or comment."

The women who weren't already seated quickly got cushions from somewhere and found places on the floor. All heads turned toward the main door leading into the hall, as seven teenagers in the service uniforms entered. They carried the cushions off the stage, and removed the chairs and harp from the platform. The service girls carried in four curved sections of a white flat table, fitting them together to make a large curved table on the stage. Then they set twenty-eight chairs behind the table, so that the goddesses on stage would be facing the women on the floor of the chamber. After puttering around, adjusting and checking the table and chairs, the attendants left. Everyone was waiting. The tension in the room was palpable. Only a few women were shifting into different positions and whispering. The mood was changing quickly from one of celebration to seriousness.

Minutes passed and I looked around to see where the dancers had gone. There they were, again, all five of them! The five beauties re-entered the stage area slowly and deliberately, like queens unsmiling, shoulders and heads held high. Each dancer carried a black silver-fringed square cushion. They gracefully took their seats on their cushions on the floor near the edge of the stage. Each wore an identical covering over her dancing gown. Their robes had a distinctly Oriental flavor: lovely black silk with bright yellow and rose flowers embroidered on the hem, and sleeves with embroidered hummingbirds dipping into them. Wide belts of shimmering light green silk encircled their waists.

Rametha saw me looking at them and whispered, "Lotsa little girls apply before the age of eight to be accepted into the Dance Troupe of the Divine Feminine. Only five of them are chosen and each is supposed to serve five years. There are ten alternates. Even to be an alternate is a privilege. It's very prestigious. Only the very best stick it out. Their training lasts from age eight to thirteen. It's really rigorous. Besides dancing it includes martial arts training, gymnastics, debating, poetry, meditation, even anatomy. Then they serve five years to age eighteen.

"The teenage service corps, though, is open to all girls. Any girl who wants to join, can. She learns to do the task she's best suited for. She studies what she wants. These girls sometimes serve the goddesses, and also the elder women. My granddaughter's one of them," Rametha said proudly. Then she hushed and moved her eyes away from me toward the main door at the rear of the chamber. I heard the sound of many voices in the hallway.

The door was opened by a tall service teenager. She resembled Rametha—a younger Rametha. Rametha poked me in the arm, and when

I glanced at her, she was grinning from ear to ear. "My granddaughter," she said. The murmuring in the hall grew louder. Rametha began poking me again, so I knew this must be it!

These must be the goddesses! I thought with growing excitement. Not quite . . .

Three service teenagers entered the room. Instead of a blue cap they each wore a wreath of pink roses braided with ribbons—the first girl with white ribbons, the second with red, the third with black. Each carried a large basket of rose petals, and they tossed handfuls of them onto the floor. As the flower girls glided slowly through the room, women shifted themselves to make a straighter path for them. They stopped just before the steps to the stage, then turned and walked past the seated dancers at the front of the stage. I thought I saw the gorgeous singer sneer at the black-ribboned flower girl but couldn't be sure. The service teenagers went out through a side exit.

Then—finally! In came the goddesses. One by one, with several seconds between them, they processed slowly past us women, so we could see them each individually. A few of them walked up the short flight of stairs to the stage; most of them took seats on the bleachers at the sides and back of the room. *Why, they look just like human women, maybe just a little larger!*

They were more matronly and handsome than beautiful: strong-featured, serious, many of them with long wavy light or dark hair, although a few had short cropped hair. Some had their hair braided and wound up in circles in the back. Their skin colors ranged from the most pale ivory to almost coal black. A number of them had tattoos or what looked like face paint. I saw two green-skinned goddesses. One goddess was small and wiry with small black-rimmed spectacles and short cropped dark brown hair. She looked like one of the youngest. She carried a plain notebook and pen, and seated herself at the table on the stage. Another looked like Rametha: soft and plump and rather vacant looking, although there was certainly nothing vacant about Rametha.

The goddesses wore an assortment of outfits, most of them gowns of a heavy fabric of various colors, some loose, some tied at the waist with brightly colored sashes. Many carried staffs, shields, small boxes, flowers, musical instruments, or other objects—*probably to show their special attributes,* I figured. One had an owl on her shoulder, another a vulture, another a parrot. The goddesses' costumes and headdresses seemed to be representative of all the times and cultures of the world. I saw several in Indian saris, and a few in Chinese-looking robes. A number looked like statues I had seen in books about ancient Greece and Rome. Some wore plain linen skirts and shawls in the style of ancient Egypt. There were a couple who looked American Indian with feathered headbands, and beadwork-embroidered buckskin clothing and moccasins. One goddess wore a skirt of writhing green serpents! *I wouldn't want to sit next to her—creepy!* A few were almost naked. A few had more than two arms.

I thought I could identify some of them from statues and wall hangings I'd seen—Isis, Maat, Green Tara.

One by one, the goddesses found their places at the hemispheric table on the stage or in the bleachers. Someone whispered that there had been a lottery for the privilege of sitting in the bleachers. I heard there were 360 goddesses present, out of thousands. There was one seat empty near the center curve of the table—I assumed it was for Sophia.

Then, Sophia entered tall and regal, her head high. Her left hand lifted up her glittering tail against her waist. With her right she held a long scepter out in front of her. It was black and studded with rubies and emeralds and sapphires. She walked through the room and up onto the stage. She was still wearing the blood-red gown and scarlet and gold belt. As she passed by me, I saw the two eyestones—front and back—and the new dragon slayer mark amulet attached to her belt. She stood behind the empty seat at the center of the stage.

Sophia waited for the clamor to subside, then spoke, "I have convened a special session of the Council of Goddesses because there is trouble brewing on Earth.

"Let me begin. The night before last, I confronted the Great Dragon, Ialdabaoth, and temporarily defeated his nefarious plans. His meddling in the politics of Earth almost caused a senseless, disastrous exchange of atomic weapons. Destruction of the Earth and World War III were barely averted, only because of the temporary destruction of Ialdabaoth and subsequent resolution of the Cuban Missile Crisis.

"However, he has already reconstituted himself. He and his demons are once again whispering in men's ears. Although the destructive madness of men instigated by Ialdabaoth was momentarily halted, men remain powerless to create the peace and safety that people desperately want. Men are obsessed with making new and deadlier weapons—weapons to kill and poison *all* the creatures and habitats of Earth! They remain ignorant of how their biology is manipulated by Ialdabaoth into adoration of missiles, rockets, and bombs. Ialdabaoth encourages this narcissistic worship and incites men to inflict agony and suffering. He wants a global bloodbath for his own perverted pleasure. Minions are willing to carry out his objective."

Despair overcame me as I thought about the endless inevitability of this cycle of destruction against all living creatures and the Earth herself, perpetrated by this "god" and the men of Earth.

"The Earth herself, Gaia, has petitioned me several times. Her spiritual development is being thwarted. Her very life as a physical being is threatened by the poisons and indignities heaped upon her daily. The nuclear testing, the weapons and bombs blasted in their wars, the chemical and biological agents unleashed into the environment are causing lethal damage and unbearable distress to Earth and to all the beings she sustains. We *must* act!"

She paused to look around the table to each goddess and then around the room, seemingly stopping at every face for a brief but intense fraction of a second. A couple of minutes passed while the women shifted uncomfortably on their cushions and benches.

Sophia continued, "Even though destruction of the Earth has been averted for now, men are *still* enamored of acquiring even bigger missiles. They will not cease their nuclear testing of bigger bombs. This Ialdabaothian enterprise reaps ever bigger profits in business. We must stop this obsession with *size* and being *number one!* Male competition for ever bigger profits and control spells the ruin of Earth."

She paused and looked around the chamber again. At one point, it felt like she was looking me right in the eyes. Images of Sophia's encounter with Ialdabaoth in his Great Hall—the gray-suited businessman—were filling my mind, and I was beginning to squirm on the bench where I was sitting next to Rametha.

Sophia then concluded: "Considering the precariousness of the fate of the Earth, we must begin by ensuring that there will be *no* more blood sacrifice, no more shedding of blood. This is because any spilling of blood feeds the un-god Ialdabaoth. The time has come for human beings to stop killing. No more slaughtering of other human beings, whether the killing is for personal reasons of hatred or in the commitment of crime; or through wars, executions, assassinations, or political actions designed to indirectly cause human deaths through famine or disease. No killing of animals, for food, sport, fur, or skins. All females—goddesses and women—must now strive to stop the flow of blood for demonic ends.

"We are gathered together today to discuss the Crisis and to discuss possible solutions. I now invite Gaia, the Earth Mother, to give a brief statement."

The goddess to Sophia's left arose. She was short and stout, with medium brown skin, looking matronly in a green, blue, white, and brown print muumuu dress. She had graying black hair, braided up with a fabric that matched her dress. Her eyes stood out so clearly, I could see their deep teal blue-green color from where I was sitting. Gaia's statement was brief and to the point:

"Dear goddesses and women, I ask that we go beyond debate to real action. Things have gotten to a crisis point. Earth and all its life could be totally destroyed. We must remember that Earth is the keystone jewel of the entire cosmos, and if this planet can no longer support life, there will be rifts and chaos in the realms all the way up to the Ogdoad. It's as simple as that."

"Thank you, Gaia," said Sophia. Gaia sat down.

Sophia raised her jeweled scepter above her head, and then pointed it straight ahead at the closed door at the rear of Goddess Chamber. The tip of the scepter was an immense ruby. All heads in the room turned as a beam of red light flashed out of it and a large red disk suddenly appeared near the top of the tall door. The disk began to pulsate with its own light and then—*then, it began to spin!* Static electricity filled the air of the Goddess Chamber. The air felt prickly and the spinning made an intense whirring sound.

Sophia said, "This disk will not stop spinning *until blood sacrifice has ceased on Earth!*" She pointed to it again with the tip of her scepter.

Sophia announced, "Thank you, goddesses and women, for being present and attentive. Refreshments are served." Sophia nodded to the assembly and sat down.

The attendants now brought in trays of food and pitchers of a green liquid. They served the goddesses at the front first. Then they carried in small tables for the rest of us—in front of the bleachers for the goddesses and in the center of the room for the women. We were told to help ourselves. The food, in bowls and on plates, looked like familiar fruit, bread, and some kind of cheese. I was quite hungry but didn't want to look greedy, so only took an apple and drank the green drink that was sweet and energizing, but unfamiliar to me. Everyone was quiet, as had been requested, while they ate. The air had a tension in it, a kind of friction from the seriousness of the upcoming debate. The crisis was heavy in the room and everyone was conscious of it.

After the meal, Sophia stood again, and announced, "The debate will now continue among the goddesses. After its conclusion, only the elder women of the Women's Council who've chosen to remain may discuss the issues with the goddesses. After this session, the women and goddesses will choose representatives who will then take their recommendations to tomorrow's meeting of the Great Council of Philosophers. That Council includes men, of course, and will be held in the Council Chambers building of La Ville de Sophie. That meeting will continue the debate about the Crisis."

Sophia again sat down. Most of the women were leaving the chamber. A few others were rearranging themselves. Service teenagers were quickly sweeping the floor and removing the dishes and leftovers. Rametha squeezed my arm and quickly told me good-bye. Then she got up and joined several older women in the middle of the chamber in conversation.

I knew it was time to leave. I stood up and glanced back at Sophia and the other goddesses on the stage one last time. As I walked to the main door I looked around at the serious-looking goddesses in the bleachers. I looked for Rametha but didn't see her. When I got near the open rear door, I stole a glance at the weird ruby-red spinning disk. *How did Sophia do that with her scepter?* I wondered. Rametha's granddaughter was standing by the door; perhaps she was the doorkeeper. I hoped she didn't see me, or *heaven forbid!* recognize her dress on me.

Then, surrounded by women with whom I'd danced, I went through the door quickly, trying to stay as far away as possible from Rametha's granddaughter. Walking down the hallway, I glanced up at the statues and shields again. Near the Women's Temple entrance I found my sandals.

42

Cracks in the Astral World

I walked out of the Women's Temple into the afternoon sunshine. The sun was falling below the line of trees behind the building. I looked around and didn't know where to go or what to do. Then I remembered I was supposed to meet Samantha by the sycamore tree on the front lawn, to ask her for directions. I wanted to go to the Temple of the Body soon to eat dinner—I hoped there'd be macaroni and cheese. I was tired and hungry. I had only eaten that one apple at the goddesses' refreshments table since breakfast at Rametha's. *What a day!*

Samantha wasn't by the tree—she was alone at the bottom of the stairs leading to the temple. The beautiful dancers were standing under the big tree, and I'd have to walk by them to reach her. I didn't really want to talk to them or ask them for directions. I felt awkward and embarrassed just standing there doing nothing, though, so I walked slowly over to them.

All five of them were there, still wearing their black embroidered robes but now with plain black tunics and trousers. *Oh my!* I thought, *there's the singer!* She looked even more glamorous close up. She resembled my beautiful older sister Peggy, both in the way she looked and in the way she carried herself. As I watched her talking to one of the other dancers, it looked like she was whispering and giggling about something secret between the two of them.

Suddenly, she stopped and turned toward me! She stared at me and pointed me out to the other dancers. I blushed and squirmed. I didn't want anyone looking at me—*especially her!*—or, worse, talking to me! I didn't know what to say or do and felt strangely apprehensive. I wished Rametha was here with me now.

The gorgeous singer walked slowly like a sinuous black panther across the lawn. She motioned her friends to follow her. Her thick black hair fell in curving folds that disappeared into her silky black robe. Her hair mingled with the silk and you couldn't tell where her shiny hair ended and the silk began. Something in her smile made me edgy.

She stopped right in front of me, looking down at me with her brilliant blue eyes. I had never seen anyone this beautiful so close up, and it made me feel slow and sloppy. Her slender left hand was pointing at me. Around her wrist was a large silver bracelet with small brightly colored jewels and beads dangling from it. Her long perfectly tapered nails were painted a splendid red that matched the crushed berry red of her lips. Her long slim fingers were adorned with brilliant blue, red, and green gems set into plain silver bands.

The jewelry—and her entire appearance—were so captivating that for a second I forgot my discomfort and wondered if the gems were real sapphires, emeralds, and rubies. I had never been close to a girl whose dress, jewelry, and makeup so perfectly matched her physical beauty. I felt tongue-tied and helpless, as though her presence bound me with invisible cords I was powerless to escape or defend myself from.

"This, my friends," she said in a lovely voice, pointing with the jeweled hand, "is the girl who brought the filthy magician into our pure city." She paused, looking first at me, then to her friends. "This," she said, her voice now like pointy icicles, "is the girl who *bit* the slimy Mephistopheles! *Yuck!* I think that's pretty disgusting, don't you? She fought him like a stinky wrestler taking on an opponent, instead of withdrawing her energy from such a gross and putrid entity."

The other girls obviously were under her control. They were all looking at me like I was a dead toad in the road, not a person. I felt icky, rejected, and despised. The traumas of yesterday and today quickly paled in significance to this. All the safety I had felt upon entering a women-only sanctuary evaporated.

"This is the girl they're all talking about, but I certainly can't understand why! I can't understand why Sophia has given her so much attention—she's done so many stupid things!" Her words bore a hole right through my heart. She was relentless. "Look at her! She can't even talk! What's the matter, is she deaf . . . or maybe just dumb? And why is she wearing that dumpy green dress, with its hem dragging in the dirt? It looks like it came out of the rubbish bin." She drew the last words out slowly, in a loud mean voice, and then she hooted an ugly little laugh, pointing at me, looking to the others for agreement.

I was mortified. I felt betrayed by own feelings. *How could I have so admired this girl?* While this humiliation was going on, I felt no anger—maybe because I had given her so much of my admiration before. She was still on a pedestal and I below. I felt only fear and self-disgust and any words I might have said simply vanished. I just stood there.

"You know, friends, she's dirty and stupid and she signed *the Book*. She failed her first test! What a fool she is! She's a failure. Why, I don't know why she's still allowed to mingle with us. She has nothing. She hasn't been trained to think, to dance, to sing . . . or even to . . . *speak!*"

My face was turning red hot in shame. I knew I was plain compared to these beautiful girls, didn't have the training they had, and had no idea how to respond to this attack. Out of the corner of my eye I saw Samantha walking away very slowly. It seemed that she, too, was afraid of Sapphire and her friends.

Then a rescuer arrived: a middle-aged woman of medium height with chin-length straight brown hair that curved toward her face. She wore glasses and was quite pretty. She was dressed in dark pants and a forest green tunic that fell to her knees; she had on brown sandals.

"Sapphire! Stop it right now. You may think you run this place, but you *don't!* You have a lot to learn about manners and respect. You won't get very far in your training until that deadly arrogance is rooted out. Arrogance is harder to get rid of than ignorance, and don't you forget it!" With that, the woman scowled at Sapphire and the other dancers. You could have heard a leaf flutter to the ground.

The woman took a deep breath. She stared at Sapphire for another moment. Turning to me, her face still serious, she said in a gentle tone, "Molly, my name is Esther. I teach Life-Force Science and Philosophy to the temple dancers and the young women of the city. Later I will present this evening's Blood Mysteries teaching."

Esther became silent. The dancers stared at the ground. One by one, they walked away, down the lawn, to the street. Sapphire was the last to leave. I saw that Samantha lingered on the lawn. Esther took my hand, and we started up the slope away from the sycamore tree.

"Molly, I'm sorry that you had so rude an introduction to some of the other young women of the city. As you will see, the astral world is not so different from Earth in having its decent folk and its bullies and boors, places of perfection and places where there are cracks and flaws." Esther looked at me intensely.

"Sapphire sees you as a threat. You must have triggered her vicious envy in some way. How did you manage that so soon?" the kindly teacher asked.

"Everything was going along great," I replied. "and then suddenly this thing happened with the Book and my blood, and, uh . . . you know about it. It seems everyone here knows more about it than I do!"

"Well, stay out of her way. She's beautiful, but dangerous because her envy and arrogance rule her. She will try to bait you. That's her way of leveling the playing field, to bring you down to her level." Esther stopped a moment to look around to see if anyone was nearby. The five dancers were no longer to be seen, and Samantha was now about twenty feet away on the lawn, watching us.

"Sapphire has to externalize the self-hatred she feels at being overcome with jealousy," Esther continued. "She envies girls who might beat her at whatever contest she fancies herself in. She is very competitive. Her mother did not indulge her as a child as much as she does now. Her mother is the goddess-caller, Ruth."

I remembered the little shadow that crossed Rametha's face when she told me about Ruth. *Hmmm,* I thought, *I wonder if Rametha had a run-in with Ruth, like I just did with Sapphire.* As if reading my thoughts, Esther said quietly, just in case someone could hear her, "Not all the women are happy with Ruth running things and Sapphire gets her way a little too often."

Esther smiled at me. "Now go and ask Samantha where to get some dinner."

I thanked Esther for helping me, and then walked over to Samantha.

"Hi, Molly," Samantha said. Her skin was olive-brown. She had pierced ears with simple silver earrings, and wore a plain pale orange long-sleeved tunic with darker orange trousers. "What did you think of Sophia's speech today? Pretty powerful, huh?" Her smile was a warm welcome to me.

I replied, "Well, I sure hope the goddesses can decide on some plan of action to save Earth from the men there. It was scary on Earth. Everyone in my city figured they'd be incinerated by atomic bombs. Boy, am I glad it didn't happen! Sophia took me to Ialdabaoth's Hall. When she called down Bladed Thunder to incinerate him, that was the most frightening thing I'd ever seen in my life."

Samantha's mouth turned down at the mention of Ialdabaoth, and she changed the subject. "Did you see my tutelary goddess? That's Saraswati, the Hindu goddess of music and the creative arts. She was the one carrying the vina. It's like a sitar."

I didn't know how to reply to Samantha partly because there were just too many goddesses and partly because I wouldn't know a sitar if one jumped on me. "I think I saw her," I answered unconvincingly. Then I added, "Sophia wants to teach me about wisdom—but it seems I've got a long way to go. I haven't gone to any real lessons yet in the Hall of Philosophy—they were canceled. Or to any of the women's Blood Mystery teachings."

"Well, let's get going. I'll take you wherever you want, then come back here with you for this evening's Blood Mystery teachings. You've missed many of the sessions, but I can tutor you."

"Uh, yeah, I guess," I mumbled, a bit uncomfortable with the topic that just wouldn't seem to go away at this place. I was clueless as to what the lessons would be about—hopefully not about periods, remembering the embarrassing "sanitary napkins" movie that was shown one evening in Girl Scouts—with all our mothers present.

"I'm really hungry. Can we please go now to the Temple of the Body for dinner?" I asked Samantha.

"Sure," she replied. "It's near the fountain."

We turned around and started walking down the temple lawn.

43

Sapphire's Curse

"How would you expect *her* to understand anything of what's going on around here!" came a familiar voice, loud from behind me. I turned, and there she was! Sapphire!

"Sapphire, leave her alone," said Samantha.

"Oh, so the big tough Samantha is gonna play bodyguard for helpless little Molly?" Sapphire chided her. Samantha froze as though she had accidentally stepped on a rattlesnake.

"Well, Samantha," Sapphire was relentless, "maybe you better tutor her *before* our lesson tonight—so she's not totally ignorant about all the Blood Mystery teachings she's missed . . . and, it wouldn't be a bad idea to give her a dance lesson or two. She's so clumsy, it's a wonder she didn't trip over that dumpy dress and fall on top of Rametha the *Big Fat Tub!*" She let out a fiendish cackle.

With that, Sapphire's four dancer friends, and even Samantha, shrunk back from her and moved away. Obviously none of them wanted any part of what they could see coming.

Suddenly, something snapped in me. A poison stew of truth, shame, and guilt boiled up. Sapphire's cruelty toward dear Rametha stirred up my own revulsion about Rametha's flabby body, and my whole body shook. I even felt shame about my own plain looks and ugly dress—the dress that kind Rametha had lent me!

Sapphire was every perfect girl who gets what she wants. Sapphire was every girl with the perfect hair, the perfect body, the big boobs. Sapphire was every girl who got any boy she chose. *Stupid boys!* I thought, with growing fury. Sapphire was every girl who enslaved boys with her phony charm. *Just like Peggy!* Here in this odd realm—where everything was supposed to be heavenly—I was face to face with everything I hated and feared in my sister Peggy back home in the real world.

I took aim and let Sapphire have it with all the pent-up fury from years of Peggy's teasing. I spoke with power and authority. "*You,* Sapphire, will end up just like Rametha, but *you* won't have a heart like she does! You will wither into a bitter old bitch because *all* you have is your beauty. *You* are the *stupid* one not to see that all beauty fades, whether it belongs to a rose or to a woman. *You* will have nothing left but a withered face and a broken body—with *no heart!*" I raised my voice at the end. Seldom had I experienced the pleasure of saying the right words at the right time.

The poison daggers in my words hit their mark with deadly accuracy. I felt it. I loved the feeling of strength that poured into me. I knew I had shot the truth into her heart, that is, if she even had a heart. *What is this bitch doing in this supposedly blessed city, anyway?* I wondered.

Sapphire was motionless. She sucked her breath in sharply. Underneath her makeup, her face was visibly turning red. I watched with pleasure the effect of my revenge on my enemy.

"What's the matter, cat got your tongue?" I taunted. I relished Sapphire's defeat, as I felt my power grow . . . But my victory was short-lived . . .

Sapphire's brilliant cold eyes, the color of her jewels and her name, shot their hatred into mine. She slowly lifted her right arm, the folds of her robe slipping back to reveal her silver bracelet glistening with gems. With deadly calm, with ice-cold composure, she pointed her index finger at me and uttered these words:

"*You,* Earthling . . . *you,* worm of filth . . . I declare you cursed unto all your generations and bloodline." She spoke in a strange uncanny voice. I knew it was a magical incantation from the chills that ran up and down my spine. I felt my blood curdle like sour milk inside me.

Suddenly, a phosphorescent green light burst around us in a million tiny jets of sparks. Just as the sparkles of green exploded, all the torches that served as street lights flared like blowtorches ten feet into the sky.

A loud crack split the air. A jagged fissure opened up next to my right foot and continued down to the street. A zigzag gash cleaved apart the paving stones. *What just happened—an earthquake?*

Startled, I jumped away from the crack in the ground. Sapphire stood her ground, unmoving, as though paralyzed.

Within seconds, it seemed there was noise everywhere. I heard people yelling and what sounded like thunder. Sophia appeared immediately, seemingly out of nowhere, about three yards away from Sapphire and me.

"What is happening here!?" Sophia shouted. "We felt it in the Goddess Council Chamber. All the torches blew out. How dare you two bring contentiousness into its sanctity! We were convening a special session to deal with the imminent annihilation of Earth, and here *you two* are falling into the same pattern as the men on Earth. Fighting—instead of using reason, dialogue, and compassion. Aggression comes in many forms—not just bombs and guns—but in speech as well."

"Sapphire!" Sophia thundered, striding to Sapphire who was still motionless. She yanked her shoulders, pulling her away from me and toward herself. "You *cursed* Molly just now, didn't you? And you did it just at the moment the sun set! You know the penalty for abuse of magical power in La Ville de Sophie! You will be sent to the Refinery tomorrow to prepare for incarnation in an Earth life. The place and time of your birth will be decided by your spirit guides. Your Earth family and fate has been decreed accordingly. You abused your power, Sapphire. You have let narcissism rule you. You are now its slave. Do you want to be reborn hideously deformed? Or into a family of beggars on the streets of India? Or raised to be a common whore in a slum?" Sapphire and Sophia looked at each other, neither one saying a word for several minutes.

During this momentary lull, as thunderous in its silence as Sophia's had been in her speaking, I stood stock still. But thousands of thoughts swirled inside my head. I kept wondering: *Why do I keep hearing about my bloodline? Sapphire has now cursed it—what can that mean? And—Refinery—what's that and why does it sound so bad?* My thoughts returned to Squeaky and Raspy when they had mentioned it. *I have to ask Sophia about that.*

Sophia put one hand on my shoulder and the other on Sapphire's. She turned both of us to face her. "And, *you,* Molly! You are my protégée! What did *you* say to trigger this girl's old habit of protecting herself with the satanic arts? Satanic magic feeds Ialdabaoth. We must talk."

Sapphire tried to pull herself away from Sophia. But Sophia looked her in the eye and said, "Sapphire, go home now. I will speak with you tomorrow and give you instructions about the next stage of your incarnation on Earth and about what will be expected of you in the Refinery."

Sapphire's face contorted into an ugly look. She pulled free from Sophia's grasp, and backed away, scowling, down the slope of the lawn. She lost her balance and fell against one of the large tree roots that was sticking up through the grass. She picked herself up right away, embarrassed, looked all around to see if anyone else noticed her fall, and then brushed herself off. I could see she'd torn her robe, and was glad it was no longer whole and beautiful. She'd cut her hand, too. Blood streaked her face as she wiped her hand against it to brush her hair out of her eyes. Leaning against the sycamore, breathing heavily, she tried to regain her composure.

Sophia let me go, and trotted down to Sapphire. *Why is Sophia giving that bitch so much attention?* I fumed.

Sophia raised her hand toward the street, pointing toward the cracked pavement. "Sapphire, leave these premises now! I will see you at your house tomorrow with your mother. We will discuss this incident and make preparations for you to leave the middle realm. Go home and wash that wound—it's just a surface cut."

Sapphire straightened up and faced Sophia. "Molly has brought chaos and violence into our city, Sophia! It's *her,* not me, who has ruined everything," she insisted, and then went on complaining in a snotty voice to Sophia. They moved away from the tree, a few yards down the slope. I could still hear them talking. Finally there was a brief moment of silence, and it seemed that Sophia's and Sapphire's conversation was over.

But then—it looked like Sapphire was going to strike Sophia! Her fist was raised over her head. Instead, she turned to look at me, and yelled, "You will pay for this, bitch!"

"Sapphire, enough!" Sophia exclaimed. "When you act like a bully, this is what you're going to get. You picked on the wrong girl!"

Sapphire abruptly turned her back to Sophia as though she were just another girl, not the Queen of Heaven. Brushing off her dusty and blood-stained robe again, she stalked off in the direction of the city.

"Come over here," Sophia called and gestured to me. When I went to join her beneath the sycamore tree, I could see some blood on the tree root. She took my hand and led me over to the temple steps. We sat down over to the side, on one of its wide white marble steps. There didn't seem to be anyone around. The sky had softened into a gentle peach-rose sunset.

"Molly, let's talk," Sophia said kindly.

Here it comes, I thought despondently.

"Molly," she began in a serious firm tone, "Esther spoke to you about how Sapphire baits you. Didn't you hear her instruction?"

I wondered how Sophia knew about what Esther had said. "Something came over me," I mumbled. "I can't describe it. I couldn't stand what she was saying about my friend Rametha." I sighed deeply. *At least I'm not crying . . . yet,* I thought miserably.

"Are you saying that you felt you had to defend Rametha?" Sophia looked at me sharply.

"Yes, of course. What she was saying was so mean. She called Rametha a 'Big Fat Tub.'" A twinge of shame surfaced in me as I recalled the memory of her large lumpy body.

"Molly," Sophia said as she looked intently into my eyes, "this has nothing whatsoever to do with Rametha. This is all about you. Sapphire has an instinct for finding a person's vulnerable spot. She slices it open for all to see, exposing their weakness to others."

"What do you mean!?" I asked.

"What happened had nothing to do with Rametha. She doesn't care what anyone calls her. She cares less about Sapphire and her mother than about the leftover flour on her breadboard. They mean nothing to her, except as an occasional reminder that this seemingly perfect world has its little parasites, flies, and rats. Rametha celebrates her body. She understands that what is important is how she feels about her body, not what other women think about it. Rametha is untouchable by others."

"Can't I go now, Sophia? I'm hungry," I whimpered, trying to wriggle out of the uncomfortable conversation.

Sophia wouldn't let up. "Rametha is a reminder to Sapphire of what her physical future holds. Sapphire can't bear the thought of her own eventual aging and deterioration and all that goes with it. She has to crush out that image within herself because it is her greatest fear. Regarding Rametha's body, your shame about physical unattractiveness and Sapphire's fear are two sides of one coin."

Now I did cry. I couldn't stand this kind of exposure. I shook my head and wept. Sophia hugged me and patted my back.

"Honey," she said softly, after a few minutes of my uncontrollable sobbing, "it looks like your life has brought you a very sharp teacher. Her name is Sapphire. The lessons you will learn through her will quicken your development as no other classroom here could do. Yes, you're in for a rough ride, but your karmic stream has drawn her into your life. You have to learn how to manage your own feelings of inferiority and how to deal with competition and intimidation."

Sophia looked at me sternly. "And don't forget, what happens here has its counterpart in your world. Now, Molly, I am afraid you have to remain on Earth *for a while*. You must learn about the uncontrollable forces that take you over. You have lessons to learn back on Earth before you can return to us in La Ville de Sophie."

I asked again, "What do you mean, Sophia?"

Sophia answered, "The rules of the city have been violated and judgment has been rendered. Sapphire, too, will return to Earth after her sojourn in the Refinery."

"Sophia, what about Sapphire's curse? Did she curse me and my bloodline for real, and forever? Can't you remove her curse?"

Sophia looked at me sadly and answered, "No, Molly, you'll have to learn about removing the bloodline curses yourself—that will be in future lessons. And don't worry, Sapphire will be in your life again—soon. You'll learn a lot from her, your sister Peggy, and others like them. These lessons will contribute more to your spiritual growth than any teachings in the Hall of Philosophy."

"How long will it be until we meet again?" I asked desperately, and then wailed, "None of this seems fair!" Anger, confusion, fatigue, and hunger were battling for my attention.

"For 'a while' is what I told you. During that time, I will not call you. No matter how often you try, you will not be able to use your dragon slayer mark to call me. Nor will you be able to enter the middle realm as you fall asleep."

With that, she got up and pulled me up, and then led me by the hand halfway up the temple stairs. I was speechless with fear and dread. I began to plead, "Why are you punishing me? Why are you making me leave? This isn't fair. I'm hungry, that's why this happened. Don't I get a trial or something? Don't I get to defend myself?" I felt betrayed and now I was being pushed out, a repeat of what had happened with Li.

Sophia shook her head slowly. "The lessons you have to learn now are about how beliefs are living inside you and can be stirred up and used against you by people like Sapphire. You must learn all about their occult anatomy, as thoroughly as a university zoologist might study animal anatomy. These lessons are best done on Earth. Don't worry, you'll be back. You're under my tutelage. This is merely a delay, not forever.

"I know you're hungry. But please don't go anywhere. Wait here until the council takes a break again. Then I will come out and talk to you some more. I may be a while, so just try to relax."

Sophia turned to go up the remaining steps, then stopped and turned back to me, "And please, Molly, stay out of trouble!"

44

Back to Earth

Sophia left me to wallow in the foul pit of this fresh misery, now mingling with all the other miseries. I could think of nothing but my multiple failures. *So much for a warm welcome in the Women's Temple! What that stinking Sapphire did to me was worse than what happened with Li!* I felt such a hatred well up in me toward Sapphire, not only for the humiliation but now for being thrown out of La Ville de Sophie, when it wasn't even my fault. *I didn't do anything except defend Rametha . . . or me, or whatever. She didn't have a right to say those things, that snake!* The more I reflected on what happened, the angrier I got. *I was the victim. I was set up. I was baited.*

What else could I do? I would never turn the other cheek to that bitch!

Anger turned to regret. *No visiting the Temple of the Body for dinner and lessons on chocolate truffles with Samantha—she abandoned me too, it seems. No Temple of the Muses, either. No Blood Mystery teachings this evening, whatever they are. No meeting the goddesses Demeter and Persephone tomorrow in the Goddess Chamber, as Sophia promised. No more magical middle realm—for who knows how long*—although right now it didn't seem so magical to me anymore.

I watched with a dismal eye as a few people strolled below me on the street, probably on their way home to dinner. The sun was now well below the horizon, as dusk settled in. A moon a little more than half full hung in the sky. The streetlight torches cast pools of pale illumination. I was getting chilly, so I hugged my knees and tried to keep from shivering. *Where is Sophia?* I wondered. *What's taking them so long? I wish I could leave here.*

I sat longer. The sky was dark, with twinkling stars. The street was empty now of people. No one was on the temple lawn. I wondered where all the students had gone, if they were home, back inside with the older women, or at some special hangout. *Once again, everyone is where they're supposed to be, except me. Here I am abandoned, left alone . . . again.*

Then I heard a tinkling laugh and a familiar male voice through the still evening air. Suddenly focused and alert, I stared through the deepening gloom. Walking down the street in front of the temple, hand in hand, were Li and Sapphire!

No! I screamed inside, *No! Not that!* I pressed myself against the wall alongside the Women's Temple stairs, praying to melt into it and not be seen by them.

Sapphire had changed her clothes and was wearing a long shimmering silver gown with a scarlet shawl around her shoulders. Her black hair made a startling contrast to the silver and red. Li carefully helped Sapphire step over the large crack from the earthquake in the middle of the street. They walked a few yards further down the street, then stopped under a street light. They apparently didn't see me.

Li was acting like a silly poodle around her, staring up at her, practically drooling, clutching her arm. His arm circled around her shoulders as though to keep her warm and hold her close to him. They were laughing at some private joke. She was glittering her charm all over him. It was so obvious that he was infatuated with her, smitten.

How could she be smiling? Sapphire laughed again at something Li said. I was furious! *Why is she with Li?* I thought. *Sophia has sentenced her to the Refinery—tomorrow!*

I was shaking. I thought I would die right there on the spot if they saw me. Sorrow and rage boiled up in me. Their laughter and delight in each other were more than I could bear. *Li never fussed over me like that,* I thought. *He never joked around with me!*

Li leaned into her face. Her head tilted back. They kissed. Sapphire stood there, her eyes closed. A smile froze on her painted lips.

I held my breath, anger and humiliation surging up from deep within my body. I don't know what happened next. I must have fainted. When I woke up, I was in another world, and drenched in a pool of grief.

Epilogue

by Violet Harmon, Molly O'Brien's stepdaughter

My name is Violet Harmon. What you have been reading is the story of Molly O'Brien, my stepmother. Before he died, I promised my beloved father, Narada Sarin, that I would accurately portray his wife's adventures in—and messages from—the spirit world. He told me that her story must be told—to women, especially, and to those men who desire to end war and protect the Earth and the soul of humanity. Father said it was critical that I get Molly's story into print as quickly as possible. If I put it off, my karma would be disastrous, he said. I would not be able to contact him in the spirit world.

Molly died of a heart attack in 2007, just before she turned sixty. My father was diagnosed with an inoperable brain tumor shortly after her death. I quit my job as a computer programmer in Chicago to care for him in his small house near one of the campuses of the University of Illinois.

For eight months, almost every day that he was well enough, he told me about Molly's adventures in the realms of the demons, the deities, and the dead. He insisted that I tape-record these conversations. He gave me several large plastic tote bins of Molly's diaries, notes, and sketches. Until then, I had no inkling of her extraordinary adventures in her current and previous lifetimes.

As I learned more about my father and his wife, however, the unexplained twists and turns in my own life also began to make more sense.

Thanks to a modest inheritance from my father, I have been able to focus all my attention on this project. Committing the last two years to transcribing Father's tapes and typing Molly's notes, I have stitched together their descriptions of the landscape of the spirit worlds into adventure stories. Dialogue has been crafted to clearly reflect and express the persons, beings, events, and ideas, the content of the conversations, and the passion of Molly's dramatic and bewildering encounters and conversations. I am confident in the accuracy of the narrative, including the scope of my own shortcomings.

I confess to the reader, however, that I remained emotionally distant from Molly. We were, in fact, repelled by each other. That said, the truth of her descriptions and interpretations is guaranteed by her integrity and honesty. I have dedicated my life at this time to the editing and publication of these volumes, not for Molly, but as a labor of love and devotion to my father. Rest assured, dear reader, I would never violate his trust and confidence that I would convey the facts without bias, malice, or distortion.

I have retained the use of the first person "I" as Molly speaking, to be as close as possible to the way her diaries were written. The beings that Molly met in the spirit world are identified with their own names and described exactly as recorded in her notes. Regarding deities, elementals, and historical figures that appear in this book, the reader can consult printed or Internet reference sources. With the exception of Molly, my father, Ben Sarin my half-brother, and myself, the names and some details of her family, friends, neighbors, teachers, priests, school, church, and so forth, have been changed at the request of members of my family to protect their reputations and identities. This book has been written with the permission of Ben Sarin, only child of Narada and Molly.

This book recounts only the *beginning* of Molly's story. She had many more adventures, both in the middle realm and in the real world. She finished high school and college. She met and married my father and had a child, my half-brother Ben, with him. In her later years, she traveled around the world and met many interesting people.

My father returned to Delhi after a scandal at the ashram he had founded in Illinois in the 1960s. After that, as a single mother, Molly raised me and my half-brother Ben. When we were young and Molly couldn't find a babysitter, we got to stay in the ashram. The ashram was limping along after my father's departure, but Marion, the ashram administrator, took care of Ben and me. Ben and I never got along. We argued and fought constantly.

Molly was pressed with trying to make ends meet—and it was often difficult. There were not many decent-paying jobs for women, even with college degrees. Molly had to take time off from work whenever Ben or I got sick. She even lost two jobs for that reason. She did substitute teaching whenever she could.

Molly eventually got some money from my father, but it was not consistent. When his money came, it helped a lot. My father sometimes sent wonderful birthday gifts from India to Ben and me like delicate hand-painted cards with peacocks and trees in lavender and pale rose, on handmade paper. Once he sent me a sari—a lovely tan and gold print. His high school graduation gift to me was an expensive trip to India.

There's more to this story and my relationship with Molly than you'd first guess. That's because Sapphire is me. After the incident outside the Women's Temple, I was judged by Sophia and sent back to Earth after completing my work in the Refinery. On Earth I incarnated as Violet, Narada's daughter and Molly's eventual step-daughter. I will not write of what I learned in the Refinery. Suffice it to say, I was forced to dig every day through piles of dust there to find gems of wisdom from my previous lifetimes before I could reincarnate. But that's another story.

I had a past-life regression a few years ago, in which I saw how I died as a hetaera in Greece. I was stabbed by a rival for the affections of a man we both loved. It became clear I had spent lifetimes perfecting my feminine wiles and arts for the purpose of attracting males who would support my desire for luxurious living. Then I had a dream of the incident that took place in the middle realm in the last chapters of this book—when I baited and cursed Molly.

As Sophia mentioned several times, the 1962 Cuban Missile Crisis corresponded with the crisis in the middle realm. Sophia's incineration of Ialdabaoth, the Great Dragon, which was witnessed by Molly, occurred on the date of the turning point of the Cuban Missile Crisis. Although nuclear testing expanded, a change of consciousness appeared in the world. By October 25, 1962, Nikita Khrushchev had agreed to withdraw the missiles from Cuba and worked out a deal with U.S. President John F. Kennedy. In April 1963, Pope John XXIII completed his "Pacem in Terris." In August of that year, Martin Luther King Jr. gave his "I have a dream" speech. A couple months later, in October, a limited nuclear weapons treaty was signed, banning aboveground testing. That same year, the book that launched the environmental movement, Rachel Carson's *Silent Spring,* was published. The modern women's movement to give women control over their own bodies can be said to have begun in 1963 with the publication of Betty Friedan's *The Feminine Mystique.* But of course, the wars continued, with the Vietnam War escalating in the late 1960s. And greed, environmental degradation, and the abuse of women continued everywhere.

After her 1962 adventures in the middle realm, Molly would not encounter Sophia for a while. Meanwhile, she went through a crisis of faith. Now Molly really wanted to *understand* what she had experienced. She began to study mythology, astrology, goddesses, and Oriental religions such as Hinduism, Buddhism, and Taoism, as well as comparative religion and the ecumenical ideas of the later 1960s. She even tackled some philosophy, and read a couple of popular books on Pythagoras—though she found much of it too academic and dry. She read all the Faust legends she could find. She read whatever she could get hold of in her high school and public libraries on these subjects. The drugstore book rack had paperbacks on UFOs, palmistry, tarot, and Edgar Cayce, as well as Dell publications on astrology, although they did not tell a whole lot about *wisdom.* However, Molly did find the wisdom passages in the Bible. She especially liked Sophia speaking in Proverbs. Molly borrowed books by Sigmund Freud from the Murphys next door, husband and wife psychologists. She babysat their young daughter, and they in turn mentored and encouraged her interest in psychology. She taught herself to meditate from a book. She did not find a spiritual teacher until she met my father, Narada.

After the 1962 Thanksgiving dinner, Molly tried to stop eating meat, even though her mother kept insisting she wouldn't be healthy and strong without it. When she got to college, Molly found many more young people who were vegetarians and it was easier for her to make the change. Narada came from a vegetarian Hindu family, and Ben and I were vegetarians in our childhood. But I did go through a very rebellious carnivorous phase after I left Molly's home. It took a while, but I was determined to acquire a liking for rare steak.

To sum up what happened after the adventures recounted in this book, Molly blossomed as she came into her own power. She eventually became a true dragon slayer as she encountered the Great Dragon over and over again in different forms.

As best I can, I am preparing her stories and the stories of those whose karma is linked to hers for publication as a series of books, of which this is the first. So reader, there will be more—much more!

Some Background

Sophia—Wisdom—has been the focus of my investigations and contemplations for many years, and the subject of both my MA and PhD dissertations, the latter of which, *Sophia: Exile and Return,* is available at: wisdomsgoldenrod.org/publications/kdamiani/

For more on both Sophia and the Dragon, please visit my Web site www.sophiaandthedragon.com. This site will have announcements about upcoming events.

- pp. 9 and 39, the poem beginning "I breathe a breath of force— " is my own adaptation of Rig Veda X.125.8,7, Vak Hymn, *Hymns of the Rig Veda,* vol. 2, Ralph Griffith, trans., 1896, www.sacred-texts.com/hin/rigveda/rv10125.htm
- p. 37, the poem beginning, "I have fallen because of Wisdom," is my own adaptation from the *Kebra Nagast,* p. 153, E. A. Wallis Budge, trans., 1932, www.sacred-texts.com/chr/kn/; www.sacred-texts.com/afr/kn/kn097.htm
- pp. 104–106. References to Sophia as Ialdabaoth's mother and to the demiurge Ialdabaoth as the abortion of the lower Sophia are from Gnosticism, an early Christian sect. Elaine Pagels, *The Gnostic Gospels* (Vintage, 1989) has more on Ialdabaoth and Sophia in Gnosticism.
- For more information on the deities, mythological figures, sacred concepts, and some of the images that appear in this book, see Manly Palmer Hall's *The Secret Teachings of All Ages, An Encyclopedic Outline* (PRS, 1978; Dover Reprint, 2010; also available at www.sacred-texts.com/eso/sta/index.htm).

Caitlin Matthews, *Sophia: Goddess of Wisdom* (1991; reprints by several publishers) is a sourcebook on Sophia. See Jane Ellen Harrison, *Themis* (1927), for more on the Spartan dragon slayer mark. The reader can also consult various other printed or Internet reference sources as needed.

- Molly's birth data: Nov. 30, 1947, 11:44 A.M., Chicago

This is a work of *fiction*. Names, historical or otherwise, locations, and events are all used fictitiously. Molly O'Brien, Violet Harmon, Narada Sarin, the members of Molly's family, et al., are fictitious characters. Any references to any cultures and religions are used fictitiously.

Mark of the Dragon Slayer with Horizontal Eight /Infinity Sign

The dragon slayer mark below has two components: the two facing crescent moons, which is the form of the scar on Molly's thigh, and the infinity symbol that Molly traces as the final part of the ritual she uses to call Sophia.

Acknowledgments

I wish to thank:

My friend and editor, June Fritchman, without whose encouragement and skill this novel would have remained an endless series of episodes; Amy O. and Paul R. ("Randy") Cash of Larson Publications for their willingness to publish this, who immediately grasped why this novel is timely, especially for girls and women; Jeanne Astor and Crow Marley for editorial assistance; Anne Kilgore for her artistry in the book design; Hrana Janto for her cover image; Rosemarie Quebral for her infinity dragon; Richard Guttridge for suggesting fiction as a medium to give voice to Sophia.

Anthony Damiani, my father-in-law, founder of Wisdom's Goldenrod, for his neo-Platonic vision that brought coherence to the multiplicity of wisdom traditions; Paul Brunton, Anthony's teacher; Manly Palmer Hall, who told me that we all need more "entertainment" so wisdom is no longer confined to religion or conversation among academics.

Inspirational minds for conversations, ideas, and support over the last thirty years: Robert Schmidt and Ellen Black, Maurice Friedman, Caitlín Matthews, Doug Greene, Vicki Noble, Michael Wagner, Johnes Ruta, Ashley Montagu, René Girard, my husband Paul Damiani, my parents John and Katherine Granville, and my mother- and father-in-law, Ella May and Anthony Damiani.

The encouraging readers of the manuscript: Michele Shean, Glenna Mahon, Wanda Kaplan, Dorothy Martindale, Barbara Elliott, Ed Lisbe, Susan Lee Meeder, Richard Nowogrodzki, Michael Sandoval, Tim Daniels, Aalexcia Fox, Rebeca-Ann Cabanillas, Lynn LeFeber and my sons Austin and Anton Damiani.

All those people on Earth who share the spiritual import of these challenging times.

About the Author

Kathleen Damiani completed interdisciplinary graduate programs at Old Dominion University and Union Institute & University, earning her PhD in 1998. She has given lectures and slide shows about Sophia for the last twenty years. Her writings can be found on her Web site: www.sophiaandthedragon.com. Sophia: Exile and Return, can be found at wisdomsgoldenrod.org/publications/kdamiani/. In this novel, her first, she has given Sophia a body and a voice.

She lives in northern California with her partner Tim. Recently retired from New York State Parks, she worked to preserve parkland and historic properties, organizing cultural events earlier in her career. She produced the Taylor Vintage Summer of Song outdoor concert series which began in 1979.

She has two sons and three grandchildren.